ENDURE SERIES: ONE

THE DEUS MOLECULE

DIMITRIO TERRANOVA

Prologue

The road ahead is endless, pockmarked with holes in some areas and completely buckled in others, where the dampness of winter has seeped beneath its surface to freeze and expand. There's snow on the ground and a stale taste in the air that hangs stagnant among the majestic pines bordering either side of the two-lane stretch of asphalt. In stark contrast to the dormancy of my immediate surroundings, something shimmers in the distance, like light shadowed by the fluttering of moth wings on a warm summer's night. No, not just shimmering, but dancing like fire, like flames. Subconsciously, and not unlike a moth, I am drawn to its light, its warmth. The allure of this distant inferno calls me closer, and I approach it, walking the double-solid yellow line that bisects the street like a tightrope.

I'm aware of the pavement behind me giving way, crumbling silently as it vanishes into the ebony nothingness below. I have no choice but to push forward as the shadows close in and funnel me toward the burning light. The silence is overwhelming as I approach the blazing flames. Shapes emerge from the hellfire, revealing the source to be a vehicle scorched to an obsidian crisp. I'm right up on it now, close enough to see inside. Resisting the urge to recoil from its intensity is becoming a struggle, but I squint through the heat and see two figures in the passenger and driver's seats, both equally charred and burnt. Not far from the wreckage lies a young girl, her skin untouched by fire yet lifeless all the same. Her once-golden brown locks are sprawled across the asphalt, soaked in blood and tangled. As I stare in horror, I'm filled with an overwhelming sense of dread. I know these people; I love them, even.

There's a sharp and sudden pressure on my shoulder, the weight of a hand. Yet when I glance down at where it should be, all I see is shadow. It is embodied and multi-dimensional but a shadow nonetheless. I swivel around in a hurried panic, breaking free from my visitor's unwarranted grip. Now, the shadow stands before me in full, like a mirrored silhouette, a stark raven-black creature in place of a reflection.

"Come home, Royce," it whispers.

I take a step back towards the vehicle but immediately feel the singe from the tendrils of fire behind me. Before I can retreat, the blackened hand of the passenger darts out and grabs my wrist. She's screaming violently, and these animalistic sounds emanating from her throat are the only indication this corpse once was, in fact, a woman at all. I struggle to free myself as her grip sears my skin, and in my panic, I notice that the shadow is closing in on me from behind.

"Who... what are you?!" I shout.

Slowly, the entity raises its arm and reaches for me, beckoning. The world crashes down on me now, its resonance a cacophonous and continuous echo. The fire grows louder, crackling and hissing among the screams of the corpse.

"Come home, Royce. You belong here; you belong with us."

The shadow's insistence is palpable. All at once and without warning, the entity engulfs me and wraps itself around me like a second skin. I'm swallowed up within its cold embrace and begin to fight with all my strength against it.

"Wait! What do you mean? Belong where? Wait!" My toes go numb, followed by my ankles, knees, thighs, and abdomen. The loss of sensation travels up my body until it reaches the whites of my eyes. Startled and shaking with anxiety, I'm entombed by the darkness, hurtling into an infinite and obscured abyss.

Rem

Time and location (present-day): 7:00 am,
ENDURE Center for Rehabilitation

My eyelids snap open as I inhale sharply. For a moment, I considered whether I had stopped breathing during the nightmare. I attempt to move but find my body paralyzed. Sleep paralysis—I was told—is a symptom of my post-traumatic stress disorder. Doctor Atticus Cais diagnosed me with this condition shortly after I arrived at ENDURE, a facility renowned worldwide for its expertise in both medical and physical rehabilitation. Even those with the most severe conditions found second chances under the attentive care of the doctor's team. After the car wreck that claimed the lives of my family, the hospital staff placed me in a medically induced coma to address the debilitating effects of the traumatic brain injury I sustained in the crash. My coma lasted three long years. When I finally awoke, I was transferred to this facility for physical and mental rehabilitation.

My eyes, the only part of my body freed from sleep, slowly glance at the bedside table clock. It reads 7:00 am on the dot, a seeming constant throughout my now six-month and counting stay here. It feels as if an internal alarm clock has been secretly implanted in my brain, triggering me to wake up at precisely the same time each morning. At least that's the explanation my now hyperactive and rampant imagination has conjured for this strange occurrence.

Something in the corner of the room moves ever so slightly in my peripheral vision, drawing my attention. Across from my bed stands the shadow from my nightmares, a shadow I've come to know as Mallen. It's a name it has given itself, one it adopted during an earlier episode of my ailment. For better or worse, Mallen is now my own personal sleep-paralysis demon. As it tilts its nondescript head and featureless face to the side, I begin to feel the tips of my fingers jitter. The sensation travels up my arms and eventually throughout my body, and with my reawakening to motor function comes the dissipation of Mallen, like early morning mist. The demon now held at bay, I sigh in relief and sit up in bed, rubbing the sleep from my eyes. No matter how many times I see it, it unnerves me just the same. Mallen is a product of my imagination, but that doesn't stop it from feeling completely real. It didn't help that I had noticed its recurring presence, which gave this figment even more substance. Before long, I was conversing with it in my dreams during the REM cycle of sleep. *Nightmares*, I remind myself solemnly. Soon after we began talking, Mallen started appearing in my room when I would wake, the boundaries between reality and fantasy blurring more each day.

I run a hand through my dark brown hair. It's getting long again, and the tone of my once olive skin looks paler today than before, something I notice as I lower my arm back into my lap. I made a mental note to visit the facility's barber. A knock at the door pulls me from my thoughts, and shortly after, Lena enters my quarters. She's the nurse assigned to care for me during my stay at ENDURE and has become a source of comfort over the past six months.

"Morning, Royce. Did you sleep okay?" she asks, her radiant green eyes piercing through the drab brown irises of my own.

I feign a smile before replying, "Like a baby."

Lena raises an eyebrow at me. "Mallen again?"

"Always." I pause, swinging my legs over the edge of the bed to stand, then say humorously, "He's not so bad once you get to know him."

She lets out a short laugh. "Oh, it's a 'he' now?"

I shrug in response, and she smiles again. It's hard to look away when she grins; she truly is stunning. Even in her sky-blue scrubs, her golden-brown hair falls gracefully, barely brushing the small of her back. Her eyes are so vividly green and regal that one might describe them as emerald. There's something hidden behind this feature of Lena's that I find mysteriously alluring. She's typically poised, but I know there's a side to her she keeps locked away for the sake of professionalism. What intrigues me the most about her is that she seems completely oblivious to her beauty.

I, of course, am a patient with no chance of catching this fish, but it never hurts to try, and I really don't have anything to lose. Besides, she flirts with me from time to time as well. It's subtle when it occurs, but it's present, restrained by that pesky professionalism. This way of thinking serves as my explanation for confiding in her and sharing my experiences with the shadow that lingers in my subconscious.

"How are you feeling today, aside from a visit from your friend?" she asks.

I walk over to the desk across the room from my bed and next to the door. The desk and the chair tucked into it are the only other pieces of furniture in my quarters besides my bed and side table. We were allowed a few other approved items based on our individual conditions, like an alarm clock and the occasional book to read. Leaning on the desk, I arch my back to stretch it. The white tile floor is cool to the touch, feeling pleasant against my bare feet. "Pretty good; no nausea or pain today," I say, knowing she's looking for an update on the side effects of my condition. Inexplicable nausea, muscle aches, and intense migraines are symptoms I've been experiencing ever since the wreck. Dr. Cais still isn't sure whether these symptoms are connected to potential brain damage sustained during the crash, but repeated MRI scans hadn't indicated anything of the sort.

"Well, that's good news!" she says joyfully. "My uncle believes your body simply experienced significant trauma in the accident and that these other symptoms will completely fade away with a little more time. Our primary focus is ensuring that your sleep paralysis is resolved before your discharge and that your body and mind are in good condition. Three years is a long time to be unconscious, and although we did our best to provide adequate coma stimulation therapies while you were under, we need to be certain."

That's a small point of tension between Lena and me. Dr. Atticus Cais, owner of ENDURE and Lena's uncle, is someone I like less with every passing day. She trusts his goodwill, but I find his methods cold and calculating. He's shrewd, always angling for something beneath the surface, or at least that's how it feels whenever we cross paths.

Perhaps my resentment was misplaced after a recent interaction with the doctor resulted in a much longer and seemingly endless stay at the facility. I have no family to return to, no job, and no home. Therefore, Dr. Cais believes it's best for me to remain at ENDURE until they can address my sleep paralysis and uncover the root of my other illnesses. When I argued that I couldn't pay any bills I was accumulating due to the lack of stable income or savings, Dr. Cais reassured me that we would sort everything out later.

"Well, I know you're watching out for my best interests," I mumble. "Your uncle, however..."

Lena sighs and gives me a stinging look of disappointment. "Royce, we've discussed this before."

I quickly backtrack, hoping to appease her and ensure our interaction doesn't end on a negative note. "I know, I know, I'm sorry. It just slipped out. Forget it entirely."

Her face relaxes, and she grins gently once more. It feels as though we're frozen in time for a bit before a second knock at the door shatters that perfect moment, and Dr. Cais enters the room.

He studies both of us, then turns to me. "Hello, Mr. Wilko, just doing my rounds." Dr. Cais pauses to write something in a pocketbook, then adds, "How are you feeling?"

Lena and I share a brief glance, a silent goodbye before she leaves the room, abandoning me to the doctor's inquiry. "I'm feeling fine, thanks. Is there anything new on the agenda for today?"

Often, Dr. Cais provides me with a daily regimen meant to challenge both the body and mind— 'Restorative therapy,' he calls it. Though I'd never admit it to him, it certainly helped me regain my strength and mental fortitude.

"I'm pleased to say no. You have your workout routine, which I'd like you to continue. Your recent MRI scans have shown promising results; all brain function is relatively normal, or at least as normal as can be expected after enduring what you have. I trust that from now on, your chess games with Mr. McAllister will be sufficient for mental stimulation gymnastics."

I know he's referring to Jonathan McAllister, the only other patient at ENDURE whom I trust and consider a friend. As soon as I could walk again, Jonathan showed me the ropes and became a mainstay in my new life. We play chess at least once daily in the lobby to pass the time and keep our competitive edge sharp. He's a few years older than me, but we have a lot in common, which makes up for the age gap.

To make small talk and hide my dislike for Dr. Cais, I respond, "Sounds good to me. Jonathan and I can use the extra time for more games of chess."

He smiles, though it appears forced. "Excellent. I also wanted to speak with you regarding—"

The doctor's cell phone vibrates persistently, interrupting his train of thought. I see a fleeting trace of worry flicker in his eyes before vanishing in an instant. "I apologize, Mr. Wilko, but we'll need to continue this discussion later. I'm needed urgently; enjoy the rest of your day." He gives me one last suspicious smile and leaves the room.

I let out a sigh; every interaction with the man is exhausting and leaves me on edge. *What did he want to talk to me about?* I wonder, then fall deeper down the rabbit hole. *What was so important that he left in such a hurry? And why did he try to hide his concern?* The questions start to jumble in my mind, a perfect cocktail of stagnation and paranoia fueled by my imprisonment in this place. Overthinking has been my strong suit long before the accident, but now it seems that I'm holding onto every potentially strange occurrence I can, hoping to squeeze out some excitement from my situation.

The lights cut out without warning, plunging my room into pitch-black silence. For a split second, I swear someone's here with me. Then, a flicker. The lights return, but now everything is drenched in an eerie red glow. I rush to the door and try to peer into the hallway, but it won't budge. It's locked. I'm trapped.

A voice suddenly crackles to life from the P.A. system. "Attention all residents: a code red protocol has been enacted. All rooms have been secured, and residents who are not currently in their quarters will be escorted to them shortly. Rooms will remain sealed until the protocol is lifted, which will be indicated by the return of normal lighting. All doors will unlock at that time, allowing you to proceed with your daily activities. We appreciate your understanding and cooperation. Remember, together, we can ENDURE anything." The P.A. system cuts out, and I am left in the flashing crimson silence. Somehow, the lack of alarms and the presence of utter quiet makes the situation even more daunting.

With nothing left to do but wait, I lay back down in bed, staring at the ceiling as it flashes in and out of existence. I think about what might be happening beyond the threshold of my room's door and quickly decide to block out those intrusive thoughts before I get too carried away. Ignorance truly is bliss; sometimes, I'm perfectly content to remain unaware. I begin to daydream about Lena and how, in a perfect world, the idea of us could somehow work.

Ever my enemy, my mind drifts—always to the same place when left alone for too long. The crash. My family. All the ways life could've turned out differently. Then Rory appears, my younger sister. I close my eyes, trying to summon her. I can almost smell that cloying perfume she loved, the one that used to drive me crazy but now feels like the sweetest scent in the world. I try to see her nose crinkle mid-laugh, to taste her banana bread, the one that made her a legend among our friends and family. But the details are slipping. Fading. I refuse to open my eyes. I won't let her go.

Somewhere between memory and determination, sleep takes me. I'm boarding a temporal train at an astral station, and I already know where it's headed, Mallen. Always, inevitably, Mallen.

CHAPTER 2

Conspirers

Time and location (present-day): 3:30 pm,
ENDURE Center for Rehabilitation

I'm back, standing in the middle of that endless, two-lane road. The wind howls, driving a brutal snowstorm that blurs everything into white noise. Snowflakes whip around me, turning the world into static. Up ahead, something tall looms on the pavement—the only other presence in this frozen stretch of nowhere. I know the drill by now. The only way out is through. So, I move forward, obedient as ever, drawn toward the unknown.

I hold my forearm to my head to shield my eyes from the blizzard, and as I draw closer, it becomes clear that the object is a door. There are no walls supporting it, just a wooden slab door and frame standing upright in the middle of the street. I grasp its knob and turn it. The door opens inward, and its frame serves as a portal, outlining a realm that differs drastically from my current location's dreary, frozen hellscape. Warmth radiates from beyond the door's threshold, and I instinctively,

14

almost involuntarily, step through. I glance over my shoulder, but the door has vanished, taking the tundra with it.

I turn back around, and three figures stand before me. Two are instantly recognizable: my mother, Olivia, and my father, Charles. The third, however, is nothing more than a blur, a shadowy silhouette. The shape feels familiar; I'm certain of it. Feminine in nature, pure of sin and wrongdoing. I clench my eyes tightly and will my mind to give form to this shadow, to reveal its identity. Just then, a flash of memory. A mere snippet of her face vanishes as quickly as it appeared, but it serves its purpose all the same. Aurora, Rory for short. It's my younger sister. Suddenly, the shadow comes to life, its edges begin to vibrate violently until it disintegrates into ash, gently drifting away in the breeze. A swift and instant pain wells in my chest, a feeling of loss, of grief... I then look to my parents, hoping they can bring her back and fix this, but they stand like statues, unmoving.

They both reach out to me, beckoning me closer still. I step toward them, but the earth beneath me shakes and quakes angrily the moment I do. With each passing second, the tremors grow stronger until my feet are swept out from under me, and I fall to the ground. The sound of earth crumbling and cracking begins to overwhelm me, a thunderous symphony of nature. I curl up in a fetal position; my parents have disappeared; I've been utterly abandoned to my fate. I clamp my hands over my ears, trying to silence the chaos, but it changes nothing, and so I scream. I scream until my throat is raw, until I have nothing left to give, until the entire world around me collapses.

Shooting upright in bed, I struggle to gain control of my breath. I'm drenched in sweat, and one of my famed migraines is stabbing at my left temple. I swing my feet out over the edge of the bed and notice the floor shining its usual pearlescent white. The scarlet glow of the code red is gone, so I'm free to leave my room. When I attempt to stand, instantaneous nausea attacks my gut, and I quickly find myself seated once more. *These episodes are getting out of hand,* I think. With each nightmare comes an increased physical reaction upon returning to the real world, and it's taking a toll on not only my mind but my body as well. I take a moment before attempting to stand again. The mixture of lemon-scented cleaning products and antiseptic threatens to open the floodgates of my esophagus. I try again slowly, methodically. The nausea attempts to creep up on me one final time but eventually passes.

I glance at the clock; it shows 3:36 pm. *Did I really doze off for that long?* Shaking the confusion from my mind, I decide to head to the lobby. If I know Jonathan as well as I think I do, he'll already be waiting at the chess table for me. He's always been punctual, and it's something he takes pride in. Before becoming a resident here, Jonathan was an air traffic controller. He's shared several stories with me, and they nearly always end with some kind of lesson about the importance of punctuality. Sure enough, when I arrive at my destination, Jonathan is there waiting, chessboard set up and ready to play.

"What's the score again?" I ask as I take a seat across from him.

Jonathan furrows his brow as if he hasn't heard my question. "Are you feeling okay? Because you look terrible."

I wave him off and ask again, "What's the score?"

"Six to five, me. Underdog goes first," he says mockingly, straightening his posture and acknowledging my feigned indifference toward my own well-being.

I settle into a comfortable position and advance a pawn as we start our conversation. "So, code red... what was that all about?"

"I don't know," he shrugs. "I've been here for just over a year and have never seen anything like that." Jonathan moves a knight, capturing one of my pawns off the board. I glare at him, then study the playing field as I contemplate my next move.

"Interesting. I'm sure it wasn't anything as extravagant as I'd like to believe. It's probably someone trying to leave without permission or a guardian." Suddenly, I feel a presence beside me, and for a moment, I think Mallen has shown up in public, hastening my descent into madness.

"Well, it wasn't exactly an attempt to *leave*, per se, but I definitely didn't have permission. I've got the next game, assuming no one else has claimed it." The man speaking pulls up a chair and sits down on it backward next to the chess table, his folded arms resting on the backrest. I can't decide whether his unkempt dirty-blonde hair, beard stubble, or bright blue eyes give him a slightly unhinged look. Other than that, he's just your typical corn-fed country boy. He extends his hand. "The name's Aiden Buckley."

I glance at Jonathan, who merely shrugs again in response, before I take Aiden's hand and give it a firm shake. "Royce Wilko, this is my friend Jonathan. The next game is all yours."

A second set of chair legs scrapes against the floor, and now we're flanked on both sides of the table by uninvited company. "Desmond Luther, I'm a friend of Aiden's," the second gentleman says as he takes a seat. He's tall and of African American descent. If I had to guess, they're both in their forties, but Desmond seems more stoic than his partner. His facial hair is well-groomed, and his shaved head is so neatly lined up it looks like he just came from a visit to the barber. Once I finish studying the two of them, I finally address the bait I had previously ignored. "*You?* You're saying you're the reason for that code red?"

He smirks. "Maybe that's what I mean, maybe not. It depends on how the rest of this conversation unfolds."

Not one to be deterred, Jonathan shifts a bishop and leans in closer to the table as I try to divide my attention between the two newcomers and our game. "Sounds like you planned this conversation ahead of time, Aiden. What does this have to do with Royce and me? Why are you two bothering us?"

Jonathan had been a straight-to-the-point kind of guy for as long as I had known him. Desmond interjected.

"Forgive Aiden; he's a little eccentric. Let me get straight to the point. You both seem like reasonable men, so I encourage you to listen to us," he pauses, and I make my next move before glancing sideways at Desmond. The entire interaction feels odd, and their intrusiveness is starting to become a bit irritating.

Why the pause? Was that for dramatic effect? Or is he waiting for us to agree before he continues? And we "seem like reasonable men"? What does that even mean? Are they flattering us or trying to manipulate us? Aiden's just standing there like some strange prop. Eccentric, he says. That could mean anything, from harmlessly weird to totally unhinged...

Desmond continues, seemingly noticing the caution in my eyes. "Aiden and I have this theory, and it isn't without merit. We've spent a few years compiling evidence to support it. It has become increasingly apparent in recent months, however, that if we want to act on our theory and find the answers we seek, we need more help. That's where both of you come in."

Did he say a few years? How long have some of these people been here? And this theory — what theory? That's either scientific or dangerously delusional, and I'm not sure which is worse. Jonathan seems calm, but I know him. He's scanning them the same way I am. It certainly feels coincidental that these two strangers need our help. Why us? Why now? It feels... deliberate. I hate that part of me wants to know more. That's how these things start: curiosity, then involvement, then no way out.

Jonathan knocks one of my knights off the board and pulls me out of my thoughts; I'm losing. He smiles slyly.

"Alright, we'll bite; what's this theory of yours, Desmond? What delusion have you two conspirators fed into?" I can tell that Jonathan isn't taking the two men seriously, but something about the calm demeanor of Desmond is preventing me from dismissing him entirely just yet.

"Not here. If you want to know more, meet me in my quarters tonight after lights out. We'll explain everything then." Desmond discreetly slides a small piece of paper across the table to me, with a room number written on it. Jonathan chuckles softly.

"Sure Desmond. Tell ya what, let us think on it for a bit. Maybe you'll see us tonight; maybe you won't. Checkmate, Royce." It takes me a moment to look away from Desmond. When I finally snap out of it, I glance at the board. There isn't a single move I can make; Jonathan has won.

"Good game," I say as I get up from the table, with Jonathan following suit.

"We understand how it looks," Aiden says as I push in the chair. "Just take some time to think it over; we'll be here when you're ready to discuss more."

I gaze at him in confusion, then turn to Desmond, who merely nods. Once again, Jonathan comes to the rescue. "Yeah, we'll do that... you hungry Royce? I think I'm going to head to the cafeteria."

"No, I'm not feeling well suddenly. I think I'll head back to my quarters for a bit; it's getting late."

It's certainly true; the nausea is starting to become apparent once again.

"It's not even 5:00 pm Are you sure you don't want to eat?"

I nod. "I appreciate it, but I'm sure. I'll find you later."

Jonathan waves goodbye. I glance at Aiden, then at Desmond. "It was nice meeting you both."

Aiden smiles and waves. "See you later," he says, lingering a moment before walking away.

I hesitate, then turn away and head back to my room. As I walk, I reflect on the interaction. Maybe they're just a couple of loons... ENDURE *is* home to a wide variety of patients... it's possible, after all. I've seen my fair share of schizophrenics who refuse to take medication, patients with severe bipolar disorder, and many other mental ailments. It's perfectly plausible that Desmond and Aiden fit that mold.

"But that's not really what you believe, is it?"

I stop dead in my tracks just outside my quarters as my stomach drops. Not because the thought makes me second-guess my own sanity, but because it doesn't feel like *mine.* I circle around, checking the hallway for anyone else. No one's around. Sweat begins to bead on my forehead. *Don't... don't do it. You know it's all in your head. Just don't give in.* I shut my eyes tightly, hesitant, even afraid. Then, despite how much my body and brain are telling me not to, I speak into the void.

"Mallen... are you... are you here?"

I continue to keep my eyes clenched shut. It feels like an eternity before I finally open them and glance around frantically. Nothing. No one. I'm still alone. I let out a sigh of relief. *Here I am, contemplating whether Desmond and Aiden are off their rockers, and yet I'm losing my own damn mind. Christ, I need to get out of here...* I regain my bearings, steady myself, and enter my room. Once I close the door behind me, I flop down on my bed once again. I suddenly feel exhausted, as if my life force has been drained. The nausea is stronger than ever, and my head is beginning to throb. I don't want to sleep for fear of what awaits me in my dreams, but I can't stay awake unless I want to puke my brains out and battle the pain in my temples. Neither option seems fair, but I settle on the lesser of two evils and shut my eyes.

CHAPTER 3

Time

Time and location (present-day): 7:00 am,
ENDURE Center for Rehabilitation

I find myself submerged in an ocean of pale white, just like always. The terrain has become a familiar place at this point, so I know what to look for. As I slowly spin in a circle, the door finally appears where I'm sure it hadn't been only moments before. I step toward it and feel myself being pulled, bare toes scraping against the indistinguishable floor beneath my feet. Whatever intangible force has dragged me releases its grip mere inches from the standalone gateway. Gathering my composure, I step through, once more into the fray.

Again, off in the distance, I recognize my parents, though this time, they stand alone, with no third silhouette beside them. Before I can move, the invisible hand lassoes me once more, roping me in to stand before my mother and father in the blink of an eye. My mother reaches out, gently placing the back of her hand against my cheek. Her touch feels warm and nurturing.

I reach up to hold her hand in mine, but the moment we make contact, she liquefies before my eyes, raining down in drops that pool on the ground. As I stare at the puddle below my feet, it begins to change. Color sprawls seemingly out of nowhere until the fluid transforms into a deep burgundy hue, resembling blood. Father has tear stains on his cheeks. There's pressure on either side of my face, holding me perfectly still, forcing me to watch as the man shakes his head in despair, then turns and walks away.

I'm out of bed and scrambling toward the trash can beside my desk in an instant, sleep paralysis suddenly absent from this old song and dance. Grabbing the receptacle, I plunge my head into its opening just in time for the vomit to rush out. As I heave, I swear I feel my sternum crack, and yet I'm grateful. Grateful that this time I'm spared my usual visit from Mallen. The ordeal seems to last an eternity. When it finally ends, I push the now-full bin away from me and slouch against the wall.

My hand comes away wet after pressing it to my forehead; I'm burning up. Something is wrong with me, *seriously* wrong. I need help; I need to get up, but I can't find the strength. Every muscle in my body aches, and every fiber of my being feels like it's on fire. Just as I start contemplating possible solutions, a knock on the door sounds—a literal gift from the gods. Shortly after my silence, the door opens, and Lena steps in. I watch as she notices me crumpled on the floor, her casual demeanor quickly shifting to shocked concern as she rushes to my aid.

`"My God, Royce! Are you okay?" Lena grabs me by the shoulders and tries to straighten my posture. "Here, sit up… come on, help me out a little, Royce," I wince as I fight back another wave of nausea, pressing my back against the wall to give the appearance that I'm not completely falling apart, but Lena remains unconvinced. "I had no idea things were *this* bad, Royce. Jonathan told me you hadn't left your quarters in two days, so I came to check on you. I never imagined that… we need to get you medical attention, have your overall health assessed, maybe run some blood work. Let's try to get you up."

She grabs my hand and tries to lift me from the floor, but I pull away with a viciousness so unforgiving that I surprise myself and leave her looking wounded. "No! No… I don't trust him, Lena. I don't…" It's getting harder to speak. Every inhale feels physically straining, draining my already empty well of energy. *Did she say two days? No, that can't be right. I've only been sleeping for a few hours… right?*

"Royce, don't be ridiculous. Differences aside, my uncle is a doctor, and you *need* medical attention. Please, let me *help* you."

I shake my head defiantly. "I trust you; *you* can help me. Not him. Please, don't tell him." The fear in my own voice surprises me even more than my earlier aggressive withdrawal from Lena. *Is that what this is? Fear? Do I really fear Atticus Cais?* Lena sighs in anger, yet somehow sounds defeated.

"Fine. I won't involve my uncle, but you need help. Here, take two of these." Lena reaches into the pocket of her scrubs, and when she pulls her hand back, she holds a dram filled with pills. She opens it, takes out two electric blue capsules, and thrusts them toward me. I take them hesitantly and hold them up for a closer inspection. Etched into their surface is an identifier code that reads, "DM1."

"What... what are they?"

Lena's eyes dart sideways and then quickly return to me as she offers a half-hearted smile. It's a subtle shift in her behavior, but a telling one, all the same; she's crafting a lie. "They're just some NSAIDs; they'll help with the fever and the pain."

I raise an eyebrow, growing more suspicious of her with each passing minute. "Who said I have a fever?"

"I'm a nurse, Royce. I can tell by your symptoms, not to mention how much you're sweating in a consistently temperature-controlled environment at seventy-five degrees. What's with all the questioning? Didn't you *just* say you trusted me?"

You're losing it Royce... letting Desmond Luther and Aiden Buckley fill your head with conspiracies... "Of course, you're right, I'm sorry. My head just doesn't... it doesn't feel right." I throw the pills into the back of my mouth and swallow. If they're poisoned, then at least I'll perish in her company. *It's not like I have a whole lot left to live for anyways...*

"Oh, don't be like that, Royce. I thought we were just starting to become friends. Am I not worth living for?"

I hear him, Mallen, whispering, like he's breathing right behind me. My eyes snap up to meet Lena's, but instead of calm, panic ignites inside me like a wildfire. Suddenly, I'm lunging away from her, a caged animal desperate to escape. "No! You're not real! Get out! GET OUT OF MY HEAD!" I scream, voice raw and ragged. My hands slam over my ears, eyes squeezed shut as if shutting out the world will silence him. Lena stumbles back, her face twisting in shock and fear, but I'm beyond caring. The darkness inside me has taken hold, and I'm drowning in it. I don't care if she thinks I'm crazy because, for the first time outside of a sleep paralysis episode, I *see* him. Mallen stands behind her, a hulking shadow with two beady red dots for eyes. Something is different this time, though. He appears less like a shadow and more three-dimensional and solid. I can now see that those menacing, diminutive eyes are set deeply in what seems to be sable black *flesh* draped over a skeletal structure that is *almost* passable as human. However, the longer I stare in disbelief, the more peculiarities I can identify that make it clear he is nothing of the human variety. He's tall and thick-bodied, but his arms and legs are gangly, each joint bulging unnaturally as if osteoporosis has taken root. His blackened hands dangle loosely at his sides, with six elongated fingers jutting out from each metacarpus but no thumbs. Mallen tilts his head at me, making it look as though his neck is broken.

"You wound me, Royce. Why are you so afraid of me when all I want is to reveal the truth? I'll leave you with Lena for now; you've got plenty of damage to contain... but don't think this conversation is over..."

and then he's gone. As suddenly as he emerged from the depths of my fractured psyche, Mallen simply vanishes.

"...Royce? Are you... are you okay? Was it him?" Lena hasn't said a word until now, remaining silent and watchful throughout the entire interaction with Mallen, just as she has probably been trained to do.

"Didn't you see him? He was right there, behind you. Didn't you hear him?"

She approaches me now, albeit cautiously, as if I'm a threat to her. *I would never hurt her...* "Royce... It's just you and me here, no one else. Mallen isn't *real*, you know that, right?"

She gently places a hand on my shoulder, and her touch grounds me almost instantly. I nod slowly and begin to regain control of my breathing.

"Yes... I know that... of course I know. Maybe you're right. Perhaps it's time we get Dr. Cais involved."

"What are you saying? Are you even listening to yourself right now? Atticus Cais CANNOT be trusted! The thoughts are becoming

more intrusive now, deafening. I just want them to stop, whether they are my own or Mallen's.

"If I go to get my uncle, will you be okay alone for a little while?"

I'm not sure, but my goal is to cause her no more concern than I already have. "I think so; the episode seems to be passing now." I still feel like absolute crap, but I am calmer now.

She gives my shoulder a reassuring squeeze. "Okay," she says softly. "Just sit tight; we'll be back soon, I promise." She hesitates before offering a half-smile, then stands and leaves my room.

I close my eyes, concentrating on the inside of my eyelids, trying not to let my focus wander anywhere that Mallen might be lurking. This task is becoming increasingly difficult with each passing day. I have *seen* him. Not in a nightmare. Not during sleep paralysis, but in broad daylight. Maybe I am a lunatic, destined to spend the rest of my days within the confines of ENDURE's walls.

As I sit contemplating my bleak fate, I think I've finally found a moment of peace, but no such luck would find me today. I hear the door latch engage, presumably signaling Lena's arrival with Dr. Cais much sooner than I expected. When I open my eyes to see who has entered my room, it's Jonathan standing before me. He quietly shuts the door behind him, a gesture that seems all too foreboding. Somehow, I muster the strength to pick myself up off the floor, albeit at a snail's pace. "Jonathan? What are you doing here?"

He smiles before responding. "I hadn't heard from you in a couple days; I was starting to worry, so I thought I'd check in on you."

It makes enough sense; there's nothing unusual about that, I think. However, the need to reassure myself and Jonathan's lackluster performance immediately trigger a follow-up sense of suspicion.

"Look, Royce, I'm really sorry about all this. I need you to understand that... but things have progressed too far. You can't let them through; I won't allow it. They'll destroy everything; I just can't."

*Let them through? What the actual fu—*My thoughts are interrupted as Jonathan suddenly closes the distance between us, and then something feels physically *wrong.* My body is hot and cold all at once. Warm fluid seeps through the fabric of my jumpsuit at my abdomen, where a dull ache starts to develop. I place my hand on my stomach where the pain is intensifying, and find an object protruding from my body. When I pull it away to inspect further, it's wet with blood. Jonathan has just *stabbed* me.

CHAPTER 4

Conduit

Time and location (present-day): 7:26 am,
ENDURE Center for Rehabilitation

Maybe it's instinctive, or perhaps it's the sheer adrenaline rush from having four-and-a-half inches of cold steel lodged in my stomach. Whatever the case, I swing hard with a right hook and connect even harder with Jonathan's jaw. There's a loud crack as my fist makes contact. He falls backward, and his elbows nearly shatter the tile upon contact while his grip on the knife tightens. The blade dislodges roughly from my gut. If the blood wasn't draining from my body at a concerning pace before, it certainly is now. I clutch my hand against the wound, a feeble instinctive attempt to stop the bleeding.

Jonathan is now on one knee, tending to the split on his chin with the back of his hand. "It's not personal, Royce. You're the conduit—their way in. We can't let them in. I won't let them in." He rises to his feet, and the look in his eyes makes him unrecognizable. This isn't the Jonathan McCallister I know; this isn't my friend. He steps forward, the knifepoint aimed in my direction.

"Jonathan, don't do this... we can talk. *Please*." I hold my hands up high, as if to calm an enraged grizzly. If I can manage to look non-threatening, maybe I can deescalate the situation.

"I don't have a choice... if I stop you, I stop Mallen," he charges at me like a wild bull. At the last moment, just before he reaches me, I sidestep and shove him forcefully onward. As Jonathan trips and crashes into the desk, I stumble and lose my balance too, my hands smearing blood across the nearest wall as I brace myself against it. I turn around, leaning back dizzily into the gore on the wall. My jumpsuit is soaked with red, and I leave a trail of maroon as I slide down its surface to the floor. The blood loss is overwhelming; I need help soon, or I fear the worst. *Is this seriously how I die? Out of all the possibilities... did he... did he say Mallen? How the hell does he know about Mallen?*

I look to Jonathan as my breath heaves, trying to prepare for his next assault amidst the chaotic confusion I'm experiencing. Something isn't right, though. He attempts to stand, but it seems he's struggling to do so. Whenever he attempts to rise from the floor, he slips and falls back down onto his hands and knees. Eventually, he rotates on all fours to face me, and I finally realize what is hindering him. When he fell, he landed on his own knife, which is now sticking out of his chest. A mixture of blood and saliva tendrils drips profusely from his mouth. He coughs a gargled, wretched sound as his gaze matches mine.

Then he starts crawling toward me, but I can't muster the strength to move, so I think it's best to conserve whatever energy I have left for when he gets close. One final push when he's near enough. I don't want to hurt him, but it's clear now that this will end only one way—my life or his. I try to plead with him one more time. "Come on, Jonathan, just stop. You're hurt, badly. I am too. This is over. Whatever *this* is." Which poses a question in itself: just what the hell is going on here? Why is this happening? How did Jonathan even get access to a hunting knife here? Why is someone I call a friend trying to kill me? *What the fuck is happening?! I'm dying... Oh God, I'm dying...* The confusion is now slipping into panic. I glance down at my maroon-spattered arms; their pallor is shocking, to say the least.

Suddenly, a hand grips my shin, moving haphazardly up my body until it firmly grips my throat. Jonathan's other hand joins in, and I tumble sideways to the floor, pinned beneath his weight. His grip tightens as blood from his mouth drips onto my face, his teeth gritting with the savagery of a man determined to take a life. The edges of my vision are starting to fade, and for a brief moment, I think this is finally it; I'm going to die here...

"I won't allow it. No more mercy, Royce. No more restraint. Kill him."

Suddenly, my vision clears, and I feel a surge of renewed energy. I grab the knife jutting from Jonathan's chest and tear it free. He exhales audibly, painfully. Then, before he can react, I sweep the blade edge across his throat. A warm spray of red spatters over me as he collapses atop my body, and that's it. Jonathan's dead. He's dead, and I killed him. I want to roll his corpse to the side and get his body off me, but the burst of energy I felt moments prior has come and gone. Jonathan is dead, and I fear I soon will be too. I start to slip in and out of consciousness. How long has this whole ordeal lasted? Where is Lena with Dr. Cais? During one of my more lucid moments, I hear the door open and shut yet again.

"Ah shit... not good." I hear the voice as if it's in an echo chamber, and it feels unfamiliar. The next thing I can consciously recall is someone pulling me out from underneath Jonathan's body by my arms. "Don't worry, we're going to get you help. I'm a friend of Desmond's; you can trust me. Hang in there." The voice sounds so distant now, almost disembodied. I struggle to stay alert, trying not to drift off, but death's warm embrace is beckoning to me...

"Not yet Royce... I'm not finished with you yet. We're just getting started."

The world goes dark.

CHAPTER 5

Desmond

Time and location (the past): 6:05 pm,
Brooklyn, New York

Desmond stands on the balcony of his two-bedroom apartment, leaning on the railing as he watches the sun set behind the Brooklyn Bridge. Work had been unjustifiably grueling today, and the pennies he and Nora had been pinching just to get by only added insult to injury. He exhales deeply and lets his head hang low, attempting to release the tension in his shoulders and allow the stress to melt away. *We'll figure things out; we always do.* He faintly hears the front door of the apartment open and wonders if Nora has gotten off work early. Her company is something he craves on days like today. She's an island in an ocean of uncertainty, something to hold onto, a reason to *survive. Pulling* himself away from the railing, he heads inside.

To his surprise, it's his son Dominic rummaging through the fridge instead of his wife. When his kid finally peeks out from behind the refrigerator door, a leftover piece of cold chicken from last night's dinner dangles from his mouth.

"Yo Dom, I was *gonna* eat that," Desmond says, pointing to the tenderloin in his son's mouth. Dominic grabs the chicken and tears off a piece with his teeth, chewing loudly.

"Snooze, you lose, old man," he shrugs, as Desmond chuckles.

"How was school today, man? You go to Gabriel's after?"

Dominic makes his way to the dining table and takes a seat as he finishes eating. "School was alright, and yeah. We got a group together and hit the court at his complex for a bit. Ran a *pretty* mean game on that punk white boy Brian too," he says with a smirk. Desmond pulls out the chair closest to his son, sits down, and tousles his hair.

"One day, your old man will be rich, and then the court will be right in your backyard, along with an infinity-edge pool, a jacuzzi, and all the *works.*"

"Sure, Pops. Just let me know when pigs start flying, and *then* I'll believe you."

"I offer you the promise of wealth, and you're just going to throw shade like that? That's cold-blooded, man. Also, you know you're half white, right? Or did you forget?" Dominic jokingly punches him on the arm, and Desmond affectionately ruffles his kid's hair again in response, laughing.

Immediately afterward, he feels a sting of shame knowing that his son will never believe they'll have more than they do now. Dominic stands up from the table and pushes the chair back into place, disappearing into his room shortly after. He's seventeen and about to graduate high school, an unavoidable fact of life that has Desmond hyper-focusing on finding a way to provide more. Maybe the kid is right; maybe this is all they are meant to achieve in life. A mediocre existence on the west side of Brooklyn.

The desperate and constant urge Desmond feels to give more to him and to Nora is palpable, yet seemingly out of reach. *Bleeding Edge*, the biotech company where he works, is cutting hours due to downsizing, and his pay barely keeps the lights on. Nora is still working to complete her doctorate program, but until she finishes, her part-time job only covers groceries each month. Once she completes her degree, she'll earn more than Desmond can even dream of. Maybe then they can finally move out of this shoebox they call home. Dominic re-enters the living area, suddenly dressed to the nines and smelling like half a bottle of cologne. Desmond raises an eyebrow.

"Where in the world are you going that has you breaking out the Retro Highs?" he asks, referencing the pine green and black Air Jordans on Dominic's feet. They're his most coveted pair of sneakers and required more than a couple of weeks of saving from his shifts at the corner market after school.

"I have a date with Marissa; how do I look? Fresh in my Jordans, no doubt?" Dominic struts about dramatically, and

Desmond takes the opportunity to hype his son up. After all, he's met Marissa a few times now, and she seems like a positive influence in Dominic's life. "Ooooo boy, dressed to impress! You get that from your dad, but don't tell your mom I said that."

Dominic chuckles. "Quit playing."

"All seriousness, son, you look great. Now get out of here; don't keep her waiting."

"Alright, see you soon, Dad. I love you."

He smiles, and for that brief moment, Desmond feels that everything will work out, as if he can take on the world with one hand tied behind his back. "I love you too."

Dominic nods and jogs toward the door as Desmond calls out after him, "Remember! Back by 10 pm!"

"I know, I know, see you later!" His voice slips through the crack in the door just before it shuts, leaving Desmond with his thoughts once more. No matter what the future holds, Desmond sleeps easy at night, knowing that he and Nora have raised such a respectable young man. Every good parent can brag about their own child, but Desmond and Nora never feel the need to do so with Dominic; it simply shows. In his words and actions, he truly is a blessing.

He rises from the table as his belly grumbles, heading for the fridge to see what's left after Dominic has raided it. Before he reaches it, a sound like firecrackers rattling off grabs his attention. It takes a moment to realize that what he's hearing is semi-automatic gunfire, and that it's close—*too close.*

Desmond races to the balcony, his pulse quickening. When he arrives and slams into the railing to look over at the street below, he does so with such intensity that he momentarily thinks he might topple over the edge. A car peels away recklessly from outside the entrance of his apartment building, a man with a bandana concealing the lower half of his face hanging out of the rear passenger window. On the sidewalk, Desmond sees a body, motionless and bleeding out. From all the way up on the seventh floor, he can barely make out the victim's shoes; they're pine green and black.

CHAPTER 6

Leverage

Time and location (the past): 6:52 pm,
Brooklyn, New York

Desmond bursts out of the apartment door, indifferent to whether it closes behind him. His first instinct is to dash toward the elevator, and he curses the habit that has formed before altering his course and heading for the stairwell. He crashes into the second door like an NFL linebacker, nearly colliding with a neighbor approaching from the opposite direction. The woman unleashes a barrage of profanities as he moves forward without slowing down, but all he hears is a loud buzzing in his ears. It's as if a grenade has detonated at close range, drowning out all sound with a violent ringing. Internally, it feels as though a grenade has indeed exploded, its shrapnel piercing every inch of his body; stinging, burning, *screaming* in agony. He's already raced down the first three flights of stairs, leaving four more before reaching the lobby.

As he rounds the corner and just before descending the next set of steps, the door to the fourth-floor swings open, and he is tackled hard. The next thing Desmond knows, he is pinned to the concrete by two men dressed in black body armor, their identities concealed behind helmets and masks. He panics like a wild animal, flailing and screaming, losing his grasp on humanity and the ability to form coherent spoken words. As he struggles relentlessly, the futility sinks in, and the sounds of the surrounding world become clear again. He can make out someone shouting his name, capturing his attention and pulling him back from the brink of insanity. "Desmond! Are you listening to me?!"

Now, as he relaxes and stops resisting, the two men lift him off the floor. The first man secures his arms behind his back with cuffs, and then the second slams his face against the cement wall of the stairwell, holding him there firmly. As best he can, Desmond looks sideways to his captors and pleads with his eyes, though his left cheek is being smashed into the wall with such force that it hinders his ability to speak. "Please! You have to let me go; my son is in danger! I'm begging you, man, just let me go!" He stomps hard on the guard's foot, only to be displeased by the steel-toed boot beneath his heel. Despite Desmond's clear failure to injure him, the man yanks his head back and slams his face into the concrete again. A third man enters Desmond's field of vision, slightly obscured by blood trickling into his left eye. Casually leaning against the wall just inches from his face, the man reaches out to the guard, tapping his shoulder in protest. "Easy, Oakley. This man is our guest, not so rough."

"Alright, so the guard with the temper is Oakley. Who are these other clowns? As if he's read Desmond's mind, the third man shifts his position, now uncomfortably close, and introduces himself in a calm Voice. "My name is Dr. Atticus Cais. My friends here are Jordan Oakley and Elliot Shaw. They work for me. I need you to listen carefully, Desmond; your son's life depends on it.'"

My son? What do they know about Dominic?! Desmond starts to struggle again, but now the man whom Atticus Cais referred to as Elliot Shaw steps in to help Oakley restrain him. "The more you struggle, the worse the outcome will be. If you silence yourself and listen, this will end much more favorably for you and your boy. Not to mention your beautiful wife, Nora. Let's consider the two of them as leverage; it may sway your decision regarding my offer."

Every part of him urges him to resort to savagery, to tear these men's throats open with his teeth if necessary, but he must reach Dominic. He's running out of time. Cooperation will be the fastest way forward. Desmond stops panting, focuses on controlling his breath, and gathers his composure before addressing his assailants. "What do you want?"

Atticus Cais smiles, and for a moment, Desmond thinks he has encountered the devil himself. "There we go, much better. It's quite simple, Desmond. You have something I want—no, something I *need*. I cannot divulge what that something is; there's a lot of red tape surrounding this… shall we say, *sensitive* matter."

Desmond grits his teeth in frustration. "How can I give you what you want if you can't tell me what it is?"

"That's the beauty of it; all you have to do is come with us. If you cooperate completely, we'll save your son's life, and no harm will come to Nora."

He's beginning to lose himself again; the ambiguous way his captor speaks pricks and irritates every fiber of his being. "Come on, man… just let me go to my son! He's bleeding out on the street!" Tears start to well as his voice cracks and desperation creeps in. Every second lost is another second where Dominic's life hangs in the balance.

"I know; he was shot on my orders. We needed a significant distraction to catch you alone. The fewer witnesses, the better."

Desmond looks up from the floor, his eyes widening as his gaze homes in and locks onto Atticus. Then, all composure is lost as he thrashes fiercely, lashing out at Atticus's throat. Desmond's fingers graze the man's neck before Oakley and Shaw subdue him. "You son of a bitch! I'll kill you! I'll kill all of you!"

Something sharp jabs Desmond in the shoulder. Moments later, Shaw and Oakley release him. He stumbles toward Atticus, falters, and drops to his hands and knees. Atticus crouches down in front of him. "I do wish you had chosen to cooperate; it'll be much more difficult to carry you out of here without being seen by civilians, but so be it."

Everything is collapsing. His vision narrows, the edges softening into darkness. The weight in his limbs, the slow drag of thought, he's been sedated. It's hitting fast. Consciousness slips through his fingers like water. Desmond's mind races as his body shuts down. Dominic, he might already be dead. Nora, missing, lost in the chaos. He doesn't know where she is, or if she's even alive. Then, the future, that fragile dream he once allowed himself to believe in. A life that felt just out of reach... now shattered. Gone.

CHAPTER 7

Falsification

Time and location (present-day): 9:43 am,
ENDURE Center for Rehabilitation

"Royce," the voice is distant and indistinct. "Royce," it repeats. Still, I can't pull a face from memory to match the sound. I stand in an endless ocean of alabaster, just as before. No walls, no floors or ceilings, only white. A strange sensation fills my body, or rather the space my body should have occupied. But in this peculiar realm, I am weightless, like consciousness without form, occupying nothing but open air. Pure white stretches as far as the eye can see, yet my sense of touch endures. I feel every gust of what I perceive as wind, every movement from surrounding objects that are just as invisible as I am. Transparent, but they exist. Perhaps they are not objects at all, but entities, living organisms trapped in the same snowy blindness I find myself floating within. Am I the only one here? Or are there others trying to cry out for help to no avail? An explanation for what is happening eludes me, but I can conclude that if there is a hell, this must be it. No fiery,

cavernous depths boiling with lava and steam, no ghoulish creatures or hellhounds imposing their will, just emptiness. Stark, white emptiness; an existence without truly existing.

Suddenly, as if my silent plea for help has finally been heard, something appears in the distance. It's small—a mere speck of black in a sea of florescence—but at this point, I'll welcome any form of company. As it draws nearer, so does the sound it produces. Humming? The closer the speck gets to me, the less muffled the noise becomes. What was once static is now beginning to form into words and sentences, and then I realize this speck is what called my name moments ago. With its decreasing distance, its shape becomes more familiar, stretching and morphing into a figure. Tall and slender, with limbs and appendages. An image that becomes clearer the closer it moves to me. Soon, I can see without any obstruction; the speck, now a full-bodied man, stands before me.

His face twists and contorts as if someone took human features and tossed them into a blender. As the cycle slows, it becomes clear that the man is familiar. The features on his flesh canvas settle, a mouth fully forms, and then my father speaks to me. "Royce," the vibrations trail off and echo into the eternity that lies before us. "Open your eyes, come home. It isn't too late to fix what's broken."

This leaves me confused. Come home? But home is nowhere, not anymore. My family is gone, and I can hardly consider the facility I had been thrust into as my home. Before I can attempt to produce any words of my own, I feel the pallid ocean before me tremble and *unsettle, an occurrence invisible to the naked eye. The everlasting white that has surrounded us now decays, yellowing and eventually cracking into dust and fragments, giving way to nothing but darkness beneath its bright exterior. As this strange world falls apart, I stare on; my gaze locked onto my father's when suddenly the cycle on his face starts up again.*

Charles Wilko's face, my father's face, starts twisting and contorting into an unholy puddle of cartilage and skin. As the process continues, nearly everything around me shatters and falls into the abyss, except for the separate patches of white that my father and I stand upon. When the face finally settles again, my stomach drops deep in my abdomen. Staring back at me now isn't the face of my father, but the face of Dr. Atticus Cais; cold... calculating... "Creationist," Atticus says, as if reading my thoughts.

The ground beneath me collapses.

My eyes open slowly; the panic that once accompanied these nightmares is subdued by their repetitive pattern. I try to sit up in my bed but feel a pang in my stomach just below the left side of my ribcage. That's right... I was stabbed... My God, Jonathan. I... I killed Jonathan... As my brain replays the scenario in a game of catch-up, my eyes take in my surroundings. This isn't my room; it seems more like an infirmary. As I glance around at all the medical equipment, I suddenly notice someone at my bedside, the entire chest of his facility-provided jumpsuit stained with blood. I instinctively jolt, which is clearly visible to the man as he raises his arms in a gesture of peace. "Whoa there, take it easy, I'm not a threat. I'm a friend; just relax. We need to talk before the nurse comes back."

I feel a twinge as I continue sitting up, my muscles somewhat atrophic and aching with every slight twist and turn. "Jonathan was a friend too…" The wariness in my voice speaks volumes, and my new guest can probably see it on my face as well.

He exhales heavily. "While that may be a fair point, I'm not here to stick a knife in your gut, even though I'm covered in *your* blood. My name is Matias Castellón. I'm a friend of Desmond and Aiden. We'll have plenty of time to discuss that later, but for now we need to operate on assumed trust."

I can't decide if it's sheer stupidity or the lack of willpower I'm left with after being betrayed and nearly killed by the only person I once called a friend here. Whatever the case, I choose to trust Matias for now. "Alright, what do you need to tell me before the nurse comes back?"

Matias scans the room as if checking for any prying eyes or listening devices, then leans in closer. "I arrived at your room later than I would have liked after Jonathan attacked you. I found you lying in a pool of your own blood and carried you to the lobby. Staff saw us and intervened, which brought us to the present situation. Thankfully, Jonathan's death was deemed an act of self-defense. So, for the most part, when they ask what happened, you're going to tell the truth. However, the one thing you need to leave out is anything he may have mentioned about the voices in his head. As far as they're concerned, you had a disagreement over a previous chess match, and Jonathan went ballistic. His chart indicates he had issues with schizophrenia and anger management in the past, so we can leverage that to assist with our alteration of facts."

Jonathan's chart? How did this guy gain access to patient records? Why didn't Jonathan tell me about his health issues? What leaves me most stunned, though, is the mention of voices in Jonathan's head. Suddenly, a memory rushes back from the assault; Jonathan had said Mallen's name. *I never mentioned Mallen to anyone other than Lena, and she wouldn't have told anyone other than Atticus about him, right? Certainly not other patients...* How then did Jonathan know about this shadowy creature that has taken up residence in the depths of my mind? This leads me to another potentially shocking revelation. "Wait... do you hear him too? What about Desmond and Aiden?" Matias scans our surroundings again before speaking. "Like I said, we can discuss this in more detail later. The short answer is no, your friends don't communicate with us. We just know that you and Jonathan aren't the first to hear them."

Them? As in plural? The door to the infirmary opens, and I imagine Matias's stomach dropping just like mine. Lena enters and rushes to my bedside. "Oh, thank God you're alright, Royce," she says, reaching for my hand, then, as if reconsidering, she pulls away and gathers herself. I can see tears forming in her eyes as she tries to hold them back; she truly cares for me. "I'm sure you've been introduced by now, but this is Matias Castellón. He lives in the room across the hall from yours. If it weren't for him, I don't know what would have happened. Matias saved you, Royce. Normally, we wouldn't allow other patients in the infirmary without illness or injury, but Matias insisted on being here when you woke up. Given the circumstances, we made an exception."

I then look to Matias as the realization settles in: I owe this man my life. I nod in appreciation, a silent thank you. He returns the gesture, taking the opportunity to share our narrative. "I heard all the commotion from my room; I just wish I had reacted sooner. Maybe if I had, Jonathan would still be with us."

Lena suddenly becomes sullen. "So, you've told him then? I'm really sorry about Jonathan, Royce. I know you two have grown close over the past few months. What happened? What led to all of this?" Showtime. I feel a bit guilty at the moment, willingly lying to Lena, but at this point, I can't be sure who to trust. If I have to rely on one of them, it's the person who doesn't have direct ties to Atticus Cais and who also saved my life, no matter how I feel about Lena. "Shortly after you left my room to get Atticus for help, Jonathan arrived and let himself in. He was ranting about... a previous chess match we had played. He began shouting that I was a liar and a cheat, and before I knew it, he was on top of me and hitting me. Somewhere along the line, he pulled out a hunting knife and stabbed me. We continued fighting until he tripped and stabbed himself as well. I was pleading with him the entire time to stop, but... eventually he began choking me and I... he left me no choice. I did what I had to, Lena. He forced my hand... I'm so sorry..." I guess the performance is easier to execute than I had anticipated because I'm sobbing now. The pain and reality of it all come rushing in. I miss my friend, and yet I can't reconcile the man I had come to know with the one who attacked me like a rabid beast.

"Of course you're upset, Royce, you butchered your best friend. What kind of monster does that? Maybe the beast isn't me, maybe it's clawing its way out from inside you."

It takes every fiber of my being to ignore Mallen's voice. Lena knows about him, but I can't let her know that Matias is aware of Mallen's existence, too. So, I focus on the pain, concentrating on sitting with it now that the dust has settled. Lena places her hand on my shoulder, and I'm certain that if Matias wasn't here, she would drop the professionalism and embrace me. "It's okay, Royce; let it out. It's understandable that you're upset. Normally, you'd have to speak with law enforcement about this altercation, but based on Matias' testimony and the evidence collected from the crime scene a week ago, they deemed this an open-and-shut case of self-defense. There may be procedural follow-up, but I want you to know you're safe."

"*Did she say a week ago*? What do you mean by a week ago? Did I lose track of time *again*?"

Lena nods her head. "Unfortunately, yes. You had to undergo anesthesia for surgery, and afterward, you fell back into a comatose state. Dr. Cais thought it best to let you recover at your own pace. It was only a week, though."

Atticus arrives just then, as if on cue, summoned like a demon at the mention of his name. "Hello, Royce. Glad to see you up and at 'em again. I just wanted to stop by to see how you were doing, though I'm sure Lena has already covered everything with you." I quickly glance at Matias, wanting to gauge his reaction to the doctor's arrival. It's subtle, but I can tell all the same; Matias hates Dr. Cais just as much as anyone else. I feign nicety again, gathering myself after releasing all my pent-up emotion. Wiping the tears from my eyes, I respond, "Yes, she has. Sorry, it's all just been... a lot."

Atticus approaches me then and, like Lena before him, places a hand on my shoulder. *His* touch sends shivers down my spine. "Don't apologize; you've been through one traumatic event after another. How you're feeling is entirely understandable. Right now, you need rest. Once Lena performs a proper health check on you, you're free to return to your room. You'll find no trace of the altercation upon your return; we've made sure of that. Take care of him, Lena." Atticus prepares to leave but pauses when he crosses paths with my new acquaintance. "Matias," he says with a simple nod. Something in his eyes shifts just slightly before he continues and exits the room. There's a history between the two, but what kind, it's hard to say.

Once Atticus is gone, Matias stands up from the chair beside my bed. "Well, I'm glad you're okay, Royce. Looks like my job here is done. I'll leave you to it, nurse. Royce, I'll see you around."

I nod. "Thank you for everything, Matias."

"Don't mention it," he says before leaving as well. With only Lena and me remaining, the mood relaxes a bit. She sits down on my bedside, finally grabbing my hand as she wanted to earlier. "You really had me worried there for a moment."

"Can you trust her, Royce? Or is she just as much a snake in the grass as her dear uncle, Atticus?"

I close my eyes and sigh exasperatedly. Lena pulls away slightly. "What is it?" she asks with that wounded gazelle look.

"Not you, it's Mallen again," I say, feeling more confident in my ability to speak freely about him now that we're alone.

"What's he saying?" she asks. On that subject, though, I feel compelled to be as vague as possible. "Nothing, just trying to cast a healthy amount of doubt on everything and anything like he always does."

"I guess that's as good a segue into the next conversation as any," Lena responds, pulling out a dram of pills—the same dram she had offered me a week ago from her pocket. "I want you to start taking these regularly. I believe they'll help reduce your side effects, and I also think they might lessen Mallen's grip on you, silencing him completely or, at the very least, muffling his voice in your head."

There was a time when I would have contested and been suspicious of her, but I'm not in the mood for arguing or dealing with Mallen's incessant prodding of my mind. With a silent nod, I accept the pills. "Yeah, that sounds good. Can I take some now?"

Lena appears surprised by my request but quickly recovers. "Of course, it's a once-daily medication. I'll have it ready for you at the dispensary every day, and they'll call for you via the intercom system if you forget." She hands me two bright blue pills, and I toss them to the back of my throat and swallow.

"Thank you; I truly appreciate all that you have done and continue to do for me."

She smiles gently. "Of course, you're my... Well, I'm responsible for your care, right?" The way she pauses mid-sentence sends a nervous chill through me, raising every hair on my body. *What was she going to say?* Not wanting to pry, I choose to interpret it as she feels something deeper for me, no matter how insane that idea might be. Instead, I simply reply, "Right."

Lena stands and steps away from the edge of the bed. "Well, my uncle is right; you really should get some proper rest, and I need to be going. When you're ready, feel free to leave. It was nice chatting, Royce; I'll see you soon."

I smile at her; it's all the response necessary to show her how I feel. She hesitates for a moment longer, then walks away. Once the door shuts, I let out a final exhale. So much has happened so quickly that it will require much more time to process and sort it all out. Now, with *whatever* medication is in my system, I can at least think it through without Mallen negating my every thought. I doubt they're just simple anti-inflammatory meds as Lena had previously suggested, but I don't care anymore. If it brings me inner peace, I'll welcome these pharmaceuticals with open arms.

As I reflect on everything that has happened, I realize I still need to check the damage the knife may have caused. I unzip my white jumpsuit and pull my arms out of the long sleeves, letting the upper portion fall around my waist. However, when I look down, I'm more confused than ever. Under my left ribcage is a small, almost unnoticeable scar. If I didn't know any better, I would think it was a birthmark. Lena mentioned that only a week had passed since the incident. So how am I almost completely healed? Things aren't adding up; Desmond, Aiden, and now Matias seem less and less crazy with each passing minute. What if Atticus Cais and ENDURE aren't who they claim to be? I continue to ponder this as I slip the upper part of my jumpsuit back on and head for my room. However, as soon as I exit the infirmary, I'm immediately flanked by two police officers and Dr. Cais, who seems just as taken aback as I am when we nearly collide. Atticus steps back, straightens his coat, and clears his throat before speaking.

"Royce, I was just coming to get you. I apologize; I didn't know that law enforcement would be visiting today—they showed up unannounced. They'd like to take your statement now. I know I said you needed rest, but unfortunately this can't wait."

Christ, I just want to be left alone for a moment... I try to hide my irritation before I respond. "Of course, I understand. I'll cooperate in any way I can."

"Thank you, Royce. If you would, please follow the officers this way," Dr. Cais gestures to the right of the infirmary, and I step down the hall. Before the two of them turn around to lead the way, I take a moment to check both names embroidered over the right breasts of their uniforms; they read Oakley and Shaw.

CHAPTER 8

Interrogation

Time and location (present-day): 11:01 am,
ENDURE Center for Rehabilitation

"You mention that Jonathan pulled a weapon on you at this point. Where did Mr. McCallister get a hunting knife?"

I look at Officer Shaw with bewilderment etched across my face. "I'm not sure how that's a question for me. I'm a patient here, not security. How am I supposed to know why another patient had access to a deadly weapon? Ask him." With an accusatory finger, I then direct my attention to Dr. Cais. I was told I would provide details of the event to assist in the officer's report of the incident, but after nearly an hour of reliving the nightmare, it's starting to feel more like an interrogation. Officer Shaw shifts his attention to the doctor, and Atticus responds accordingly. "I do have security looking into this matter, but I'm ashamed to say that we have no leads yet. While some patient rooms are equipped with cameras, Royce's is not one of them. It's an invasion of privacy, one we only support if the patient poses a danger to themselves or others. Had this happened in Jonathan's room, we would have everything recorded. In any event, Jonathan McCallister never left the facility after he was admitted. He must have received outside assistance from an employee. We are interviewing every employee to get to the bottom of this. I also have my most trusted staff members interviewing the security personnel themselves to ensure that none of them were responsible as a double measure."

Officer Oakley writes something in his notepad. He's acting as the scribe while Officer Shaw conducts the questioning. He looks up from his pad to address Atticus. "Please report back to us with any findings as soon as possible."

"Of course, officer," Atticus replies curtly.

Officer Oakley nods, and then both he and Officer Shaw stand up. Oakley moves toward the door while Shaw approaches Dr. Cais with an outstretched hand. "That should be all for now. We hope to hear from you soon, Doctor, and feel free to reach out if you need anything from our side." Atticus shakes his hand. "Thank you for your time, officers." He walks the two of them out, then shuts the office door behind them. Before returning to his desk, he subtly opens the blinds that cover the office windows, as if waiting for the officers to be out of earshot. After a while, with a heavy sigh, he walks over to his chair and sits across from me, hands steepled in front of him. Atticus then turns his attention back to me. "Royce, you and I need to discuss another aspect of this scenario privately."

I raise an eyebrow. "Alright... what might that be?"

He sighs once more, as if suddenly burdened by my trauma. His entire demeanor shifts from that of a caring doctor to a father trying to have an extremely difficult conversation with his son. He flips open his laptop, and I hear his fingers clack four different keys. "First and foremost, I want you to remember that I'm here to help you, Royce. However, if I am to do so, I need you to be completely honest with me."

Where on earth is he heading with this?

"Some evidence hasn't quite added up, especially regarding how Jonathan was here for so long and then suddenly acquired a knife. One begins to wonder if the knife was already in your room when the fight started, given your limited time here and ability to have sneaked an item past the initial screening upon arrival."

It takes all my strength to avoid letting my jaw drop visibly. "You can't be serious. I came to this place unconscious, in a coma. How could I have slipped a six-inch blade past your security without being conscious?! What exactly are you suggesting? Foul play? Do you think I somehow orchestrated this? To what end?" I begin to lose my grip, allowing the frustration of it all to take over. Given how utterly absurd the accusation is, I can't quite hold back.

Atticus gestures for me to compose myself. "I understand that it may not sound very plausible, but we must be certain. This is a very delicate matter, and we can't leave any stone unturned. I just want to be sure that if you know anything else that you haven't told me, you'll come clean for all our sakes. So, I'll ask you directly; is the knife yours?"

At this, I throw my arms up in disbelief; *this asshole can't be serious.* "No! Of course it isn't! Christ, was I not the one who got stabbed?!"

"Stabbed, yes, but Jonathan McCallister is *dead.* Yet here you are, incredibly alive and well." His personality shifts once again, and I remember how I perceived him in my earlier dream: *cold... calculating.* The air between us lingers momentarily, tense with frustration. I rise from the chair. "You know what? Fuck you."

Before I know it, I'm out in the hall after slamming the door to Dr. Cais' office. *Who the hell does he think he is?* I'm filled with rage, my ears burn, and my heart is beating rapidly. How could he even begin to insinuate that this whole ordeal is somehow my fault? Lena had already told me the case had been considered self-defense, no questions about it. I know that my leaving without being excused will most likely have consequences, but at this moment, I don't care. Leaving seems a better option than reaching across the desk and throttling Dr. Cais.

My thoughts distract me long enough that by the time I pull myself away from them, I've entered the lobby. I look across at the chess table, instinctively expecting to see Jonathan waiting for me there. Instead, I find Desmond, Aiden, and Matias. Desmond and I almost immediately make eye contact, as if he has been waiting for me. That must have been the case, because he then stands slowly and subtly nods his head to the left, gesturing for me to follow. I cross the lobby as Desmond walks down the adjacent hall and notice Aiden and Matias trailing behind us. They keep just enough distance to make everything seem natural. Eventually, Desmond enters a room, which I assume is his. *Well, no turning back now, Royce. Let's hope you're smarter than you look.* When I reach the door, I hesitate before grabbing the handle and entering the room. I scan for a camera, but there isn't one. In fact, his room is a mirror image of mine. To the right of the entrance, there's a desk and chair, while a bed with a side table is located in the corner opposite them. *So, he isn't dangerous, at least according to the staff...*

Desmond is sitting on the edge of his bed. "Have a seat," he says, pointing to the chair tucked under the desk across from him. I follow his instruction, and shortly after, Aiden enters the room. Matias is the last to come in, locking the door behind him. It realistically can't keep any of the staff out; it's more of a placebo to create an illusion of privacy. At the very least, it will buy them some time if they are up to anything suspicious.

"We need you to listen closely because we must assume that at any moment, security could come barging in to break this up.

Moreover, the longer we're all missing, the more suspicion will spread. Let's begin with Jonathan. At first, he was working with us to bring you into the fold." Desmond's information overload is unwelcome after my conversation with Atticus just moments before, but it seems I'm stuck in it now with no way out.

"Bring me into the fold? The fold of what, exactly?"

Desmond looks at Aiden, then Matias. They both nod, giving him permission to proceed. "The four of us have been here for quite a while... long enough to notice inconsistencies in the staff's routines, discrepancies in their practices... participation in activities that appear less than rehabilitating in nature. The gist is that we don't believe Atticus and his staff are who they claim to be."

"Then who are they?" I ask demandingly.

Aiden chimes in, saying, "That's what we're trying to find out."

Matias supports their stance from his position at the door. "We have evidence, but right now it's all circumstantial. What we do know so far is that no one seems to leave this place, *ever.* You either die of old age, or one day you just up and disappear without a trace. When we've asked about those who do, all the staff plays dumb and pretends not to know the patients we've all seen them interacting with before."

"Have you ever noticed that there are no windows in this facility?" Desmond asks, taking the driver's seat once more. Now that he mentions it, there truly isn't any way to see outside the facility. There are windows that look out into the courtyard, but the courtyard is enclosed by concrete walls that stand at least twelve feet high. I scratch my chin, a nervous habit I kicked long ago, agitated by this current conundrum. "I've noticed that... What does all this have to do with me? Why include me in your conspiracy theory?"

"Because, Royce, you're special. So was Jonathan before he lost his damn mind," Aiden says nonchalantly as he paces back and forth.

Desmond tries to clarify. "When we learned that you were hearing voices, just like Jonathan, we decided that we needed to establish contact with you. So, we sent Jonathan to do that. As he got to know you, the voices in his head became more pronounced. Eventually, he began to lose his grip on reality, became combative with us, and told us that he didn't trust you anymore. The voices in his head warned him that you were a bad omen."

"'Harbinger of death' was the exact term he used," says Matias.

Desmond continues, ignoring the interruption. "When Aiden and I approached you at the chess table that day, it was because we no longer trusted Jonathan. We were trying to intervene because we were afraid he might do something drastic. So, we had Matias keep an eye on you to ensure your safety."

"I did a great job, considering you got stabbed," Matias adds.

I stare him straight in the eye. "Hey, I'm alive. I wouldn't be here without you. I'm forever grateful to you; it could have been much worse." He nods, but still seems guilty about his timing. "Jonathan was important to Atticus. We haven't seen the doctor or Lena interact with anyone as deeply as they did with him. Not until you arrived. Then, when we discovered you were hearing voices too, we realized it couldn't be a coincidence."

"It's *a* voice," I corrected him.

"Could you repeat that?" Aiden asks.

"You keep saying that I hear voices, but I don't; I only hear *one* voice." *Out of the fire and into the frying pan, I suppose...*

"It named itself and calls itself Mallen. I've started referring to it as a 'he,'" I say, making air quotes, "it's just easier to humanize it. But it's not human... not at all."

All three of them exchange fleeting glances, as if they're trying to determine whether I'm batshit crazy or not. The irony of how the tables have turned isn't lost on me at all. So, I figure that if I'm going to share details, I might as well give them every last bit. "I also... recently, I've *seen* it. I don't mean just in my dreams; I've seen it *in real life*. It's like an afterimage of my dreams burned into my reality."

The room becomes so silent that you could *hear* a church mouse, if one were present.

"Well, *that's* fucking creepy. Are you sure this guy isn't a basket case like Jonathan was, Desmond?" Aiden asks, breaking the tension. I respond before Desmond can pass judgment. "I'm not crazy. I know how it sounds. Lena is aware of it too. She recently prescribed me some medication that seems to keep Mallen at bay. She told me they were anti-inflammatories to help with my headaches and nausea, but I don't believe her. I think whatever Mallen is, they know about it. Maybe that relates to your suspicions about what they're truly doing at ENDURE?" *Listen to yourself, Royce. You're becoming a full-blown conspiracy nut. It wasn't long ago when you dismissed these people as lunatics, and now you're having a brainstorming session with them.*

"Regardless of the situation, the time for speculation has ended," Desmond states, proceeding to speak when no one interrupts him. "No more circumstantial evidence. We're breaking into Atticus's office to see what we can find on his computer. There has to be hard evidence somewhere in the facility, and that's our best chance."

I recall my earlier conversation with Atticus and how he had pressed just four keys before his laptop unlocked. "The computer is password protected, but I know his password is only four characters long."

Matias steps forward and asks, "How did you find that out?"

I shrug. "When I was in his office a little while ago, he opened his laptop, and I heard him tap only four keys before it unlocked. The way he hit them was kind of distinct," *almost too distinct... I* think, as an afterthought.

"See? You're already proving to be an asset," says Desmond. "Let's not waste any more time; I say we break in tonight."

The thrill of secrecy is fading now, replaced by logic. "Are the three of you sure that's a good idea? Don't you think they're on high alert given everything that's happened recently?"

Desmond reflects on this before responding. "Maybe, but the longer we wait, the greater the risk that one of us could disappear overnight. Remember, we've all been here much longer than you. We've been cautious, but Atticus isn't foolish. Chances are he's a bit suspicious of our digging into his affairs. This is a four-person task; originally, Jonathan was going to help us. Now, it falls to you, Royce. We need your assistance. If we're wrong about this, the worst-case scenario is just adding some extra time to our stay here. If we're right? It could mean life or death. Jonathan's dead; that's certain. For all we know, every other patient who's gone missing over the years is dead too. I don't want to fall victim to the same fate."

This is crazy. I shouldn't be considering this... yet something in the back of my mind urges me to go for it. Whether it's Atticus's recent accusations and the need to prove that he is the villain in Jonathan's story rather than I, or just blind curiosity, remains to be seen. One thing is certain, though: I won't discover anything if I don't help Desmond and the others. "I'm in; let's see what's on that computer."

CHAPTER 9

Aiden

Time and location (the past): 5:51 pm, Aurora, Colorado

Aiden hunches over the engine bay of a Ford F-250. It belongs to a fancy lawyer from out of state and is a brand new 2018 model with all the bells and whistles. Old or new is of minimal consequence to him; he can repair any vehicle thrown his way. That fact is the only thing in his life he's sure of. The fool who owns the truck has had it for about five months and has made multiple business trips from Kansas to good old Colorado without ever having general maintenance performed. The oil is black, and that's just the start of Aiden's problems. It wouldn't be long before the idiot ran the truck into the ground for good. Stupid is as stupid does, something his mother always tells him; a bit of a mantra growing up. He finishes his work, screwing the new oil filter into place and wiping the grease from his hands as he glances at his watch. It's nearly six o'clock in the evening. He hears the side door of the garage swing open and perks his head up to see who has entered.

"Buckley! Where are you?"

"Right over here!" Aiden shouts back. It's his boss, Brandon Buchanan, who is every bit as stupid as his name suggests. Aiden has worked at this repair shop since he turned sixteen. Back then, it was owned by Brandon's father, Daniel. Old Dan was an upstanding citizen; always kind, always fair, and he did his best to see things from the perspective of anyone he did business with. One day, shortly after Aiden turned twenty-five, Daniel Buchanan collapsed on the job from a heart attack. Despite all his positive traits, staying in shape was never one of them. When that happened, Brandon inherited the shop. Another of the few negative aspects of Daniel Buchanan's character was that he spoiled Brandon, his only child, to no end. This, of course, made him grow up into one of, if not *the* most arrogant bastards Aiden had ever met. Now at the age of twenty-three, Brandon thinks he's on top of the world. As the owner of a tiny repair shop in the middle of nowhere-Aurora, Colorado, he's made quite a fortune for himself; where else will people go to get their vehicles serviced? It's the only shop for miles around.

"Buckley, what in the hell are you still doing here?"

"My bad. Just had to finish changing the oil filter." *Little shit.* It's a wonder Aiden hasn't beaten the hell out of this kid over the years, which he thinks Dan should have done long before his passing. Maybe then Brandon would have a modicum of decency. He'd gladly take jail time to teach Brandon a lesson. Suddenly, as if daring Aiden to act on his intrusive thoughts, his boss's anger shifts into bemused mockery. "What the hell are you still doing here?" he asks again, a sort of chortle following the question.

"I'll clock out right now, Brandon."

"That's 'sir' to you, Buckley. Besides that, I'm not asking what you're doing here still clocked in; I'm asking what you're still doing *here*. You're thirty-one years old, man. Are you ever going to do something with your life? Or will you always be a shitty mechanic making shit money in this shop? Jesus Christ, it's just sad! Get out of here, Buckley... I'll see you in the morning, and probably every morning after, until the day you're six feet under." Brandon slaps him on the back before walking away, likely to irritate instead of commend him.

Aiden squeezes his grease rag so tightly during the confrontation that his knuckles turn pale and glow bright white. He drops the towel on the floor and walks out the back door of the garage, intentionally not clocking out. Brandon Buchannan isn't the sharpest tool in the shed; he hardly ever pays attention to payroll. It only takes Aiden ten minutes to get home. According to his phone's GPS, it should have taken sixteen, but the perks of being in the middle of nowhere mean you don't really have to worry about cops pulling you over for speeding, since they hardly ever come around. He pulls up to the house, shuts off the engine, and hops down from his truck. As he walks through the front door, a bevy of delicious scents wafts through the air. He makes his way to the kitchen. "Smells great, Ma," he says, then wraps his arms around her slender shoulders and hugs her affectionately.

She's preparing chicken breasts and mashed potatoes on the stove. His mother spends so much time in the kitchen that she nearly always carries the scent of one dish or another, the aroma getting caught in the thick Italian curls of her greying hair. She winces slightly before realizing it's Aiden who has embraced her, a telltale sign of the trauma she has suffered at the hands of his father. "Thank you, darling. How was work?"

"Same old, same old. Where's Cash?" Aiden asks, noting his younger brother's absence.

"Oh, he's out chasing some girl again; he should be home soon."

"Hopefully before the food gets cold," he replies, releasing her and walking to the dining table. He removes his coat and drapes it over the back of a chair, then inspects her visually while her back is turned, checking for new bruises. When it comes to fathers, Beau Buckley did an adequate job fulfilling his paternal duties during Aiden and Cash's formative years when he was sober. However, once he got drunk, that was a completely different story. Under the influence of alcohol, Beau was belligerent and even violent. Aiden couldn't count the number of times he came home to find his mother battered and beaten, lying on the floor in tears. Financially, Beau always provided; throughout their childhood, Aiden and his brother consistently had new clothes, and the thought of not having a warm dinner on the table every night never even crossed their minds. In essence, they all hated Beau for the monster he kept locked away inside himself, the one he unleashed whenever whiskey lowered his inhibitions. Despite their hatred, they knew they needed him to survive. Without him, affording the essentials would have been impossible. Their mother barely makes enough to cover the utilities, and the thought of supporting herself as well as two children is laughable. Not to mention, Aiden was never strong enough growing up to face his father in a fair fight. Now at thirty-one, he's still unsure how that confrontation would go, and Cash, barely twenty, isn't old enough to stand up to their dad. As a child, Aiden learned to turn a blind eye to the abuse, knowing that any interference would only lead to further abuse for his mother and then a beating for himself. They're trapped as they always have been, and Aiden has no way out unless he chooses to abandon his mother and Cash. He feels like it's happening less often lately, or perhaps he's just become so numb to it all that he hardly notices it anymore.

"Is that Buchanan boy still bothering you?" His mother's voice pulls him away from his dark thoughts.

"Buchannan will always give me trouble, Ma. People like him thrive on making others miserable."

His mother steps away from the oven and walks over to the table, carrying two plates. She sets one down in front of Aiden and takes a seat with the other.

"As long as you don't let him reach that goal, that's what matters, dear. Now, eat up and relax."

Aiden smiles at her and takes a bite of mashed potatoes. "So, is this girl who has Cash's attention the same one from last week?"

Aiden's mother laughs. "Of course not! You know your brother!"

Aiden knows his brother well. At twenty, Cash Buckley is sharp for his age, charming, good-looking, and fully aware of it. Aiden jokes he's got a new girl every week. He wishes Cash were around more for their mother's sake, but remembers he wasn't much different at that age, so he cuts him some slack. When Cash is present, he's caring, devoted, and that's all Aiden really asks. The three of them have been through hell, and it's forged a bond nothing can shake. Sometimes Aiden wonders how life might've turned out differently, but he believes there's a reason for everything. Cash is a good son, a good brother. The only thing Aiden wishes he could change is the pain his brother endured growing up. Then, the front door slams. Their father enters, reeking of liquor—the kitchen stills. The warmth vanishes, replaced by a quiet, heavy tension.

"Hey, pop, how was your day?" he asks, trying to gauge Beau's mood.

"Quiet," his father snaps back almost immediately as Aiden stands from his chair. "Dad, let's not do this tonight. Why don't you go lie down? I'll make you a plate and bring it to the sofa."

"Boy, I said shut your damn mouth!" He stumbles to the right as his shout echoes, and Aiden knows his father's stupor all too well; he's drunk, and heavily so. Beau steps forward, but Aiden doesn't move, though he remains as cautious of his father's proximity as a gazelle would be to a hungry lion.

"What did I say about sneaking off in my truck, boy?"

"I'm sorry, Dad, but I was called in to work on short notice and had to take the truck."

"Oh, you *had* to?"

"If you still want help with the mortgage and the bills, then I need to work, Pop. And you know that Brandon is looking for every reason he can to fire me. So yes, I *had* to." Silence fills the small void between them for a moment, a moment that seems to stretch on far too long for Aiden's comfort. Finally, a poorly expressed smile creeps ever so slightly onto Beau's lips. He takes a few stumbling steps forward and places a hand on Aiden's shoulder. Beau's touch makes every hair on his body stand on end. "Well then, I guess I should be thanking you for your help instead of chastising you, huh?"

Cash enters the front door of the house just in time to see Beau's fist shoot up and, in the blink of an eye, hook Aiden across the face. Aiden spirals and hits the linoleum hard. Beau takes a swig from his cherished bottle, seemingly produced out of thin air, then crouches down and speaks softly while Aiden clutches his hand to his cheek.

"Dad, what are you doing?!" Cash protests. Aiden immediately raises a hand in warning. "Stay out of this, Cash! I mean it!" Luckily, Beau seems oblivious to his other son; his full attention is fixed on Aiden as he hovers over him. "If you ever take my truck again without asking, next time I'll leave you with far more than a handprint on your face, understood?" Aiden fights back his rage, *determined not to show any weakness. Don't let him get a reaction out of you.*

"I want to hear you say it, boy!" he screams, specks of saliva flying from his mouth.

"Understood, sir."

He smiles again, that crooked, sadistic grin. "Good." Beau stands, pivots on his heels, walks through the kitchen, and vanishes into the living room. Aiden lies on the floor a moment longer to ensure his father won't return for round two. Cash approaches him slowly. "Hey man, you okay?"

"Yeah... yeah, I'm fine."

Cash helps him to his feet, and when he stands again, his eyes land on his mother. She remains at the table, fork in hand, staring blankly at her food as silent tears stream down her expressionless face. Her entire body shakes, but aside from the barely noticeable tremors, she is frozen still. Cash must have noticed this too, because he storms off after their father before Aiden can stop him. Almost immediately, there's a loud 'thud' from the next room.

Aiden freezes for a moment, then runs to the family area when the shouting starts. When he rounds the corner, his stomach drops and Aiden stares in silent horror. Now it's Cash who has been brought down to the ground by their father. He's begging Beau, who stands over him with a .44 magnum in hand, to put the gun down. Aiden can see that Cash is crying, clearly in a state of shock. Yet he can't hear any of it. It feels as if his body has just shut down, like he's a captive audience of one, forced to bear witness to the events about to unfold. Cash slowly reaches a pleading hand out to Beau in a desperate attempt to soothe a situation he doesn't understand. Beau lifts his leg and kicks out violently, sending Cash flying back into the sofa with a distinctive 'smack.'

It's at that moment everything comes rushing back, and Aiden's senses explode into action. before he knows it, he's across the room, throwing his entire body into his father as hard as he can. They both crash down, Beau hitting his head on the fireplace mantle. Before Aiden's actions even register, he finds himself on top of his father. Blow after blow lands, causing little damage at first, but suddenly, Aiden starts to feel the bones in his father's face cracking under the weight of his fists. Beau grabs him by the front of his shirt and thrusts him backward into the coffee table. Its glass center shatters into a million pieces as the wooden frame splinters in half simultaneously. He stands up, placing his palm against his forehead. When he pulls it away and sees red, his face flushes with even more anger.

"Have you lost your mind, boy? Huh?! You think you can step up to your old man? Then step up, kid! Come on! Show me what you've got!"

CRACK! Porcelain shatters behind his father's head. Fragments from a vase thrown by his mother are scattered across the living room floor. This momentarily distracts Beau, but that brief pause is all Aiden needs.

"Don't you touch those boys, Beau!" Their mother screams, tears flowing freely. Beau turns to face her. "Now Delilah, dear, why the hell would you do that? You are one stupid bitch," he says, a little too calmly for comfort before advancing towards her. One step, two, three, and then a clear and distinct 'ka-chink' breaks the air behind him. Beau stops, laughing as he turns around. "Aiden… now listen to me. You put that down. You put that down now." Somewhere in the chaos, Aiden has begun to cry. He aims the gun, both hands wound tightly around its grip. Through choked sobs and broken whimpers, he speaks. "I won't let you hurt us anymore, I won't."

His father takes a step toward him, and Aiden stiffens his arms. "Don't come any closer, please don't come closer."

"Aiden, I'm only going to tell you one more time: put that gun down. Aiden!" The anger returns in Beau, who is clearly done trying to smooth things over with calmness and feigning concern. Everything happens quickly, so suddenly that Aiden almost doesn't process it. Beau lunges forward, then BANG! BANG! BANG! He crashes to the floor, arm outstretched and reaching just short of Aiden's foot, blood slowly pooling out beneath him like molasses. The gun trembles uncontrollably in his hands, snapping Aiden out of his stunned stupor; he lets it fall to the floor. His mother rushes to Cash and starts to check him for injuries, appearing numb to the horror that has just unfolded in her living room. Aiden tries to move but can't; his legs and arms just refuse to work, no matter how much he wills them. Delilah finishes inspecting Cash, helps him up from the floor, and then rushes over to Aiden. Cash follows closely behind her, and when they reach Aiden, the three of them embrace tightly, as if letting go would mean the end of the world. Aiden closes his eyes then, trying to forget; but he can't, and he never will for the rest of his life. As if the earlier chaos isn't enough, there's suddenly a loud knock at the front door. Delilah looks up from their huddle, panic etched on her tear-streaked face.

"Who could that be?"

"I have no idea. Stay here with Cash, Ma, I'll go see who it is." Aiden kisses his mother on the forehead and ruffles his younger brother's hair before standing up, the adrenaline fading and the reality of his father lying dead just a few feet away sinking in. The floorboards creak under his weight, the house's old age echoing the pain it has witnessed over the years. He reaches the front door and opens it without checking who is on the porch; there's no need to fear anyone on the other side, not anymore. A slender but fit gentleman stands before Aiden. He is of average height and clean-shaven, with a short crop of dark hair and aviator-style sunglasses perched on the bridge of his nose—an accessory Aiden finds odd, considering the nearly set sun resting on the horizon. The man extends a hand to greet him.

"Aiden Buckley?"

"That's me. But I'm not sure I know you," Aiden replies, refusing the offered hand.

"I apologize, my name is Jordan Oakley. I am here to present you with a business proposal."

Aiden hesitates, now acutely aware that he has just killed a man—his father—and the last thing he needs is for Jordan Oakley to find out. "Got all I need right here, good day to you, Mr. Oakley." Aiden swings the door shut, but Jordan Oakley stops it by placing his foot between the door and the frame. He turns back to the door and, with reluctance, opens it once again.

"You and I both know that isn't true, Mr. Buckley."

"And just how would you know that, mister?" Aiden steps out onto the porch now, shutting the door behind him. "I don't take too kindly to strangers interrupting my dinner."

"I mean no disrespect, Mr. Buckley. If you'll just listen to me, I'm sure we can reach an agreement and possibly find a solution to what happened a moment ago; I heard gunshots."

Aiden raises an eyebrow and crosses his arms, trying to hide the fact that his heart rate has just increased tenfold; he isn't amused and certainly isn't in the mood for any bullshit. "You've got five minutes; make them count."

Jordan Oakley smiles crookedly, clearly pleased at the opportunity to explain himself. He reaches up, removing his glasses and revealing his vibrant blue eyes. "I'm here to discuss something my corporation has been working on for quite some time now. It's known as the Experimental Nuclei Derivation and Unification Research Endeavor, but for the sake of brevity, we'll simply refer to it as ENDURE."

CHAPTER 10

Homicidal

Time and location (present-day): 3:16 pm,
ENDURE Center for Rehabilitation

I lay in bed, staring at the ceiling for hours—much longer than I should have—reflecting on the decision made yesterday. The potential consequences of it all, how we could pull it off, and what we would do if the information we hoped to find turned out to be real. *What would we do? How does someone even begin to expose this place as... as what?* There are far too many unanswered questions swirling in my mind to reconcile these new ones.

The plan Desmond discussed with the group after I agreed to join their evidence-hunting party was shoddy at best. Tonight, after lights-out, we were supposed to sneak out of our quarters at 2:50 am, then meet in one of the halls branching off the lobby. Security guards would be on patrol, so we'd have to play chicken with them throughout our expedition. From there, we'd all waltz over to Atticus's office and pray the door was unlocked. It had badge access only, and none of us wanted to risk stealing a badge from an employee, much less from Atticus himself. Not to mention, if we stole one and it didn't have the proper permissions to enter the Doctor's personal workspace, it would surely set off some alarm that an attempt had been made. No, stealing a badge would be far too risky. So, blind hope and optimism were our best and only chances. If the door ended up being locked, we would find a solution; no matter what it took, we would leave with answers. At least that had been the alternative proposed by Matias. I hadn't spent much time around the three of them, especially not Matias, but something about his tone of voice during our scheming left me more than a little apprehensive. The man seemed constantly on edge, as if he had some sort of vendetta to fulfill.

As I mentally make note to keep a close eye on the behemoth that is Matias, the door to my quarters swings open after a flurry of knocks that I recognize as Lena's personal greeting. She brushes a loose strand of hair from her face as she sits at the edge of the bed, playfully slapping my covered leg.

"What are you doing in bed? It's three in the afternoon! Sit up. I brought your medication; Shannon at the dispensary said you hadn't stopped by today, so I figured I'd bring them with me." She holds out a cup with two lightning blue capsules at the bottom, then pulls a small bottle of water from her physician's coat. With a sigh and more effort than should have been necessary, I prop myself up on one elbow, pop the pills into my mouth, and wash them down. Lena squeezes my leg, her touch now sending nervous waves of heat throughout my body. "I know it's only been a day since we started you on this medication regularly, but do you feel like it's helping you deal with Mallen?"

I nod, and a sense of relief crosses Lena's face. "I slept through the night, woke up, and I haven't seen or heard from him yet. So far, so good."

She smiles at me, and for the first time since Jonathan's death, I smile back, however fleeting it may be. We are clearly on the same wavelength, as her next question addresses the subject that has been brooding over my life like a storm cloud. "How have you been coping? I mean, with all the Jonathan stuff?"

I sit up completely now, swinging my legs over the side of the bed so that I'm sitting next to her. "I... I don't really know. I think I'm okay. It's not my first encounter with death, but this time just felt... different."

"Different how?" she asks as I lock eyes with her, and I can see that she understands and shares in my pain and anguish.

"When it comes to my family, I remember nothing. Just the car swerving off the road, and then nothing, until I woke up here, years later. But with Jonathan... it's the opposite. I can't forget. Every time I close my eyes, I see him, his bloody corpse, the emptiness in his stare. And the rage... God, the rage in his eyes right before I killed him. Like the lights were on, but no one was home. You know?"

She sits in quiet contemplation for a moment before responding. "I understand… can I share something with you? Something I haven't mentioned to anyone outside my family?"

My curiosity piqued, I turned my body inward toward her, wanting her to know that she has my full attention. "Of course, you can trust me."

She gently tilts her head in a solitary nod and exhales slowly, as if bracing herself for the pain this story will bring up. "A few years ago, my father… he killed my mother. Then he took his own life." The air in the room becomes heavy with the weight of her statement, and I do my best to conceal my shock. "Lena, I'm *so* sorry; that must have been incredibly difficult for you."

"It was… my parents meant everything to me."

"I know it hurts to talk about it all, to remember… but do you know what happened? Why he do what he did?" I can see the tears welling up in her eyes now, how she fights with every ounce of her being to suppress them.

"In that regard, it was a very similar situation to your altercation with Jonathan. There wasn't really any warning—no signs that anything was different about him until a few days leading up to the incident. No one suspected he was homicidal." Teardrops are flowing freely down her cheeks now, though silently. I want to reach out; I feel an innate need to hold her tight and never let her go, but how can I? She wipes the tears away as she tries to lighten the mood. "Oh gosh, look at me pouring my heart out to you. I didn't mean to unload my trauma; I just wanted you to know that I understand what you're going through more than most. I'm here if you need anything, Royce, always."

She takes my hand, holding it in a gesture that feels kind and so familiar that my stomach drops. I glance down at our intertwined fingers, then quickly look away as if embarrassed she'll see the confusion in my eyes; in that moment, it feels like I've known her for a lifetime. When she releases my hand, I feel a sudden pang of sadness. *Get a grip, Royce, for Christ's sake, man.*

"The same goes for you, Lena. I'm always here for you." She smiles, and I notice her fidgeting with a pendant that hangs from a sterling chain around her neck. "What's that? Your necklace, I mean," I ask as I point to it. She holds it up, admiring it. "Oh this? It's a pendant of Pax, the Roman goddess of peace. Atticus gave it to me after my parents were gone, he found it amongst my mother's belongings. He said it was supposed to be a constant reminder that, although life can sometimes be painful, peace is almost always on the horizon. It was waiting for that peace to arrive that I struggled with growing up.

She laughs, and I do too. "So, how about now? Have you found that peace?"

Lena stares at me for a moment, the grin formed from lingering laughter still perched upon her lips. Then, suddenly, the corners of her mouth begin to turn downward into a frown. She averts her eyes from my gaze, leaving me baffled. *What did I say? Or what does she know that I don't?* She stands up from my bedside abruptly. "I should probably get going; I've been gone too long. Get out of your room; it will do you good to stretch your legs. I'll see you soon, Royce."

She walks toward the door, and suddenly, I remember our plan to be carried out later tonight. "Lena, wait! I have something to tell you..."

She stops with her arm outstretched, reaching for the door, and I panic. *You can't tell her, you fool; it could jeopardize everything!* Even so, the urge to divulge what Desmond had planned, to bring her into the fold, and to be honest *with* her is overwhelming.

"Well? What is it?" she asks, as I become painfully aware that we've been sitting in silence for one second too long.

"It's... never mind. Have a good rest of your day. I'll see you later." I can feel my face flushing red, and I look away, ashamed of my choice. She gives me a bewildered look, then exits my quarters. Just before she leaves, I swear I see her beginning to cry again.

CHAPTER 11

Cleanse

Time and location (present-day): 3:01 am,
ENDURE Center for Rehabilitation

"Where the hell is Aiden?"

Desmond whispers, the irritation in his voice palpable. Matias and I met Desmond promptly at 2:50am as agreed the evening before, but now it's 3:01am, and Aiden is still nowhere to be found. The man's ears must have been burning, because almost immediately after Desmond's words leave his mouth, Aiden scurries down the hall with an apologetic wave of his hand. He stops directly behind me, and Desmond glares at him. "You're *late*," he hisses. Aiden shrugs in response. "Better late than never, right?" he grins, and Desmond gives him a gentle thump on the back of the head.

"Quit wasting time," Matias whispers from the front of our group, peering around the corner into the lobby. He scans the area one last time for any signs of activity, then turns and gestures for us to huddle up before speaking again. "Alright, Desmond had me conduct some reconnaissance over the past week. There are usually two security guards patrolling the facility throughout the night, and their route can be quite sporadic. Planning for it isn't really an option, so we need to stay extremely alert. If we get caught, Desmond and I will handle the talking. We've devised a cover story that requires minimal confirmation from you two if it comes to that. Follow Desmond, and let's get moving."

Desmond nods and moves to the front of the group. Aiden is next in line, followed by me, with Matias taking up the rear. After ensuring the lobby is clear of guards again, we begin to make our way across the room. I feel my heart skip a few beats as my stomach drops. *What have you gotten yourself into, Royce? Just turn around and walk away; it still isn't too late to bow out of this...* and yet, my feet propel me forward right on Aiden's heels. As if I were developing a rapid sense of loyalty to this ragtag group of potential invalids, I find myself blazing ahead on Desmond's path despite the multiple alarms ringing in my head telling me to stop. Darker scenarios begin to weave their way into my thoughts as we continue slinking about in the facility's shadows. These thoughts are not Mallen's, but they could be if it weren't for the medication keeping him locked away in the recesses of my mind. *What if we're right? What if we're right and discovering what they're hiding here gets us killed? Or worse? What could be worse than death? Torture? Imprisonment? Are we already imprisoned?* I bump into the back of Aiden, who has stopped in front of me. Deep in my frightful mental descent, I had entered autopilot, not realizing we had reached our destination without any interference.

Aiden turns to check on me. "You okay, man? Groggy or something?"

I nod, not wanting anyone to know I momentarily lost my confidence. "Yeah, sorry about that..." Standing there outside Atticus' office, the door now seems imposing, like a tombstone waiting to have my name etched on its surface.

Desmond beckons Matias over to the door, and Matias taps my shoulder as he passes. "Keep a lookout behind us," he says. I nod, keeping my eye on the hallway we came down. My attention is quickly diverted from my duties by a string of profanities that quietly leave Matias' mouth shortly thereafter. It becomes clear that the door to the doctor's office is locked.

This is unsurprisingly obvious to me, though it seems to get under Matias's skin at an unreasonable level of intensity. He starts glancing around like a frantic animal, his head swinging back and forth as if weighing all his options. Suddenly, he pulls his leg up to his chest, kicking out with his heel against the locked door. Matias previously said we would get answers one way or another, and it seems he intends to keep his word. He jiggles the handle after this initial assault, but the lock still holds the door firmly shut. He slams the bottom of his foot into the door a second time, with even more force than before.

Aiden grabs Matias by the shoulder. "Are you out of your mind? You're being way too loud; you're going to get us all caught!" Matias aggressively shrugs Aiden's hand off his shoulder without a word and lashes out with his foot for a third time. I glance over at Desmond. He stands in silence, pinching the bridge of his nose in frustration at the entire ordeal. He clearly understands that Matias is beyond reasoning at this point; there's no sense in trying to stop him. Either our goose is cooked, or it isn't, but we have zero say in the matter now. A fourth time, and much to our shock and awe, the door jolts open, caught by its soft-close mechanism and left to lazily drift back toward us.

We stare at each other in a circle of disbelief for a moment, and then hurriedly enter Atticus's office, minus Aiden, who stands watch at the now disfigured doorway. My heart rate is through the roof, driven by some combination of fear and excitement; this is it. Whatever Atticus has on his computer has the potential to finally settle whether I'm completely delusional for believing this conspiracy theory or not, whether Mallen is simply a figment of my imagination or something more.

I make my way to the doctor's desk and sit down in his chair with a bit too much haste, something Desmond notices. "You know what you're doing?" he asks.

"I'm younger than all of you, which means I'm faster than all of you on a computer." It's flimsy reasoning at best, pulled out of thin air to put me at the forefront of the exposed truth, but it's sound logic nonetheless. Desmond concedes, and I tap the keyboard to wake the computer, only to find myself immediately fraught. The computer is password-protected, because, of course, it is. *A toddler could have planned better for this, you imbecile...*

"Any ideas?" Desmond asks, pointing at the screen.

"I don't know; a password is personal—something unique to Atticus, or maybe something important, like..." I trail off, retreating into my thoughts once more. If I get this wrong, who knows how quickly Atticus will be notified? We're in too deep now, though; no sense in giving up. "... I have an idea... just *one*..." With an inhale of anticipation, I enter the assumed password, and the desktop flashes to life, all its tiny icons like treasures to be plundered. Sitting in shock, it takes a moment for me to realize that we've done it; we're in.

The desktop is home to a plethora of folder shortcuts, all dated. Beside the dates, most folders have only two words: Deus Molecule. "Deus Molecule?" Matias asks, seemingly to himself.

"Here," Desmond says, producing a flash drive from somewhere within his jumpsuit and handing it to me. "Copy everything, Royce."

I take the flash drive, then hesitate. "Wait... where did you get this?"

"Royce, we *really* don't have time for questions," Desmond says. That's a valid point by all accounts, but something in his tone and demeanor raises red flags. I nod but tuck the question away in my subconscious to address later. After copying all the files on the desktop, I search through the computer's hard drive for anything incriminating. It takes just moments, leaving us time to dig deeper into the mysteriously labeled Deus Molecule folders. I open the folder with the earliest date I can find; if we want answers, it's best to start from the beginning. Inside, there are several smaller folders, each titled with first and last names. In this one alone, there are at least thirty. As I scroll through the names, one catches my eye. It reads, "Mason Cais." I glance over my shoulder at Desmond and Matias, both of whom seem to notice the familial ties as well.

"Open it," Matias says with that same insane fire dead-set in the depths of his eyes. I nod and then click on it. When I do, it opens an MP4 file in a video player. The video begins to play, seemingly from a camera in the upper corner of the room. At the center sits a man who appears to be in his forties. It takes me a moment to notice the thick leather straps binding him to the seat at his ankles and wrists, or that this is no ordinary chair. It seems to be made of solid steel and has some sort of mechanical function. As I glance around the snow-white room in the video, I start to realize that it's a laboratory of some sort.

The door to the room slides open with a chime, and someone enters. As he walks toward the captive, I immediately recognize him.

"That's Atticus," I say, pointing to him on the screen. He holds a tablet in one hand, lifting it to his face to study. The man in the chair hasn't moved a muscle.

Then, as if addressing us directly, Atticus begins to speak. "The date and time will be noted in this documentation for later reference. Our subject is Mason Cais, age forty-four, male. This is day eighty-two of trial one." The word "trial" sends a shiver down my spine, yet I watch intently. "Nearly three months have passed since the Deus Molecule within my brother's DNA was discovered and awakened, and much to our dismay, the side effects have been rather… unfavorable. Mason's mental state is quickly declining into psychosis. We've spent the past few months trying to isolate the mutagen that caused this new block in his DNA sequence to emerge so that we may study it further should the worst come to pass; today, we succeeded." Then, Atticus removes a syringe from his coat pocket. Within its barrel, I can make out a viscous blue liquid. Atticus admires the substance as he holds it up to the light. "I hold in my hand, for all intents and purposes, the Deus Molecule in its purest form, or DM1 as we've labeled this refined version. We are currently experimenting with other methods for administering DM1, but an intravenous injection has been at the forefront of our experimentation. After all, entry into the bloodstream is the quickest way to see how our subjects react to DM1 and, therefore, the fastest way to compile and record data and results. As stated before, Mason's condition is worsening by the day, and I fear he is not long for this world. The activated Deus Molecule in his DNA has given him unfathomable abilities, but the cost of these gifts is physical in nature. His body is deteriorating, aging at a rapid pace, and his mind is rotting internally. He hasn't communicated, ingested food or water, or much less budged for the past three days. If we didn't know any better, we'd say he was brain-dead, but his scans show the opposite; his brainwave activity is rampant and hyperactive. We are uncertain of what will happen if we inject our refined Deus Molecule into his bloodstream, considering the naturally occurring Deus Molecule is already active inside of him. However, we have nothing to lose. Time is of the essence; the looming threat of Mason's premonition is becoming a reality more and more each passing day, and thus, sacrifices must be made." Atticus then reaches up with his free hand to remove the cap from the syringe's needle.

"Jesus Christ..." Desmond mutters under his breath, his eyes glued to the screen as well. I'm not sure any of us are prepared for what happens next, but I'm certain it scares me more than it scares them. Atticus reaches for Mason's arm, seemingly to inject him with the DM1, but the man's arm shoots out and grips Atticus' wrist, breaking the leather restraint as if it were nothing more than tissue paper in the blink of an eye. The doctor tries to hold onto the syringe, but the crushing power of Mason's grip forces him to release it with a wince of pain, and it falls to the floor.

"Hello, doctor Cais. It's lovely to finally meet you; formally, that is."

I jolt backward away from the monitor as my stomach drops at a hundred miles an hour. *That voice—I know that voice! It's him... Mallen... Suddenly,* I feel dizzy, a cold sweat forming on my forehead.

"His voice sounds... unnatural," Matias says, providing a much-needed distraction from the whirlwind of thoughts racing through my mind.

I look over at Desmond before I speak, locking eyes with him. "I don't know what Mason Cais sounds like, but I DO know that voice..."

"Aw hell... don't say it... That voice in your head? What did you call it?" he asks, his eyes growing wide.

I nod solemnly. "That's Mallen. There isn't a single doubt in my mind about it."

Atticus's pained and panicked voice draws our attention back to the video feed. "Mason, let me go at once! What are you doing?!" he shouts.

"I'm afraid there's no Mason here, doctor, not anymore. Tell me, do you really think you can stop what's coming? You and your army of lab rats?"

Atticus visibly steels himself, relaxing a bit and no longer resisting Mason's vice grip. "You... are you the entity that lives inside my brother? I believe you and I spoke once before, a few hours ago," Atticus states, reflecting on his previous visit to his brother.

"Yes... indeed I am. It took time, this one resisted. Strong-willed, mentally fortified... But in the end he was only human, and all humans break sooner or later. Such fragile little things... I am what remains. You may call me Mallen."

"Holy Mary, mother of Joseph," Desmond says, his hands clasped nervously behind his head. "Well, Royce, I guess this means you aren't batshit after all. I don't really know whether that's good or bad in the grand scheme of things, though." I don't respond; I can't, or at least I don't know how. Mallen. He's *real*, and I have *proof*.

The video plays on. "Pleasure to meet you, Mallen. I'd introduce myself, but you already know who I am, so I'll skip the pleasantries. What is it that you want with my brother? What do you know about his premonitions? What can you tell me about The Nine?" The doctor was probing, desperately seeking answers.

"There is nothing I require of him, not anymore. I thought he might be strong enough, but sadly, that was not the case. As for the latter, these are no premonitions. Premonitions are merely strong feelings; what Mason has seen are visions of a future that will come to pass. You cannot stop it; humanity will reap what it has sown."

Atticus continues to push, seemingly unfazed, but I know better. "Your reference to humanity implies that you are not of this world. If that is so, then how are you speaking to me now? In a language I can comprehend?"

Bemused, Mallen opts to give Atticus a morsel of information. *"I am very much of this world, doctor. We were here before you, and we will remain long after. Telepathic brainwaves, courtesy of Mason's dilapidated mind. I do not speak a language you can even begin to fathom; you are simply hearing my words in your native tongue, translated in real-time."*

Atticus scratches his chin, considering the entity's explanation. "Fascinating… tell me then, Mallen. If you do not require my brother any further, what is it that you *do* require?"

Mason's head cocks unnaturally to the side before Mallen speaks through him again. *"A suitable vessel, doctor. Though Mason's decline is of no consequence to me, you will unwittingly provide me with a new viable candidate soon enough."*

I can feel Matias' eyes boring silently into me, but I dare not look. Desmond nudges my arm. "A vessel? Royce... does he mean... does he mean *you*?" he asks, and for the first time, I think I hear a quaver in his voice. I don't answer, too distracted by the old recording.

The indignation is clear on Atticus's face. "What makes you so sure, Mallen?"

A gurgled cackle escapes from Mason's throat. "Surety, in contrast to certainty, implies room for error; there is none. You will, in time, provide me with everything I require. When you do, The Nine will arrive and cleanse humanity's filth from the surface of this planet."

Atticus locks eyes with his would-be brother. "And if we fight back against this cleansing? What you speak of is a declaration of war on our very species. What makes you think we will go quietly into the night?"

Mallen laughs hysterically, growing more amused as the interaction continues. "There it is, that obscene vanity you humans cherish so dearly. The idea that you humans are the very peak of evolution standing atop the food chain, is an idea misplaced. The Nine are indestructible, its concomitants including me, untouchable. We are *essence*, intangible. You cannot fight back against something you cannot see doctor; cannot kill something you cannot touch. This is not the start of a war; a war consists of two sides affecting each other equally until one side finds themselves at a disadvantage and is annihilated by their opposition. This is much simpler than that; this is an extermination. *It will be an extinction event for the ages...*"

Mason Cais's body shakes with a deep, foreboding laughter, a guttural sound that I can imagine growing in resonance as it vibrates against the walls. He's a man possessed, his behavior no longer his own.

Atticus does his best to feign a measured tone in response. "Mallen, was it? I cannot, in good conscience, allow this future you speak of to come to fruition."

Mallen's laughter halts suddenly. Instantly, the ankle straps disintegrate as he rises from the chair, his other bound hand tearing through its restraint and grasping Atticus by the throat before he can react. Atticus starts to rise, his toes barely brushing the floor as he fights for air. *"What makes you think you have a choice?"*

A loud bang makes us all nearly jump out of our skin as we watch. Mallen releases Atticus, stumbling backward as the doctor crumples to the floor in a fit of coughing and hacking. Mason Cais' hand goes to his stomach, and when he raises it to his eyes, it is red with blood. Atticus pulls out a handgun hidden beneath his lab coat. Mallen's attention returns to Atticus, and there is suddenly a second bang. I see Mason's head jerk back, and then he falls to the floor, lifeless as well. Moments later, the door to the room slides open once more, and armed soldiers enter with assault rifles at the ready.

"Secure the room; I'll secure the doctor!" One of them shouts orders as he approaches Atticus, sweeping his rifle from left to right. The others — four in total — assume individual tasks. One checks Mason's jugular for a pulse, while the other three find positions around the room to stand guard, even though there is clearly only one entrance to the lab. When the soldier examining Atticus lowers his weapon, letting it hang from his shoulder strap, I can see his face clearly.

"What in the... that soldier... I *swear* that's one of the cops who interviewed me after the whole Jonathan ordeal..."

"A cop... who is *also* a soldier? That's not possible... unless they're military police?" says Matias.

"What makes you say that?" I inquire.

"I have experience in the field, but those uniforms in the video don't necessarily look like standard military issue for any MPs that I've ever met," responds Matias, whose newly revealed past at least somewhat explains the man's deep-seated issues with aggression. I wonder if Matias's outburst relates to post-traumatic stress disorder, but I brush the thought away to focus on the matter at hand.

"They wore standard city police uniforms during our interview, though I'm not sure which city it *was for.*" *Or state, for that matter...* It dawns on me just then that I'm not even aware of *where* in the world this facility, in which I have spent the past several months, is located. I had just blatantly *assumed* I was still in California, but who really knows *anything* about ENDURE at this point?

Matias scratches his chin in thought. "So they're pretending to be something they aren't... but why?"

I decide that I prefer the silent, inquisitive Matias to the barbaric version that had smashed the office door minutes ago. However, in the coming days, I can't be certain which iteration of this man will be more helpful. I then think back to the interview with the police officers. "What was his name? I saw the badge, but I can't recall... Shaw, maybe?"

Matias jolts visibly. "Did you say *Shaw*? Are you positive?"

"Yes, I think so. Why do you ask?"

He's acting erratic once more, leaving me even more confused amongst the whirlwind of information we're uncovering. Matias' gaze drops to the floor before he responds, avoiding the subject. "It's... nothing, look, something is happening," he says, gesturing back to the video.

As strange as his behavior is at the moment, I feel that anything happening on the computer screen takes precedence, so I decide we can revisit the Shaw situation later. We watch as the suspicious soldier-cop, possibly Shaw, helps Atticus to his feet. The other soldier who had checked Mason's vitals approaches them shortly thereafter, and though I don't get as clear a look at him, something in me says that this is possibly the other cop from my interview, but I choose to keep that to myself for now. This one's name I remember, though: Oakley.

"The test subject has no pulse, doctor. He's dead," he says.

Atticus, clearly upset, begins to pace back and forth on the video feed. "How am I going to hide this from Lena..." he asks quietly to himself as he tries to calm down, and then it clicks.

Just as it should have the moment he called Mason his brother, it finally clicks. "My God... that was Lena's father. Atticus killed her dad." I immediately begin to question what I'm seeing. Lena had said her father killed her mother and himself. So, are my eyes deceiving me? Or is this proof that she can't be trusted? My statement has Matias and Desmond exchanging glances, which worries me. "What is it?"

"You might want to keep your distance from her... We don't know how much she's involved in this," Desmond says, trying to show some empathy for my friendship with Lena.

"Lena wouldn't..." I begin, but I'm immediately interrupted.

"Wouldn't she? Seems to me like you thought with your heart instead of your head. She lied to you Royce, just like Atticus..."

I try not to visibly jerk. The medication is wearing off. I attempt to refocus on the video, but Aiden hurriedly enters the office. "Guys, we gotta go; I see flashlight beams." Matias springs into action, leaving the office and disappearing in the blink of an eye with Aiden.

Desmond grips me by both shoulders and looks me in the eye. "You have it all on the flash drive, right? The video? The other files?" I nod, and he continues. "Good. Let's go, quickly... Wait; what was the computer password?"

I hesitate to answer but do anyway. "... Lena... the password was Lena."

Desmond lets out a disappointed sigh. "We'll discuss this later; let's get moving."

I pull the drive from the computer tower, ignoring the pang of guilt I feel for trusting Lena and defending her, and then tuck it into my sock under the arch of my foot. It isn't comfortable, but it's well hidden. I hurry after Desmond out of the room, which now feels more like a macabre dungeon than an inconspicuous office. As we round the corner into the hall, I collide with a body. We're too late; the guards have found us. I fall to the floor and try to crawl away, but the guard is stronger than I am. He attempts to pin me to the floor, but I roll over to face him. Then I see the same "cop" who had interviewed me, the same "soldier" from the video of Mason's execution: Shaw. I stop fighting, partly in shock and partly to avoid making a bad situation worse. My main objective now is to ensure that they don't find the USB drive.

"GET UP," he grunts angrily as he lifts me from the floor. I look around and see Matias being put into restraints by another guard, one whose name I'm more than willing to bet is Oakley.

The man has a large red mark under his left eye, and his nose is bleeding; Matias hadn't gone down without a fight. I lost sight of Aiden and Desmond in the scuffle, but it seems they have escaped, hopefully unidentified. Shaw pins me to the wall, pressing my face into its surface. I feel the restraints being clasped to my wrists, binding my hands behind my back. He pulls me away from the wall and then shoves me down the hallway. I get one final glimpse of the man I think is Oakley leading Matias around the corner, leaving me alone with Shaw.

He speaks, and somehow this man seems even more menacing than Atticus. "Dr. Cais would like to have a word with you."

CHAPTER 12

Matias

Time and location (the past): 4:28 pm, an-Nasiriyah,
Dhi Qar Province, Iraq

Matias stares out past the bronze-tinted horizon as the sun begins to set, his M16A4 resting with most of its weight distributed onto his shoulder strap. He's about seven miles west of the city, but he can just make out the Euphrates River, a silvery thread barely visible in the distance. The fighting these past few days has been intense, and the tactics used by this new enemy are... irregular, to say the least. Every muscle in his body aches, and it's all he can do to avoid sliding down the side of the "Tracks" onto the sand beneath his feet. The FMC AAV-7A1 amphibious assault vehicle, mostly referred to as Tracks among the U.S. Marine Corps, is cool to the touch. However, with all the gear he's carrying, the eighty-degree weather might as well be in the hundreds, and therefore the caress of its cold steel does little to soothe his exhaustion.

He's undoubtedly tired and likely dehydrated to boot. Matias is a skilled infiltrator, but this war is spreading even him thin.

Five days ago, President Bush issued Iraqi President Saddam Hussein and his two sons an ultimatum: leave Iraq willingly within the next forty-eight hours or face removal. The government had known shortly after the events of September 11, 2001, that Afghanistan, not Iraq, was the source of the most horrific terrorist attack on U.S. soil the American people had ever witnessed. Regardless of this, Matias and his battalion were sent to Iraq. There were suspicions that Saddam's regime was building and stockpiling weapons of mass destruction while sponsoring global terrorism, causing an increasing concern among U.S. Government officials. These weapons were believed to be biological, chemical, and nuclear in nature. Hussein had violated sixteen United Nations resolutions requiring him to disclose the fate of the weapons of mass destruction that had once been in his country's possession and refused to allow international inspectors to search for them and verify their disposal. It was the conclusion of the Bush administration, along with many experts worldwide, that Iraq still harbored those weapons with aggressive intent. Based on that alone, Matias understood the necessity for lethal force and rapid deployment. That forty-eight-hour window had come and gone, with the Iraqi president even mocking President Bush's ultimatum, and so Matias and his company, like many others, were sent to do what he did best.

Amidst the desert winds on the outskirts of An-Nasiriyah, Matias experiences his first moment of reprieve since boots hit the ground three days ago. His thoughts suddenly dance to his daughter, Anika. Though he's going through the motions with her mother and isn't sure their relationship will survive this war, Anika remains a beacon of hope. Even if he has nothing else to return to at the end of this, he will always have her. Matias is jolted from his thoughts and thrust back into reality when a young girl, no older than fifteen, seemingly appears out of thin air before him, waving her arms frantically. *Where did this kid come from?* Matias wonders as the teen shouts in Arabic, clearly distressed. He stands up straight, pulling his back from the assault vehicle to address the girl.

"Kid, I don't speak Arabic. I don't understand what you're saying, but you need to step back," he says, pushing an open palm toward the child to indicate that she should leave. This doesn't deter her at all, and she continues her tirade, which grows increasingly urgent. "Kid, seriously, get back, *now.*" Matias reaches out to gently nudge the girl away, and in an instant, a woman appears at the teen's side. She is much more erratic, dropping to her knees and sobbing uncontrollably as her rant mixes with that of the girl. The cacophony begins to attract the attention of onlookers, and before Matias can react, a crowd has gathered.

He becomes aware of a soldier he vaguely knows beside him. Jordan Oakley is his name, a corporal he has seen in passing over the past few days. The fear in Oakley's eyes is apparent, almost seeming feigned; it's a look Matias has grown accustomed to, the man searching for any reason to pull a trigger. "Ma'am, get back now or we will open fire!" Matias stiffens as soon as the words leave Oakley's mouth. The commotion draws two more soldiers who approach from behind the Tracks. He recognizes one as Sergeant Barringer; the other is Gunnery Sergeant Elliot Shaw. Matias and Shaw have served together for a few years now and are as close-knit as two soldiers can be. He sleeps comfortably at night during deployments, knowing that Shaw always has his back. As they approach the vehicle, Oakley has his sidearm drawn and aimed directly at the woman's head.

"Whoa, calm down! Do not open fire! Holster your weapon; these are civilians," Shaw says as Matias's attention now shifts fully to Oakley, away from the woman and teenage girl in front of them.

"Negative, sir! You've seen how these animals fight!" Oakley screams back shakily. All too quickly, Matias realizes what's happening. The Iraqi forces favor suicide bombings as a war tactic. It's barbaric and something that American soldiers have rarely experienced on the battlefield since World War II. It is clear to Matias that Oakley fears he is about to become a statistic.

"Soldier, she has a *child* beside her, holster that shit *NOW*." The inflection in Matias' voice clearly indicates to Oakley that it's an order rather than a request. Even though he lowers his weapon, the woman continues shouting incoherently, and the girl begins to cry uncontrollably. It's all spiraling out of control, and Matias realizes it. He does his best to soothe them as the bustle and noise from the surrounding crowd start to overwhelm him, claustrophobia creeping in.

"Everyone needs to calm down; we will figure this out together! Just calm down!" he shouts into the crowd, looking beyond the woman and the teenager as he makes a soothing gesture with his hands.

"She's got a vest!" yells Shaw. In the millisecond that Matias' gaze leaves the woman to address the larger group of people, she removes her shawl, revealing a vest layered with C4 and a detonator clutched firmly in her left hand. Now, *everyone* has their weapons drawn, including Matias, though he has no recollection of ever unslinging his rifle from his shoulder. The woman begins to raise her voice, shouting louder as her tone becomes more aggressive than fearful.

"Drop it! Drop it now!" Matias points the tip of his rifle at her detonator, then gestures towards the ground, hoping she'll take the hint.

"Half Colonel! The situation is critical; we need to put her down!" Oakley bellows, his prior ferocity returning in full force.

"DO NOT open fire! That is an ORDER!" Matias repeats. The girl clings to the woman's dress, her eyes wide and terrified as tears continually stain her cheeks. The woman's arms flail sporadically, and Matias fears he is running out of time to find a peaceful resolution, but that *damn girl...* she's an obstacle, one Matias isn't prepared for. If it weren't for this teenager, the woman would already be dead on the sand, a bullet between her eyes.

"To hell with your fucking orders!" Oakley's sidearm discharges and the woman drops like a bag of bricks, a hole burrowed into her skull.

Matias' heart skips a beat, and then he's on Oakley like a fierce attack dog, pinning him against the side of the Tracks. "Are you out of your fucking mind Corporal?! I gave you a DIRECT order! What if she had a dead man's switch? You could've just killed every fucking one of us and caused mass civilian casualties!"

"Lieutenant Colonel!" It's Sergeant Barringer this time. Matias turns to see the Sergeant pointing toward the woman's body, and his heart drops into his stomach. The young girl crouches beside the dead woman, the detonator now held in her adolescent hand.

"Easy kid, just put that thing down, it's dangerous. You hear me? Danger, put it down," he says as calmly as possible.

"All due respect sir, shoot her or I will!" It's Oakley again, and Matias decides he's had enough of this guy's insubordination.

"Shaw, get him the fuck out of here!" Matias demands. Shaw nods, grabbing Oakley by the vest and disappearing behind their transport. Matias takes a moment to catch his breath and calm his nerves. The last thing he wants is for this child to fear him; that would only spell trouble. However, the longer this confrontation continues, the more likely everything is to go up in smoke. As a precaution, he begins to slowly back up, edging toward the front of the Tracks and around the left bumper. Now, with his rifle steadied on the vehicle's surface, Matias is painfully aware that he still isn't safely out of the blast radius, but he feels more secure than before, so it will have to do. He leans back to check the status of Oakley and Shaw but doesn't see them anywhere. He assumes he hasn't seen them come back out from behind the Tracks and that they are somewhere in the sea of civilians, haplessly attempting crowd-control.

Just as he turns to face the girl again, there's a flash of white. The next thing Matias knows, he's face down on the ground. Everything around him is muffled by an incoherent buzzing. His muscles had ached before this incident, but now… now everything is on fire, throbbing and burning, a pain that he feels in his bones. He lifts his head from the coarse sand and sees the tracks, now rolled onto its side, scorched and blackened. Beside the rear wheel, he sees the lower half of a limb, perhaps an arm. Not far from there, he observes the upper part of Barringer's body. Matias cocks his head painfully in the direction the girl had been next to the woman's body moments ago, but all that remains is a dark obsidian stain on the sand, surrounded by charred gelatinous bits of flesh and bone. Civilian casualties abound, far too numerous to count. Matias still can't locate Oakley or Shaw, but he assumes they're gone, disintegrated in the blast. Rolling onto his back, he attempts to stand but quickly senses something is amiss. Glancing down, horror floods over him; both of his legs are gone, messily blown apart around the knee joints. His senses start to flood back, and he can hear people shrieking in pain and terror, weeping all around him. He can smell the scent of seared flesh and the odorizing taggant chemical of C4 compound in the air, and then the adrenaline begins to fade, and the pain hits. It's unforgiving and unrelenting. Matias' howls of sheer agony are so sharp that he feels like his lungs might collapse and end it all right there on the blood-soaked dunes. If only he had decided how to handle the situation, maybe none of this would have happened… but that damn girl… that teenager… She had reminded him of his daughter back home, Anika.

CHAPTER 13

Invitation

Time and location (the past): 8:49 am,
Snohomish, Washington

Matias jolts awake, stifling his screams as sweat beads heavily on his forehead. His breaths are labored, and his body convulses in a barely containable manner. He reaches over to the nightstand beside his bed, sitting up to grab the bottle of water he had placed there the night before. As he begins to guzzle down the liquid, he wipes the sweat from his brow. *Some fucking dream...* A knock resonates from his bedroom door, which opens gently a moment later.

"Are you okay, Dad? I heard you shouting..."

"I'm fine, honey, just a bad dream," he replies without looking at her.

Anika walks over to him, grabs his wheelchair on the way, and lines it up beside the mattress. Matias waves her hands away as she offers to help him.

"I can do it," he says, shaking and wincing throughout the process before finally settling into the seat of the apparatus.

It had been six months since her father was medically retired. Although Anika is glad to have him back at home, he seems miserable- a mere shell of his former self. It hurts her to see her old man like this. It's as if her father is metaphorically missing a piece of himself because he's now missing something literally. She thinks that having him home safe and sound is a Godsend, nothing short of a miracle; however, Matias views his luck as more of a curse than anything else. It's punishment, the retribution he must endure for not making the right call and for allowing so many to die. Anika has tirelessly tried to convince him that war never makes sense, that it wasn't his fault, and that he shouldn't blame himself for what happened in Iraq. However, she can never reach him. She watches as he rubs the scar tissue over the stubs of his kneecaps, where the surgeons stitched the skin closed after his double amputation. Her heart breaks for him, and it's all she can do to choke back tears. She mustn't cry, though, if not for her own sake, then for his.

"Do they hurt at all today?" she asks, trying to return to business as usual.

"Just a dull ache, nothing major," her father replies. She nods once more, then positions herself behind the wheelchair and grips the handles. "That's good. Let's get some grub in ya; I made breakfast."

"Thank you, sweetheart. I love you," he says, reaching a hand up and over his shoulder to rest atop her own.

She smiles and replies to him, "I love you too, Dad, more than anything... the food is getting cold, let's get to the dining room and dig in." As she begins to wheel him out of the bedroom, all Matias can think about is how that beautiful smile will attract a plethora of foolish boys that he'll have to chase off in the years to come, *not that it would be much of a chase...* The impulsive thought robs him of any momentary happiness he's just experienced, and he sits in grim resolve as Anika wheels him down the hall to the dining room.

"So, that bad dream you had... was it the same as usual?"Anika had been his sole caretaker long enough now to have experienced more than her fair share of night terrors and rough morning wake-ups. The source is almost always the same. Matias doesn't enjoy reliving his time in Iraq through his nightmares, but what he prefers even less is reliving them willingly while awake, so he simply nods in response. "I'm sorry you keep having to face those moments, but hopefully the delicious meal I made for you can pull your focus away from all those bad memories."

Matias feigns a smile as Anika pushes him to the dining room table. She kisses him on the forehead and then heads into the kitchen. It doesn't take her long to return with a plate full of food; she has truly outdone herself. There's French toast topped with her homemade whipped cream and raspberries, eggs benedict with sliced avocado beside it, pepitas cooked to perfection, and thick-cut bacon slices that smell delectably of maple. "Bon Appétit!" she says, her mock French accent sounding anything but authentic.

Matias laughs, a genuine and hearty laugh. "You have a true talent for cooking and baking. Have you ever thought about opening your own restaurant?" he asks before taking a bite of French toast.

"I'd love to, but I'm only seventeen. I don't think they allow seventeen-year-olds to open restaurants in Seattle. I guess I'll just have to put that dream on hold for a while." He has devoured nearly half of the French toast by the time she finishes speaking and thinks it just might be the best French toast he has ever tasted. "Well, I suppose so," he says between bites, "but just promise me you'll never stop pursuing that dream, okay?"

"When have I ever let anything get in the way of what I want? People often tell me that I'm nearly as stubborn as my father." She winks and returns to the stove to prepare herself a plate.

She has a point: Anika is headstrong, a trait she takes directly from him. In fact, there isn't much of her mother in the girl, and as petty as it seems, Matias is thankful for that. Some people, try as they might, just aren't good at their core. Matias feels that his former wife fits snugly into that category. She left while he was deployed, long before his injuries occurred, and did so in a deplorable fashion by simply packing her bags and skipping town one night while Anika slept down the hall. When his daughter called and told him the next morning, she was inconsolable, which left Matias feeling a fury that could rival that of the God he no longer believed in. How could someone just up and abandon their child that way? Especially one as kind-hearted and respectful as Anika? It hardly matters now; Matias is home, and he won't be leaving her ever again. If he dedicates his life to *anything* from here on out, it will be to that girl. "Hey, what do you say we head to the store once we're done with breakfast? Could use some more groceries, especially if you're going to be outcooking Gordon Ramsey on the daily."

Anika chuckles at his remark. "Sure thing. Finish your food; I'll go grab some clothes for you to change into."

Matias nods as she returns to his bedroom to rummage through his closet and drawers. There is no longer any privacy between them, and her searching through his underwear drawer is the least of his concerns. With the distraction of Anika gone, the thoughts come flooding back. What was the right call? Could I have saved them all? Should I have shot that little girl? It's always like this; unless there's constant and unending interference, his mind immediately snaps back to that day. Living through something like that is too much for even the most seasoned soldiers to process. Although Matias has a tough exterior, he isn't anywhere near unfeeling enough to escape that situation mentally unscathed. It haunts him day in and day out, and when night falls and he shuts his eyes, it culminates in nightmares. Anika returns, the necessary interruption to divert his thoughts once more. "Uhhh, Dad? There's a man in our living room... he says he's here to see you..."

His head snaps toward the front room of the house. "You let a stranger into our home? Anika, what have I told you about checking the peephole before you open the door?"

"I didn't let him in! He must have let himself in, and he scared the shit out of me when I walked past the living room!" she protests.

"Watch your mouth," Matias says sternly.

"Sorry. Anyway, he's sitting on the sofa waiting for you," she says, handing him a stack of folded clothes. As he takes it from her, he immediately feels something that doesn't belong among the jeans and flannel shirt. It's his Sig Sauer P365, discreetly tucked within the folds of his clothing. *Good girl.* He raised her to be suspicious of strangers, and evidently, the lesson has stuck like glue. He looks her straight in the eyes.

"Stay right here. Do you have your phone with you?" he asks.

"Yes, sir," she responds, all business.

"Good. If you hear *anything* bad happening in the other room, run out the back door and call nine-one-one. Don't stop running until you're with law enforcement, understand?" Anika nods, and Matias begins to roll himself into the living room, the stack of clothes that hides his handgun resting on his lap. When he enters the room, he sees a man sitting patiently on the sofa just as his daughter has promised. He looks to be in his thirties, wears a tailored suit, has short, cropped, dark-brown hair, and aviator-style sunglasses perched on the bridge of his nose. When the man notices Matias he removes his glasses, revealing piercing blue eyes.

"Hello old friend, it's been a while."

Matias hides his shock. After a moment, he recognizes this man, having been through hell and back with him. It's Elliot Shaw, who has been dead for *six months*. Regardless, he's entered Matias' home uninvited and will be offered no quarter. "What the hell are you doing here, Shaw? How are you alive? I saw you… no… no, I never did see you die… Do you make a habit of coming back from the dead and inviting yourself into people's homes?" The man rises from the sofa, straightening his suit as he does so, while Matias' dominant hand instinctively moves toward the pile of clothes resting on his thighs.

"I apologize for entering your home without permission; it was rude of me. Old habits, and all that… It's just that time is of the essence. I now represent a company called ENDURE. While we're on the subject of invitations, I'm here to offer you one you can't refuse." Shaw steps forward, and Matias' hand finds the grip of his Sig Sauer, though he does not reveal it just yet.

"With all due respect, Shaw, I'm not sure I know you anymore. Come any closer, and you'll find out just how quickly and surely I *can decline* that invitation."

His old ally's hands raise in protest. "No need for all of that. Again, I'm only here to make you an offer. If you refuse, I will walk back out your front door, and you'll never see me again. I promise, it's as simple as that."

Matias glares at him. "Why don't you tell me how it is that you're alive first? I swore you died in the same blast that took my legs. All the reports had you and everyone else listed as K.I.A."

Shaw nods. "I know what the reports say; ENDURE falsified them. I can't go into too much detail since most of what we do is classified. If you agree to my offer, I can explain further." Matias hesitates, then reluctantly signals the man to continue. Elliot Shaw smiles and presents his proposal. "Tell me, Matias; how would you like to walk again?"

CHAPTER 14

Hinderance

Time and location (present-day): 12:00 pm,
ENDURE Center for Rehabilitation

I'm not clinically insane; the ever-growing pain in the arch of my left foot, where the flash drive digs into it, confirms that with every step I take. The security guard who apprehended me threw a fabric bag over my head, then led me to a random room after our botched escape from Atticus' office and locked me inside until morning. The only thing I can recall from the long walk is that at some point before reaching this room, we had entered an elevator. Whether we rode it up or down, I couldn't tell, but we were inside for quite some time before the chime signaled and the doors finally opened.

I could have screamed and cried, but all I could manage was to replay Mallen's voice in my head repeatedly... *The Nine will arrive and cleanse the filth of humanity from the surface of this planet. It will be an extinction event for the ages...* What did he mean by that? Who were The Nine? This single statement lives rent-free within the confines of my mind until the clock strikes twelve noon. Then the guard returns to retrieve me, and a conversation via a portable two-way radio reveals that the cop, soldier, or *whatever* he is, is indeed named Elliot Shaw. How can this guard be the same cop who interviewed me after Jonathan's death? How is he the same tactician from the Mason Cais video files? The only thing I'm certain of is that this Oakley character who disappeared with Matias was usually present wherever Elliot Shaw was. They're both working under Atticus' instruction, but it seems that in whatever capacity they do so, they operate as a unit.

Based on what I overheard on the radio, I'm finally being taken to Atticus Cais, just as Elliot promised. It's one of the few things he's said since capturing me. The rest has been limited to commands like "Don't move," "Stay put," and the occasional "Quiet" when I protest his iron grip. The cuffs bite into my wrists, sharp enough now to draw blood. Before we leave, he slips the bag back over my head. Then we walk, silently to the elevator. Inside, we stand encased in stillness as it moves in some unknown direction. I know this ride takes time, so I press my luck. "Where are you taking me? No, better yet, where were we? Did we go up or down last night?"

"Be quiet," is Elliot's response- one that I intentionally ignore.

"What's *really* going on here? Are you even part of law enforcement?"

"Last warning, shut your mouth," he replies, but I don't feel even close to compliant enough to follow his command.

"How about you give me some answers, *Elliot*."

He punches me hard in the gut, and I crumple to the floor, gasping for the breath that's been knocked clean out of my diaphragm. It's unexpected and certainly catches me off guard. It's also intentional; the badge on his chest, which I first noticed when I put a face to the name during the interrogation about Jonathan, only displays his last name: Shaw. I learned his first name by listening in on what he probably assumed was a quiet and private conversation through the two-way radio. My goal is to strike a nerve and get him talking more. While it comes with a physical toll, the purpose of this charade has been fulfilled. "I warned you. Do *not* call me by that name again; there will be more where that came from if you do. I can't kill you, but I *can* make you wish you were dead."

That's at least good to know; my life isn't in danger, not any *immediate* danger anyway. As the air returns to my lungs, I press the man even harder. "Sorry, won't happen again… but what *can* I call you then? Officer Shaw? Mr. Shaw? Black Ops Shaw? Nurse Shaw?"

"Just Shaw, but preferably, you just shut your mouth as instructed."

I brace for another impact, but luckily do not receive any new blows. "Okay Shaw, I'll shut up now… *If* you tell me where that Oakley guy took Matias." Some part of me is worried; maybe my life isn't at risk, but that doesn't mean that Matias will be treated in kind.

"I don't know what it is about the cuffs and the bag over your head that make you think you're in any position to negotiate." Shaw makes a valid point; I really don't have the upper hand in this situation at all.

"True, but you know I can take a punch now, and I could just go out of my way to irritate the ever-loving shit out of you until you answer me." The fabric sack muffles my speech, and I silently hope it's only increasing Shaw's irritation.

"Or, if you keep talking, I might just gag you too. The ball's in your court." The elevator slows to a stop with a cheerful, juxtaposing ring, and I hear the doors slide open. Shaw lifts me from the floor and guides me forward.

"Alright, you win. Shutting up," I say, forfeiting the fight for now. Shaw clearly isn't going to give me any more information than necessary. At this point, I'll just have to play along, wait, and see if maybe Atticus has more to reveal. After all, even if they don't know about the flash drive hidden in my sock, they must know that we accessed Atticus' computer. We had *seen* the things they did, the atrocities they committed, and might *still* be committing. That gives me an advantage.

"Or they could just kill you and toss your carcass in the incinerator. Advantage gone."

I bristle slightly, hoping Shaw hasn't noticed. The effects of the medication Lena gave me are dwindling fast; Mallen will take up residence in my mind again soon if I can't get more of it. As for Lena, that's a whole other mystery to unwrap. Can she be trusted? If I live to see her again, I'll have to confront her, if only to better understand whether she's as twisted as her uncle or not.

I hear a beep followed by the mechanical sliding of a door. Shaw nudges me a bit further, then firmly sits me down in a chair. He tears the bag from my head, and the harsh light in the room temporarily leaves me blinded. When my eyes finally adjust, I suppress the urge to gasp aloud. The room looks identical to the one Mason Cais died in- the room where Atticus killed his own brother and where the doctor now sits across from me. I become painfully aware that I'm seated in the large, mechanized steel chair where Mason had been held captive. Nothing lies between us but open air, and the knowledge that I could have been secured to the seat like its previous victim, but am not, helps me to subdue the animalistic instinct to escape.

I glance to the right and see Shaw standing guard beside the entrance to the room, resembling the "Black Ops Shaw" I mentioned earlier in jest. He's clad in full military gear, so completely sable against the iridescence of the white room that it's hard to distinguish the finer details of his kit. A helmet and balaclava conceal everything but his icy blue eyes.

In contrast to the contraption I sit upon, Atticus is only about ten feet away from me, sitting on a simple metal chair, the kind you'd find in a college cafeteria. He's hunched over in silent thought, with his elbows resting on his knees and his chin on his clasped hands. His eyes study me as if he's contemplating the best angle to approach the forthcoming conversation. The moment builds to a crescendo of tension, and he finally speaks. "Hello, Royce. I assume you know why we're here, in this specific room?"

I nod hesitantly. "I do. *You* know that *we* know."

"No need to be coy, Royce. What exactly do you *think* you know?" He's trying to provoke me again, but I won't fall for his tricks like I did with Jonathan.

"Well, I know what we saw in those video files. You killed your own *brother*, Lena's *father*."

Atticus nods solemnly. Or did he? That's another thing eating away at my sanity, along with Mallen's grim prophecy. Had Lena lied to me? Was Mason even her father? After all, it's perfectly plausible that Atticus has or had other siblings. Hopefully, my leading of Atticus will answer at least one of these questions.

"Is that what you saw? I think you know, just as I do, that at that time, Mason had long been dead and gone. I know it speaks to you, Royce, so let's not dance around the subject; Mallen poses a threat to everyone and everything you have ever held dear. I did what I believed was necessary to stop it. I failed, but at the time, it seemed like the right course of action."

"You did what you thought would save yourself, regardless of how you choose to manipulate the situation. Your attempts to gaslight me into believing what you want will not get you very far, Atticus." My words are laced with venom, the doctor's name slipping from my lips in a sharp hiss.

He chuckles under his breath, and a hint of disappointment lingers in his tone. "If you say so, Royce. The nitty-gritty of it all is that you simply don't know. You don't know *anything beyond* what I *want* you to know, because if you did, you'd understand why I must do the things I do. Do you really think a man of my caliber would be so foolish as to make the password to his work computer, which contains highly sensitive material, the name of his beloved niece? You saw what I wanted you to see, and then we intervened. Nothing more, nothing less. The question you should be asking yourself is *why.*

That couldn't be true, could it? This is just another one of Atticus Cais' attempts to gain the upper hand with falsehoods; it has to be. But if it isn't, though… I have to be certain. "Okay, I'll bite. Tell me then, why? Why would you bother revealing any of this to me?"

"It's actually quite simple," he replies as he rises from his chair, beginning a slow and methodical walk around the room.

"You wouldn't stop. You and your group of misfits. I couldn't allow contact with Mallen to be disrupted, but as long as that thing was gnawing away at your sanity, you weren't going to stop digging."

There's a glimmer of hope in Atticus's statement; he didn't want Mallen to stop speaking to me. Did Lena prescribe the medication that kept him at bay behind the doctor's back? I set the thought aside for later contemplation as Atticus continues.

"So, I decided to give you a nibble, a crumb of information. In return, you gave me leverage." The realization strikes me like a ton of bricks, and I can barely restrain myself from lashing out at the doctor.

"What did you do to him? Where is Matias?" My anger is palpable, yet Atticus laughs. The bastard *laughs*.

"It's cute how attached you are to these people- people you hardly know! Wake up, Royce! They're strangers to you! It's moments like this that make me question how so much of this could depend on a foolhardy young man like you..."

"So much of *what*?!" It's a slip, a chink in the armor I cannot help but expose. The expression on Atticus's face tells me that he has almost said too much. I can see that he is trying his best to maintain his composure.

"It's crucial for you to understand that the work we're doing here must continue without hindrance, Royce. So, here is what will happen from this point forward. Shaw will take you back to your quarters shortly. You must never speak of this again unless I approach you about it. You are more than welcome to continue spending time with Desmond and Aiden, but rest assured that if it involves all of you sticking your noses where they don't belong again, I can have them removed from this situation as swiftly as I did with Matias. I have eyes and ears *everywhere*, Royce. This is *my* facility, and I strongly advise that you don't forget it."

Atticus had railroaded the conversation so well that I almost forgot the question at hand- *almost*. "Where is he, Atticus? Where's Matias?"

The doctor exhales deeply, regaining his calm and composed demeanor. "Matias is alive, for now. If you want him to stay that way, you must do what I have asked of you."

I'm backed into a corner, and it feels awful. I have no choice but to follow the doctor's instructions, but I refuse to leave the confrontation empty-handed. "So, I take all this to mean that I can't leave here? I'm effectively your prisoner?"

"Yes, that would be a correct assumption," he says coolly, as if he isn't openly admitting to the crime of abduction.

"Then that means you *need* me for something."

Atticus smiles grimly. "Tread carefully, Royce; that last bit is yet to be determined."

My stomach lurches at the remark; perhaps I'm not as safe as I initially thought. "Just answer one thing for me. Answer this one thing, and I promise I'll return to my quarters afterward and play whatever part you expect me to play."

"I will consider your request, but I promise nothing."

I'll have to accept it. At this point, that's all I'll receive. "Jonathan... I... what happened? Why did he try to kill me?"

A brief flash of something appears in Atticus' gaze- pity, perhaps. Whatever the case, he answers quickly. "Jonathan McCallister is a prime example of why our work must continue. Mallen took hold of Jonathan long before it latched onto you. Mason and Jonathan represent two sides of the same coin, illustrating what happens when someone is not adequately conditioned to withstand this *entity's* influence over them. But you... there's something different about you, Royce. I won't lie to you and say you're in good hands or that you're safe. Mallen is a volatile force of nature, yet I have no choice but to see this pseudo-observational study through to the end, regardless of the outcome. Whatever reasons Jonathan had for attacking you were his own, not Mallen's. My guess? He was afraid- afraid of what Mallen intends to achieve *through* you. Jonathan attempted to kill you out of *mercy*; it may have been the last sane thing he attempted to do."

It's a heavy burden to bear. When I thought Jonathan had suffered a psychotic break from hearing Mallen in his head, it was easier to come to grips with what happened. Yet here's Atticus, telling me that Jonathan, *not* Mallen, made the decision to take my life. Quite possibly for all the right reasons, but it stings, nonetheless. I don't know what to say, choking on every word when I try to respond, and instead, I just sit there in mute acceptance.

Atticus finally breaks the silence. "I apologize if that is a hard pill to swallow, but I believe it is the truth. After all, that is what you've been seeking. I appreciate your continued cooperation moving forward, Royce. I assure you this is all for the greater good. Perhaps in time, you'll come to realize it as well. Shaw will escort you back to your quarters." Just like that, the doctor turns on his heel and leaves the room, the tinny whir of the door signaling his departure.

"Stand up," Shaw demands as he approaches me. I comply, feeling defeated and lost. He slips behind me and throws the bag over my head once more.

CHAPTER 15

Confrontation

Time and location (present-day): 4:47 pm,
ENDURE Center for Rehabilitation

I aggressively fidget with a chess pawn, rolling it back and forth between my fingers. This small piece of wood and I are the same; pawns in a game controlled by those far beyond our purview. As Aiden and Desmond debate across the table from me, I pay little attention. All I can focus on is Atticus' revelation: that we have little to no control over anything that is happening within the facility, even during the times when we think we do.

After Shaw left me in my room, I refilled my Mallen-killing medication at the dispensary and then made my way to the chess table. It had become our unspoken meeting ground, and I knew that if Desmond and Aiden weren't there when I arrived, they would be soon enough. Ultimately, I arrived first, which inevitably gave my mind time to rehash my interaction with Jonathan that led to his death. It's better, if only a little, than hearing Mallen's sharp words slicing through my brain like a knife through butter. I began picking at the details, justifying Atticus's take on the scenario until it became the only plausible outcome: Jonathan attempted to kill me, all to put a stop to the thing living inside me like a parasite. Jonathan had failed. I survived the ordeal, but now I felt dead inside.

"What do you think, Royce? After all, you seem to be Atticus's center of attention in all of this," Desmond says.

I blink absent-mindedly at Desmond, having heard little of what was said. "I'm sorry, I kind of zoned out. There's a lot on my mind. What were you saying?"

Desmond nods, no trace of frustration on his face. "I get it, what we found back there... it was a lot to handle for anyone. I can't imagine what's going on in your head right now. Aiden and I were just saying that considering everything, it might be best to disband our group for a while and keep our distance from one another. It sucks, but for now... for now, Atticus won."

Aiden expresses his agreement. "Especially considering none of us know what happened to Matias."

That's true; there's no two ways about it. We found evidence that Atticus, along with who knows how many others working for ENDURE, had been conducting experiments on human subjects. Yet, this evidence proved to be useless. Using it in any way would be sentencing Matias to death.

"I do," I utter, but then I correct myself. "Well, not exactly. I was just told that he's alive, and that our cooperation will help keep him that way."

Aiden's head droops. "Damn… I guess that seals the deal, then. Time to back off. At least we know we aren't lunatics. I'll see you fellas around, I guess."

Aiden stands from his chair, gives a disheartened wave goodbye, and disappears into the crowd. As I watch him go, Desmond knocks his fist on the table to get my attention. "Hey man, I just wanted to say thanks for helping us. Even if we all die of old age trapped in this godforsaken facility, at least we found evidence proving us right. Speaking of which, do you have the flash drive on you? Why don't you let me take that? I have plenty of places to stash it, and you have enough on your plate."

The device that covets the truth of our circumstance is still very much with me. I refused to let it leave my person until we were all together again. Once I had been escorted back to my room, however, I adjusted the flash drive to give my aching foot a break, the small rectangle now tucked just above my ankle. Making sure I am not being watched, I bring my left leg up so that I'm sitting semi cross-legged in my chair, then discreetly retrieve the flash drive from my sock. I then hand it to Desmond under the table. Once I feel him take it, he nods. "Alright, I'll keep this safe, Royce. Just keep your head down. This isn't the end; we just need to regroup and get our bearings. I'll reach out to you again when the time is right."

We both stand from the table, and Desmond places a silent hand on my shoulder, pausing for a moment before he turns and begins to walk away. A thought strikes me like a lightning bolt, and I spin around, catching him by his wrist. "Wait!" I blurt out as quietly as possible, trying not to draw attention to us. Desmond looks at my hand clasped around his wrist, then at me, bewilderment written all over his face as I let go of him. "I almost forgot to ask you about the flash drive; where did you get it from?"

Desmond's face contorts in response, resembling something akin to sorrow for a millisecond before his eyes dart behind me. I turn around to see Lena headed my way, and a terrible wave of stress washes over me. I had known that this confrontation was coming, but I had thought it would be on my terms. Seeing her now sets my nerves ablaze, but not in a good way, not in the way it did before. I turn back around to get my answer from Desmond before Lena is within earshot, but he's already gone. It's a behavior I would have found strange if not for his fear that Lena is working with Atticus, a possibility that seems even more believable now.

"Hey, Royce," she says as she stops behind me.

I swivel around, swallowing my anxiety and trying to act as calm as possible. "Hey Lena, how's it going?"

She gives me a look of dissatisfaction, conveying her unspoken message: *don't beat around the bush.* "Can we go somewhere more private to talk?" She asks, wasting no time at all.

"Of course. My room?" I offer, and she nods, gesturing for me to lead the way. The walk there is quiet and, for the first time ever, daunting. The small cube I call home is the only place that feels safe here now, but at this moment, the idea of Lena staring me down from across the room, the tension taut like a tightrope... in this moment, the thought of being trapped in that cube with her is pure hell.

We reached my room within minutes, but the moment we stepped inside, time seemed to warp, stretching each second into something unbearable. The air was thick with unsaid things. I made my way to the edge of the bed and sat, trying to quiet the storm of expectations in my head. Before I could get lost in them, Lena moved closer and lowered herself beside me. She turned slightly, her right knee brushing against mine, her hands folded delicately in her lap. There was a quiet intensity in her presence, a closeness that felt both comforting and overwhelming, like standing at the edge of something you can't name but deeply feel.

She reaches out and takes my hand in hers. When she does, all my suspicions wash away. Last night's events become a distant memory, and the thought of not being able to trust her with my life, while still present, seems laughable. I stare at our interlaced fingers for a while, and when I finally look up to meet her eyes, they're welling with tears. Her lip quivers as she speaks. "This is *so hard*," she says breathily through hitched inhales and exhales.

I squeeze her hand, trying to reassure her. "What is? Talk to me, Lena. I don't care about all the other stuff right now. I just want to know that you're okay."

She leaps off the bed, practically throwing my hand away. "No! I am *far* from okay! None of this is okay, Royce!" She begins pacing back and forth now, her hands clasped behind her head, her footfalls heavy with rage. "I am *trying* to hold it all together; I really, *really* am. For you, for my uncle, for everyone but *myself*. Every day we continue this, every day I play along with this charade, I feel further and further away from myself. And all the while, *YOU*," she halts abruptly, an accusatory finger shakily pointing in my direction. "You don't even *remember*. But then, how could you?"

There's a pause, and then Lena collapses to the floor, sobbing uncontrollably. I get up from the bed, feeling awfully confused, but my need to console her overrides everything else. *To hell with the rules; it's all a damn lie anyway.* I go to where she has shrunk onto the tile and get down on my knees behind her. Wrapping my arms around her, I pull her in close, hugging her as tightly as I can. Lena grabs onto my forearm, clinging so firmly to me that it hurts. Her nails dig into my skin, but I refuse to let go.

After a while, the sobbing lessens, fizzles out, and becomes more of a whimper.

"Come on," I say gently, "let's get you off the ground." I help her to her feet as she snuffles away the last of her tears, and we walk back to the bedside. Once we sit down, I embrace Lena again, rubbing her shoulder soothingly. She leans into me, nestling her head against my chest. "Lena, I need you to explain. I want to help; I want to understand, but I can't do so without your help."

She looks up at me, staring into my eyes, a hesitance reflected in her own. Then suddenly, without warning, Lena's lips are pressed against mine. She pulls me into her embrace, and we tumble backward onto the bed. My synapses are firing at what feels like supersonic speeds; what the hell is happening? There are so many reasons I don't want to resist this, and yet as many times as I have fantasized about this exact situation, it never begins with Lena broken down in tears on the floor. It feels right yet somehow wrong at the same time. I try to interject verbally between passionate grazes, but physically, I cannot pull myself away. This moment, this perfect moment, is the only normalcy I have felt in years. Words can wait until tomorrow. I'm not leaving this place; Atticus said so himself. There will be enough time to discuss everything later. For now, what I need is a break—a break from secrecy, a break from espionage, a break from all the insanity that ENDURE has brought into my life. So, when Lena begins removing my clothes and the fleeting thought of stopping her dances across my mind, I push it far away in favor of a different notion: *to hell with the rules... the rules can wait until tomorrow, too.*

CHAPTER 16

Royce

Time and location (the past): 8:02 am, Murrieta, CA

The sun began to rise, casting a fiery orange glow atop the grove of trees that spread far and wide at the bottom of the falls. It's my twentieth birthday, and I have finals next week. After copious amounts of studying, fun has been the furthest thing from my mind when it came to celebrating this day. I wanted nothing more than to shut off my brain and enjoy a relaxing day exploring nature. My younger sister Rory argued that a hike to the top of Tanaja Falls was anything but relaxing. I contended that it was my decision, and in the end, she begrudgingly agreed.

We arrived early that morning to beat the heat, knowing that the hike wasn't long or rigorous, despite how Rory felt. Reaching the top took no time at all, and we had spent the past hour or so cooling down from the short trek and enjoying the views. Despite only being 1.6 miles out and back, Rory had complained the whole way up the trail. She was two years younger than me, and although she usually gave me a run for my money when it came to being the energetic sibling, she had tuckered out earlier than usual today. Our mother, Olivia, had hung back and kept a steady pace with Rory, while my father, Charles, and I practically jogged to the end of the hike, wanting to enjoy the falls before anyone else arrived. Now, I sat atop a large boulder with my dad, far too high a climb for either Rory or my mother and watched as they explored along the stream that fed into the waterfall below.

"What a sight, that sunrise," my father said, pointing out at the glowing sky in front of us as the light glinted off his green eyes. My father pulled a rag from the pocket of his shorts and dabbed the sweat from his forehead before running it over his short, dirty-blonde hair. With his hair now slicked back and out of his face, he tossed the used towel at me. "Gross!" I said with a chuckle, slinging it back in his direction. "Definitely worth getting up early for, though," I agreed as I averted my attention back to the scene before us. "I think Aurora would disagree with you, but we have to forgive your sister; she's still a lazy teenager after all." I laughed again as my dad reached over and patted me on the back.

My thoughts began to wander as I reflected on how other kids endured tough upbringings or had no parents at all. Remembering that always made me appreciate how attentive and kind my own were. Rory and I were always their top priority, no matter the situation.

"Twenty years old; you sure are growing up fast. Pretty soon I'll be a crotchety old man and you'll have kids of your own." My father said, his gaze unwavering as the sun now peeked over the horizon.

I scowled at the idea; children had never really been on my agenda. "Yeah right! Besides, you're going to live until you're one hundred." I shoved him playfully as we laughed more.

"Hey, I've been meaning to tell you that your mom and I really admire the way you watch over your sister. Remember, family always comes first; don't ever let anything stop you from believing that. If anything were to happen to your mother or me, it would be up to you to ensure Rory grows up to be a healthy, well-rounded adult."

"She's eighteen, Dad, I think 'well-rounded' set sail a long time ago. Nothing is going to happen to you and mom anyhow, so don't even pay it a second thought." I said, momentarily panicked by the remark, worried that my father may have been alluding to a serious conversation around the corner. "You're not about to tell me one of you has some sort of terminal illness, are you?"

My father nearly choked as he sipped from his water bottle. "No, not at all! All I'm saying is, growing up, my brother didn't treat me nearly as well as you treat your sister, and I'm proud of you. It's hard being the older sibling, but you never lose your patience with her."

I chuckled as I fidgeted with a rock that had parted from a crack in the boulder. "She certainly tests my limits from time to time, but Rory's my sister. I love her, I love all of you. That's what matters, right?"

Dad smiled. "That's exactly right. I know that you were sometimes bullied at school when you were younger; I'm just glad you didn't treat your sister the way those kids treated you in return."

I dropped my gaze as I reflected on the past. "Well, those kids were *assholes*, whose parents didn't raise them to be respectful. Rory and I are just lucky that we had you and mom as role models."

"You've always been a little different, Royce. It's human nature to respond to things that we don't understand with fear and aggression; those kids back then didn't know any better, didn't know that *you* were better."

I raised an eyebrow; that was strong praise, even for a father as involved and caring as mine.

"I don't mean that in a narcissistic way. You're better than most anyone I've ever met. People are likely going to treat you differently all throughout your life. Maybe you're smarter than them, or more physically capable. Maybe you're faster and more adaptable. Regardless, they'll put you down, not because you deserve it, but because they're afraid. Afraid of what someone like you can achieve when you put your mind to it, afraid of what you might do with all that expanding knowledge in your head. No matter what life throws at you, just always remember to be better than that, to be something better than those who want to knock you down a peg. You're capable of greatness, Royce; your mother and I knew that from the moment you began speaking your first words. Don't ever let this world tell you otherwise. You got it?"

Somewhere deep down, I knew he was right. I had always been more advanced than my peers. I was sharp as a knife when it came to mental acuity, intuitive in matters of the heart, and particularly skilled in anything and everything that was physical in nature. I was forming full sentences at only one year old and started walking without a single stumble at just five months. As I progressed through school, I eventually began skipping grades. My teachers and the school administrators ultimately put a stop to that, citing the bullying I was a victim of and knowing that skipping grades further would only result in more mistreatment. At first, the speed at which I was growing up had scared the hell out of my parents, but as time went on and my repertoire of skills grew exponentially, my parents realized they had created someone special. Or at least that's what they had always led me to believe. How much I believed in that statement was up for debate, regardless of the facts. "I got it, Dad. Thanks," was all I said in response.

My father gave me a final pat on the back and stood up. "Good, now let's get back to your mother and sister. It's time to pack it up and head home."

I nodded and followed suit. My father crawled back down from atop the giant stone, and I took one last glance at the sunrise to store in my memory bank, knowing that this conversation would stay with me for years to come.

As we began to descend back down the mountain, Rory and I inadvertently swapped hiking partners. This time, I took up the rear with my mother, Olivia, while Rory, eager to get back indoors, surged ahead with my father. I inhaled the crisp morning air, reflecting on how much I truly enjoyed being here. It was peaceful; the sounds of birds chirping, sunlight beaming through the trees to illuminate the foliage below, and the streams and rivers flowing gently throughout the forest. There was an unmatched tranquility about this place.

"So, twenty today, no longer a teenager! How does it feel?" My mother said, pulling me away from my reverie.

"I don't know, the same, I guess," I responded with a shrug.

She laughed. "Yeah, get used to that. The years pass by faster and faster the older you get, and eventually you just stop caring altogether."

"Well, if that's the case, I guess you and Dad can practically blink and age a year."

Mom scoffed. "Gee, thanks Royce! I bet you woo all the women at school with that overwhelming amount of charm!"

I chuckled and shoulder-bumped her. "Relax, I'm only kidding!"

"You better be," she said, squinting at me suspiciously.

"All jokes aside," I said, the tone of my voice now serious, "are you feeling okay lately? You've seemed a bit… off recently. Something on your mind?"

My mother's playful façade was immediately gone, and seeing her falter pained me deeply. "Well, at least you're attentive, might make up for the lack of charm… It's nothing really, just what I said before. The years seem to be flying by too quickly to count. Soon you and Rory will be out on your own, with families and homes… I just worry that I didn't properly prepare you both, that maybe I wasn't the best mother I could be."

I shot her a bewildered look, one that brought a smirk to the corner of her mouth. "I can tell you with absolute certainty that you're *overthinking*. You and Dad have done an excellent job raising us. We both love you and couldn't ask for better parents. I don't want you to ever question that. I'm content with where I am and how I got here, and I know Rory is too. You both have always been loving and supportive no matter what, and that's all a child can ask of his parents."

She smiled genuinely. "Guess I was wrong after all; my son *can* be charming when he wants to be."

She laughed as I rolled my eyes at her. "Way to ruin the moment, Olivia."

I found it strangely endearing that my mother felt this way, that the thought of having made even the smallest mistake in raising my sister and me had crossed her mind. The sky was always the limit for her when it came to spreading positivity. She could never be too kind, too good, or too loving; she always felt she had more to offer. We continued talking until we reached the car, where I gave her a reassuring hug and told her that I loved her. After that, I clambered into the back seat of our GMC Acadia. Rory slid in from the opposite side, and I immediately fulfilled my duties as a big brother.

"You smell awful, like dirty socks and manure," I said as she closed the door.

Rory's long, wavy brown hair whipped around in a flurry as she gasped and punched me in the arm. "How *dare* you!" She hissed, daggers behind her blue-green eyes. "Plus, if I *did* stink, which I don't, it would be *your* fault for picking the lamest birthday activity of all time!"

My mother shot me a sour look in the rearview mirror. "Royce, be nice to your sister," she said before resuming her conversation with my father.

I looked over at Rory, who stuck her tongue out at me. I simply smiled in return. Rory would never quite understand, but moments like this were why I chose to escape the monotony of day-to-day life on my birthdays. Here, with the four of us in this car, it felt like we were little kids again. It transported me back to simpler times, times not riddled with huge, life-altering decisions like which university to attend after community college or how much money to save for a down payment on a house.

"It sure is beautiful, I'll give you that," Rory said, staring out the window as the car bumped along unpaved roads. As vain and materialistic as she could be, Rory always managed to find beauty in everything; she could discover something stunning in a pile of garbage if you asked her to. It was one of many aspects of her personality that I admired, as I tended to be more of a pessimist in that regard. Rory suddenly looked back at me, sullen. "You know, I'm really going to miss you when you're gone."

And just like that, one of those huge, life-altering decisions came into play, refusing to allow me to experience life as it once was. "I'll still have all the normal breaks, Rory, I'll come home for the holidays. Besides, I won't be gone forever. I'll have my associate degree by the end of this semester, so by the time I go to university, it should only take two years to get my Bachelor's. I'm not *dying*."

She chuckled. "It's not that! It's just... I don't know, I've been thinking a lot about the future. I mean, how often do we see

Uncle Gerald? He's Dad's brother, and we see him a few times a year at best. I just hate thinking about that being you and me eventually. We do so much together! I hate how that won't be the norm soon."

"Don't think about it that way then. We'll both have our own lives soon enough, but we'll still see each other. I'd never cut you out of my life, and I'll see you more than once a year; there's no way I'll be that busy."

"Promise," she demanded.

"I promise. As a matter of fact, how about I make you a deal?"

Rory perked up, placing her hands on her hips, and speaking in a mock western accent. "A deal, you say? Well, I just might be inclined to accept your offer, mister."

I cringed at the horribly executed drawl but laughed anyway. "How about every Christmas in the future, once we have families of our own, we all get together and come back here to Tanaja Falls for a hike? Mom, Dad, your family, and mine. We can spend the holiday together as a tradition. We'll see each other throughout the years, but this trip will serve as the cherry on top every winter. How does that sound?"

"That sounds like a mighty fine deal, sir, I'd be obliged to accept," she said in the same playful accent as before. However, I have one small change I'd like to propose.

The accent had disappeared, and I knew Rory had entered negotiations mode. "Go ahead, what is it?"

"Hiking sucks, Let's spend Christmas at a cabin in Big Bear instead, where it actually snows!"

I sighed and smiled. "I suppose that'll work too."

Shortly after we made our commitment to one another, Rory passed out for the remainder of the drive home. I, however, replayed our conversation in my head until we pulled into our driveway. Then, I continued to do so throughout the night. When my head hit the pillow, I could not find sleep. Instead, I stared at the ceiling, riddled with guilt. How could I possibly fulfill such a promise to Rory? The truth was that neither of us had any idea what the future held. I could end up moving out of California, not to mention the many darker outcomes that could plague our lives between now and then.

By the time I had to roll out of bed for college the next day, I had only slept for a total of two hours. I was exhausted, but with finals next week, I had no choice but to pull myself together. By the time I drove to campus and sprinted into the science building, I had missed the first twenty minutes or so of my organic chemistry lecture. Luckily, the professor for this course had taken a liking to me and wouldn't fret about my arriving late. I took a seat in the back of the class, partly because it was closest to the door I entered through and partly because I didn't really enjoy being around the other students.

Many of my classmates came from affluent Ivy League families who had financed their entire education, something

I couldn't relate to. Parents would often boast about their children, highlighting their brilliance. Mine never did, and I had no illusions about the truth, even if I pretended otherwise. By the time I graduated from elementary school, I was solving algebra meant for tenth graders. I skipped a grade in middle school and reached college-level reading and calculus early. After skipping eighth grade, I started high school at twelve.

Most students didn't know how to react to someone younger excelling at everything, so the district chose to place me in the standard track to reduce bullying. While it eased the pressure, the mistreatment never stopped. Had others known I could've skipped high school entirely and graduated college by their senior year, the resentment might've been worse. I got through it and took a break before college. While my parents still idolized me, my college peers didn't care, and that indifference was oddly refreshing. It felt as if I didn't exist to them, which was a nice change of pace.

Surrounded by the usual stereotypical cliques on campus, I was a fish out of water. The cheerleaders, the jocks, the goths, the metal kids, the nerds... There was no single category that I truly fit into. So, I accepted their lack of acknowledgment, kept my head down, and minded my own business. Considering I was never much of a people person, college was a win-win for me. I wrote down the homework the professor assigned as the lecture came to an end and then melded into the sea of other young adults as we headed for the exit. As I stepped through the threshold of the door, I almost crashed into someone. I sidestepped to avoid her, stumbled, and nearly fell, barely catching myself on the doorframe.

"Sorry, that was my bad," I said while checking to see if I had dropped anything. "It's no problem at all, I was the one who wasn't watching where I was going."

The unusually kind response caught me off guard and simultaneously drew my attention. I looked up at her for the first time since the interaction began.

"My name's Lena, nice to meet you," she said, extending her hand.

Hesitating briefly, I contemplated how long was *too* long before accepting a handshake. I felt wave after wave of confusing emotions, her unnatural beauty placing me in a state of shock. I accepted her hand, and immediately thought that I had waited far too long to do so.

"I'm Royce, the pleasure's mine."

Lena giggled shyly, causing my face to flush bright red. She was a brunette with startling green eyes- so bright, I thought, that the green hues of the aurora borealis paled in comparison. As she turned to go, my stomach dropped as if I were on a rollercoaster ride; I felt an incessant need to stop her.

"How are you liking organic chemistry?"

She stopped and turned back to face me. "It's not my favorite, but it's a necessary evil."

"What's your field of study?" I continued.

"I'm majoring in Biomedical sciences with a minor in computer science."

"Biomedical sciences? That's... learning about the human body and how it works to develop new medicinal products and treatments, right?"

She smiled, though I could tell she was a bit taken aback by my textbook definition. "That's right. You're cute *and* smart? That's a rare combination."

"Mentally gifted," I said, making air quotes with my fingers. "At least that's what my parents tell me."

Lena laughed. "How old are you anyway?"

"I'm twenty. I graduated high school when I was fifteen, but I took a break before starting college courses here."

"Wow, that's impressive. I'm twenty-three, so I guess I'm not quite as intelligent as you are, but at least I'm on track, right?"

"Right," I said with a smile.

Lena raised an inquisitive finger to her lips. "Don't you play on our football team as well?"

"Running back, yeah."

"Well, you're just a jack of all trades, aren't you?"

The blush spread across my face like wildfire. "I guess so."

It fell silent for a long moment that should have felt awkward but didn't. There seemed to be a natural, unspoken comfort between us.

"Well Royce, I better get going; I don't want to be late to class. It was nice getting to know you, albeit briefly."

"Same, it was great talking to you. Maybe… maybe we can get together sometime and study? Chemistry isn't my strongest subject." It was a lie, but I was eager to see her again.

"I'd like that, here," she pulled a pen out of her pocket, then reached toward me as if asking for something. Confused, I stood there, staring at her outstretched arm. Finally, she grabbed my hand and scribbled on the back of it. "Call me," she said with a wink, then walked away.

CHAPTER 17

Hurt

Time and location (the past): 2:24 pm, San Diego, CA

The wrinkles in my shirt would have been evident had it not been for the deep blues of its pattern that blended them into its linework. I finished buttoning up my flannel, checking my hair in the bedroom mirror one final time before we left for the day's events. It was Memorial Day, and we had a family barbecue to attend. I sat down at the foot of the bed, slipping on my shoes and tying the laces.

"You look handsome," said Lena as she walked into the room.

"Looking good yourself," I said as I stood up and faced her.

She placed her hands on the back of my head and pecked me on the lips. When she pulled away, she stood there for a moment, staring at me with her arms still wrapped around my neck.

"What?" I asked.

"Nothing, I just love you."

I smiled and kissed her again. "I love you too. Now, let's get through this barbecue so we can start packing for our trip."

Lena pranced away, giddy as a schoolgirl, and began to peruse the clothing in her closet. "Hawaii is supposed to be so beautiful this time of year, I'm so excited!"

"I'm just glad you still want to go with *me*. I thought for sure after five years together you'd get sick of me and kick me to the curb," I joked.

Our wedding anniversary was yesterday, but Lena's parents insisted we not leave for our trip until after the annual barbecue. It was a family tradition- one I didn't understand, and one Lena had grown tired of. Seeing her family made her happy, though, so I grinned and bore it yearly.

Lena whipped around to face me, feigning a look of disgust. "How dare you think a woman as loyal as I am would ever call it quits after a measly five years! It would take *at least* six years for me to even *consider* leaving! Besides, I love your sister too much to abandon her."

I laughed and slapped her thigh as I exited the room. "Oh whatever! Come on, we need to get going, then you can spend all the time you want with Rory!"

I shouted over my shoulder. Over the past couple of years, what had started as a Cais family tradition had turned into a joint one. Now, both of our families attended these tedious affairs. Rory was excited to see Lena, as they were two peas in a pod and got along like old friends. My mother and father also enjoyed the company of Lena's parents, which left me as the odd man out during these events. I didn't mind, though, as long as I met my annual family-outing quota and had the rest of the year before the holidays to avoid any drama. The drive to Lena's uncle's house was roughly fifteen minutes, but we had told them we would arrive by 2:30pm, which is what the clock on the stove currently read. I walked back toward the bedroom to retrieve Lena when she appeared in the doorframe.

"I'm ready," she said as she stumbled into the hall, still trying to slip on a shoe one-handed.

I rolled my eyes sarcastically and opened the front door, shooing her through it and to the car. Once I began to back out of the driveway, Lena's demeanor shifted drastically. She became suddenly withdrawn and quiet. I knew why; this happened whenever there was a family gathering. The only question I debated every single time this occurred was whether to talk about it or ignore the issue entirely. With our vacation on the horizon, I decided this was something I wanted to address before its effects on Lena carried over and continued during our trip. I sighed as I took a right turn, then pulled the car over. She looked at me confused, as if she didn't know what was going on, though she most certainly did.

"You do this every year, Lena; we don't have to go if it's too much for you; there's no shame in it."

The feigned confusion vanished from her face, replaced by an eerie stillness. "I know, I just... mom and dad would be upset if we didn't."

"I can handle Mason and Kaylee; besides, they have my mother and father there to keep them sane. If you would just tell them what happened, what your uncle tried to do, then I'm sure they would understand," I contended.

"How Royce? How do I look my father in the eye and tell him his brother tried to sexually assault me?"

I pursed my lips in frustration, treading carefully through my thoughts before responding. "I can't answer that, it's for you to decide how to approach it. All I know is that I think you should tell them. At the very least, it would get us out of these damn barbecues every year if your father decided he never wanted to see Atticus' face again," I kidded, attempting to lighten the mood. Much to my dismay, my wit brought no change to Lena's disposition.

"I don't know... maybe I'll tell them, but probably not today. I'll just keep my distance from Atticus and try my best to pretend he isn't there."

"Alright, but if at any point you want to leave, just text me and I'll find an excuse, okay?"

She nodded, and after a moment, I pulled back onto the road.

The incident with her uncle Atticus had occurred two years ago during the same gathering. Lena had left everyone in the backyard to use the restroom inside, but when she arrived, her uncle caught her in the hall. She attempted to squeeze past him, only to be pinned against the wall, his hand finding its way up her dress. Lena was no delicate flower, though, and that earned Atticus a swift knee to the groin that left him crumpled on the floor.

She came to me afterwards, cool, calm, and collected, but I knew her well enough to sense when she was fighting back tears. We left shortly after, and she told me what had happened on the drive home through strained sobs. Atticus had been grotesquely intoxicated that day, but that fact hadn't earned him any sort of reprieve as far as I was concerned. Drunk or not, he had taken a pass at her, at his own niece. It was deplorable to say the least, and a decision influenced by alcohol was an honest one at the end of the day.

She never told anyone else; it was a secret only I had access to. I had barely liked the man before but had remained cordial. Now, though my distaste for him was confidential, I could tell that Atticus knew I wanted to hurt him- hurt him bad. I refrained, however, if only for Lena's sake and the impact it would have on the family dynamic. It was Lena's decision to keep things hushed, and I had to respect that. However, I decided long ago he would only receive one get-out-of-jail-free card. If it happened again...

I shifted the car into park as we came to a stop in the driveway of her uncle's house, my thoughts having distracted me the whole way there. It was a grand structure located in the Rancho Santa Fe Golf Club gated community. At the front of the house, two great marble pillars flanked dual handcrafted mahogany doors. Those doors, like gates to a castle, sat atop a multi-tiered stone pathway that wound through a colorful flowerbed. It was a shame to know that such a feat of architecture was tainted beyond repair by the man who called it home.

I reached over and grabbed Lena's hand, squeezing it for emphasis. "Remember, if at *any* moment you want to leave," I said, looking her dead in the eyes so that she would know how serious I was.

"I text you; I know. Thank you, Royce."

I brought the back of her hand to my lips and kissed it. "You never have to thank me for looking out for you."

After taking a few deep breaths, Lena exited the vehicle, and I followed in tow. Lena's mother greeted us at the door, pulling us both into a suffocating hug.

"Kaylee, you're squeezing the life out of me," I said, struggling for air.

She released Lena fully while keeping her grip on my shoulders. "It's been nearly a month since I've seen you, Royce. You should have anticipated this."

She was right. Between work and school, I didn't have much time for family, let alone the in-laws. In fact, the barbecue being a sort of mandatory meeting was the only reason I wasn't home studying at that moment. "Fair enough, it's good to see you, Kaylee. How's Mason doing?"

She flinched at the question, a barely perceptible reaction that only I had caught. "He's doing okay. We have another appointment in about an hour, so we'll be leaving early. We were hoping Lena could take the car and follow us there, and you could get a ride home from your parents since Mason's doctor's office is right by our house. Would that be okay with you?"

It was the ticket out of this barbecue that I wanted and that Lena needed. Less time around her creep of an uncle while still maintaining our image among the family for having shown up regardless of our busy schedules. "That's great, and of course, I'm sure my parents won't mind at all. Let me know what the doctors say," I responded, trying to reassure her that everything would be okay as she made a sweeping motion towards the backyard with her arm.

I took the hint, ending the conversation as we headed to greet the rest of the family. Lena's father had been experiencing some form of mental illness for a few months now. The problem was that none of the doctors they had seen could pinpoint exactly what the illness was. Some said schizophrenia, while others suggested that he was suffering hallucinations as a side effect of his prescribed anxiety medications, but no solid diagnosis could be made. Kaylee had remained particularly quiet about what his symptoms had been beyond this.

When we stepped out into the expansive yard, my eyes immediately found Mason's. He was looking back at me as if he had been waiting for my arrival. I had always felt nothing but admiration for Lena's father- along with a sense of sorrow over his recent condition. However, in this moment, I felt a chill travel down my spine; something about the way his eyes bore into mine was unnerving, to say the least.

"I'm going to run back inside and grab something to drink. Do you want anything?" Lena's voice pulled me back to reality.

"Yeah, I'm gonna go talk to your dad and catch up. Can you bring me a glass of whiskey? The good stuff he hides in Atticus' office?" I said, winking.

Lena knew I was referring to the bottle of Johnnie Walker Blue Label that Mason would bring every year and hide in his brother's desk drawer. It was a tradition of our own to share a glass whenever we got together, and I knew that because of our tardiness, he'd already be on his second pour.

Lena nodded and kissed me on the cheek before walking away. When I turned back to Mason, he was still staring me down, as if he were looking straight through me. I waved, then headed in his direction while exchanging pleasantries with family members I recognized but whose names I could not remember along the way.

Atticus's backyard was a lush, sprawling field of green, with massive trees spanning its length. They filtered the sunlight in patches across the lawn, making it look like something out of a fairytale. The irony of this home's beauty was never lost on me; the façade Atticus had built around himself never dissuaded me from his rotten core. A continuous planter lined the perimeter, filled to the brim with a plethora of vibrant flowers, like the ones beside the pathway in front of the home. Atticus's wife, Madelyn, had been known to have a green thumb. Since the divorce, he had hired a team of gardeners to maintain the flowers, and everyone in the family knew it was his way of hanging on to an aspect of his life that could never be repaired. I had no delusions about the cause of their divorce; it had occurred shortly after Lena's incident with Atticus. This left me wondering exactly how much Madelyn had known before packing her bags and skipping town.

I passed Atticus without so much as a glance, then pulled up a chair beside Mason, who was sunbathing fully clothed just out of earshot of everyone else. "Hey, long time no see. How have you been?"

"We need to talk, Royce," said Mason, cutting straight to business.

It turns out my intuitions hadn't been far off the mark; something was certainly off about him. "Sure, about what?"

"Keep your voice down, son, and make sure to smile."

I was confused but complied with his request anyway, faking a grin to prevent my face from revealing the contents of our conversation. "What's going on Mason?" I asked as he glanced away briefly, seemingly in Atticus' direction.

"Royce, promise me you'll keep her safe. No matter what happens, promise me that."

"Mason, you're stressing me out," I said through gritted teeth before feigning a laugh. "Tell me what's going on."

"It's my... condition, Royce. You know Atticus is a doctor, but you don't know everything about him. There are many other... skills he possesses but can't discuss publicly. Something is going to happen soon, something we can't stop... but Atticus thinks my condition might help, might give him some answers. If it doesn't... well, your name has come up a few times as an alternate solution."

At this point in Mason's ramblings, I couldn't hide my bewilderment any longer. "My name? Alternate Solution? You aren't making any..." I stopped my sentence short as it occurred to me at that moment; Lena had never returned with my drink.

I turned to look for Atticus, but he was no longer seated with the rest of the family. "Hold that thought, I need to check on Lena."

I stood from my chair and walked hurriedly back to the house. I wasn't sure what foreboding scene I was about to walk into, or if I would find anything nefarious at all, but I walked with purpose all the same. If Atticus placed another hand on Lena, I swore to myself it would be the last thing he ever did. I stormed through the kitchen, making my way toward his office where I figured he would have trapped Lena. As I neared it, I heard whispering through the closed door and slowed my approach. It was Atticus and Lena speaking, and while she sounded angry, she did not sound like she was in distress.

"No, absolutely not. You stay away from him, Atticus. I mean it," I heard Lena whispering, her voice laced with a menacing aggression.

"Lena, you don't understand the ramifications at play here. If we don't do this—"

She cut him off, raising her voice to a level of ferocity that I rarely saw her display. "DO NOT touch me. You don't ever touch me."

At that point, I had heard enough. I opened the door, none too calmly. "What is going on here? Lena, is everything okay?" I asked her, though my eyes stayed fixed on Atticus. He stared back at me as if silently pleading for forgiveness, but he would receive none.

"Yes, we were just leaving anyway, my father's appointment is soon." Lena walked over to me, placing her hand on my bicep. "Leave it be, Royce, let's just go."

I couldn't tear my eyes away from Atticus, and he seemed to suffer the same affliction. Finally, Atticus broke the silence, albeit unwisely. "Royce, I—"

"You're lucky Lena is here, you're *very* lucky," I said before he could finish his sentence.

Lena tugged at my arm. "That's *enough*, Royce, we're *leaving*."

She pulled again, and I staggered backwards out of the office without taking my eyes off her uncle. The sense of rage I felt had become overwhelming. We made our way back through the kitchen and stopped as we stepped into the backyard once more.

"Did he touch you, Lena?"

"No Royce... I mean yes, but not like that. He placed his hand on my shoulder; that was it. Then I yelled at him."

I nodded in silence, still seething and trying to regain my composure. "What were you two talking about anyway? You sounded upset. Who were you telling him to stay away from?" I asked, finding their discussion and my earlier conversation with her father equally strange.

Lena's eyes widened at the question. "You heard all that? I... Royce, there's something I need to tell you."

"Okay? So, tell me?" I said, attempting to mask the irritation in my voice.

Before she could say anything else, we both noticed her parents approaching. "Lena, honey, we need to get going so we aren't late for your father's appointment!" Kaylee hollered as she crossed the grass with Mason.

Lena sighed heavily. "I'll explain everything when I get home tonight, okay? Just know that I love you, and I'm on your team, through thick and thin."

"On my... Lena, what are you talking about?" I urged her to explain, but it was too late.

Mason and Kaylee had reached us, and the walls went up. We both acted as if nothing out of the ordinary had occurred moments before. "You ready sweety?" Kaylee asked her daughter.

Lena nodded and then leaned into me, kissing me goodbye. "I'll text you when we get there, okay?"

"Sounds good," I replied, though I felt anything but good at that moment.

"I didn't even get to spend any time with you!" Rory shouted as she ran up to us, my parents following behind.

She still lived with them, even at twenty-three years old. It was a decision made out of necessity on her part and hospitality on my parents'. Rory was just as smart as I was, though she often concealed it. She graduated from college after four years with a degree in biology and a goal of becoming a veterinarian but decided she wanted to specialize in exotics. This would require further schooling, and my parents allowed her to live with them and pay a modest rent to save money for her own place.

Lena hugged Rory tightly, holding onto her as they conversed. "I know, I'm sorry. Why don't you stay the night tonight? Your parents are taking Royce home anyway. When I get back from the doctor's office, we can snuggle up on the couch and watch a movie."

Rory responded cheerfully, "Only if it's a horror film!"

"Deal," Lena said as the hug concluded. Watching the two of them interact always brought back memories of Rory as a little kid; Lena simply had that effect on her.

My father seized the opportunity to speak next as we moved inside, the imposing front doors that led to our freedom a straight shot through the kitchen. "Well, if you all are leaving then we'll pack it in too. It was great seeing you guys, drive safe, it's supposed to rain later. Royce, you ready to hit the road?"

"Yeah, you sure you're okay driving me home?"

My father gave me a distasteful glance. "You're my kid, of course I'll take you home. Besides, you're getting Rory out of my hair for the night, that's the least I can do."

"I *heard* that," Rory said, a scowl upon her face.

My father and I both chuckled. "Fair enough, thanks dad."

Though the smile our laughter left behind quickly faded, I looked towards the foyer and caught a glimpse of Lena as she mouthed, "I love you," one last time before she slipped through the doorway and out of sight.

CHAPTER 18

Luck

Time and location (present-day): 8:49 am,
ENDURE Center for Rehabilitation

Lena's left arm was wrapped snugly around my torso, her fingertips grazing the small of my back as my eyes flickered open. Still fighting the last wisps of sleep as I awoke, my brain struggled to comprehend the situation. I hadn't been accustomed to this kind of human interaction in a very long time. I became aware of her bare body pressed against mine, stomach to stomach, her left leg draped over my right, keeping us intertwined. I glanced down to where her head lay less than an inch away. She was still sound asleep in my arms, seemingly at peace with the world. Her hair fell in loose tendrils that beautifully framed her face. As I studied the soft features that accentuated her cheekbones, feeling her chest rise and fall against my own in steady, rhythmic beats, I knew then that I would kill for this woman; I would do whatever it took to protect her, in this life and the next. Her eyes opened slowly, as if my silent vow had lifted a curse that had kept her in a deep slumber. Lena's gaze locked with mine. Much to my chagrin, there was still sadness behind her viridescent eyes.

We lay there like that for a while, staring at each other, communicating without speaking, until Lena broke the placidity between us. "I need to tell you," she spoke gingerly.

"Tell me what?" I asked as I gently brushed the loose hairs from her face, tucking them behind her ear.

"*Everything,*" she said, stifling a sob as the tears returned once more.

As eager as I was to hear what Lena had to reveal, the guilt of not having discussed my own findings in her uncle's office was weighing on me more now than ever. "I have something to tell you, too; I think it might be best to let me talk first."

She nodded, then adjusted her position slightly so that we could have this conversation face to face rather than melted into one another.

Without further hesitation, I unburdened myself. "The four of us... myself, along with Desmond, Aiden, and Matias, broke into your uncle's office the other night. We wanted answers and we were sick of feeling insane. Atticus' goons caught us, but not before we uncovered some video files. Lena... we found something really *bad* on that computer."

Now, her attention piqued, she sat up in bed, pulling the covers up for warmth. "Bad how?"

I paused, unsure of how to explain without sounding outlandish, before realizing that version of our excursion didn't exist. "Like 'human experimentation' bad. I know what you told me about your parents, but Lena... I saw... I saw Atticus experiment on your father, injecting him with something he referred to as 'The Deus Molecule', or DM1. I saw Atticus kill your dad."

Lena sat frozen for a moment. Her gaze was locked firmly on the wintry-white tundra of linens that covered her. Then, she exhaled steadily. "That's not *exactly* what you saw... looks can be deceiving."

Involuntarily, I scooted away from her. "You knew?"

She climbed out of bed at my question, hurriedly finding her clothes and dressing herself. "I told you I need to tell you everything, and everything has a lot to do with what you found on that computer."

"You lied? About how your parents died? Lena, who does that? For Christ's sake, please help me make sense of what you're telling me!" My heart rate accelerated, and I felt the pulse in my jugular with every rapid beat.

"I didn't lie, Royce! It's... it's complicated. Look, you've told me what you needed to tell me; now just listen. I have a lot to explain, and it's going to sound absolutely batshit, but it's the truth. Just let me talk, okay?" She stopped shuffling about to look me in the eyes, now fully clothed. I opened my mouth to yell, berate, to do anything to siphon the anger and confusion from within me, but then I stopped. Taking a deep breath, I nodded, and she continued as I listened. "The world beyond the walls of this facility isn't what you remember it being. Look, I'm sure you and the others have already found out what this place isn't. On paper, it's a center for rehabilitation, but remove the red tape and ENDURE is a government-run facility dedicated to scientific research and development. We're completely off-grid, what's known as a black site. The work we're doing here is of the variety that no one else wants to do, that no one else is capable of."

Though I hadn't been sure what to expect when I began my search for answers, clandestine government agencies had never appeared on my mental bingo card. I certainly didn't expect Lena to take the revelation of Atticus putting a bullet in Mason's head in stride; and yet, here we were. "What work, Lena? Why are we here?"

"In a single word?" she paused, then said, "Mallen. We're here to stop what he, what *it* has begun. Mallen is a far more dangerous force than you realize."

"So… you know what he is? Which is what exactly, alien? Some sort of spirit from the underworld? Please, shed some light as to what type of fantasy-bullshit-turned-reality is plaguing my mind." I pleaded, a hint of irony in my tone.

"I can't do that, unfortunately, because we still don't really know. We have a working theory, though. We think Mallen exists on an alternate plane of reality from ours, that it has existed there for millennia, quite possibly since the dawn of time itself. It wasn't until my father's illness began, until Atticus found the Deus Molecule in his DNA, that Mallen was able to bridge the gap between our dimension and its own. Now that it has, it seems hellbent on wiping us off the face of the planet. The scariest part, though? Mallen isn't alone, Royce."

I raised a brow, half expecting Mallen himself to interrupt our conversation. Then again, the sadistic nightmare creature was more than likely getting a kick out of watching me squirm from his home in the depths of my psyche. "What do you mean he isn't alone?"

"Mallen seems to be a herald of sorts. It's, for all intents and purposes, a henchman. There have been numerous references throughout our interactions with it to a group it calls, 'The Nine'. Based on what's happening out there in the world, we now are almost certain that The Nine aren't a matter of who, but rather what."

My head was spinning, but I did my best to absorb as much information as possible while Lena continued to spill ENDURE's secrets. "A year ago, a monolith sprouted out of the Earth seemingly overnight on Ross Island in Antarctica. At first, it didn't seem to do much of anything. Then the second monolith appeared in Nairobi, Africa a few months later. After the second monolith appeared, their effects became noticeable. Where these monoliths rose, death followed. They somehow affected the mental stability of the populace surrounding them, to the point where people began killing each other in the streets. Royce, I'm not talking about just grown men and women waging war on neighboring countries. I've seen *children*, torn to pieces by the *bare hands* of their parents... whatever sway these things have over us, however they're spreading this... infection, they're turning us into rabid animals. The havoc they're wreaking... it's *unspeakable,* horrific beyond your wildest imagination. Dig into the deepest darkest crevice of your mind, and then dig deeper. That's what is happening outside these walls. If left unchecked, they'll cause humanity to eradicate itself. These monoliths must be The Nine that Mallen keeps mentioning, and based on the existing pattern, the remaining seven will show up on different continents around the world. These things are networking, Royce, creating an invisible blanket that spans the globe, leaving nothing untouched by its influence. Once the ninth monolith arrives? The worldwide population has already dropped to roughly four billion... you do the math."

I stood from the bed and slipped into my jumpsuit, then began to pace around the room nervously. "You're right, that does sound batshit. All of this Mallen and monoliths nonsense aside, what does any of this have to do with me, Lena?"

She looked me dead in the eye, as if contemplating whether she had already exposed too much, then continued anyway. "You were told that you were in a coma for the past three years, but that isn't exactly true either. Royce, you... came out of a sort of stasis, and you were like that for far more than three years. More precisely, you were placed into cryostasis because you have the Deus Molecule in your DNA, just like my father had. It's hard to explain in a short period of time. I'm sure Atticus has sent someone to retrieve me by now... but there's evidence that the Deus Molecule is the key to stopping Mallen and The Nine. The fact that you can communicate with it and are seemingly still healthy, much less alive is already a testament to that idea."

My vision began to tunnel as sweat beaded on my forehead, my face numbing more with every passing second. *Alive? Was my death a known possibility in all of this?* Clearly, Lena hadn't noticed the crushing pressure I was experiencing, because she proceeded to drop another truth bomb immediately after telling me some multi-dimensional being was laying waste to civilization in its entirety.

"Royce, you don't remember, but you and I... we... we had a life together. We were happy, so happy... We were about to take our five-year anniversary trip to Hawaii, but then..." Her voice trailed off; her expression was haunted by the ghosts of her past. It sounded unbelievable, yet at the same time, it explained the connection I had always felt with her. Somewhere in my subconscious, I had loved Lena from the moment I laid eyes on her. Our former life together had to be the reason I felt so comfortable with her and why I trusted her to a fault. Though trusting Lena now seemed to be one gigantic oversight.

A thought occurred suddenly, one that made it feel as if Lena had spit in the face of whatever we had shared between us prior. "Shit... does that mean... the car accident never happened? Is... is my family even dead? Is anything I've been told since waking up here true?"

Lena raised her hands in a soothing gesture, blinking away more tears. "Royce, stay calm. Yes, that's true... You were in a horrible accident with your family; what we didn't tell you, though, was that you... well... you died in that accident too, Royce."

At the mention of my death my legs grew shaky, and I nearly fell to the floor, catching myself on the edge of the bed. "If I died, how am I here? If you aren't lying about your father's murder suicide, then *how* do you explain that video? How did I watch Atticus shoot a man in the head that you claim was already dead prior?!" My voice had elevated; I was panicking and couldn't contain it.

Lena flinched visibly at my liberal use of the term that had supposedly caused the entire upheaval of her life. "Royce, please. I know this is a lot to take in, but I need you to try to relax. My father... he did the things I said he did... he went berserk and killed my mother, then turned the knife on himself... or at least at the time, I thought my father had been responsible. Atticus had been studying his condition for nearly a year prior to that incident, and he couldn't afford to lose all that research if my dad were to succumb to his illness. So, he developed a workaround, a way to continue unearthing all he could regarding the Deus Molecule, even if my father were to die. It wasn't highly ethical, but… desperate times… you know how the rest goes."

"What *work around*?! How do you work around your subject being deceased?!" I shouted.

Lena exhaled evenly, biting her bottom lip so hard at the end of her breath that the skin around it glowed white. "Royce, what Atticus did to my father… he did to you. He did it to others, too, but the results were mediocre at best and catastrophic at worst. It never worked properly until you. Again, it wasn't ethical, but it truly was the only way. Royce, you're—"

The door unlocked and opened without warning, with Oakley and Shaw closing it behind them as they entered. "Lena, stop talking and come with me, NOW," said Shaw, pointing firmly. Her cheeks flushed a deep red as she promptly obeyed his demands.

"Hey, wait a damn minute!" I demanded. I couldn't let them leave with her. This was my chance to completely lift the veil that shrouded ENDURE in mystery. I stepped forward, and then Oakley cocked back his fist and smashed it into my nose, sending me to the floor. The punch came out of nowhere, leaving me in shock as I applied pressure to stop the blood from flowing from my nostrils.

"Atticus warned you to quit sniffing around with that nose of yours, Royce," Oakley said, his voice lowering an octave at the utterance of my name, "and you're pushing your luck."

As I looked up, I saw Shaw escorting Lena from my room.

Oakley crouched down beside me, a contorted grin on his face. "If you're a good little guinea pig from here on out, *maybe* you'll get lucky, and we won't come back for you or one of your friends. Take it easy, *Royce*," Oakley said in that strange manner again.

He stood and began to walk toward the door. In that exact moment, with the bridge of my nose throbbing and my head racked with too many emotions and thoughts to process, I fixated on one thing and one thing only: that peculiar way he kept saying my name, as if his tone were insinuating that Royce wasn't really my name at all.

Just before he exited the room, he paused and raised a quizzical finger. "Oh! I almost forgot! I've got something for ya!" He rummaged in his pocket for a moment, then took out something with an uneasy excitement. "Here you go, don't go losing it." Oakley flicked something towards me, and it tap-danced across the tiles as he exited my quarters.

I crawled over to the item on my hands and knees, then scraped it off the floor for further inspection. Just as quickly as I had picked it up, I dropped it in disgust.

It was a fingernail, torn cleanly from the cuticle.

CHAPTER 19

Shaw

Time and location (the past): 2:45 pm, San Diego, CA

Shaw chewed absentmindedly on a toothpick, his seat reclined and one foot resting on the dash. In the driver's seat to his left, Oakley played Tetris on a burner phone. The armored vehicle was parked just beyond the tree line at the edge of the road that the Wilkos would be traveling down. From the outside, their transportation looked like a standard black SUV, but it was custom-fitted to withstand a hit, and a hard one at that. Shaw waited patiently yet apprehensively. Soon, Atticus would call, signaling them to carry out their orders. Almost every day, he had to remind himself that what they were doing was for the greater good. They were fighting a war—something he was very familiar with—and in war, people died. Often, those people were innocent, just in the wrong place at the wrong time. That was exactly the predicament in which Royce Wilko's family had found themselves. Atticus only needed Royce, but he unfortunately was traveling in a vehicle with his younger sister and parents, which now put their lives at risk too. He glanced back over at Oakley.

"You ever feel like what we're doing is kind of fucked up?"

Without taking his eyes off his game of Tetris, Oakley replied. "You're too soft, Elliot. How you survived Iraq, I'll never know."

He sat up, returning his seat to its regular position. "I'm serious. Do you ever think about the whole picture here? What if Atticus is wrong? What if we're abducting people, killing people, and he's *wrong?*"

Oakley sighed and dropped the cellular device into the vehicle's cupholder. "You mean like our government was about Iraq? Half the orders we've ever received were probably based on shoddy intel and half-cocked plans. Guys like you and me, Shaw? We aren't paid to ask questions. We're paid to get the job done. So long as I get my money, I couldn't care less. It's a dog-eat-dog world; you either eat or be eaten."

Shaw shook his head, removing the toothpick from his mouth and fiddling with it in his hand. "I don't know man... the shit we did in Iraq... It was messed up. What we did to Matias was bad enough, but that woman and her daughter? They were innocent, Oakley. That girl had to have only been, what? Thirteen? Fourteen?"

Mentioning their past service together hadn't elicited the response from Oakley that he had hoped for. Instead, the man seemed chuffed as he reminisced about their time as Marines.

"So what? Who was that girl to me? For all we know, she could have grown up to join ISIS. The point is, you need to worry about yourself more and these strangers and acquaintances less. Besides… you can't tell me that you don't enjoy it sometimes…" The statement was left open-ended, not posed as a question but still fishing for an answer, nonetheless.

"Enjoy what? Killing?" Shaw asked, slightly appalled by the notion.

Oakley shifted in his seat, more absorbed in the conversation now than ever. "Yeah, man. Think about it; the power that comes with taking a life… It's like nature's ecstasy. Knowing that you can do what others are too weak to do at any given moment in time. Knowing that you can just snuff out an individual's existence in the blink of an eye… it's *electrifying*. Then there's people like Jonathan and Matias; as far as the world is concerned, they're already dead. We can do *whatever* we want to them, and no one would know; there would be *zero* consequences."

Shaw looked at his partner in bewilderment. "You're a fucking lunatic, you know that?" His tone insinuated that he was joking, but in the privacy of his thoughts, Shaw wondered just how many screws Oakley had loose in that head of his.

"I'm a realist, Shaw. I'm *honest* with myself and my desires. Sometimes, I get the urge to open somebody up, really see what makes us humans tick, you know? Hell, if Atticus ever gives me the opportunity, maybe I'll slice open your old buddy Matias."

Shaw was about to interject when the phone rang, signaling Wilko's imminent arrival. A large part of him was thankful for the interruption; he could only imagine where the conversation would have gone if it had continued.

"Start her up," He told Oakley, finding it hard not to stare at the man in revulsion.

They both buckled in as the armored vehicle hummed to life; then Oakley shifted it into drive. Shaw noticed a small speck appear through the tree line, growing closer to them with every passing second. It approached from their right on a path perpendicular to their location. "Hold," said Shaw, ensuring that Oakley didn't jump the gun. The Wilko's car was closer now, about half a mile away. "Hold," he repeated. When it approached within a quarter mile of their vicinity, he gave the okay. "Floor it!"

The tires squealed as they fought for traction against the mossy ground cover, Oakley's foot pressing the gas pedal to the floorboards. The wheels gained traction, and in an instant, the SUV collided with Wilko's car, t-boning its left front fender. The impact caused it to spin hard and its windows exploded with spectacular force. A body was thrown out of the left rear passenger window just before one of the front tires blew, sending the car end over end multiple times. It all happened too fast for Shaw to identify who had been ejected. After three rolls, the vehicle skidded a couple of feet further, the metal on asphalt screeching like nails on a chalkboard before finally coming to rest on its side. His brain tricked his body into producing adrenaline associated with the experience of being in a vehicular accident. However, their transportation remained virtually unscathed, and neither Oakley nor Shaw had been injured in the crash aside from some minor whiplash.

"You good?" he asked Oakley.

"Right as rain, let's go," his partner responded, and they unstrapped themselves and got out of the SUV.

The roads were clear of any other traffic and would remain so; Atticus had made certain of that. With their pistols drawn, the two men approached the overturned car cautiously as its engine bay billowed smoke into the afternoon sky. Nearing the wreckage, Shaw was now able to identify who had been launched from the rear seat before the vehicle began its vicious roll. It was Aurora Wilko, Royce's younger sister, her body motionless on the embankment at the edge of the road. She was either dead or unconscious, so Shaw decided to circle back to her after checking on the other passengers.

He signaled to his partner to check on the parents in the front seats while he went to retrieve Royce from the back. Luckily for him, there was a moonroof that extended to the back seats, which had shattered almost entirely in the collision. He could already see Royce through the jagged opening as he approached and was thankful that he wouldn't have to clamber on top of the car, which was now technically on its right side, to pry open the door and pull the man out. Shaw walked up to the twisted hulk of metal, reached inside through the broken glass roof, unstrapped Royce's seatbelt, and pulled his body clear of the wreck. He noticed a flicker of flames coming from the engine, creeping out around the crevice between the mangled hood and the front bumper.

"Check on them quickly, this thing might go boom," he said to Oakley, pointing at the fire.

His partner nodded and peered through the cracked windshield to assess the parents while Shaw placed a finger on Royce's jugular, checking for a pulse. Before he could confirm whether the man was alive or not, Oakley's weapon discharged. He quickly stood up, leaving Royce on the pavement as he jogged over to his colleague.

"The hell was that?" he asked as he approached his partner, immediately noticing a bullet hole in Charles Wilko's head.

"They're alive, *both* of them. Well... he's not anymore. You want to do the honors?" Oakley responded, gesturing now to Royce's mother, Olivia.

Shaw grabbed Oakley by his collar. "Our orders were to secure Royce, and leave the rest to the ICT, not to execute survivors!" he growled at the man, with the degree of Oakley's insanity now painfully obvious.

Oakley shoved him away. "Oh, lighten up, Shaw! Atticus would be none the wiser, just put a bullet in the mother. No survivors means less paperwork and less cleanup for the ICT."

Shaw glared intensely at his associate. "Follow orders, Oakley, or I'll report you to Atticus."

Oakley tutted, then stepped in close to Shaw. "Look, Shaw; I like you, I do, but you seem to think that you're still my superior. This isn't Iraq, and we aren't in the Marines anymore. You and I are *equals* now. So, as your equal, I'm going to make you a deal. What I do on these ops? It stays between the two of us, so long as the mission gets completed. Everything between receiving our orders and then? Well, who's to say? Otherwise..." He lowered his voice and spoke in a hushed tone. "Maybe I visit that family of yours one night."

Shaw glowered at him, fully aware that Oakley meant every word. Before he could respond, someone interrupted the conversation, startling them both more than they were willing to admit.

"Please... help me..." It was Olivia Wilko, pressed against her shoulder strap and dangling from the passenger seat. Blood crusted her face in trails, originating from her scalp, where Shaw assumed she had suffered a head injury during the crash.

Quickly, he turned back to Oakley and scowled. "If you go anywhere near my family, I swear I'll *fucking* rip you apart Jordan, is that clear?"

Oakley shrugged. "Depends; do we have a deal or not?"

They stared each other down for what felt like hours before Shaw begrudgingly gave in to the psychopath. "Do what you need to do, but I follow the orders I'm given, to the letter." He turned and began to walk away.

Only a few seconds later, he heard a second gunshot and knew that Olivia Wilko was dead. Oakley jogged up beside him before he reached Royce. "You're right, that thing is about to explode. Let's load him up into the transport and clear the area. What about the daughter? Did you check her for a pulse? Maybe I should make sure she doesn't get back up."

"She's *dead*, Oakley." Shaw snapped. "I checked her pulse myself. Help me grab Royce before this car explodes and we're dead too." It was a lie, but Oakley hadn't been paying attention to anything other than his own bloodlust when they first approached the scene.

The man rolled his eyes in response as they stopped in front of Royce's body. Oakley crouched down and grabbed his legs while Shaw bent down and took hold of his arms. "Like I said, Shaw; you're too soft."

They tossed Royce into the back of the SUV, then cuffed his wrists and ankles. Shaw became painfully aware that he might have miscalculated. It didn't seem like Oakley believed that he had made certain Aurora Wilko was deceased. Either way, they both re-entered their vehicle and pulled away from the crash site.

Shortly thereafter, the Wilko family's car detonated. The fireball that consumed it would burn away the evidence that Oakley had executed Royce's parents well enough, unless someone specifically went searching for foul play. Shaw knew that wouldn't happen, though; everything ENDURE did fell into the category of foul play, so they wouldn't be looking to out their own employees.

As they waited for the Incident Containment Team and Atticus to arrive, Shaw looked out his window at where Aurora lay. He was glad that Oakley had let it go, that his deranged partner in crime hadn't been curious enough to check her pulse himself. Aurora hadn't been a teenager, not like that poor girl in Iraq, but she was still young, still a kid in Shaw's eyes. Whether she was gone or not, he had no desire to add another dead child to his roster. At least this way, he could tell himself that Oakley had been the one behind the wheel, that Oakley had killed her. Even so, that little untruth wouldn't be nearly enough to stop the image of her still corpse from haunting Shaw's dreams for many, many nights to come.

CHAPTER 20

Atticus

Time and location (the past): 3:17 pm, San Diego, CA

Atticus had Oakley and Shaw on standby, hidden somewhere along the route that connected Royce's home to his own. It wasn't long before they called to inform him that the task had been completed and that Royce was now in their possession. The time after the Wilkos left the barbecue was used to clear out the rest of Atticus's family members prior to Royce's procurement, with Atticus climbing into his car and departing his home almost simultaneously along with his final guest. Murdering your in-laws was a gruesome chore, even if it meant saving the world. Of course, the death of the Wilkos was never planned when they mapped out Royce's abduction. Rather, Royce's family had all been casualties of what was essentially a high-risk, high-reward smash and grab. In this scenario, however, the Wilkos' vehicle had been the glass case, and Royce, the priceless jewelry contained within it.

He had tried to take measures earlier to prevent these crude tactics from becoming necessary, but when he asked his niece to convince her husband to come voluntarily, she had stood firm in her refusal. Atticus had explained to Lena that if her father were to succumb to his ailments, an event he feared was imminent, Royce would be their only remaining hope. Hope for what, of course, Atticus had forbidden himself to disclose. He had taken certain liberties regarding how much information he divulged to Mason, his wife Kaylee, and Lena on the matter, but the details he revealed were nonetheless limited in scope. Convincing his niece to allow him to take her husband for an unknown amount of time, then informing her that there was a very real possibility she would never see him again, was a hard pill to swallow; Atticus knew this. When combined with the fact that Lena had only a minor understanding of what his overall work entailed, there was no conceivable way to assure her that the atrocities he was committing in secrecy would all be worth it in the end.

There was also the issue of his past unsolicited advance towards Lena, which had understandably caused quite a rift between them. This act, this one brief decision, had been and would remain the biggest regret of Atticus's life; and Atticus was a man with much to regret. He'd known that the moment he made the choice, but Lena resembled her mother Kaylee so much now, a woman who, during their teenage years, had been the object of Atticus's affection. The two of them had shared so much together and had been happy for a long while, but the heart wanted what the heart wanted; and Kaylee just so happened to want Mason in the long run. So it was that Atticus had to watch the woman he loved not only leave him behind but do so for his own brother. If Kaylee had simply left altogether, it would have been an easier blow to deal with. However, her being with Mason meant that Atticus had to see her regularly, and every time he did, that wound was ripped open again, exposing raw nerves to the harshness of his reality. In his drunken stupor a couple of years earlier, his inebriated brain mistook Lena for Kaylee. Attempting to commit acts of adultery with your brother's wife, while frowned upon, wouldn't have been nearly as bad as trying to reach up your niece's skirt; but the damage was done before the alcohol-induced haze lifted and he realized who stood in front of him that day.

The rest would be cemented in his mind as an act so unforgivable that he'd contemplated ending it all for weeks thereafter. In the end, he deemed his work too important to leave it in the hands of anyone else, concluding that he would live in shame until he could solve the problem humanity now unknowingly faced. Atticus counted himself lucky that Lena had kept the incident between the two of them and was willing to let him explain. While the explanation did little to alleviate his guilt, it aided in mending their relationship, if only slightly. At the very least, Lena had reached a point where she could now exchange pleasantries with Atticus and be in the same room as him. It wasn't much, but he'd take what he could get.

Regardless of what Lena had said, Atticus suspected that Royce knew what had occurred. The young man had been particularly cold and distrustful towards Atticus ever since that day. None of that would matter now, though, as he had found a loophole that would allow him to involve Lena in this endeavor without any red tape or confidentiality issues. If all went well, Lena would soon be employed by ENDURE and have unfettered access to what they did in the shadows.

Atticus rolled down his window as his car came to a stop at what appeared to be a checkpoint set up by city officials; in reality, these were men and women he employed who had established a ten-mile perimeter around the "accident." A short woman with dirty-blonde hair tightly secured in a ponytail approached his vehicle. Her name was Lauren, and Atticus knew she recognized him, but security protocol still required a verbal passphrase to confirm his identity.

"Good afternoon, sir. Where are you headed?"

"Home for the day, officer."

"Where might home be, sir?"

"Oh, about… ten miles north, give or take… as the crow flies."

She nodded as the act ended and waved him through, satisfied with the expression given. When Atticus pulled up to the wreckage, an ICT, or "Incident Containment Team," was already hard at work. Most of the excess debris had been cleared from the road and surrounding areas, as had the retrofitted SUV Oakley and Shaw had used as a battering ram to bring the Wilko's journey home to a screeching halt. The only evidence of the crash that remained was the Wilko's vehicle, burnt to an obsidian crisp and flipped onto its side. Atticus could see two equally charred corpses in the driver's and passenger's seats. His stomach turned at the thought of Royce's younger sister's cooked body dangling from her seatbelt in the back seat… until he saw Aurora's body, untouched by fire, lying on an embankment nearby. She appeared battered and bruised, most likely having been ejected from the sedan upon impact. Atticus silently thanked whatever God might exist that she hadn't suffered the same fate as her parents; at least her death was less grisly. He saw Oakley exit a large SUV. They made eye contact, and Atticus walked over to him.

"Where is he?" asked Atticus.

"In there," responded Oakley, pointing over his shoulder at the vehicle.

Atticus nodded. "Was there any trouble?"

"None at all. The parents died on impact and the girl was ejected; she should've worn her seatbelt. Shaw and I will get the package prepped and delivered to the facility pronto."

"Yes, thank you Oakley. I'll reconvene with you two shortly."

Oakley's head bobbed in confirmation, amused. He always seemed thrilled at the opportunity to commit acts of violence.

Atticus hoped that wouldn't become problematic down the road. Oakley hopped into the passenger seat, and the SUV departed with their prize shortly thereafter.

The doctor surveyed the scene once more, shocked by the efficiency of the ICT. By the time he finished his brief conversation with Oakley, they had already removed the Wilko's destroyed car, presumably having taken the bodies of Charles and Olivia for disposal. All that remained now was the girl on the embankment, Aurora 'Rory' Wilko. Atticus set a course for her limp body as he contemplated how to explain all of this to Lena if she ever found out what he had done here today. Officially, Royce and his family would all be victims of a drunk driver who struck their vehicle at high speeds through an intersection after running a red light. Regardless of how efficient ENDURE was at clandestine operations and cover stories, Atticus had a nagging feeling that one day he'd have to come clean to his niece, and he dreaded the thought. It would all be much easier once she was brought onboard, though, and Lena would contribute a much-needed skill set as well. With a background in both biomedical and computer sciences, Atticus would be able to offload all the cybersecurity and software engineering tasks from his plate and onto Lena's.

His thoughts came full circle back to Rory as he reached the spot where she lay upon the grassy noll. Hovering above her, he stared down at Rory's unmoving corpse. He was sorry that things had to be this way, but survival meant sacrifice. Atticus froze for a moment, fixating on the young girl's hand. *Had she... no, she couldn't have...* For the briefest moment, he thought Rory's finger had twitched. Just the slightest movement, but he could have sworn... his personal phone rang, breaking his concentration.

"This is Atticus,"

The caller identification was spoofed, showing an area code for New York that Atticus had grown accustomed to since Mason's condition had worsened. When he answered, the voice on the other end of the phone was not who he expected, but belonged to Kaylee instead. "Atticus, we're at Mason's appointment, but he's not... he's not himself."

Atticus turned away from Rory. When Mason and his family had left earlier that day for his "doctor's appointment," they had actually driven to a secure ENDURE black site instead. The "doctor" in this scenario was Santosh Ravi and her team of scientists and technicians. All of them were contracted with ENDURE, entrusted with the sole purpose of conducting weekly check-ins on Mason, particularly focusing on his brainwave patterns.

"What do you mean by 'not himself,' Kaylee?"

She sighed, and Atticus could sense the tension on the other end of the line. "He keeps referring to something he calls *Mallen*? Do you know what that is?"

Atticus' heart plummeted as he began to jog back to his car. "Kaylee, give the phone to Doctor Ravi and get yourself and Lena as far away from Mason as possible, do you understand? I will come find you after I've seen him, but you need to leave that place, right now."

He nearly fell into the driver's seat, the rear wheels struggling to find traction as his foot pressed the gas pedal to the floor, sending it screaming like a banshee down the street.

"Stay away from... Atticus what's going on?"

"There is *NO TIME* for questions. Give the phone to Doctor Ravi, grab Lena, and leave, *NOW.*"

There was a moment of irritated silence, then Kaylee reluctantly did as she was told. "... Fine, but you better explain yourself later, Atticus."

A mixture of muffled sounds and movements filled the phoneline as Kaylee passed the device to the doctor. "This is Sabina, are you on your way?"

"I am. Is he restrained?"

"The technicians are affixing the restraints as we speak, but Atticus... I don't know that he's coming back this time. There is no trace of your brother left on his most recent scans; his brainwave patterns are almost entirely consistent with those of The Boundless."

"Understood. Assign a team to guard Kaylee and Lena around the clock, Sergeant Major Argerich's unit if he is on site, I trust him implicitly. I want a security detail on them twenty-four-seven from here on out. My niece and Kaylee are the *only* priority that supersedes Mason, is that clear?"

"Yes sir."

As soon as the words left Doctor Ravi's mouth, Atticus hung up and focused on driving as the speedometer climbed ever higher. If this was it—if Mason really had crossed the point of no return—then Royce would become the subject of Atticus' undying attention much sooner than he had originally anticipated. His grip tightened around the steering wheel, and Atticus just hoped he could get to Kaylee and Lena in time; hoped he could reach them before they found out first-hand what Mallen was capable of.

CHAPTER 21

Lena

Time and location (the past): 5:15 pm, San Diego, CA

The car rocked gently back as Lena shifted it into park. She felt completely drained and just wanted to go home, lie down, and shut out the world for a change. She had promised her mom she would visit, though, promised her that she would try to find normalcy again; something Lena was certain would be impossible without Royce. She was nearing a year without him now. Nothing had been the same for Lena since they left last year's annual barbecue in separate vehicles, and she never saw him again. She had gone with her parents to her father's doctor's appointment while Royce hitched a ride home with his family. If it hadn't been for a drunk driver, they all would've made it back safe and sound that night. The woman had run a red light and t-boned the Wilkos' car at one hundred and three miles per hour; everyone, including Royce, had died on impact.

To make matters worse, things at her parents' house had been anything but free of stress lately, and it left Lena with a headache day in and day out as she tried to alleviate it all. A few weeks ago, her mother had called and expressed concern over her father's mental health. She claimed that Lena's father had not been himself recently and that she had begun to fear for their safety. Lena thought her mother's reaction was a gross over-exaggeration of her father's recent behavior; he had been this way for as long as the Wilkos had been… well… dead, something she found excruciatingly painful to think about, and even more agonizing to say aloud. As far as Lena was concerned, it was quite possible her dad's condition had caused this change in behavior long before that tragedy, and they just hadn't noticed until now.

She exited her car with a sigh of exhaustion and walked to the front door. As she removed her parent's house key from her purse to let herself in, she contemplated whether she had been too harsh on her mother. When Kaylee first came to Lena with accusations that her father might end up harming them both, it had infuriated her. Lena had yelled at her mother, even cursed at her… she brushed the thought aside. Today was a new day, as so many had been before, and she didn't want to enter the home with a predisposition for argument on her mind. Lena opened the door, calling out gently as she did so.

"Mom? I'm here," she said, receiving nothing but silence. As she made her way through the house, she peeked her head into the kitchen, but no one was there either. "Dad? Where are you guys?" Almost immediately after the question left Lena's mouth, she heard what seemed like a wet cough from the living room. Her feet carried her further down the hall until Lena suddenly stopped dead in her tracks, just short of the archway on her left from which she was almost certain the sound had come. Through that archway was a thick, crusty smear of what appeared to be gelatinous merlot seeping into the carpet. What struck her as odd, though, was the pattern of it, how it dragged across the floor and rounded the corner into the living room. All at once, her heart sank. This can't be happening. Lena's mind raced as she became aware of what sounded like whispering on the other side of the wall. It was incoherent jabbering, a conversation held by only one participant.

"Dad?" Lena called out again, believing the voice to be her father's. No response, though the whispering became more rapid, escalating in volume. She took a deep breath, then moved through the hall and rounded the corner into the family room. Lena let out a sharp, poignant shriek of horror, cupping her hand over her mouth in an attempt to contain herself. There was blood *everywhere.* In front of the fireplace, roughly ten paces away was her father. He knelt behind her mother, who lay on her side facing the archway where Lena stood in shock. His arms, drenched up to the elbows in a viscous red liquid, extended outward from his sides, forming what looked like a grotesque human crucifix. His palms hovered face-up as if in prayer. A trail of blood trickled slowly from the corner of Kaylee's mouth as she hacked and sputtered.

Her mother's weary eyes found Lena, and she summoned what little strength she had left to plead with her daughter to leave. "Lena... baby, run... Run as fast... as you can..."

As if suddenly and acutely aware of Lena's presence, her father's head twitched in an agitated, unnatural fashion. His arms dropped, freed from whatever mysterious ritual they had previously been entangled with, and he stood up from the floor. When he turned around to face Lena, every inch of her father was spattered with her mother's gore. In his right hand was a butcher's knife that was equally stained. Lena searched her father's eyes, hoping for any hint as to what had occurred, any sign that he still inhabited this body; but they were devoid of life. For a split second, she thought she saw a flicker of consciousness, of anything other than emptiness, but in a flash, it disappeared, and he turned his attention back to Kaylee. He kneeled once more, bringing the knife to bear and raising it slowly above his head. Lena's eyes grew wide with fear and welled with tears as she tried to speak but choked on each attempt. Her brain couldn't process what was happening, and if she hadn't known better, she would have sworn she had suffered a stroke. She found herself completely immobilized, either by disbelief or sheer terror.

"Mason... put it down... please... not in front of... our daughter. Whatever is going on... we will get you help, Mason... just let us help you..."

As Kaylee wheezed in raspy breaths, Lena saw the blade begin to tremble in her father's hand, noticing for the first time through her own tears that her father was silently crying himself. In fact, his whole body spasmed as if a current of electricity were running through him. For the fleetest of moments, Lena thought that maybe her mother had gotten through to to him, that she had broken whatever spell he was under; and then he plummeted the cutlery into her temple. Again, and again, and again. With the first stab, Kaylee's eye closest to the gash where the blade entered rolled back in her skull inhumanly. By the fourth blow, Lena could hardly recognize her mother through the carnage. Somewhere in her subconscious, she knew she should run, but no matter how hard she tried to escape the scene, her own body held her hostage.

Suddenly, her father turned to face her again, and the expression on his face reflected pain, anguish, and misery. It was the look of someone who could never undo the actions they had taken, someone so deep in their regrets that they could never find their way out. He turned the weapon inward, pressing its point slowly into his sternum as his face contorted through a multitude of emotions. The knife had sunk into her father's chest down to its hilt before he stilled and fell like a bag of bricks, a wet thump on the now deeply saturated carpet indicating the curtain call for the horror show Lena had witnessed. All at once, it became quiet—utterly and uncomfortably quiet.

Lena stood in silence for what seemed like an eternity, staring not at the violent scene in front of her, but at her feet. She willed them to move, to twitch, to do anything. The tears had stopped, and she made no sound; she was broken, like a watch that someone had forgotten to wind. An hour passed before her body finally began accepting requests from her brain again. When she could finally move, she could only think of one thing to do. Lena slowly backed out of the living room, walked down the hall, and out the front door. Then she did what her mother had pleaded; she ran, as fast and as far as her feet would take her.

CHAPTER 22

Pax

Time and location (the past): 4:43 pm, San Diego, CA

"Thank you for agreeing to meet with me, Lena. I know that being alone with me is… difficult." Atticus sat across from his niece at a local café, a small round table for two separating them.

"Yet you originally asked to meet me at my home, alone. Quite the misstep in calculations for a man with your intellect, don't you think?" she scoffed.

Atticus faltered at her jab but quickly recovered. "Yes, I admit that was incredibly daft of me, I apologize. I asked you here so that I could give you something… something your mother left you in her will. I would have done so sooner, but I wanted to wait until the wound wasn't so… fresh."

After Lena had cursed him out, citing the absurdity of him stepping foot in her home, they decided to meet at this location around the corner from Lena's house instead. She had been absentmindedly swirling her cappuccino in its mug with a stir-stick for the better part of fifteen minutes, avoiding eye contact with him.

Now, at the mention of her mother, Lena's brow raised, a spark of interest twinkling in her eyes. It had been a year since her parents' murder-suicide, and Atticus had handled all their postmortem affairs for Lena, knowing it would be far too much for her to deal with. He also knew she would never fully recover from losing both of her parents, as well as Royce two years prior. Regardless, he felt that enough time had passed; it was now or never. Lena's expertise was needed at ENDURE, and as long as he executed this pitch properly, he would have it. He pulled a small box from his coat pocket and slid it silently across the table to Lena. As she opened it, he studied her expression.

"It's a pendant of Pax, the Roman goddess of peace. Though I'm sure you already know that; your mother hardly ever took the thing off after your grandmother gave it to her. I remember her telling me that it was her reassurance that no matter the storm she weathered, there were always blue skies full of peace just beyond the horizon." That, of course, was a lie. Atticus had given that pendant to Kaylee and imbued it with pointless meaning. When she left him for Mason, she had lied to her husband about its origin. As Lena turned the necklace over in her palms repeatedly, Atticus could tell there were some deeply rooted memories clawing their way to the surface. He continued to analyze her in silence, giving her the opportunity to speak, though she never took it. The girl was lost in a sea of emotions; she was vulnerable.

"I'm sorry, Lena. I know this must be hard for you. I can't change the past. Not with your parents, not with Royce, and certainly not with me. I want you to know, whether you believe me or not, that I will never do anything to hurt you ever again. I gave up the drink that day and have been sober since. You know why I did what I did, but that is no excuse, and I will regret it until the day I die… but I'm not here to reflect on the past today, Lena. What I want to talk about is the future."

Yet another lie; Atticus knew with certainty he would hurt her again, but it would be a different kind of hurt, a necessary one. As she endearingly played with the necklace, lost in thoughts of better times, Atticus felt a pang of guilt. One day, his sweet, innocent niece would find out that he had caused the death of her beloved husband. One day, Lena would know that Atticus had killed her father in self-defense and indirectly caused the death of her mother as well. If all went according to his plan, this day was just around the corner…

Lena finally looked up from the pendant of Pax and, for the first time, met Atticus's gaze. "Thank you for this, Atticus."

He nodded and knew in that moment it was his time to strike. He bent down and pulled a file from the satchel at his feet. Placing it on the table, he inconspicuously nudged it in Lena's direction. Hesitantly, she grabbed it. Before she could flip the file open, though, Atticus placed his hand over it, holding it shut. "Take that home, read it in private." he said, his stare firm.

"What is it?" Lena asked, her confusion outweighing her curiosity.

This was it; time to execute. "It's a job offer. I could use someone with your talents at ENDURE, Lena. Your experience with biomedical and computer sciences would be a huge asset to us. I'm sure you'll find the pay to be more than generous. You will never struggle a day in your life again, financially speaking of course. I need someone to handle our cybersecurity and software programming, someone who I know is intelligent enough to make sure we never fall victim to a cyberattack. The information we are dealing with is highly classified and can never leave our servers. As far as the biomedical aspect of this all goes... you'll just have to trust that I have plenty of use for your knowledge in that area. If you accept, however, you won't ever have to blindly trust in me again. You will have full access to everything and anything ENDURE concerns itself with."

Lena sighed, the weight of the decision bearing down heavily on her conscience. "Fine, I'll bite... ignoring the shiny bells and whistles you just dangled in front of me, why would I ever agree to work with you considering our past?"

This was it; her decision would hinge on what he said next. "You're the best there is. Top of your class in every subject. Skills aside, I feel I owe you for the emotional trauma I have caused you," he paused, fully aware that Lena could never know that said trauma extended far beyond that drunken encounter so long ago. "I don't need to ask you if you miss your parents, Lena… if you miss Royce. It's clear you do… and how could you not? So… what would you say if I told you I could bring them back?"

His question rang in Lena's head like the tolling of the Liberty Bell. How could he possibly achieve what he had alluded to? There was no way to cheat death. Humanity had tried for centuries and would continue to try for centuries more, but the impossible would always remain just that: impossible.

"That's a lovely idea, Atticus. It's also an insane one. It's simply not possible." Lena stood from her chair, leaving the folder on the table beside her unfinished cappuccino. "Look, thank you for the pendant, but I think we're done here." She began to walk away, but Atticus sprang up and caught her by the wrist. Lena yanked it away, revolted, but the action had served its purpose; she stopped and turned to face him.

"Lena, I've already *done it*. Furthermore, I can *prove it*."

She searched his eyes for the lie but found none in his bemused smile. Atticus appeared flattered with himself, a look she had come to know well over the years she spent growing up with him as her uncle. He was either telling an inconceivable truth or had lost his mind and convinced himself of this absurd notion. Of all the things Atticus was, though, Lena knew he was a genius, a fact she admitted to herself begrudgingly in that moment. She stared at him a moment longer before grabbing the file from the table. The look on her face was a mixture of anger, confusion, fear, and intrigue. "How, Atticus? How can you prove it?"

He gestured for her to sit back down, but she ignored it. "Please Lena, it will all make sense soon, if you'll just hear me out." He gestured again with more insistence. Finally, she complied and took her seat. He nodded his thanks and followed suit.

Steepling his hands in front of him, he contemplated the best way to explain. "The day of the barbecue, the day you lost Royce and went with your parents to Mason's appointment... your mother called me concerned about Mason. That was the reason she took you and left."

Lena rolled her eyes. "Get to the point, Atticus; my patience is running very thin at this point."

"That day Lena, your father never left that room. He never returned home to your mother," he said, his gaze unwavering.

Lena threw her hands into the air. "Atticus, have you lost it? What do you even mean? My father was around for an entire year after that day before... you know what I'm saying."

"Lena, you're not understanding. If you accept my offer though, you will." Atticus leaned across the table and whispered. "The man that returned home that day looked like Mason. He sounded like Mason; he had the same memories as Mason, but Lena; that man wasn't your father."

CHAPTER 23

Descent

Time and location (present-day): 10:06 am,
ENDURE Center for Rehabilitation

"I trusted you, Lena. I'm coming to realize that was a huge mistake."

She sat in Atticus's office across the desk from him, staring into the woodgrain of its handcrafted mahogany design. It reminded her of the grandiose front doors attached to Atticus's home and how she found his affinity for the material generic and gaudy. Oakley and Shaw flanked either side of her. When she looked around the office, there was no sign of the break-in that Royce had mentioned, but that was to be expected. If ENDURE wanted to cover something up, they did so with rapid efficiency.

Without diverting her gaze from the desk, she responded in a monotonal fashion. "Sorry I grew a conscience, uncle."

Atticus sighed audibly. "Lena, you knew what this was going into it. If you didn't have the stomach for it—"

He was interrupted by Lena's attempt to stand, but Oakley caught her by the shoulder and shoved her downward into her seat. Rage filled Lena to her very core, her face flushing red instantly as she looked to Atticus. "Are you *fucking* kidding me? Tell your goon that if he places his grubby paws on me again, I'll claw his eyes out of his skull." Lena said, looking up and to her left to glare at Oakley, who in turn shrugged.

"Sorry sweetheart, doctor's orders," Oakley said, winking, a mannerism that repulsed her.

Atticus continued before Lena could respond. "Lena," said Atticus, refocusing her. "If you were anyone else... if you weren't my niece... Do you have any idea what the consequences of your actions would entail? I could have you—"

"—Killed?" she asked, finishing the sentence for him. "Since when has blood relation ever stopped you from killing, uncle? Since when has *family* ever stood in the way of your research? You killed my father. He was your brother; you killed him anyway. Then, you allowed your faulty Echo to murder my mother. Hell, it could've murdered me all those years ago too, could have prevented me from being such a thorn in your side. You know what? Go right ahead. Put a bullet in my head right now, Atticus. If you do, you just better pray to whatever twisted God you believe in that Royce doesn't find out, because if he does? With that... *thing* living inside of him that you are so obsessed with? He'll move heaven and hell to rip you apart, limb by limb."

Atticus chortled in disbelief. "That's your gamble? That Royce would find a way to utilize Mallen to avenge your death should I order it? What exactly would become of that, Lena? Don't be so nonsensical. I would never harm you. As far as your father goes, what I did to him was a mercy. There was nothing left of Mason at that point; only Mallen remained. If I hadn't put those bullets in him, Mallen would have used your father to murder me, and then it would've killed everyone in this facility. I had to stop it while it was still weak, still learning how to navigate its new host."

Atticus paused, and stood from his desk to pace around behind his chair. It was as if he were briefly transported miles away before continuing. "Kaylee, though... Kaylee will always be one of my deepest regrets. There were signs that the Echo wasn't ready, but I sent it home to her anyway. I thought having a version of Mason, even if it wasn't the original in your lives, was better than not having him at all. I just didn't know how to tell either of you about your father's death; I didn't want you two to have to go on without him, and well... what's done is done."

He stopped once more, taking a deep breath of stale air before returning to his seat. "All I'm saying now is that you cannot continue to allow your emotions to stand in the way of our progress. We are closer than ever before to figuring this all out. It's bad enough that I need to perform damage control now due to you revealing far more than I ever planned to Royce, but then prescribing him DM1, Lena? You knew that with a steady dose of DM1, Mallen's ability to communicate with Royce would cease to exist. Going behind my back to effectively halt my research, preventing me from learning more about Mallen in hopes of finding a way to stop it? And all for what? For the sake of one man? If you can even call him that..."

Atticus massaged his temples as Lena's nose scrunched up with fury. "That *thing* that you are so intent on letting walk around in Royce's skin is *killing* him. You promised me you could bring him back; you never said you were doing it just to take him away again."

Atticus was a man of composure; it took far more to disgruntle him than the average human being. Nonetheless, the sleepless nights, the endless hours dedicated to this endeavor, and the constant data analysis and experimentation... Lena had finally pushed him too far. When he snapped, his voice echoed throughout the room in thunderous prose. "WAKE UP LENA. THAT THING IS NOT YOUR HUSBAND. YOUR HUSBAND DIED WITH THE REST OF THE WILKO'S WHEN OAKLEY SMASHED AN ARMORED VEHICLE INTO THEIR CAR!" It had slipped out before Atticus could catch himself. He knew one day it would come to this, and yet, he still hadn't been prepared. "... God... DAMN IT!" He swept both arms across his desk in a fit of mania, a decanter of whiskey flying across the room and smashing to pieces on the floor. Atticus stared at the shimmering glass shards as his chest heaved, and all he could see was another broken promise, the caramel-colored liquid symbolizing one of many lies he had fed Lena in the past. It took everything in him to meet Lena's eyes again.

When he did, hers were wide with the revelation of betrayal. "What? What do you mean when Oakley... they said it was a drunk driver? The police... it wasn't police, was it? You... you used ENDURE to orchestrate it all? You *willfully* took my husband from me? *Murdered* his entire family?"

Atticus' brain tried its hardest to conjure up an excuse, a way to rid himself of suspicion and refute her accusation. For once in his life, all the knowledge in the world couldn't save him. "I asked you, that day at the barbecue. I pleaded with you to convince him to come willingly. I told you he was our only hope, and you denied me, told me to stay away. So, I took matters into my own hands. Oakley had admittedly been a bit overzealous in his retrieval; my intent was never to kill the Wilkos, Royce included. It was unfortunate that things played out the way they did."

Lena began to seethe. Her chest rose and fell visibly with each furious breath. "*Unfortunate?* You *fucking monster!*" Lena sprang from her chair, and this time, when Oakley tried to prevent her from getting any further, she shifted her weight to the side, dodging his hand and ramming her elbow upwards into his nose as she stood. It gushed blood as he stumbled backwards, taken off guard. Lena threw herself across the desk, now stained with whiskey and spattered blood, and tackled Atticus to the ground. Her fists made contact anywhere they could, raining down blow after blow, as Atticus held his arms in front of him for protection. At some point, her fists un-balled, and she began to claw at his face like a wild mongoose. Shaw approached her from behind, wrapping his heavily muscled arms around her, restraining Lena.

"I'll fucking kill you! If it's the last thing I do, I swear I'll fucking kill you Atticus!" She yelled, spittle flying from her mouth as she writhed in Shaw's arms. Almost immediately after she vowed to end her uncle's life, Lena's teeth sunk into Shaw's bicep. He held on as long as he could before letting out a scream of pain and releasing her. Lena fell to the ground, then quickly clambered toward the door. Oakley turned to grab her, but Atticus intervened.

"Stop!" he shouted as she fled from the office. "Stop," he repeated, quieter this time, completely and utterly defeated. "Just let her go... let her go... there's no time for this," he said between strained breaths. Atticus leaned on his desk, gasping for air as his heartbeat began to slow down to its normal rhythm. A trickle of blood started to drip from below his right eye, where Lena's nails had sliced at his cheek. He gathered his thoughts and what little composure he could muster before addressing Oakley and Shaw. "I want Royce's DM1 pulled from the dispensary, immediately. He *will* continue his interactions with Mallen. He *must* if we are to figure out a way to stop this threat." Atticus' thoughts then trailed to the many hindrances he had suffered over the past few days. From Royce and his band of misfits rummaging through his office to discovering that Lena had prescribed medication for Royce without Atticus' approval... The anger had been stewing beneath the surface for some time, but Atticus had kept it at bay. Now, however, after Lena had shared a bed with his test subject, exposing many of the skeletons Atticus kept locked in his closet... Now the vexation was finally boiling over.

He needed to act. He needed to demonstrate power, making it clear to both Royce and Lena that he would tolerate no further impediments to his work. Atticus didn't hesitate as much as he hoped he would before making his next decision. "Royce and Lena are off limits, at least for now, but I want you to make an example out of one of the others."

Oakley stepped forward; his upper lip was now crusted with blackened ichor. "What kind of example are we talking about here boss?"

"Eliminate one of them."

At the confirmation of the kill order, Shaw interjected. "Matias?" he asked, but Atticus shook his head.

"No, as far as Royce is concerned, Matias could already be dead. Hell, he *will be* soon enough. One of the other two."

Shaw raised a brow. "Sir, need I remind you that—"

"I haven't forgotten about the deal we made," Atticus interrupted, "but we've gotten what we need from him. I never claimed to be a man of my word. You have your orders. Eliminate one of them; I do not care which."

There was a brief hesitation before Shaw nodded, patting Oakley on the shoulder to signal him to follow. Atticus noticed the smirk on Oakley's face as the two exited the room, reaffirming his thought that the man enjoyed killing a little too much. He also knew, though, that was why the two of them worked so well together. Like a handler and his canine, Elliot Shaw was the steady grip that kept Jordan Oakley on a tight leash until his violent temper was deemed necessary. Years of helming this torturous task took its toll, one Atticus knew to be both physical and mental in nature. With this thought in mind, Atticus couldn't help but wonder if this was the beginning of his descent into insanity; he wondered if he had any shred of humanity left at all... or if the chaos had finally consumed him whole, leaving behind nothing but a husk of the once great man he had been, but would never be again.

CHAPTER 24

Imminent

Time and location (present-day): 2:48 am,
ENDURE Center for Rehabilitation

I can feel the heat swelling around me, the air coming to a near boiling point; tendrils of fire twine around my body, enveloping my person, threatening to devour me entirely. Though conscious of the constant rise in temperature, there isn't the faintest burning sensation; the flames warm caress isn't harming me in the slightest. I search for signs of life, but all I can see before me is an endless sea of golden scorched Earth. A voice suddenly shatters through the roaring blaze, clear as day.

"You can't stop what's about to happen. It's important to know that this isn't your fault." A silhouette begins to form in the distance but remains unrecognizable. The voice though; that's familiar.

"What do you mean?!" I shout, my scream competing to be heard over the raging ocean of red-hot heat.

"*They're going to kill me, and there's nothing you can do to prevent it. All you can do is use it to drive yourself forward, to honor my memory.*"

A sense of dread starts to settle in my chest. "Who are you?! I can't see you!"

Levelheaded and calm, the voice replies. "*You know who I am; deep down you know. Death will come for me, and you'll try to stop it, but you'll be too late.*"

Upon speaking the last few words, the voice changes, contorts. "*Wake up Royce; try to save your friend, try to be the hero of your story... but you and I? We both know the truth. No matter how much you lie to yourself, you'll never be able to lie to me. I will always be there to remind you that you are no hero. You'll never be anything more than a failure seeking redemption. Time and time again, death has come for those closest to you; and time and time again you failed to stop it, and will continue to do so. Just like those who came before you. You are restricted by the bonds of physicality, Royce, but we... we are Boundless.*"

I awake on the floor in the middle of my room, unsure of how I ended up here. Thinking about it further, I can't even recall turning in for the night. The last thing I remember is going to the dispensary for my medication, only to find that Atticus had declined the refill. Without those little blue capsules, Mallen began to slowly seep back into my mind and then... I feel a dull ache throb in my skull as I recall bits of my dream. Picking myself up off the floor, I make my way to the door and peek out into the hallway. It's silent, dark; early morning, probably somewhere around three o'clock. I slip back inside and shut the door gently.

These dreams keep getting weirder and weirder. What *had* I dreamed about though? Glimpses of it all came and went, little flashes here and there, but I can't put them together to see the full picture. It's like opening a puzzle box only to find you're missing pieces after completing it. Fire, that I remember vividly enough. The endless heat, surrounding me entirely. I also can recall a brief conversation with Mallen, my unwanted shadow. There was something else in the dream that I can't place though, *someone* else, I'm sure of it. I had spoken with someone prior to Mallen, but I can no longer hear the voice clearly, can't put a face to the words. Something about it frays my nerves, has me on edge. The more I try to ignore it, the more a sense of urgency arises, gripping me so tightly I swear I'll suffocate in its hold.

I need to calm down, focus on what I had seen before in the dream. Meditation isn't something I'm keen on, but at this point I'll try anything to rid myself of the overwhelming anxiety I'm experiencing. So, I sit back down in the middle of my room, the cold floor biting at my feet as I cross my legs and close my eyes. I inhale deeply, hold the breath in, then slowly exhale. My heart rate slows, the suffocating weight begins to lift, and the silence thickens. A few more breaths, repeating the same rhythm of inhalation and exhalation; and it all comes back in a flash. The images flood my head in a violent flurry, like fast forwarding through a movie at the highest rate of speed. At the end of it all is the voice; all too familiar, and this time, a face to match. My eyes snap open. At some point, I had begun to sweat profusely. My face is flushed and red, my pulse racing once more. *God no, this can't be happening. This can't be real. It's just in my head, just a dream, nothing more.*

"Rest assured, it's real, Royce. Consider this little premonition a sort of… gift… but know that I will come to collect later."

"Oh, just shut the hell up!" I yell aloud, praying that Mallen will listen for a change. Impatiently, my fingertips begin tapping rapidly against my thigh in nervous indecision; I can trust my gut, or I can trust Mallen… I leap from the floor and run out the door as fast as I can. A feeling that I can't even begin to explain washes over me as I sprint down the hall; someone is about to die, that much is imminent, and I know who.

CHAPTER 25

Eventuality

Time and location (present-day): 3:12 am,
ENDURE Center for Rehabilitation

Something about their presence in his quarters seemed to chill the room more, if only slightly. He sat on the edge of his bed. Jordan Oakley perched on the desk chair across from him, a suppressed pistol resting on his leg and targeting center mass. Leaning against the wall beside him was Elliot Shaw. It stayed like that for a while; all darkness and empty air between the three of them. Finally, Shaw broke the tranquility surrounding them. "This isn't how things were intended to happen, but hopefully you understand; orders are orders."

He laughed at that, a sound of disdain laced with disbelief.

"What about this do you find amusing?" asked Shaw.

"About the current situation? You two and me? Right here, right now? Not a damn thing. I'm just wondering how much more death and decay you people are going to spread around before you stop buying into your own bullshit." He shook his head in disgust.

Shaw sighed and drew in a breath. "Look, you don't know what's really going on here, and you wouldn't believe me if I told you. If you had to kill a few to save the many, I'm sure you would do just that. That's all this is. Nothing personal about it.

The bed creaked as he leaned forward to rest his elbows on his knees. "Then tell me."

"What?" asked Shaw, clearly perplexed by the request.

"You said I don't know what's really going on here, so tell me. The way your buddy has that pistol trained on me, there's an eventuality that I won't be leaving this room once our conversation ends. So why don't you tell me what I don't know? I think I at least deserve an explanation as to why I'm about to be murdered in the middle of the night."

Shaw crossed his arms, letting out a bemused chuckle under his breath. "Jesus Christ, bartering until the very end. That's very like you."

"What would you know about me? I'm just one of many cattle in a thinning herd to you…" He clung to the last word as the reality of his situation set in.

"Everything," Shaw said confidently.

"Is that so?" he asked, convinced it was a lie.

"I would hope so; I helped create you, after all."

At the drop of that remark, he stared at Shaw, perplexed. "What the hell is that supposed to mean?"

Shaw's tone grew serious as he spoke. "Let's just say, you're not who you think you are. Your whole existence has basically been one big lie, a means to an end. You're nothing but a tool created to serve a larger purpose. Or at least that was the intent. Now, however, it seems only one of you has a chance in hell at preventing the impending doom we're faced with."

He pondered curiously about whatever the "doom" Shaw mentioned could entail before prodding the man with more conviction. "Enough with the allusions, just give me some answers. Why are you keeping us trapped here like prisoners? What is the Deus Molecule? Why were you experimenting on people? I want some fucking answers!" He had slightly lost his patience, but who could blame him? His entire time at the facility had been spent wondering if he was insane, and just recently he concluded that he wasn't.

Yet here was Shaw, spewing a bunch of crazy, vague comments that made him question his sanity all over again. "Fine, you win. I can give you answers, but not all of them. Four questions, start whenever."

That caught his attention, and he didn't hesitate to take the dangled carrot. "Alright. Question one; why can't we go home? I've never seen anyone leave the center."

"This facility *is* your home. Next question."

"The fuck is that supposed to mean, Shaw?"

"You've asked me for answers; and I'm giving them honestly. Helping you understand them was not part of the bargain. *Next question.*"

He held Shaw's gaze for a moment, contesting his argument, but ultimately, he gave in. The answers he sought could either be revealed before he found himself dead and gone, or he could enter his unmarked grave knowing nothing more than he did now. "You said only one of us could possibly stop what's coming. Who? And what exactly is it that they're capable of stopping?"

"As for who, you know him as Royce Wilko. Regarding what it is that he might be able to stop; for the sake of simplicity, we'll call it an autonomous contagion. One that, if left unchecked after it reaches full maturity, will eventually cleanse the Earth of humanity entirely. You get two more questions."

What in the actual fuck is going on? Beyond confused, he mulled over what Shaw had just revealed to him. It was a lot to digest under pressure, far too much to take in while knowing he was mere moments from death. One thing was certain: that voice in Royce's head—the one he referred to as Mallen—was at the center of all of this. He had hoped that the others would somehow catch on to his situation and come to his rescue to stop Oakley and Shaw if he bought some time, but his demise seemed all but inevitable now. There was no point in trying to make sense of it all. "You said you helped create me, that I'm not who I think I am. What do you mean by all of that?"

"I'm afraid that falls under the category of inquiry I can't answer."

"Oh, come on man! Just tell me!"

Oakley raised the pistol from his lap, but Shaw motioned for him to wait. "I've been gracious enough to allow you the privilege of dying a little bit less in the dark than you were moments ago, don't take that for granted. Ask your next question."

Gracious? What a joke. "Alright, tell your attack dog to take it easy... I'll ask a different question."

"I'll wait," Shaw said, nodding to Oakley, who in turn lowered the gun. He sat in deep contemplation, knowing that if he had only two questions remaining, they better count.

"Where are we?"

A facility owned and operated by a government-funded research program, codenamed ENDURE."

"I meant geographically."

"I cannot answer that."

"Jesus fucking... fine. One question left, right?"

"That's right."

He didn't need to think about it; his final question became clear the moment Shaw told him that the fate of the world practically rested on Royce's shoulders. "You said only one of us could stop this... 'contagion'... said that someone was Royce... what can he do that the rest of us can't?"

Oakley stood from the chair, never letting his aim fall below chest level as Shaw removed himself from the wall. "I shouldn't answer that question, but I suppose it won't do any harm once you're disposed of. The simple answer is that Royce Wilko, in layman's terms, has the ability to see into the future."

He erupted with laughter, more amused than he thought possible considering the circumstances. "You've gotta be kidding me, right? You expect me to believe that?"

On the contrary, I told you from the beginning that you wouldn't believe the answers you were given."

"So, you're saying this guy can tell the future, he's... what? A prophet or some shit?"

"To an extent, yes. It's far more complicated and much more scientific in nature than how you so delicately describe it, but yes. Royce Wilko can glimpse snippets of events yet to come. More precisely, Mallen can show him these things. If we can hone this ability, if we can find a way to control Mallen, we may be able to save our species from an otherwise unpreventable demise."

He shook his head once more, an ironic smile perched upon his lips. "Well pal, you lost at your own game, because you just answered a fifth question."

Shaw raised an eyebrow as Oakley cocked his sidearm. "How so?"

"I wasn't sure if I had lost my mind all over again. Thought that maybe I was the lunatic in the room after all. Now though, I can say with one hundred percent certainty that you are, in fact, the one who is bat shit crazy."

Shaw smiled, amused by the comment. Oakley approached their hostage, raising the weapon and pressing the cold steel of its suppressor to the man's temple.

"I *am* going to miss that dry sense of humor when you're gone," said Oakley, speaking for the first time since entering the room. Tensions rose as a grim resolve settled in him.

He looked his captor dead in the eyes, teeth gritted. "Go to hell," he growled.

"I'm sure I will; Goodbye, Aiden." Oakley pulled the trigger.

CHAPTER 26

Immaculate

*Time and location (present-day): 3:31 am,
ENDURE Center for Rehabilitation*

My heart thumps rapidly in my chest as I dash through the maze of hallways leading to Aiden's room, but I don't feel it; I can't hear the thudding of my feet on the concrete flooring, and I can't see anything other than the path directly ahead of me. A primal instinct has taken control; the urge to protect those close to me pushes me onward with every passing breath. As I run through the lobby, I realize that of all the absurdity I've experienced since awakening from what Lena had revealed to be cryostasis, none of it has come close to the feeling driving me now. It's hard to explain; I know there's no plausible evidence that something is wrong, and yet I also know that something isn't right.

Rounding the corner and leaving the lobby, I take note of the placards beside the patient's doors lining the hallway on both sides, immediately searching for Aiden's name. One by one, I quickly glance through the nameplates: Fields, Moss, D'Souza, Hardy, Zakimi, Jones, Swaving. When I reach the end of the hallway, I'm in utter disbelief. Aiden's room was in this exact corridor, I'm certain of it. My pace slows as I turn around and begin walking back in the direction I came from, but then something catches my attention. I stop in front of one of the doors, reading the listed name aloud.

"Dejanovich..." *No... that's not possible... unless...* The door in front of me had led to Aiden's room before, there wasn't a doubt in my mind. Yet the name now engraved on the golden plate beside this room told a different story. *Maybe I'm crazy after all...* I think, if only for a fleeting moment. Resolving my mental conflict, I choose to trust my instincts and knock on the door. A moment passes, but no one comes to answer. I inhale deeply. "Screw it." I test the handle; the latch releases, and the door swings open, allowing me to step inside hesitantly.

"Hello?" I call in a whisper, trying to make sure not to draw attention to my possible intrusion. As I slip further into the room, it becomes clear I'm the only living thing present in the vicinity. I peek my head back out into the hallway; there isn't a soul in sight. So, I retreat into the room once more and close the door as silently as possible. Looking around, I take in my surroundings as best I can in the darkness. There's a desk accompanied by a chair and a twin-sized bed, the same furniture in my own quarters, but something about it seems off. The bed isn't just made, but freshly so. It looks as if it has never been laid in. I make my way over to the desk, running my fingers across its wooden surface. Not a speck of dust has settled atop it. The room in its entirety looks as if it hasn't seen a visitor until this very moment, immaculate in every aspect of the word.

Beginning to suspect foul play, I surmise that I'm not insane; I simply hadn't made it here in time. Someone had cleaned up, and they had done one hell of a job. They had either taken Aiden and ransacked his room, or worse. If this were the case, however, something isn't correlating properly with my dream. It had been all but right; something had gone horribly wrong, and Aiden was missing as a result, but what about the fire? The unrelenting heat? If my dream had been something more... a vision of sorts, then that almost certainly meant that Aiden was...

A sudden jolt of panic surges through me as the handle on the door moves. It opens, and four silhouettes enter the room, unrecognizable in the shadows. One of them shuts the door, sealing themselves inside with me. My body tenses, and I feel Mallen brimming at the edges of my mind, begging to take control. Two of them stand guard by the door, while the other two approach the desk, moving closer to me. I assess them in the darkness like a nervous predator deciding when to lunge at its prey. The overhead lights suddenly illuminate the room, flooding everything in phosphorescent white. I glance at the intruders and immediately feel the color drain from my face. Elliot Shaw stands at the entrance to what had once been Aiden's quarters, and beside him is Jordan Oakley. Closer to my position in the room is Atticus Cais, with *Desmond* in tow. He tries to speak almost immediately after our eyes meet.

"Royce, this isn't—"

"Silence, Mr. Luther," the doctor interjects. He looks Desmond in the eye, as if telling him to stay put, then slowly approaches me. "Mr. Wilko, it seems that you and I have come to a sort of... impasse. I'm here before you now to help ease your mind so that we may find mutual ground."

"What does Desmond have to do with all of this?" I ask.

Atticus chuckles impatiently to himself, pinching the bridge of his nose. "Desmond is here because he is part of the bigger picture, a picture I need you to see clearly by the end of our conversation."

I sneer at the doctor. "Forgive me if I feel none too inclined to believe any of the drivel that pours from that venomous mouth of yours, Atticus." I sense Mallen taking control, if only for a moment, with a single statement, and then I shove him back down into the caverns of my thoughts. It takes everything in me to hold him at bay as Atticus trains his eyes on me, studying me, trying to gain an understanding of where my mind is.

"You're so certain that I am the only one in your midst that has betrayed you, but Desmond here is no more your ally than I am, Royce. He has used you just the same as I have."

Desmond's gaze drops to the floor. "Royce, that's not true," he says, though the defeat in his voice reveals a hint of truth in the doctor's words.

"Where's Aiden?" I ask, ignoring Atticus's attempt to divert my attention; I will worry about Desmond later, but right now, Aiden is my priority.

"You needn't concern yourself with Mr. Buckley." Atticus clasps his hands behind his back as I battle Mallen with even more ferocity.

"Answer the fucking question." Atticus raises a brow as if caught off guard, then gradually regains his composure. "We *must* do something about that temper of yours. Just relax, Royce, and we can discuss this matter further."

I've tried as hard as I can, but I'm losing the fight with Mallen, and it is becoming increasingly evident the longer we converse. "I'm not going to ask you again; answer me or I swear to God, I will close the gap between us and tear your eyes from their sockets."

"Royce, you need to think rationally and logically for a moment. If you attack me, Shaw and Oakley will have to forcibly remove you. I simply want to— "

I'm on him before he finishes his sentence, clenching his neck with a strength I know isn't my own. It's a moment of clarity I never expected; Mallen hates the doctor as much, if not more than I do. My hands squeeze so tightly around Atticus's throat that I think I might rip it wide open. "WHERE IS HE?!" I demand, screaming like a savage. A vicious kick catches me in the ribs but does not deter me. A second comes, then a third, and finally, I release the doctor as I tumble to the floor beside him. I hold my ribcage, hacking and wheezing; Mallen has abandoned me to my pain for now.

Atticus picks himself up from the floor, caught in his own fit of choking and coughing. When I look up at him, his face has turned so red that I imagine fumes bellowing out of his ears; it brings a momentary smile to my lips, which disappears when I roll over to see who had been kicking me. Desmond huffs and puffs, coming down from the adrenaline high that had been punting me from atop Atticus like a stray dog. "I'm sorry Royce, you have to understand I—"

"ENOUGH!" My attention turns back to Atticus all too late as he begins to advance towards me. There's no use trying to defend myself; I can barely breathe, much less stand. I'll take whatever abuse Atticus is about to dish out and then use it as fuel to stamp the man out of existence later. He reaches the spot where I lie on the floor, crouches down, and grabs me by my collar with both hands. Atticus lifts me up, pinning me forcefully against the nearest wall. "Do you want to know where Mr. Buckley is? Is that what you desire? Fine, so be it! He is *dead*! Aiden Buckley! Matias Castellón! Desmond Luther! Royce Wilko! They are *all* dead!" He stares daggers at me, his gaze frozen and locked onto my confused eyes.

A moment later, Atticus shoves me aside and storms off in the opposite direction, his hands gripping the back of his neck in distress. I stumble and find my footing, brushing the wrinkles from my jumpsuit and coughing out the last bit of discomfort caused by the previous blows to my midsection. Though I am perplexed, I'm also intrigued; or perhaps it's Mallen who's interested in what Atticus said. Hell, maybe it's both of us. The only certainty is that the doctor's guard is down, and now is the time to bombard him with questions if I want answers. Atticus is now the second person to tell me I was previously dead; I need to understand what that exactly means.

"What in the hell are you talking about? How can Desmond or I be dead? We're both standing right here in this room with you."

Atticus turns around, exhaling heavily, dropping his arms back down to his sides and trying to calm himself. "You are *not* Royce Wilko."

"Atticus, maybe—" Desmond tries to stop him, but he is cut off by the doctor once more.

"Silence your tongue! That is the last time I will tell you!"

"I wouldn't threaten him if I were you," I warn, regaining my strength, *Mallen's* strength, little by little.

Atticus laughs once more. "You run to his defense, even though he has betrayed your trust. How ironic."

"I don't believe Desmond has done that, but we'll cover that later. Let's get back on topic here," I say, trying to bring the doctor's focus back to me.

Atticus turns back toward the desk, pulls the chair out, and takes a seat. "Your tenacity knows no bounds, Royce; I will give you that. I originally planned to keep this operation shrouded in secrecy; however, I've come to realize that you will not rest until you have the answers you seek. I thought giving you a taste via those video files would quell your desire to poke around my business… However, I did not foresee Lena exposing ENDURE's secrets further. Against my better judgment, I've decided to tell you everything you wish to know. My hope is that in doing so, it will allow me to gain your trust and cooperation."

"Highly unlikely but go on," I say defiantly.

Atticus smiles anxiously. "We'll start with what I've already shared with you. I understand that those research videos you watched involving our administration of DM1 into Mason's bloodstream were very difficult to witness, and that they may have caused you to view me in a certain… negative light. I also previously assured you that everything I have done has been in the best interest of you and everyone else involved, including Lena's father. Mason asked me to help him, begged. I never would have harmed him if it wasn't necessary. By the time I…

by the time I did what had to be done, there was nothing left of him, of my brother. He had spiraled out of control, lost his mind, lost what made him Mason Cais."

I say nothing in response and won't look him in the eye, but I almost feel that Atticus is being sincere... almost.

"Much like what Lena revealed against my orders, what I'm about to tell you may sound unbelievable, but it's the truth. Whether you accept it or dismiss it as fiction is entirely your choice. Just understand this: I won't let anything, or anyone, stand in my way. If you choose to oppose me after hearing what I have to say, I'll do whatever's necessary to ensure my research continues without interference."

I can feel his stare boring into me throughout his diatribe, like a parent lecturing his child. If Atticus thinks his slightly veiled threat has achieved anything other than irritating me, he is sadly mistaken. "Enough. Start talking about what we're here to talk about, no more stalling."

Atticus nods, exhaling steadily as he prepares for another lengthy monologue. "Ten years ago, Lena's father came to me pleading for help. He said something was wrong with his mind, but he wasn't sure what. He didn't know when, where, or how the onset of symptoms had occurred. All he knew was that it was getting worse, much worse. Knowing my background in biomedicine, he asked me to diagnose his sickness and to provide him with a cure. So, naturally, I was inclined to help; the man was my brother, how could I say no? I gathered a team of my best employees, and we began to perform various tests on Mason. No matter what we tried, though, we could not find the proper diagnosis for his ailment. Then one day, my protégé Elliot Shaw noticed something rather... peculiar in Lena's father's genetic code; what we discovered was so much more than a mere sickness; what we found lurking inside of Mason's DNA held the key to our survival, the prevention of our extinction; what we found in Mason was the Deus Molecule."

CHAPTER 27

Mason

Time and location (the past): 12:21 pm,
ENDURE Black Site 7

Mason's right hand shook violently as he extended his arm, reaching for the door handle. He tried desperately to steady it, grasping at the trembling hand with his left one, which wasn't faring much better. He stood outside the entry to the ENDURE location, one of multiple biomedical research facilities led by his older brother, Atticus. It was here that Atticus and his team experimented with all sorts of medicinal substances to create cures and remedies for a broad spectrum of diseases and ailments, primarily focusing on cancers.

Atticus had always aspired to be the first biomedical engineer to find the cure for generalized cancer, a feat that Mason was sure everyone in the field strived to accomplish. However, it wasn't until recently that he discovered his brother's motive for finding that cure extended beyond the generality of the matter.

The painful visions that had plagued his mind revealed to him that Atticus had a personal stake in the matter... It had been roughly a month since the aching in Mason's skull had escalated to unbearable new heights, and he decided that it was probably best not to dismiss it as simple migraines. Not to mention the things he had seen; like dreams, only much more than that...

He grabbed the handle, still shaking, though a little less than before, and then entered the building. Mason could only imagine what was going through the receptionist's head as he neared the front desk. Dressed slovenly in dirty clothes and with his hair a mess, beads of sweat speckled his forehead as she stared at him on his approach. A ripe smell followed him wherever he went, since he couldn't stand being in the shower anymore. Ever since this sickness had wrapped its slimy hands around him, there was constant noise in his head. Whenever he tried to shower, the continuous pitter-patter of the droplets hitting the basin of the tub was enough to make him scream. He reached the desk and did his best not to frighten the poor woman. "Hello, I'm here to see Atticus Cais."

The receptionist feigned her best smile and responded. "I'm sorry sir, but Dr. Cais does not take walk-ins. I can schedule an appointment if you'd like?"

I'm his brother. Please, it's urgent."

She hesitated and then reached for the phone. "One moment please sir."

He nodded, then gritted his teeth; another pulsing wave of pain washed over him. It felt like being zapped by an electric current. He squinted and looked away, trying to hide the agony. Whatever was ailing him was getting worse by the minute; Atticus had to help him, or no one could. The receptionist hung up the phone and then addressed Mason.

Dr. Cais will be with you momentarily. Please feel free to help yourself to refreshments and have a seat in the waiting area.

"Thank you, miss."

She nodded, and Mason turned to take a seat but stumbled and fell to one knee. Panicked, the receptionist stood and rushed around the desk, the sound of her heels on the tile floor sending shockwaves of torment throughout Mason's body as he struggled to regain control.

"Sir, are you okay? Should I call 9-1-1?" the receptionist asked.

He tried to respond, to tell her no, but words wouldn't come out. Then suddenly, a firm grip clasped his forearm, lifting him back up to his feet. "Mason, it's Atticus, are you alright?"

He dug up the last of his strength and mumbled, "Need... quiet..."

Atticus nodded. "Amanda, place all of my meetings on hold until further notice, inform my clients that I have an emergency to attend to."

The receptionist nodded.

"Can you walk Mason?" Atticus asked.

Mason nodded, then cringed from another surge of pain.

"You need somewhere silent? I know just the place. There's a park across the way, should be all but vacant at this time of day. Let's head there; take your time, nice and easy." Atticus directed him, and they walked out the front doors and down the steps. When they arrived at the park, the air was crisp and cool, the spring breeze soothing the cacophony of chaotic sounds in Mason's head, if only momentarily. Atticus had been right; it was just the place to go to help silence the storm within his mind. The pain, although still present, had subsided significantly. They sat upon a bench near a pathway lined with sweetgum trees. Atticus hadn't turned his attention away from his brother since they arrived, staying as quiet as humanly possible to help expedite the alleviation of Mason's suffering.

Once certain that the pulsating in his temples had almost disappeared, Mason began the conversation. "I apologize for that; I didn't know..." He trailed off. What did he know? Not much; something was severely wrong with him, and he had no real way of explaining what that might be. At least not in a fashion that would make a lick of sense to someone as logical as Atticus.

"Mason," Atticus paused, waiting for his brother to look him in the eye. "What exactly is going on here? I thought you were going to keel over dead in my lobby for Christ's sake."

Mason laughed, but it was cut short by a knife-like stab at the base of his skull. "I don't really know how to explain this all without sounding crazy, so I've decided to show you instead. Atticus; this *needs* to stay between the two of us. I'm trusting you because you're the smartest person I've ever met, but what you're about to witness… this is unknown territory, even for you."

"Mason, I'm not quite sure what you're—"

"Your phone is going to ring in exactly three minutes. It's going to be Uriah Gholston; he works for your genetic engineering division. He's going to tell you that he's come down with the flu and can't make it to work today."

"What? Slow down, Mason. What exactly are you talking about?"

"Just watch. Only about two minutes to go."

Atticus stared at him, bewildered, but Mason simply held up a hand, signaling him to be patient. They sat there like that for what felt like quite a while, eyes locked; then Atticus' ringtone began chiming from the pocket of his coat. Hesitant, he reached in and answered the phone. "Hello, this is Dr. Cais speaking."

Mason sat, intensely focused on his brother as he waited for the call to end.

"Understood, rest up and get well soon, goodbye." He hung up the phone and attempted to speak, but confusion got the better of him. Mason smirked, yet Atticus remained completely unaware of what he had just witnessed. "How do you know Uriah?"

"I *don't*. Atticus, something happened. I don't know how or when, but I've gained this… this ability. I can *see* the future, or at least bits and pieces of it."

"Mason, that's impossible," Atticus sighed in frustration.

"You *literally* just witnessed it, Atticus! I told you; it sounds crazy, but it's *true*."

Atticus stood from the bench and faced him. "If this were true, Mason, then— "

Mason stood up abruptly, placing a hand on Atticus' shoulder. "You have stage three cancer. You're visiting your physician tomorrow for a check-up, but you and I both know what he's going to tell you. The cells have metastasized and escalated your condition to stage four. You've been working on desperately finding a cure for cancer all this time for the common good, and ironically enough, you now need the cure if you are to continue your research. You haven't told anyone about this. How could I possibly know, Atticus?"

Atticus stood in shocked silence. He stared at Mason, mulling over all the thoughts racing through his head. What he was hearing sounded insane; and yet, the scientist in him couldn't find any reason to denigrate the accuracy of his brother's predictions. "Say I believed you; why have you come to me with this?"

"Something's wrong. My head feels like it's about to explode. These… visions have started to blur the line between reality and… I guess the future. They're becoming less detailed and less accurate. I'm hallucinating, seeing things that aren't there, things that haven't happened, or rather haven't happened yet, hearing voices... I'm losing my mind, Atticus, and it's taking a toll on my body as well. I came to you with the hope that you can cure me, hoping that you can figure out what exactly this is before it's too late."

"Too late? You don't think..."

"I don't know, but the pain increases immensely with every passing day. The human body can only take so much. Please, Atticus, *help me.*"

He stared at Mason for a moment, something like compassion in his eyes, and yet behind them lay something dark in nature. It confused Mason, but his priorities were elsewhere. Atticus turned around. "Let's go."

Mason raised an eyebrow. "Go? Go where?"

"Back to ENDURE. There isn't time to waste if you fear your life may be at risk. We start here and now. I agree with your earlier sentiment; this needs to stay private. What happens from here on out stays between the two of us, and a select number of employees who absolutely must be involved moving forward. You cannot tell Kaylee or Lena. At least not until we know what we're dealing with here. Those are my terms if you want my aid in this matter."

Mason nodded. Truthfully, he didn't care what the terms were, as long as it resulted in at least some sort of relief. "Whatever it takes."

Atticus smiled. "Then welcome to ENDURE. We'll figure out what's wrong with you, I promise. If what you're saying is true, then who knows what we'll discover along the way. We're experiencing an unprecedented discovery in both the scientific and medical fields, charting unexplored terrain as it were. Hopefully, we'll find a way to cure you of these unfavorable side effects, and then maybe, with enough research and experimentation, we can reverse engineer this peculiar condition for our own purposes."

Our own purposes? Mason found his brother's choice of words unnerving, but his priorities lay with his own well-being, and so he brushed it off as paranoia. He was right to worry, however, because in Atticus's mind, the gears were turning. The things they could achieve if they had the foresight to witness events before they occurred... the disasters they could avoid... the potential of it all was limitless. If they could harness this strange new ability and use Mason's phenomenon as a tool for good, they could build a perfect world together. Atticus would let Mason believe that curing him was at the forefront of his efforts, but his ulterior motives were clear: if what Mason had told him was true, then Atticus would utilize his gift for the betterment of mankind. For that to be possible, he knew where he had to start: finding the cure for his cancer no matter the cost, even if it meant Mason's life.

CHAPTER 28

Echo

Time and location (present-day): 3:46 am,
ENDURE Center for Rehabilitation

"My reasons for helping my brother were somewhat selfish, I see that now. If only I had known... In the weeks that followed, I would come to find that there was a much more pressing reason for our need to understand Mason's affliction."

"What happened after you agreed to help him?" I ask, intent on learning as much as possible.

The doctor's description of Mason's illness sounds eerily familiar to my own, albeit dialed up to ten. Compared to Atticus's accounting of Mason's condition, my symptoms have been mild. I figure if Atticus is still willing to feed me answers, then I'm not going to quit prying. He leans forward, elbows resting on his knees as he continues addressing me. The doctor looks exhausted, if only from recounting these events.

Then we began to study his condition, compiling all the information we could regarding the symptoms Mason exhibited under our watch. I won't bore you with the details of the many hours poured into sleepless nights of research, but before long, we had cured cancer with the help of Mason's visions, and I was free to continue my studies. Just like that, this sequence of DNA that we discovered, which didn't belong; what you now know we would come to dub the "Deus Molecule," helped us cure a disease that had left scientists puzzled for centuries, and it helped us do so overnight. The more time that passed, though, the worse Mason's condition became and the more fragmented his visions were. He could see glimpses of events to come, but they weren't whole ideas at that point; they were more like puzzle pieces; if he couldn't find every single piece, the image they created would remain unseen. Mason's mind was becoming less reliable and deteriorating into pure insanity with every passing day. His body was not far behind that, and so we feared the worst. My team and I took drastic measures, which eventually led us to human experimentation."

"You mean on Mason, on Lena's father?" I glance over at Desmond, if only to observe his reaction. There is an eerie calmness in his eyes; it's as if he already knows all there is to know.

"Precisely so. What choice did we have? It was a simple decision, from a pragmatic point of view; do nothing and Mason dies, or experiment on a willing subject and he would at least have a *chance* at survival. We thought it best to attempt to learn something potentially unfathomable from his case while possibly saving his life, rather than allowing any knowledge we could gain from the matter to deteriorate along with him. What we found after weeks of experimentation yielded tremendous potential, until..."

"What? Until what?" I ask, urging Atticus to continue.

When Mason briefly mentioned hearing voices, I dismissed it as hallucinations, but those voices... they were so much more. As his illness progressed, these voices unified and became one; became Mallen."

My heart sinks as I realize I'm most likely destined for the same grim fate as Mason Cais, that I'm the next victim of Mallen's icy embrace.

"Did you miss me, Royce? Without those pesky little pills, you won't be able to fight me much longer."

I jump visibly as the voice booms from within, clear as day.

"You hear it now, don't you, Royce?" asks Atticus, noticing my discomfort. I lock eyes with him as the question falls from his mouth, giving no answer, but he continues anyway. "I know you do. Just like you know that it is no mere hallucination, nor a figment of your imagination. That voice in your head is as real as you are, as real as I am, just less... tangible."

My body trembles, adrenaline coursing through me as my brain struggles to choose between fight or flight. "Explain, tell me what he is. I need to know what Mallen is…" I say through shaky lips.

Atticus nods in compliance. "'The Boundless': that's how Mallen refers to his own kind. Lena told you a lot of what we already know, which unfortunately isn't much. From what we gathered during our experimentations with Mason, The Boundless are the original inhabitants of Earth. They're intelligent and powerful, but that is all we know for sure; everything else is just an observation. Trust me, I know how it sounds," says Atticus, as if listening to my thoughts. "Nevertheless, it's the truth. As I mentioned before, Elliot discovered the Deus Molecule in Mason's genetic code, and we then discovered it was present in a vast number of human beings. The difference was that in Mason, the gene was active, while in everyone else the gene remained dormant. It was the activation of this gene, of the Deus Molecule that enabled Lena's father to glimpse bits and pieces of events yet to come, and enabled him to communicate with The Boundless, with Mallen. Once we realized that fact, we began acquiring other carrier subjects of the dormant Deus Molecule, attempting to activate it and replicate Mason's condition."

Other carrier subjects… The thought sends a chill down my spine as I realize I likely fall into that category, along with every other patient in the facility.

"Now you're beginning to understand, Royce. You're Atticus' plaything... though you really should thank him; after all, you and I would never have been acquainted without his assistance."

I grit my teeth, ignoring the beast. "Why was the active Deus Molecule causing Mason so much pain? Why would you choose to put others through all of that?"

Atticus stands up from the chair and begins to pace in front of the desk. "The active Deus Molecule unlocks the fifty percent of the human brain that the average subject cannot access; however, there is a reason we aren't able to utilize our brains to their full potential. The human body cannot endure the increased brain activity; it shortens our lifespan by nearly sixty percent. The Deus Molecule gave Mason abilities unfathomable to most, but it was also killing him, deteriorating his body at an accelerated pace. Prior to Mason's expiration, though, he learned from Mallen that we were nearing an extinction-level event, the end of humanity. With Mason being the one and only person we knew for certain who could establish contact with these beings, we scrambled for a solution. We had to find other carriers and successfully activate the dormant Deus Molecule within them before Mason perished if we were to learn more, but every time we tried, the subjects weakened far quicker than Mason and eventually died. In desperation, we continued testing other subjects while also utilizing what resources we could to keep Mason alive until we could communicate through him with Mallen and find a way to prevent the coming apocalypse, until..." Atticus's voice trails off, and it doesn't take a genius to figure out why.

It was rare for me to witness the kind of fear I was seeing now in Atticus's eyes. I finish the thought for him. "Until you realized that The Boundless are the cause of our destruction, the harbingers of our death. Mallen wasn't warning Mason about our extinction; he was *basking* in its inevitability." Silence fills the room. I realize then that for once, Atticus and I feel the same: powerless. How can we hope to stop something we can't see? How are we meant to stave off a force of nature we can't even touch? Although Atticus is my captor, in this moment, he is as scared as I am. "So, Mason died, and you never found a solution. Your experiment failed, and you were unable to activate the gene in other carriers, such as myself. How does that lead us here? If you couldn't activate the dormant gene within us, why am I still here? Why are the others still here?" I point to my would-be ally, Desmond, as an example.

It isn't until the question in its entirety has left my mouth that the dawn of realization grips me. "Unless... you *did* find a way to activate it."

Atticus nods as a self-approving smile spreads across his face. "Our initial experimentation failed, yes, in that aspect you are correct. However, finding a cure for cancer and other terminal diseases was never at the forefront of ENDURE's motivations. It served as a facade for something else entirely. ENDURE isn't just a word, it's an acronym. It stands for Experimental Nuclei Divergence and Unification Research Endeavor. What we had truly been working on in secrecy all these years was a way to prolong human life by taking certain portions of a subject's DNA and piecing those bits together with the DNA of a younger, healthier host body. That was a goal that we had all but accomplished by the time Mason had come seeking my assistance, minus a few complications here and there."

I hold up a hand. "Wait a minute, stop; what do you mean 'host body'?"

Atticus sighs, exasperated. "It means exactly what you think it means. I told you already; you are not Royce Wilko, and the subject who was terminated moments ago in this very room was not Aiden Buckley. You were grown in a vial, then later in a tube, the walking embodiment of a dead man's memories. You're a clone, Royce, what we at ENDURE refer to as an Echo. Subject RW-117."

CHAPTER 29

Monoliths

Time and location (the past): 6:07 am,
ENDURE Black Site 7

Mason sat in a chair in a cold, dimly lit room made entirely of concrete. He had come to know this room well over the past three months. His wrists and ankles were bound by leather straps, securely locked in place. He was hungry and thirsty, but not for what one would expect. He craved peculiarities—things he should not: motor oil, sea water, sand.... most disturbingly, blood. His senses conjured their aromas, flooding his nose with tantalizing wafts of things he knew he shouldn't have an appetite for; but that awareness was tucked in the deepest recesses of his mind, where the last remnants of sanity resided, desperately trying to claw their way to the surface. His eyes darted back and forth until something caught his attention, lurking in a heavily shadowed corner of his enclosure. Mason's pupils dilated as he tried to focus on the silhouette, attempting to discern its true form to no avail. Suddenly, Mallen's deep, rumbling voice growled and echoed from the shadows, explosive in volume.

"Why did you leave her! The girl trusted you, loved you, and you abandoned her!"

"No... I didn't leave! I had to get... better," he whispered to his unwelcome company.

"Look at you... so willing to blatantly lie, futilely attempting to safeguard yourself from the truth. She was so young when you cast her aside, not to mention her mother."

Mason squinted his eyes shut with such force that he thought they might implode. "It's not real, it's just in my head... get out of my head... get out of my head!" He screamed in hopes of assistance but knew it was a lost cause. Behind their glowing white exterior, the concrete walls were twelve inches thick, soundproof by all notable accounts.

"Open your eyes Mason, open them to the truth of your reality. You left her all alone in this world, and because of you she will suffer the same fate as you. You've imprisoned her to a life that will never be her own, made her a slave to your mistakes, to Atticus' twisted science."

"She's not alone... she has her mother..." he grumbled, his voice straining against the agony; the misery evident in every spoken word.

"Maybe for now, but you've seen the events yet to unfold. Soon enough, she'll have no one left. No one to keep her safe, to tell her everything will be okay. When that day comes, the beast you call family will come for her, just as he came for you. The same monster who put you in that chair will so gently sit her down as well, and will tell her that everything will be just fine. Tell me, Mason; do you feel fine?"

He clenched his eyes shut more firmly than before—a feat he would've previously thought impossible. Silence followed, a moment of stillness in the eye of the storm, until he could feel heat on his neck, coming and going in steady breaths.

"OPEN YOUR EYES!"

Reluctantly, Mason's eyes snapped open, yielding to their true master. Though shaken, Mason nearly overlooked the woman standing before him, her appearance unfamiliar. She hunched over, resting her hands on her thighs as she smiled gently. "Well, don't you look worse for wear?" It was a bizarre statement, irrespective of his current circumstance.

"Who... who are you?" asked Mason, the confusion momentarily providing a brief reprieve from his breakdown.

"What? You don't recognize her, Mason? Are we so eager to forget? As if somehow that will wash away all the pain? All the regret?" Mallen's disembodied voice returned, coiling around him like a snake.

"I don't know her… get out of my head!" He pleaded again, his voice now coarse and gravelly from the aggression in his words.

"YOU KNOW HER! SAY HER NAME MASON!"

"Please… please go away…" Defeated, he now spoke in low, sobbing weeps.

"No, I won't let you off the hook that easily. Tell me her name. Speak her name, and I will leave; I want to hear you say it. I want to hear the pain and sorrow in your voice; I crave it, long for it."

Mason stared into the ivory floor, begging it to crack, to give way and allow him to fall into a bottomless pit beneath. There was no way out, and Mason couldn't bear it any longer. "Lena… her name is Lena." He lifted his head slowly, and when his gaze met Lena's, he wept. She slowly began to fade away into wisps of air without a word until nothing remained. If there was anything Mason could be thankful for, it was that at the very least, Mallen had kept its word; the voice had subsided, returning to its slumber within Mason's broken and tattered psyche. He had dealt with the omniscient machination of his mind on multiple occasions in the past, and each time it presented itself more violently and aggressively than the last. It quickly became evident that Mallen would never leave; it had set up camp and pitched its tent within the crevices of his brain, where it fully intended to live out the rest of its non-tangible life. Mason could never hope to rid himself of it, so he did his best to survive, to live with it constantly accentuating his worst fears.

The steel door at the far end of the room began to grind and whine as it slid open on its automated track, distracting Mason from his recently concluded psychotic episode. Once fully open, Atticus stepped through the threshold, and the gateway sealed behind him once more. He calmly made his way over to Mason. "Hello Mason, how are you feeling today?"

He panted, exhausted from his encounter with the darkness within him. "Atticus, please... please just end this, I'm begging you." His brother's expression told him all he needed to know; Atticus was never going to stop. He had discovered something through Mason's phenomenon, and the potential ramifications of halting the experiment now meant death and decay on too massive a scale for Atticus to give up without finding the answers he sought. Mason only wished he had kept his mouth shut and had never told Atticus of the horrors that Mallen had unveiled.

"Mason, you know we can't do that... this is bigger than you and me. Now please, we need to focus. We have an incomplete puzzle laid out before us and limited time to find the missing pieces. Let's go over what we know again, starting from the beginning."

Mason sighed and hung his head low, fighting back tears as they pushed forcefully behind his eyes, threatening to flow freely. "I... I remember seeing multiple large structures of some sort… like monoliths. Something about them was ominous; they radiated some form of strange energy, unique in nature to each individual tower. I saw visions of the Earth, and this… this cloud of mist eating away at it, draining the color from the grasslands and turning the oceans grey. I saw people *dying,* watched the life being sapped from them until nothing remained. I saw loved ones, *tearing each other apart,* like savages… So many emotions: sadness, anger, hatred, fear," Mason paused for a moment, seemingly lost in his own mind. Atticus noticed the mannerism immediately; there wouldn't be much time left to extract information from his brother before he lost the plot entirely.

Mason became animated once more, continuing his previously broken train of thought. "Mallen told me it was all caused by those monoliths. That they had arrived as an omen, a reckoning. They've come to wash away our sins, to cleanse this planet of disease, to cleanse it of us… They've been here all along; sleeping, dormant, lying in wait for many millennia, longer, even. They know all, see all… The Nine shall cull this planet of the human infection that has been left to fester upon its surface for far too long… The Nine… The Nine…The Nine… The Nine…" His rantings faded into oblivion, entangled in his own mind.

Atticus watched as his brother began to rock back and forth in his chair as much as the restraints would allow, uttering the same two words under his breath, "The Nine." He pondered who or what they could be, knowing that the chances of Mason answering this question were now slim to none. It didn't take a scientist to deduce that his younger brother had finally fallen off the deep end, and that these were now the ramblings of a madman. Atticus wasn't one to waste valuable resources and time on a lost cause.

No, their experiment had reached its end, and it was time for closure. He would give Mason until the end of the day and then grant him his final wish and end it all. Atticus had been wrestling with the idea for weeks, knowing full well that Mason could never return home again, at least not the real Mason. His Echo had already been generated in their lab, and with the amount of funding it took to create each carbon copy, there was no way in hell Atticus could justify not utilizing it to the brass.

True, he ran ENDURE, but everyone had someone to answer to, even him. It was genuinely the best and only option available to him; after all, the real Mason was hardly able to function properly, now in the final stages of his decline. It was in everyone's best interest to send his Echo home to Kaylee and Lena; they would have Mason back, happy and healthy, and none the wiser about the replacement of their loved one, and the real Mason wouldn't have to endure this condition any longer than necessary. Atticus waited for the episode to subside a moment longer but quickly realized that Mason wouldn't be returning to the realm of reality any time soon. He placed a hand on his brother's shoulder.

"Rest Mason, give your mind some time to relax. I'll see you soon." Atticus turned and headed for the sliding steel door as it screeched open, retreating into the wall. He stopped just outside the room, glancing back at Mason with pain in his eyes. Then, he walked away as the door slid shut, sealing away Atticus's most sinister demons in the ebony dark.

CHAPTER 30

Nine

Time and location (the past): 10:43 pm,
ENDURE Black Site 7

"The Nine... The Nine...The Nine..."

Atticus pinched the bridge of his nose in frustration as he sat in front of his sibling. Sixteen hours had passed since their last conversation, and Mason's condition had remained unchanged. He mumbled those two words repeatedly like a broken record. "Mason, who are The Nine you speak of? Please, listen to my voice, we need your help."

"Not who..."

Atticus nearly fell out of his chair as Mason finally spoke, causing a break in the repetition. He pounced on the opportunity like a cat seizing a mouse. "Then *what* are they?"

"The monoliths, nine in all. A sublunary equivalent to the circles of hell. There is more truth to myth than we like to believe; details may differ, but the subject remains mostly the same."

"What is it that you think these monoliths are capable of?"

Mason's eyes were wide, filled with terror and yet somehow ecstatic. "Aggression, terror, isolation… They amplify pain, feed off emotion. It's brilliant, really; the influence of The Nine will cause humanity to exterminate itself, it's hands-free genocide!" Mason cackled to himself, but the laughter sounded contorted and unnatural.

"By 'they', you mean these… monoliths; they are The Nine, correct?" Atticus asked, seeking absolute clarification.

"Yes… yes…" His brother was spiraling again, Atticus could tell. He needed more information on these monoliths and tried desperately to obtain the necessary details from Mason. "Good Mason, thank you. I have only a few questions left for you. There isn't any time to waste, so please, I beg of you; dig down deep, get a grip on your psyche. Where are these monoliths? How do we find them and destroy them?" Atticus stood from his chair and came closer, crouching down in front of his brother so their eyes met. "Mason, please. I know you're in there."

With his head hung low and fingers twitching slightly, Mason began to laugh once more. It was a low, foreboding, and guttural sound. He slowly lifted his head, staring straight back at Atticus with more clarity than he had shown in weeks. "He's told you all I will allow. Know this, doctor: The Nine are coming, and they will offer no forgiveness, no reprieve. Humanity is a blight on this world, an inferior infestation, undeserving of a place to call home. When the culling is complete, this decaying sphere will grow and thrive once more. Your species had its chance and squandered it. This is your eviction notice, Atticus. You, and the rest of your vermin ilk, would be wise to find a new home before it is too late."

Atticus' face was stone, vacant of any emotion, but he was covered in a cold sweat. Whoever or whatever was speaking to him now was not Mason. "What are you?"

"I am beyond your comprehension. Your kind has abused the blessings of life and wasted the benefits it so willingly provides. We will tolerate this no longer. Be seeing you soon, doctor." Mason's head suddenly dropped as he fainted, possessed one moment and nearly dead the next.

"I'm sure you will," Atticus sighed, uncertain if whatever he had been speaking to could still hear him. This interaction proved that Atticus had made the right call; he would return in a few hours and put a bullet in Mason's head. Whatever this thing inside him was, Atticus wasn't about to let it take his soul. Before doing so, he needed to speak with Elliot. He left Mason, slack-jawed and secured to his seat, and headed for the bioengineering lab. Hopefully, his protégé would have an update on the status of the Echo project. Kaylee would be expecting her husband home tomorrow.

After the first month and a half of their research, it became increasingly difficult to find reasons for why the two of them would be gone for most of the day, every day. So, Atticus changed his mind, and together, he and Mason told both Kaylee and Lena what they had been up to. It was a hard sell at first, but Mason convinced his wife and daughter of his strange new reality the same way he had convinced Atticus. It was hard to argue with a man who could successfully predict the future. They knew that Atticus was desperately trying to cure Mason's strange affliction, but the extent to which Atticus was willing to involve them ended there.

To Atticus's knowledge, the Echo project was on track and nearing completion. All that was left to do now was to field test it before sending it out into the world. Somewhere deep down inside himself, Atticus felt a pang of guilt; he was mere hours away from murdering his brother, and yet the sorrow that should have washed over him was all but absent. He knew that he had to stay focused. If what he had been told ever came to pass, grieving over his loss would only delay the discovery of an opportunity for survival. Atticus also knew that if he couldn't stop whatever this was, he would have far more losses on his hands than just Mason. He had done all he could for his brother, and in the end, it would be more a mercy to take his life than to allow that thing dwelling within him to gain full control. He would make this right; he would find a way. The only thing that truly frightened Atticus was the lengths he was willing to go...

Atticus entered the bioengineering lab and was greeted immediately by Elliot Shaw, who had been waiting for his arrival. They shook hands, and then Elliot motioned him over to a large table. Sitting atop its metal platform inside an artificial womb was the Echo that would serve as Mason's replacement. The womb was a thick plastic containment sheath, filled with a liquid nutrient supplement that supported the healthy growth of each clone. Its appearance resembled that of a shark egg, semi-opaque and leathery. To the untrained eye, it might seem strange to see something so human-like packaged in a vacuum-sealed bag like a slab of meat you'd find at the market, but Atticus had gotten past the odd nature of what they were creating here a long time ago. A tube fed through the surface of the package and connected to a breathing apparatus secured to the Echo's face, providing just enough oxygen to keep it functioning and alive while suspended in REM sleep.

Elliot motioned to the bagged clone. "I pulled it out of cryostasis eight hours ago. Are you ready to wake it, sir?" asked Elliot in a tone that was all business. He was a practical man who remained professional even while making history.

Atticus nodded, and Elliot began the process. He flipped a switch connected to a built-in control panel on the face of the table, and a secondary tube toward the foot of the sheath began to suck the nutrient supplement out and into a biohazardous waste containment unit. Once this was done, he unsealed the bag and increased the oxygen levels being pumped into the Echo's mask. Atticus stared at the naked, slime-covered body curled up as if it were a child in a fetal position. Mason's memories had been implanted during the clone's transfer from the test tube it began life in to the portable sheath it now called home. If everything worked properly, it would wake in a state of delirium, but it would identify as Mason Cais instantly, never knowing its true nature. Once Atticus could confirm that Mason's Echo truly saw itself as its DNA donor, they would place him under anesthesia, wipe this interaction from the implanted memory chip, and reawaken it in a more controlled and stabilized setting. The clone would open its eyes believing it was Mason Cais himself, and that he had simply dozed off during an outing with his brother Atticus.

Its eyes flickered to life, and Atticus couldn't help but smile. Turning to Elliot, he saw the same astonished look upon his face—a sight just as rare. He reached out and squeezed his subordinate's shoulder endearingly. "We've done it Elliot, we've really done it."

The Echo began to shift in its bag slowly, attempting to produce words with its quivering lips. "Wha...where..."

"Shhhhhh," Atticus spoke softly, leaning down towards the new and improved Mason. "There's no need to worry, you're in safe hands. Can you tell me just one thing? What is your name?"

The Echo reached toward its face, gently wiping the sleep from its eyes, then looked at Atticus with familiarity. "What do you mean? It's me, Atticus... it's Mason..."

He smiled once more. "Of course, my apologies brother." Atticus stood upright and beckoned Elliot away from the table, speaking in a hushed tone. "He's still delirious, place him under anesthesia before he comes around fully. There's much work yet to be done."

CHAPTER 31

Existential

Time and location (present-day): 4:02 am,
ENDURE Center for Rehabilitation

Silence falls all around as we sit in what had once been Aiden Buckley's quarters—or so I had thought. If Atticus is to be believed, then I had never truly known Aiden Buckley; rather, an "Echo" that had assumed his identity. About halfway through the doctor's story, I begin to wonder if it's all an elaborate lie, another mind game. I look at Desmond, whose face is a portrait of contrition; not a single visible emotion in his eyes as they bore into the floor beneath his feet. If any part of Atticus's story consists of truth, it's that he killed Lena's father; that much I know to be true. I silently swear that I will make Atticus pay, and discern an ever-increasing feeling of contempt that dictates his time of reckoning will come sooner rather than later; whether that contempt is mine or Mallen's remains to be seen.

"That just about covers it all, Royce. I've told you the truth and nothing but. How you decide to proceed from here on out is your choice entirely."

I turn my attention to the doctor and away from my murderous thoughts. "You haven't told me everything."

Atticus furrows his brow. "No? What have I left out then?"

"The monoliths. Your story makes it seem as if you weren't buying everything Mason had said to you, at least not until your conversation with Mallen. So, was he speaking the truth? Or was it more psychotic ramblings?"

Atticus stares at me stiffly, his muscles tense and his demeanor hesitant as if he is weighing his options. "The first monolith appeared near McMurdo Station on Ross Island in Antarctica about a year ago. The second, nearly six months ago in Nairobi, Africa. So far, these are the only two that have made themselves known to us, but we suspect a third will appear soon enough."

I shake my head. "I'm not buying any of it. I mean, come on; who would? Only someone who was truly insane would believe a story like that. Or maybe..."

Atticus raises his brow once more as I muse. "Maybe... this is all a test. Maybe you want to see how willing I am to accept this nonsense without any proof. Maybe you're just trying to reassess my mental health."

The doctor lets out a heavy sigh as he detaches himself from the wall he's been leaning against. He makes his way toward the room's door, and Desmond, who has remained frozen throughout the entire conversation until now, steps forward. "Atticus, don't. I'm begging you."

He turns his attention to the man I know as Desmond, the man who, if Atticus is to be believed, could be an experiment pulled from the pages of a sci-fi novel just as he claims I am. "I wish I didn't have to go to such extreme lengths Desmond, I truly do. However, RW-117's continued attempts to interfere with the work being done here have become… meddlesome to say the least. I could only use you to divert his attention and steer him in the wrong direction for so long. The time for misdirection passed after that little break in you encouraged. Imagine what would have happened had you not been able to retrieve this and deliver it safely to me, Desmond," Atticus says, pulling the flash drive with all the evidence we need to put ENDURE in the ground from his coat pocket. He waves it around like some sort of trinket won at a fair. So, it is true; Desmond has been a traitor the entire time. "This is now, unfortunately, what needs to be done, Desmond. It's either this, or his termination," the doctor finishes and points directly at me.

Termination? Is this bastard contemplating my death right in front of me? Unbelievable. I want to intervene, but Desmond continues before I can get a word in. "If you do this, there is no going back. God only knows what Mallen can make Royce do under enough duress. Please, *do not* do this."

"I'm sorry, I am…" Atticus sighs, then nods to Oakley and Shaw, who subsequently leave the room.

Then, Desmond looks at me with the slightest hint of tears in his eyes. "I'm sorry, Royce, I want you to know that. Believe me when I say that I was left in the dark just as much as you were up until recently. They… they have my *son*, Royce. Told me they would kill him if I didn't cooperate, and Nora… God only knows if she's still alive, it's been *so long*… I didn't… I couldn't have known the heinous shit they were doing behind closed doors. Please… forgive me when all this is over." The tone and fluctuation in his voice strikes a nerve, and I suddenly find myself fearful and vulnerable, but there's no time to digest what is happening, and no time to prepare for what's on the other side of that door.

It opens wide, and through its threshold come Shaw and Oakley with a new visitor. They lead in the newcomer, whose hands are cuffed behind their back, their face covered with a black cloth bag. This prisoner wears the same jumpsuit all patients at the facility wear, though theirs seems dull and aged. After they enter, two more men follow suit. Equally notable and jarring are these men's uniforms. They are dressed head to toe in military garb, complete with armor, like the suit Shaw had worn when he dragged me to Atticus' office a few days prior. Their faces are covered with balaclavas and their heads protected by helmets. What shocks me the most, though, is that they are armed with assault rifles, held at the ready, and sidearms holstered and strapped to their thighs. I look to Shaw, who makes eye contact but then quickly averts his gaze. If I didn't know better, he looks almost ashamed of himself.

Atticus approaches the prisoner and stops to stand beside them. "It's time now, for you to understand. This will be my final attempt to convince you to see eye to eye with me, to realize just how important your cooperation in this matter is. I've been honest with you since we've entered this room. What is about to happen will prove that, irrefutably. As I told you, you are subject RW-117, our newest and most promising Echo of Royce Wilko to date. The clone beside me now is subject RW-116, the Echo who came immediately before you. He had shown much promise, but unfortunately descended into psychosis like Mason, Jonathan, Royce, and all their successive variants. Instead of exterminating this Echo, as is standard procedure when they are no longer of use, we put him in cryostasis in hopes that we could revisit and correct his defects later. Now that we have you, however, there is no further need for RW-116."

Atticus turns to Shaw, who meets his gaze and nods in response. Shaw grabs the bag that conceals the prisoner's identity, pulls it up and off his head, and then I feel my blood run cold. Pins and needles prickle my skin as I experience a numbing sensation throughout my body. Standing before me, with tears staining his cheeks and pleas for help muffled by a gag, is *Royce*.

A picturesque, breathing reflection stares back at me with as much confusion in his eyes as I feel in my mind. A cold sweat begins to seep from my pores as my doppelganger's breathing escalates into hyperventilation.

Then, in one fluid motion, Oakley removes his sidearm, points it at RW-116's temple, and pulls the trigger. The clone falls to the floor, limp. Somewhere along the line, I unconsciously feel the warmth of blood splatter against my face, but I'm too shocked to care. Paralysis takes control of my entire body as an existential crisis grips every fiber of my being. All I can do is stare helplessly at the bullet hole in RW-116's head as it oozes a deep auburn, the bullet hole in *Royce's* head, in *my* head.

CHAPTER 32

Dominic

Time and location (present-day): 4:23 am,
ENDURE Center for Rehabilitation

"So, you see, RW-117, I have not lied to you in this instance. You are a clone, as is the Echo lying at your feet, and as are many of the other patients you see here within the facility. We began recruiting people for this experiment years ago. People who came as willing participants to our cause, but as time progressed and the situation regarding the monoliths and the Boundless worsened, we began to take a more unorthodox approach to finding candidates for our program. We learned how to test for the Deus Molecule and began studying people from afar whom we had confirmed carried it within their DNA."

Atticus pauses, a flicker of shame crossing his face before he continues. "When that stopped being a successful tactic, I turned to those in my personal life and began secretly collecting DNA samples from them for testing, which led me to Royce Wilko.

We watched him for months before deciding to take him on as a subject. Lena being married and in love with him understandably created hurdles for us to overcome. So, on one fateful day, with the help of Jordan and Elliot," he says, gesturing to his two lackeys, "we followed Royce as he left a barbecue at my home with his family. Lena had gone with her mother and Mason to a scheduled appointment at one of our facilities, creating the perfect opportunity for us. Jordan and Elliot ran the Wilko's off the road, disposed of the rest of the family, and abducted Royce. Was it immoral of us? Certainly, but it was a necessary evil because, from Royce's sacrifice, we received you, subject RW-117. And you... you just might be the key to saving us all. Would you not sacrifice the few to save the many? To preserve our species' existence?"

I don't respond, can't find the words. I don't know what to think, what to feel, what to *do*. I had tried so hard to pull back the curtain on Atticus's secrets that I never once stopped to consider whether I really *wanted* to know them or not. Now, the answer to that question is infallibly no. We sit in silence for a while, clinging to Atticus's last words; Desmond near the desk, turned away and unwilling to look at the horrific scene before him, rife with guilt. Atticus, staring intently at me, begs with his eyes for confirmation of an alliance and loyalty to his cause. Oakley and Shaw are near the door, along with the two nameless soldiers. Their emotions undetectable behind their facemasks, the doctor's ever-watchful gargoyles; and at the center of the chaos is me, staring down at the corpse at my feet with whom I once shared memories, feelings, and thoughts. The river of blood continues to pool profusely around the young man who, at one point in time, had been known, similarly to me, as Royce Wilko.

A sudden movement from Atticus finally disrupts the quiet yet misplaced peace surrounding the scenario as he approaches me. He places a hand on my shoulder, and to my surprise, I allow it, instead of flinching away from his vile touch.

"I can see that this has all been quite the disturbing and perplexing experience for you. You know what you are now, but that in and of itself can be a bit confusing. Come with me, and I will explain things in a way that is easier to understand, and then we will discuss the impact you could have on the future of humankind."

I don't move a muscle willingly, but when I find myself being escorted from the room by Shaw, I don't resist either. Receding into myself, I disappear into my mind where I can process everything safely and securely—or at least as safely as Mallen will allow. For once, I find myself begging for his incessant chatter to help me think of anything other than what I had just seen, but he's been eerily quiet throughout the ordeal. My body is nothing more than a means of transportation for the time being, for both Mallen and me alike.

As Shaw opens the door to escort me out, Atticus nods to Oakley and the other two guards. "Jordan, grab Desmond and bring him along as well. The five of us can all chat in my office now that we have a mutual understanding. It will be a far less upsetting environment for RW-117 to consider his options." Atticus turns to his remaining two cohorts. "You two, get this mess cleaned up and dispose of RW-116's body."

The two nameless men nod and spare no time between receiving their orders and carrying them out. Shaw and I continue out of the room and down the hall as Oakley follows with Desmond beside him, and Atticus at the rear. As we walk, I think about Aiden. Have I become so distracted by Atticus' song and dance that I've forgotten what drew me to that room in the first place? Aiden was dead, that was clear. Why Atticus ordered his death, however, remains a mystery. It doesn't matter anyhow; the real Aiden Buckley had died a long time ago, just as Royce Wilko had.

The Aiden I had known was nothing more than a carbon copy, like me... but I still *feel*. I think freely and experience life the same as every other human, if I can call myself that... How then, am I to discern how *real* I and the other Echoes truly are? This level of confusion is a sensation I have never known. Trying to reconcile that the memories I have of my past are those of a dead man, that they're something I haven't truly lived is frying my brain on a molecular level.

Then there's Lena. She has known all along that I'm not the real Royce Wilko, not *her* Royce... but she and I still share the same connection. I love her just as Royce always loved her, and she clearly feels the same way. For the briefest of moments, the thought of her envelops my senses, and all I can do is hope for her safety, hope that Atticus's cruelty doesn't extend even farther than I imagine. I feel myself beginning to resurface slightly, and then I think of Desmond's treachery. It ignites a fire within me, and for the first time since leaving my quarters in a desperate yet futile attempt to save a life, I address him. "Your son, what was his name?"

I hear a sharp inhale of surprise from behind me as Shaw tightens his grip on my forearm. Hesitantly, Desmond replies, "Dominic. The last time I saw him, I wasn't even sure he was alive... that was so long ago..."I nodded, more so to myself than anyone else, knowing Desmond couldn't see the gesture.

"You stabbed me in the back, Desmond."

"Royce, man... you have to—"

"I would've done the same thing. I don't know what it's like to be a parent, but I know that if it were Lena, I would've made the same choice. I forgive you."

I hear him stifle a sob from behind. "Thank you," is all he can muster.

We round the corner that leads us to the hall leading to Atticus' office. "How do you know though? If you are ever reunited with your son, how will you know that Dominic isn't an Echo like you and me? You said when you saw him last that you weren't even sure he was alive. Do you really think you can trust the word of that *snake* behind you?"

If Atticus hears me, he doesn't bother to make a retort.

"I guess I wouldn't... and it wouldn't matter. Whether I'm Desmond Luther or not, I feel like him. I think like him, act like him... even if Dominic is like us, Royce, he wouldn't be any less human than the original." Desmond's words are the inspiration I need, just as my forgiveness has been his absolution; as far as Desmond is concerned, I *am* Royce Wilko.

If he feels this way, and Lena does too, then there's still hope that I'm more than Atticus' plaything, that I'm real. "What about you, Shaw? Oakley? How do you know Atticus didn't grow you two goons in vials as well?" I ask, feeling reinvigorated and a bit more like myself again.

"There isn't any reason for him to clone us; we don't carry the Deus Molecule in our DNA," Shaw says matter-of-factly.

"That is correct," Atticus confirms from the back of the group, not bothering to lower his voice.

I wonder why none of the other patients have left their quarters to see what all the commotion is about. "Why aren't you being quiet? Aren't you worried others will hear and ask questions?" I say over my shoulder.

The facility is currently in lockdown, which changes nothing noticeably. This is different from the code red you experienced when your late friend Aiden last attempted to escape. Those codes are used to initiate a publicly announced security exercise, one that is known to patients and staff alike. A lockdown is used only among ENDURE staff to maintain silence in the facility and ensure that nothing, particularly gunfire, can be heard by those not directly involved in whatever incident might be occurring. When Jordan shot subject RW-116 moments ago, no one outside of that room heard a sound. It's an effective method of addressing any unexpected mess, as long as no one is outside of their quarters during the incident. In those scenarios, it's much more difficult to manage things, since we then must adhere to the rules of our own charade. Once lockdown is initiated, the walls are instantaneously soundproofed via nanotechnology embedded directly into every inch of this building. This facility is truly magnificent, but I digress."

Atticus speaks to me as he would to a colleague, and it makes me sick to my stomach. "Where do we go from here, Atticus? I still don't trust you."

He chuckles to himself, once again seeming exasperated by me. "You don't have to trust me, RW-117, you simply have to help me prevent the annihilation of my species."

"Quit calling me that," I snap back, "... and it's *our* species."

I can sense the lack of resolve in his response. "Very well...
Royce."

The five of us come to a stop outside Atticus's office door. The
doctor shuffles past us to the front of the group, then sweeps an
arm wide in welcome as he opens the door before us. "We can
discuss this further in my office, after you."

It's a veiled command rather than an invitation. Shaw prods
me between the shoulder blades, and I stumble forward through
the threshold. I let out a fatigue-heavy sigh; it's going to be a long
morning.

CHAPTER 33

Subterfuge

*Time and location (present-day): 4:31 am,
ENDURE Secure Sublevel*

"I know you have no reason to trust me."

Lena says, handing the prisoner a key fob and cellphone. He looks disheveled; his hair is greasy and unwashed, his face is bruised with many abrasions covering it, but the worst of all are the multiple fingernails that have been ripped off, no doubt due to Oakley's interrogative persuasion methods. She tries to stay on task and look past it all.

"Unfortunately, there isn't enough time to convince you, so you'll just have to try your hardest. That fob there will unlock the electro-magnetic restraints around your wrists and ankles. The cellular device has only one phone number programmed into it that goes to my secure line. Late tonight or early tomorrow morning, Jordan Oakley will be here to execute you. I need you to steal his keycard and get him to tell you all his access codes, write them down in the phone's notepad. Can you do that?"

The man nods but does not make eye contact. It's affirmative enough for Lena, though, so she continues. "Good. They're planning on putting Royce on ice if they can't convince him to cooperate, and if I know Royce, and I do, there's no way they'll be able to. So, it's imperative you find out exactly where they're keeping him once they take him. Use whatever means necessary to get this information. If you must kill Jordan… Well, let's just say the world wouldn't be worse off with one less revolting excuse for a human being such as himself. Just ensure that if you do, you hide the body well. The longer it takes to find him, the longer your cover stays intact."

One eyebrow raised, the captive replies, half intrigued and half skeptical. "And once I do all this? Then what?"

Lena points to the phone. "Find a way out of the facility and use that to call me. Jordan has the utmost clearance; once you have his access codes and keycard, there isn't an inch of this facility you won't be able to access. It's important that you focus on getting the hell out of here, though; that needs to be priority number one. We *will* come back for the others, but I need you to get that card and access codes to me first. Do you understand?"

The man gives Lena a bewildered look that enrages her. She adds more fury to her voice before repeating herself. "I said… *do you understand?*"

He hesitates a moment longer before sighing and responding. "Yeah, I got it. Just know that if you're yanking my chain, I'll be sure to repay the favor tenfold."

She nods. "I know everything there is to know about you, which means I also know that you stand by your word. I promise you; I am trying to help. I'll see Atticus and this company burn to the ground if it's the last thing I do. When we first started all this, I believed in my uncle's vision… I should've known better. It was foolish of me, and I don't know how I'll ever forgive myself for following in his footsteps for as long as I have, but I will do so no longer. I'm counting on you; Royce and the others will be as well."

He turns the fob over in the palm of his hand. "You know, I never would have taken subterfuge to be your style; it looks good on you. Go on, get out of here. I'll take care of the rest. Besides, Oakley and I have history, and a lot of unfinished business. I've wanted to ring Oakley's scrawny little neck for as long as I can remember. "Make sure you leave Atticus a letter of resignation on your way out," the man chides.

Lena produces a small and unique laugh. "My exit and subsequent return won't be formal enough for any of that. I'll see you on the other side."

He nods to her, and she turns around to leave. When she reaches the door to his cell, she stops. "Oh, and Matias?"

He glances up from the fob and meets her gaze, waiting for her to follow up.

"Good luck."

CHAPTER 34

Dominion

Time and location (present-day): 5:03 am,
ENDURE Center for Rehabilitation

Desmond and I sit beside each other, a joint force once more; all that remains of our band of would-be heroes. Aiden is dead, and for all we know, so is Matias. Shaw and Oakley stand at attention on either side of the office door, while Atticus waits for our inquiries from across his desk. He has been uncharacteristically forthcoming with information. Although I still don't trust the man, I'm beginning to understand his perspective, which is a far cry from agreeing with it. Desmond has been fixated on the incident involving my predecessor Echo for the past fifteen minutes, and Atticus is losing his patience regarding the matter.

"Desmond, it had to be done. Royce had to know the risks involved in hindering our work here, and he had to know that we were no longer hiding the truth. You know as well as I do that without him, humanity will fall. We are already standing on the brink of extinction; our very existence is dangling on the precipice of death."

"So, you murder the previous Echo from his cycle *right in front of him?* That doesn't seem just a *bit* extreme?" Desmond talks to Atticus as if he were a disgruntled employee. I have to remind myself that, in a sense, that's exactly what he has been. Both men have lied to me; the difference is that one of them was forced to, while the other has a soul.

"One might argue that eliminating Aiden's Echo in a show of force was an overreaction as well, but whatever gets results the quickest will always be my first choice. Time is of the essence, now more than it ever has been before. If I had known that you would grow so attached to it, I would have never embedded you as a patient. Maybe this was a job better suited for Elliot or Jordan; both can set aside emotions and make logic-based decisions."

I have never felt so insulted in such a brief time. Atticus just referred to me as an 'it' in the same breath that he admitted to ordering Aiden's death during what had essentially been a temper tantrum.

Apparently, Desmond shares my distaste for the comments, as he now turns on the doctor, his cheeks flushed red with heat. "*It?* Listen to yourself, damn it! We are *humans,* people! Born in a different manner, but human nonetheless. You treat us as if we're monsters and you're Dr. Frankenstein. We *feel,* we think, we live and breathe, the same as you do! You took your brother's life after he came to you for help, trusting you to fix him. You *murdered* Royce Wilko's family in cold blood as nothing more than a means to an end. You've killed *children.* Had I known *any* bit of that from the beginning, I would've killed you myself long ago to spare the world from the evil you've become. Tell me, at what point during all of this did you lose sight of your own humanity?"

Desmond stares at him bluntly after finishing his tirade. He surveys his surroundings as if he hasn't realized he stood up from his chair during his verbal assault.

If he has been trying to insult Atticus, seeking to elicit an emotional response from him, then he has succeeded. "I acted in self-defense when I killed Mason! He left me no choice! There was nothing left of my sibling when he died! That *thing* had taken control and would've stopped at nothing to butcher us all! As for Royce's family, this is the preamble to *war,* and in war there are *casualties.*"

Desmond rolls his eyes as if Atticus cannot see what's right in front of him. "It would've stopped at nothing, and so you played right into its hands and killed your brother. Then you continued killing others in the name of your research. You did *exactly* what it wanted. Mallen *played you* like a God damn fiddle."

Silence fills the air between the two of them as I take everything in. It's a rare sight to see, but I can tell Atticus knows Desmond is right; the Boundless has a singular goal: to turn humanity against itself, effectively wiping out our species without lifting a single finger. From what we know, they aim to do so via the monoliths, which are essentially biological weapons. Mallen, however, has merely manipulated Atticus into killing his own kind. The man has poured so many years of research and experimentation into figuring out what the Deus Molecule is, how it works, and what effects it has on its subjects, and yet through it all, he's learned close to nothing regarding Mallen and the Boundless. Everything about this enemy remains shrouded in a haze of mystery. Atticus has come no closer to figuring out who or what they are, but the monoliths are another story. At least half the picture is painted when it comes to 'The Nine', but I know the doctor well enough to understand that Atticus won't be content until he solves every piece of the puzzle.

"There's a puzzle of your own that needs solving too, isn't there, Royce?"

I'm careful not to acknowledge Mallen's arrival. Desmond and Atticus continue their argument, and luckily, they're paying little to no attention to me. I can't speak to Mallen, but then contemplation inspires a new idea: If he can speak within my mind, then maybe I can respond in a similar manner. So, I think; not to myself, but rather *at* Mallen.

"What do you mean? What puzzle?" I say, receiving no response.

For a moment, it seems the notion has failed, but then suddenly Mallen's voice rings out in my head crystal clear. "Royce knew Atticus Cais far before all of this... which means YOU know Atticus Cais. He was never an ally, never someone you held in high regard. Think, Royce... think back to those little family get-togethers, think back to what he did, and WHY you despise him so. Remember what he tried to do to your darling wife, Lena. He's a monster of the foulest breed, Royce; remember... REMEMBER!"

And then, I do. As if Mallen's command has opened a vault locked long ago, Royce's memories flood my brain, melding and fusing with my own, *becoming* my own. I remember my family. My father Charles, stoic and admirable. My mother Olivia, caring and tender. Rory... my younger sister; she had been my whole world... it's as if I'm watching my entire life flash across my mind's eye in an instant. The barbecues, the life Lena and I had built together, vividly hanging behind my eyes in multiple mental images like photos. I remember how we met in college, how her mother Kaylee used to squeeze the air from my lungs every time we embraced after long absences from one another. How Mason had warned me at the last family get-together that Atticus had plans that involved me. Then, I remember what he had tried to do to Lena, all those years ago, and Mallen's rage fills my body. I'm aware now that everyone in the room has noticed the change in my demeanor, noticed that part of *me* is missing. Shaw attempts to raise his sidearm slowly, but I spot him instantly. Whatever he sees in my eyes deters him, and he holsters his weapon.

Atticus attempts to calm me. "RW... Royce, I can see that Mallen is trying to gain control. Normally, this would be a great opportunity to gather data, but right now, I need you to do your best to stave it off. You and I can come to an agreement, find a way to work together to rid you of that monster inside you, and then rid our world of whatever plague it plans to unleash upon it. You just need to stay in control, Royce."

I'm standing now, but I do not recall leaving my chair. I place a hand to my forehead and dig my fingers into the skin. Pain pulses at my temple, increasing in frequency with every passing second. "I remember, Atticus..." I mumble through gritted teeth.

"Remember? What do you remember, Royce?" the doctor asks.

The agony is becoming unbearably intense so rapidly that I fall to my knees, both hands clutching my skull. I try to respond, but the words escape me.

"Royce, what do you remember?" the doctor repeats.

"I remember... I remember EVERYTHING!!!" I lash out at the desk, and the solid mahogany furniture flies toward Atticus, pinning him to the bookshelf at the back of the office. The doctor lets out an audible cry as Oakley and Shaw spring into action, but I'm witnessing this from somewhere else. It feels as if I have been afloat in the middle of an ocean, and now, *now*

I'm sinking. Struggling for air as I claw fruitlessly against the current. I can see what is happening up above the surface, but the ferociously undulating waves blur and confuse my surroundings. I can't remember the last time I took my medication… then, the realization that this has been Mallen's play all along strikes me; he had intentionally been reticent so that in the chaos I would forget about his presence within. Biding his time, he waited for the perfect moment to strike. Mallen has done it; my mind, my body… they're his dominion now.

"SUBDUE HIM!" I hear Atticus shout, but it's a deadened and distant sound, obscured by the bedlam I'm drowning in. I catch a glimpse of Oakley, my hands around his throat, the whites of his eyes reddening as the crushing force of my hold ruptures the finer vessels in them. As usual, he's smiling as if fueled by the chaos. The scene before me fades to black as I drift in and out of consciousness. When I next manage to break free from Mallen's hold, I see Desmond on the floor, his right eye swollen and bloodied.

"Don't hurt him… please…" I think weakly.

"Can't you see, Royce? This is it. The beginning of the end."

I stop fighting. Whether by choice or weariness, I can't determine. As I cling to what little consciousness I have, I feel a slight prick on my neck. Soon thereafter, I find myself adrift in a ruinous and never-ending void. Its pitch-black immensity is all-encompassing. I find comfort there. Suddenly, it's clear that this is where Mallen has always beckoned me to, the pocket of the universe he has been content to stuff me in. It feels familiar, feels like...

"Home... welcome home, Royce."

Kindling

*Time and location (present-day): 5:29 am,
ENDURE Secure Sublevel*

After Lena left him, Matias waited patiently for his captor to arrive. It was a strange thing: the tranquility a man experienced after committing to killing another. When Oakley did show his face, Matias would do what Lena had asked of him, and then he would ensure that the bastard would never torture anyone else again.

During the time they had held Matias here, Jordan Oakley had been his keeper. Although his military experience fortified him against many tactics, Oakley's methods had been especially... deranged. He had removed many of Matias' fingernails in their entirety, shoved needles into his body down to their ends, even strung Matias up by his ankles after sedating him and left him hanging like that for days. The worst of it, though, had been the shock therapy treatment he received two days ago; it lasted for three hours, on and off.

All of this was done in the name of retrieving information—information that Matias did not have; but Oakley already knew that. This torture had been nothing more than an excuse to exercise his sadistic nature, the same nature Matias had seen hints of all those years prior in Iraq. Matias had killed many times before in his past, but he never enjoyed it; he never felt the rush of adrenaline that he imagined Oakley experienced with every death. This, though, he would relish until his own dying breath.

Shaw is another matter entirely; he and Oakley working together doesn't make any sense. Matias would get an explanation from him if they ever came face-to-face again; he swore it. As if beckoned telepathically, the lock on the cell door chimed excitedly, opening to reveal the silhouette of none other than Jordan Oakley. "Morning Matias, did ya miss me?"

"Immensely," he snarls back. Matias feels ravenous, his most basic animal instincts begging to take over... but every predator knows to wait for the right moment before attacking its prey, and he'll do the same.

Oakley enters the room and shuts the door behind him. "I've got some bad news for you today, pal. You know your buddy, Aiden?"

Matias meets his gaze. "What about him?" he asks measuredly, revealing no hint of distress.

"Well, he bit the dust a couple of hours back, I pulled the trigger myself. His brains painted the floor a lovely shade of red."

Matias begins to seethe with anger, trying to keep himself in check. "You're lying..."

Oakley pulls a phone from his pocket, approaches him, and turns the screen toward Matias. "No, not at all. See for yourself, the security feed recorded it all in glorious detail."

Matias watches the video as it shows Oakley cock his weapon, place its muzzle against Aiden's temple, and pull the trigger. He looks away and mumbles under his breath.

Oakley leans in closer, holding his hand up to his ear. "What was that? I didn't quite hear you, friend."

Matias looks up once more, staring straight at him. "I said I'm gonna *fucking* kill you," and then he spits in Oakley's face.

The man retreats, taken aback by the assault. As he wipes the saliva and mucus from his cheek, Oakley begins to laugh. "I guess I should've expected that... Anyway, that isn't the *only* bad news I have for you today. Don't you want to know why I'm here? Aside from informing you of dear old Aiden's untimely passing?"

Matias wants to close the gap between them and rip the psychopath's carotid artery out with his bare teeth, but he has to get this right, has to make sure he's able to finish the job. "Go to hell Oakley."

His enemy smiles menacingly. "Not before you, Matias; and I'm here to deliver you to the devil myself. Let's go for a little walk."

Oakley pulls a syringe from his pocket and approaches Matias. Attacking now hadn't been his plan, but he can't risk being sedated. So, Matias waits for Oakley to get close enough, then presses the button on the fob. There's an audible 'clink,' and the anklets and cuffs restraining him fall to the floor, just as Lena had promised.

They both freeze for a moment, equally surprised, and then Matias charges, throwing all his weight into Oakley as the syringe flies from his hand. They hit the ground with a smack, and a tussle ensues, but this is no fair fight; with Matias now free from his shackles, Oakley doesn't stand a chance. He reaches for his sidearm as soon as he can, but finds it isn't in his holster. Matias had gotten to it quicker and skidded it across the floor.

Oakley tries his best to keep the hulking mass of muscle that is Matias Castellón from gaining the advantage, but it isn't long before he finds himself pinned beneath the giant, receiving blow after blow to the face. Matias hammers away, punch after punch, until he feels the fight drain from Oakley's body. When Oakley finally goes limp, Matias lifts himself up and off the battered lunatic. He looks around the room to locate the sidearm and sedative without securing Oakley; he won't be going anywhere quickly. He finds the items and retrieves both.

The syringe remains capped through the ordeal, and Matias tucks it away for potential use later. He checks that the weapon Oakley has brought him is indeed loaded, then cocks it and walks back over to the shattered man. His captor-turned-victim hasn't moved an inch. The slow, steady rise and fall of his diaphragm is the only sign that Oakley is still alive.

"Scrape yourself up off the floor, Oakley, we're still going for that walk." Matias says, kicking the downed man in his thigh. He groans in response before coughing spastically and choking on blood. After this fit, the guard somehow finds the strength to roll over onto his hands and knees. Another bout comes over him, and he begins hacking once again.

"For the love of God, Oakley, it's just your face. Be glad I left your ribcage intact. Now, GET. UP." Matias commands as he bends down, grabs the back of Oakley's shirt collar, and lifts him from the floor like the discarded piece of rubbish Matias knows he is. "Now where, exactly, were you planning on taking me to finish the job?"

Though it appears to be a struggle, Oakley laughs. A strange whistling sound accompanies each breath he takes; Matias broke the guy's nose. "I hope you know you're just prolonging the inevitable, Matias. You're a dead man walking."

Matias sighs, presses the sidearm to Oakley's shoulder, then pulls the trigger. It goes off with a loud 'CRACK!' and Oakley doubles over, falling to his knees as he squeals in agony. It's a carefully placed shot, avoiding any arteries or veins. Matias will make him suffer, but he isn't going to kill him just yet. The move is also a calculated one; chances are that any passing employees expect to hear at least one gunshot from behind Matias' cell door after Oakley arrived... they'll assume Oakley has completed his task and continue with their work. If not, well, at least he's armed now and can go down fighting if it comes to it.

"I'm *really* not in the mood for any more of your bullshit, Oakley. Now *up.* You're going to take me wherever it was you had planned to, or the next one will go in the back of your skull."

For once, all the mock bravado drains from Oakley's expression. He nods, then manages to get up without assistance this time. Matias could have obtained the necessary information from him here in his cell and then disposed of Oakley, but that won't give him anywhere to hide the body.

Something tells him that with all the people he has seen ENDURE make disappear over the years, they have a system in place for disposal. As Oakley leads him down the hall of the sublevel, his suspicions are confirmed when they stop outside a large room. The identifying placard beside its doors reads, "Incinerator."

Fortunately, it's a very short distance they traveled, but Matias isn't trying to press his luck by staying out in the hall. He nudges the back of Oakley's head with the muzzle of the gun, and the guard scans his keycard on the control panel beside the door, granting them access to the room.

Before Oakley can return the keycard to his pocket, Matias snatches it from his hand. "I'll take that; you won't be needing it any longer."

They enter the room, and the door closes quietly behind them. It appears to be a morgue, filled with medical equipment. To the right is a plethora of mortuary refrigeration units, and to the left is a row of autopsy tables. In the center is a large cremation furnace. Oakley turns to face Matias, and as soon as he rotates, the behemoth of a man latches onto his throat with his free hand. Quickly, he walks Oakley backward, his heels just barely scraping across the floor until he finds himself crushed against the side of the machine.

"This was your plan? Put one between my eyes and then toss me in the cremator?" Matias growls.

Oakley struggles for air but still manages that wry smile of his. "It's what we do with all the clones we no longer have a use for."

Matias instantly releases him and steps back, more than a little shocked. "Clones? What are you on about?"

Oakley chuckles and wheezes, hunched over with his hands on his knees. "That's right Matias, or haven't you figured it out by now? You're a clone. The lot of you. I can tell you the rest if you want; I figure only one of us is leaving here anyway."

Matias snickers sardonically. "Clones, huh? Give me a break man. Enough of your nonsense. There is one thing I want to know though; how did you and Shaw make it out of that explosion?"

Oakley's brow twitches with momentary confusion before he responds. "Ah! You mean Iraq! With the 'suicide bomber'!" he says, making air quotes with his hands. "Yeah, that whole thing? It was a set up. Shaw and I were already working for ENDURE at that point in time. You were meant to die that day so that Shaw and I could steal DNA off your corpse. The second you had Shaw drag me away, we booked it for the dunes! That woman and her child? Our hostages. The girl didn't detonate that vest; *I did.*"

Matias wants more than anything in the world to not believe him, but he does. He's fighting all his demons now, preventing himself from beating the man to death through sheer power of will. "I need your access codes, all of them. Now." He prods Oakley's wounded shoulder with the sidearm.

Wincing, Oakley nods. "Wouldn't you know it? I can never remember the damn things. They're written down in a travel journal. It's in my left pocket."

Matias isn't sure if Oakley is playing an angle or not, but he remains cautious. "Reach for it, *slowly.*"

Oakley raises his right hand and complies with Matias's request with his left, reaching into his pocket to retrieve a small booklet. Matias yanks it away from him. As promised, it's filled with codes and other potentially useful information.

"Come on, Matias. I just told you that you're a clone; an Echo is what we call you. Don't you want to know more? Don't you want to know about that creature living inside of Royce Wilko's Echo?"

I don't give a damn about anything you say, Oakley. I only need one more thing from you: where is Atticus keeping Royce?

Oakley rolls his eyes in response. "Seriously? That's *all* you want to know? That just so happens to be the *one* thing I can't tell you."

His patience had been running thin, but now, Matias's tank has run dry. He pockets the gun, then immediately thrusts an upper cut into Oakley's sternum. He feels the man's ribs crack, and based on the involuntary whimper that follows, Matias knows Oakley is regretting his actions. Without hesitation, Matias clenches the back of the man's neck, dragging him like a ragdoll to the stack of mortuary refrigeration units. He opens a random door in the middle of the top row and slams Oakley face-first against the unit beside it, pinning him there by the back of his head. Matias then uses his free hand to grab Oakley's left forearm, raising it so that his fingers rest inside the refrigerator's opening.

"Tell me where Royce is, Oakley," he demands.

Oakley tries to shake his head in refusal against the crushing force of Matias' palm. "I can't do it."

Quickly transitioning the grip of his right hand from Oakley's head and across his body, Matias reaches over and slams the door shut, guillotining all four of the man's fingers within the metal box, sparing only his thumb. Oakley shrieks and flails like a wild animal caught in a trap. With his good hand, he claws at the handle of the refrigeration unit to free himself, but Matias pounds his fist against the door, holding it firmly shut.

"WHERE IS ROYCE!" Matias screams, now extremely concerned that backup will arrive for Oakley before he can get his answers and escape.

"I CAN'T! HE'LL KILL ME! PLEASE! OPEN THE DOOR!" Oakley is now sobbing, crying like a baby. For all his gusto and violent nature, it's clear that he has never experienced the consequences of his own savagery.

Leaning in close, Matias whispers. "Listen to me you piece of shit; I'm going to kill you. Either way, you're dead before I leave this room. Now, I can continue to make it slow and agonizing, or you can tell me what I want to know, and I'll end it quickly. "So, what's it going to be?" Matias asks, yanking the man's head back by his hair and forcing eye contact.

With his lip quivering, Oakley stares back angrily. He hesitates for only a moment before the pain intensifies beyond what he can handle. "FINE. HE LOST CONTROL! THAT THING TOOK OVER SO WE HAD TO SEDATE HIM AND PLACE HIM INTO CRYOSTASIS! THE LAB HE'S BEING STORED

IN IS HERE ON THE SUBLEVEL, ROOM NUMBER 7682! I SWEAR! PLEASE! PLEASE GET MY HAND OUT OF THIS THING!"

With the shrillness of his cries increasing, Matias is expecting company at any moment.

"Sure thing, Oakley." Matias places his hands on both of the man's shoulders from behind and then pushes downward with all his might. There's a ripping, squelching sound as the flesh of Oakley's fingers tears apart and he falls to the floor, writhing and howling in anguish.

"Fingers for fingernails. Seems like a fair trade, no?" Matias asks rhetorically.

Oakley's pinky and ring finger have been severed completely, while his middle finger has been degloved. his index finger hasn't fared much better, sinew and bone visible as it dangles limply, contorted in all the wrong directions. Matias waits for Oakley to flop onto his belly, then quickly drops a knee into his back, pinning him down as he retrieves the sedative from his pocket and injects it into the muscle of the man's unwounded shoulder. It takes roughly two minutes for his screeching to lessen into a subdued mewl.

"Why haven't any of your buddies come to help you, Oakley?" Matias asks, still kneeling on his spine.

He replies drunkenly with slurred speech. "First shift doesn't start until six...we're the only ones down here..."

Matias laughs heartily at the irony. "And you thought you were going to come down here, play your twisted little game with me, then kill me without anyone finding out that you tortured me first? Karma truly is a bitch, Oakley."

His breathing has become shallow now. A pool of blood saturates more and more of the floor with every passing minute as his shoulder oozes, his nose drips, and what remains of his left hand gushes.

"Please… kill me… please…" Oakley pleads through rasping breaths.

Matias crouches beside him. "I never thought you'd ask." Hooking his fingers into the waistline of Oakley's pants, Matias lifts him from the floor. The man bobs limply with each step Matias takes as he carries him to the incinerator and drops him beside it. Matias releases the safety and presses the button that controls the furnace door. It lifts with a mechanized whir.

"You said… you'd make it… quick." Oakley gasps, fear invigorating him slightly.

Matias gets down on his knees and searches through Oakley's pockets. He takes the phone containing evidence of Aiden's death and tries to unlock it. It requires a fingerprint, so he grabs Oakley's good hand and presses the man's pointer finger onto the screen. It opens, and he navigates to the settings to disable the lock. Finding nothing else of use, he lifts Oakley into a fireman's carry and tosses him down onto the conveyor belt.

"You said—"

"I know what I said... I lied," Matias retorts, cutting off Oakley's final plea.

He presses another button on the control panel, and the conveyor belt comes to life. As Oakley is slowly carried forward and into the primary chamber, he tries to sit up, but the sedative is too strong. No matter how much he struggles to escape, it's impossible.

The conveyor stops, but Oakley isn't quite inside the machine just yet. Matias pushes against the bottom of the man's boots, bending his legs at the knees so the door will close unobstructed. At Matias's behest, the aperture hums again and seals Oakley inside.

There will be no remorse; this is the death a monster like Jordan Oakley deserves. Matias presses a button labeled "start," and it lights up green. The hissing sound of gasoline filling the chamber is music to Matias' ears. Jordan Oakley will burn alive at one thousand five hundred fifty degrees Fahrenheit like the devil he is. The flames roar to life, igniting in a beautiful display of vigilante justice. Matias watches through the viewing window as Oakley's flesh crackles and embers fly around haphazardly inside the retort. He reflects on Aiden... the woman, her daughter in Iraq, and all the other lives that this demon has ended. As the fire scorches his body, Oakley's brain has ignored the effects of the sedative; he feels every lick of the blaze's tendrils. Adrenaline pounds through the man's veins, engaging the most primal fight or flight response within him, but it's no use. His clothes burn like kindling while his muted screams fade to a dull whine, and eventually, stop altogether.

CHAPTER 36

Redemption

*Time and location (present-day): 10:16 am,
ENDURE Center for Rehabilitation*

Five long months have passed since Desmond last saw Royce, though in the final moments of that interaction, it hadn't even really been Royce. He had moved with such speed and acted with such ferocity... Desmond was certain at one point during the altercation that Royce would have killed him if Shaw hadn't successfully administered the sedative. He now understands, thanks to Atticus' explanation, that Mallen, the Boundless within Royce, had taken control. The doctor stated that he had never witnessed such a level of control over a subject; although he hadn't expressed it at the time, Desmond could see it clearly on his face; it terrified Atticus.

As he sits with the chessboard and its pieces set in their positions before him, he makes his first move. He then reaches across the table and moves one of the opposing pawns; there's no one else there. No one left to partake in this morning routine. Matias had been taken and never heard from again, Royce had been placed into cryostasis after the attack, and Aiden... He wonders if things could have been different. If he could have fought harder against Atticus or even found a way to sabotage him from behind enemy lines.

After everything he has done to misdirect the others and keep Atticus' research endeavor afloat, the doctor still hasn't provided any proof that Dominic is alive, and Desmond is beginning to lose hope that he is. Maybe he has been manipulated into a fool's gambit. After all, trickery is ENDURE's specialty. If Dominic is dead and gone, then he has betrayed the closest thing he has had to friends in years for absolutely nothing. It's a gut-wrenching feeling; one he isn't sure he'll ever be able to recover from.

He moves a bishop on the board, then drops his hand into his lap, fidgeting with a small brick in his pocket through the material of his jumpsuit. It's his one shot at redemption, should the opportunity ever arise: a secondary flash drive containing all the evidence they recovered of ENDURE's human experimentation. Desmond had copied the data to it prior to giving the original USB to Atticus. If the doctor wants to use leverage against him, then he had to have some of his own. As he moves a knight in a play against himself, he notices a member of the nursing staff heading in his direction. Desmond has seen her around and remembers her name as Viviana.

When she arrives at the chess table, the woman hunches over beside him and whispers in his ear. "Trust no one," she says, then slips an envelope into his lap and walks away casually.

He quickly pockets the note and surveys the area for any wandering eyes. Rising from his chair, he stretches slowly, trying to act as inconspicuously as possible. He walks to the opposite side of the table, resting his hand on the seatback. "Good game, Aiden," Desmond says softly.

Once a moment or two has passed, he slowly heads back to his room. On the outside, he appears calm, but inside, he's screaming with anticipation. What's in this envelope? Who sent it to him? When he finally reaches his quarters, he sits down at his desk and tears it open with haste. Inside, he finds a letter and reads it intently.

Desmond,

I'm sorry if this message isn't highly detailed, but we need to keep a low profile. I know what you're thinking, but I need you to trust that I am on your side. I'll fill you in on absolutely everything as soon as possible. What you need to know now is as follows: Matias is alive. Hopefully, by now he has escaped with my assistance. I have disagreed with the direction my uncle has been steering this company for quite a while, but he's finally gone too far. As such, I have been quietly recruiting like-minded employees behind his back while skimming funds from the company. I have amassed a noteworthy workforce of my own, as well as considerable resources. It pays to oversee ENDURE's cybersecurity and programming. It won't be long before they notice that I've siphoned funds, but hopefully by the time they do, the viruses and malware I've riddled their systems with will have done their jobs. Once I confirm that they have, Matias and I are coming back for you, Royce, Aiden, and all the others that my uncle has terrorized. If my hunch is correct, then Royce has been placed into cryostasis by now. We can still save him if we act quickly enough. As far as your son is concerned, I'm sorry; I truly do not know if he is alive or not. I can tell you that I met him, but that was a long time ago. We will do our best to help you find him, I promise. Once we are all together, we can topple this organization, find Dominic, and bring my dear uncle Atticus to justice for what he has done. His crimes can no longer go unanswered; he will pay for all the lives he has affected. I will see you soon. Stay safe, be discreet, but most importantly, be ready. I am counting on you, and so is Royce.

-Lena

Desmond folds the letter as small as he can and tucks it into his sock. Lena hadn't known about Aiden's death, and Desmond feels a pang of guilt at the idea that he will never leave this place. If what she wrote is true, then Desmond has a way out. More importantly, the stagnation of Dominic's welfare and whereabouts has shown movement. Lena doesn't know whether Dominic is alive or not, but if she met him, he had been at this facility, which meant he had survived the attack by ENDURE all those years ago.

He feels renewed hope; all Desmond has to do now is wait, and so he does. Once more unto the breach, he'll bide his time until Lena and Matias arrive to spring him from this prison once and for all. Hopefully, he'll leave here with his son by his side, but if not, he'll die trying to find him. The thought is so revitalizing that he can't help but smile to himself.

CHAPTER 37

Contractors

Time and location (371 days post-cryostasis): 2:42 pm,
ENDURE Center for Rehabilitation

The ride to the ENDURE facility was not very pleasant. Sergeant Major Blake Argerich and his team had to cross through an "M Site," the rudimentary codename for monolith locations assigned by the military, to complete their journey. The monoliths are massive towers that have sprouted up and out of the Earth, wreaking havoc across the continents they now inhabit. There are currently four that he knows of, but intel has it on good authority that there are still more to come. They're an unprecedented threat; no officials from any government worldwide have offered a solution or a way to destroy the damned things. NATO had held multiple national conferences to address the problem, and in all honesty, it was probably the most unified he has ever seen the world's superpowers. Members from the United States, China, Russia—hell, even the North Koreans were all working around the clock to find a way to prevent these monoliths from wiping out humanity altogether.

In certain parts of the world, nothing has changed at all; the sun shines brightly in the morning, and the moon's calm glow illuminates the night sky. When Argerich and his team drove through the M Site, however, it felt like stepping through a door into the apocalypse itself. The air was unbreathable, not that they needed to worry about that within the confines of their high-tech transport. Looking out the window as they traveled, Argerich could barely see ten feet ahead through the haze. It was a surreal experience, and he's more than glad to be far, far away from the place now. The haze they had seen was caused by a sort of spore emitted by the tower-like structures, similar to how a plant disperses its pollen; inhale it, and you're in for one hell of a bad time.

Reportedly, each of the four monoliths that have appeared so far has differing effects on those who fall victim to their strange infection. The M-1 site, where the first structure appeared, caused mass paranoia among those who inhaled the organic mist. After only four days of exposure, everyone within range of its effects was dead, killed by one another or themselves. M-2 produced different effects, and so on and so forth with the other monoliths, but the outcome was the same: death on a massive scale. The most terrifying aspect of the whole situation is that the circumferences of each site seem to intersect. Government officials in the research field of their respective countries all agree. Eventually, as more towers arise, there will be nowhere safe from their influence. Nowhere will be untouched by the deadly pollution produced by the monoliths.

Ironically enough, nothing played out the way the masses assumed it would once this threat became known. The government, or at least the American government, didn't attempt to cover anything up; they had been open about what was going down from day one, likely because they had no clue what was happening at all. No one had been left in the dark, and that scared the living daylights out of Argerich. It meant the people who were supposed to help the masses solve problems like this were seeking help themselves in containing the decay of the human population. He's torn from his thoughts as their transport screeches to a halt in front of a tall steel gate.

"Well, I'll be damned, welcome to Hefner's mansion ladies and gentlemen," Sergeant Jenn Vargas says sarcastically. Argerich is fond of her; the woman has balls of steel and nerves to match his own.

"No one told me this was a party, I would've brought goodie bags," Lance Corporal Anthony Owens chimes in. He's still green, having only linked up with Argerich's crew a few months ago, but the kid shows promise. He's fearless and one hell of a phenomenal tactician.

"Lock it down and focus up, we don't know what we're walking in on." Master Sergeant Katrina Lozano responds, reeling in their attention. She's Argerich's second in command and has earned her keep throughout her years of active duty as a Marine. Argerich had served alongside her in the field before linking up again in the private military circuit. It's a way for hardened soldiers like the two of them to pool extra cash when Uncle Sam's money just isn't cutting it, which is pretty much all the time.

"Just a bunch of nerds and their science experiments Kat, I think we can handle this just fine." Private First-Class Rene Freeland sees herself as untouchable, and to be fair, there's no evidence suggesting otherwise. The woman has survived altercations that Argerich himself would consider impossible to navigate.

"If Kat says lock it down, you lock it down, Freeland." That was Staff Sergeant Isaiah Fajardo, the final member to complete their group. He's quiet and mostly keeps to himself, but the man has the utmost respect for the chain of command. However, that chain is murky at best when dealing with private military contractors. His true contribution is that he possesses more brains than the rest of them combined.

Argerich has heard enough bickering and finally interjects. "Alright kids, listen to Kat and play nice. Science experiments or not, she's right; we don't know what we're walking into, and considering the current state of the outside world, I'd like to err more on the side of caution than not. Keep your guard up and stay focused."

They pass through massive steel gates, and their vehicle comes to a halt outside a large building. It's a single-story structure that sprawls far and wide over the patch of land it occupies, with a biodome surrounding it to prevent any airborne pathogens from affecting those within. Aside from O2 re-breathers, the biodomes are the only mass-produced and government funded defense against the spores emitted by the monoliths. With no monolith active nearby, however, it's clear to Argerich that whoever owns this facility is planning ahead and not taking any risks. This makes him wonder what kind of oxygen supply these people are holding. Pure oxygen has become something of a commodity since officials announced the production and distribution of re-breathers for those impacted by the presence of the monoliths. The supply isn't running thin yet, but by the time the remaining monoliths rear their ugly heads, Argerich fears there won't be enough to go around.

"We're here." Argerich moves to the Humvee's door and exits as the driver opens it from the outside. ENDURE sent their own company vehicle to retrieve them under the pretense that their location was classified information. When they got close enough to their destination, the windows in the Humvee automatically shifted to pitch black, blocking Argerich's view of the outside world. Fancy tech, no doubt, which made him wonder what kind of funding this company was receiving and from where.

As he steps out, followed by his team, a tall, middle-aged man approaches him, extending a welcoming hand. "It's a pleasure to see you again, Sergeant Major. I'm Dr. Atticus Cais, welcome back to ENDURE."

Argerich shakes his hand firmly, slightly confused; if he had worked for this guy in the past, he didn't remember. "The pleasure's mine, sir. I apologize, but do we know each other?"

The doctor clarifies. "Formally? No. You've done some work for me in the past. However, we never met face-to-face. I assure you though, I was always extremely satisfied with you and whatever outfit you commanded, which is why I chose you specifically for this job."

Argerich nods, though it doesn't clarify much. He's completed so many jobs for numerous clients that they all just blur together at this point. "You have us working some sort of security detail here, but you haven't been too forthcoming with information. What is it that we're guarding?"

Atticus smiles; it seems forced by all accounts. "I apologize for the secrecy, the work we are doing here is... delicate in nature, and of the utmost importance. We have a high-value asset within the facility, and that is who you'll be keeping watch over."

Argerich scratches his chin. "Just how important an asset are we talking? And guarding from whom? How you answer these questions might cause the cost of our labor to increase, especially if you're expecting opposition."

The doctor shoos away Argerich's suspicion with a wave of his hand. "Heavens no, nothing of the sort. This particular asset needs guarding from himself more than any outside instigator. We just need you and your team to make sure he isn't harmed, and that means protecting him from himself as well as from others."

Argerich nods again, but he doesn't like this guy's demeanor. Atticus seems stressed out and worried, which unnerves him, if only slightly. There's the faintest shimmer of sweat on the doctor's forehead, and it isn't the forty degrees they're currently standing in that is causing it. "Alright, we'll do the job. If things go sideways though, the price may need to be re-negotiated."

"Money isn't a problem Sergeant Major, that I assure you," says Atticus. The doctor motions for him and his team to move forward. "Shall we?"

Glancing to the side, he catches Katrina's eye. The look she gives him says, *this guy is fucking weird, abort.* The two of them have developed a silent link, where just a look can convey what the other is thinking. He shakes his head 'no' as they proceed through the front doors of the building, but Kat isn't willing to back down that easily. She approaches him as they walk on, leaning in close to whisper in his ear. "You sure this is a good idea? The man seems… unhinged."

Argerich agrees, noticing Atticus's right hand twitching against his thigh. He confirms that she isn't the only one with suspicions. "Yeah, I got that vibe too. Let's just feel this out a bit before we make any rash decisions."

She concurs and slows her stride to match Isaiah's speed. "What's your take on this so far?" she asks him, receiving a shrug in response.

Job's a job; as long as he pays us at the end of the day, I'm content."

Katrina rolls her eyes. "How fucking modest."

Freeland approaches from behind and places a forearm on Kat's shoulder. "This place looks... downtrodden."

Kat bats a bewildered eye at her. "Downtrodden? Is that a word people still use in this century?"

Freeland glares at her. "All I'm saying is that with the amount of cash we're supposedly pocketing from this job, you'd expect something a bit more... impressive."

Kat can't argue with that; the facility does seem run-down, as if it had been built long ago in the sixties and only minimally maintained since its conception. They passed through the lobby long ago and have taken multiple twists and turns down the hallways of the building while the doctor chats Argerich's ear off.

Jenn Vargas doesn't like the guy either. His entire act seems to her like precisely that—an act. "Why do I have a creeping suspicion that this guy is hiding something, Owens?" she asks as they walk on.

"You're suspicious of everybody, Sergeant. Hell, I'm surprised you even trust *me*."

"I don't," she replies, prompting a laugh from Owens.

"Case in point, Sarge."

They round a final corner, and at the end of the hall stand the two large, bisected doors of an elevator. The doctor stops just short of the lift and turns around to address them. "We will now descend to sub-level A, where the asset is being held. The NDA you all signed before being hired on for this job was in reference to everything you're about to see. Understand that the terms of that NDA are to be honored and followed with zero room for error, or every one of you will stand trial for treason."

Treason? This guy has that kind of pull? Guess that narrows down the source of funding... Argerich thinks to himself. "We understand, doc; we're here to work. We couldn't care less what freaky shit you have in your basement."

Atticus turns to address him. "I wouldn't be so certain of that just yet, Sergeant Major." The elevator doors slide open, and he motions them inside.

They file in one by one, and Vargas grows increasingly anxious. "I hope you know that if you try any shady shit, we'll put you down like a rabid dog," she says to Atticus.

"Stow it, Vargas," Argerich interjects, shooting her an aggressive look from across the elevator as the box begins its descent. "Please excuse Sergeant Vargas, she isn't what you'd call a people person."

Atticus raises his hands slightly in a no-contest fashion. "No offense taken here. I assure you; I am not attempting to mislead any of you. If you'll just be patient, you'll soon see why I have kept everything involved in this operation under lock and key."

Argerich immediately noticed upon their arrival at the facility that the doctor had come to greet them alone, without any security of his own in tow. Indeed, if he harbors any ill intent towards them, he has no means of causing them harm that they can't unleash upon him ten-fold. The elevator slows to a smooth halt, and the doors open wide.

Argerich steps out first, with his team following suit and the doctor bringing up the rear as he explains what they are seeing. "What you saw upstairs was merely a front for what we at ENDURE are truly devoting our time to."

"You don't say..." Argerich's voice trails off as he takes in his surroundings. The underground portion of the facility is gigantic. The room into which the elevator opens seems to be a lab of sorts, sprawling nearly two hundred meters in every direction, and almost every inch of the space is occupied by equipment and the appropriate technicians to operate it. There must be hundreds of ENDURE employees in this room alone.

Atticus makes his way to the front of the group and continues forward, serving as their tour guide in this new and confusing world. "As you can see, our work here is scientific in nature. We all know of the impending doom our species faces unless we find a way to prevent the monoliths from spreading their disease. We've successfully merged our research on DNA cloning with new research geared towards this ever-growing crisis to develop what we think will be a solution to the presenting problem. I cannot officially delve into the details of said solution, but that is the gist of what we are doing here; developing a way to fight back, to fight for our survival."

Argerich struggles to find his words as he observes the area. "It's clear that your operation is government funded judging by the tech I see here. You must be working on some 'first of its kind' stuff down here if that's the case."

Atticus says nothing, neither confirming nor denying that statement. When they finally make it past the aisle that funnels them through station after station and their respective workers, they stop in front of two double doors. They're made of a thick metal that looks like titanium alloy. A keypad on the wall to the left controls the doors, enabling them to slide open and close on a mechanical track. Standing beside the doors is a short woman with glasses who gives a polite wave hello.

"Beyond this point is the asset. These doors remain locked at all times. If anyone needs to exit, speak to a technician or use the intercom beside the door. For anything concerning me, your contact is Dr. Santosh Ravi," Atticus says, gesturing to the silent woman nearby. "She'll relay your messages. We operate around the clock, there's always someone here. No one should feel trapped."

"Doesn't want us to feel trapped after he explains to us that he's trapping us, just peachy..." Owens says under his breath. Kat throws an elbow into his ribs, a silent implication to shut up.

"How long does this job last?" Argerich asks.

"For now, we're projecting at least three days. Should we need to prolong your stay, we will readdress the terms of our agreement accordingly," Atticus replies.

"Sounds good," says Argerich, though in truth, it sounds awful. The entire situation seems far from comfortable, but Argerich and his company have never been paid to be comfortable.

Atticus smiles that same unsettling grin again, and Argerich wonders whether taking this job was a good idea or not after all. "Alright then, if you have no further questions, I will leave you and your team to it. If you need anything, just ask Dr. Ravi and she'll be happy to accommodate."

Dr. Ravi smiles at them, her act much more genuine than Atticus's, then shuffles away and continues her work.

Atticus enters a code into the keypad. The doors begin to slide open, not too discreetly. The gears grind and then cease loudly as the doors come to a halt, and Atticus motions for Argerich and his team of PMCs to enter. Hesitantly, they step inside. Atticus types a code into the keypad once more, and the doors begin to close. The Sergeant Major catches one final glimpse of Dr. Atticus Cais before the two doors meet and seal shut; that same, shit-eating grin he wore when they first met plastered on his face.

CHAPTER 38

Reckoning

*Time and location (372 days post-cryostasis): 9:46 am,
ENDURE Secure Sublevel*

Argerich sits on a stool in the corner of the room, chowing down on a granola bar as the morning grinds on. Atticus had sent down a care package earlier, seemingly trying to make their stay more relaxed. That, of course, didn't work one bit, but it did calm the grumbling in Argerich's stomach, and that was better than nothing. The first night of their guard duty had gone smoothly enough, albeit mind-numbingly boring compared to their usual assignment.

He stares across the room at the giant, iced-over tube that encases their VIP; it looks like something out of a sci-fi film. RW-117, that's what the technicians are calling him. Argerich can't see through the glass; ice crystals obstruct anyone's view of what slumbers inside. He's both curious and horrified by the sarcophagus. Out of all the jobs he and his crew have taken, this one is certainly the strangest. He sees Freeland heading his way from across the lab, crumples up the wrapper from his granola bar, and tosses it into a nearby bin.

"How goes it, Freeland?" he asks her as she leans her body against the wall next to him.

"Same old same old, bored as hell. At least this job is over and done with come tomorrow. This place makes my skin crawl."

"Yeah, easiest cash we've ever earned, though. The lack of gunfire is nice."

"The lack of gunfire is dull."

Argerich chuckles in response. "Don't worry, I'll make sure the next offer I take into consideration places us right in the shit."

Freeland straightens up. "Now that sounds like fun," she says and turns to leave.

"Hey Freeland," Argerich calls, stopping her as she turns back around to listen to him.

"Send Kat my way."

Freeland nods and heads back across the lab. Argerich has his team spread wide across the room. There isn't much to do, and because of that, he wants to at least look like they're earning their pay by strategically placing bodies and building a perimeter throughout the area. Every hour or so, his team reports to him at staggered intervals, although there's never any change in the situation. The last time Vargas visited him, she gave Argerich a report of, "All clear, the coffin hasn't sprouted limbs and made a run for it yet." In all honesty, he can't wait for this contract to come to an end so they can all be on their merry way. The sooner he can leave this place, the sooner he can forget about it.

Katrina appears from behind a large monitoring station on a direct course towards him. "You rang, boss?"

"Yeah, I wanted to—"

The lights shut off in the room, interrupting him and plunging them into all-encompassing darkness. Before Argerich can get his bearings, the lab is flooded with a pulsating crimson fluorescence.

"The fuck is going on?" he hears Kat ask one of the technicians as he speeds by.

Argerich takes note of the tag on his shirt, which reads Alexander Sierra, as the technician responds, "Something's gone wrong, RW-117 is unstable!" Alexander shouts back to Kat as he hurries about his business.

Finally, Argerich rises from his stool with a sigh; he knew the peace and quiet earlier had been too good to be true. "On me Kat, I want everyone converging on that coffin."

She nods and radios their teammates as they proceed towards the cryo-pod across the room from their current position.

"Weapons up and trained on that thing," Argerich commands into their comms as he unslings his FN MK 17 from his shoulder. The sand-colored, fully automatic rifle is weighty in his hands; heavy but not excessively so—just how Argerich likes it. He believes his primary weapon should feel comfortable for immediate use straight from the rack, and therefore, he has made limited modifications to the gun.

Kat nods and brings her HK416 to the ready. It's configured to be a bit lighter in weight. Its frame is a sleek matte black, and she's attached a muzzle brake to its barrel to reduce recoil. Speed is the name of her game, and all of her firearms are configured to be as quick on the draw as possible.

By the time Argerich and Kat reach the pod, the rest of their team has already formed a perimeter around the asset, weapons aimed steadily at the tube. Argerich takes up position beside Isaiah. "Hope we don't need to use that thing," Argerich says, gesturing towards the M1014 semi-auto shotgun in Isaiah's hands, its bronze body with black accents contrastingly elegant in light of the situation they find themselves in.

"Neither do I, but it's here if we do," says Isaiah.

Employees of ENDURE are frantically milling about in the red haze that surrounds them, checking monitoring systems beside the tank containing RW-117, entering codes into portable data pads, and adjusting the oxygen flow and fluid rates being pumped into the pod.

"Do you people know what you're doing?" asks Owens.

"Everything is perfectly fine, I assure you," Doctor Ravi responds as she pushes through the growing crowd.

"It sure as shit doesn't seem fine Ravi," Owens snaps back.

"Please remain calm, we will have the situation contained as soon as—" Dr. Ravi is cut off by a loud bang. Everyone stops dead in their tracks, turning their attention toward the source of the noise; it had come from the pod.

"Uhhhh Sergeant Major? The fuck was that?" Asks Vargas, clearly on edge.

Before Argerich can respond, another thud from the pod echoes throughout the lab. "Focus up Vargas," he says, just before a third thump sends a large splintering crack down the glass facade of the coffin and shakes the room.

Argerich's voice fills the lab as he gives his orders. "Weapons up! We want the asset alive; aim to disable if necessary, but DO NOT shoot to kill!" He expects Dr. Ravi or one of her technicians to interject, but instead, they all remain silent and terrified.

They have no fucking clue what's happening, Argerich thinks to himself. Another strike against the glass pane makes the crack spiderweb. Before anyone can react, the casing shatters, and large shards of glass spray outward with explosive force. One of the larger splinters hits the technician named Alexander in the chest, causing him to crumple to the floor screaming.

"You and you, get him to the entrance!" Freeland yells, pointing at two nameless technicians. They comply, helping Alexander to his feet and heading for safety together.

Cold fumes billow from the makeshift opening in the coffin, obscuring Argerich's view of the asset inside. He and his team have all their weapons trained on the pod, waiting for some big ugly monster to poke its head out of the mist, but nothing of the sort occurs.

After a moment's hesitation, Dr. Ravi approaches the open coffin. "Alright, all non-essential employees need to evacuate the area as a safety precaution. Elizabeth, report to Dr. Cais immediately, ask him how he would like us to proceed." A technician whose nametag reads Elizabeth Dana nods and hesitantly leaves. A handful of other employees eagerly follow her, glad to be exiting the area.

Dr. Ravi turns to Argerich as the condensation from the tank thins. "Sergeant Major, I need you and your team to—" Her words fall short, and Argerich swears he feels a swift burst of air pass by all of them. Dr. Ravi's gaze is still locked firmly on him but appears empty and devoid of life.

"Hey doc, what's wrong?" Argerich asks, his focus still on the pod and its yet-to-be-revealed contents. Dr. Ravi gives no reply, verbal or otherwise. Argerich turns to Vargas and motions for her to approach.

She walks forward, addressing the woman. "Hey, Ravi, anyone home in that head of yours?" Vargas nudges the doctor with the muzzle of her rifle. When she does, the woman's head falls from her shoulders and hits the floor with a crude thwack, her body collapsing as blood spurts from severed arteries in her neck.

Vargas jumps back, startled and pale. "JESUS CHRIST!" she shouts as the remaining ENDURE employees scatter and flee in hysteria, their screams echoing throughout the room. Vargas's sentiment neatly encapsulates Argerich's thoughts. Shit has just gone fubar in the worst possible way, and he isn't even sure how or why.

"What just happened?!" asks Isaiah, panic seeping into his usually calm demeanor.

"I… I'm not sure," Argerich responds, genuinely confused and more than a little horrified. He's no stranger to violence or combat, but an enemy you can't see or hear is always something to fear.

Full-blown pandemonium has gripped the entire lab now, and all the remaining techs who were ordered to stay put have begun sprinting for the exit. Clearly, all the ENDURE employees feel their lives are threatened; they know something Argerich and his team do not. Then suddenly, there's a distinct sound from behind Argerich and his team: broken glass crunching under the weight of someone's feet. Amid the scurrying employees, with his back toward them, stands a man. He's naked and hunched over, trembling slightly.

What in the actual fuck? Argerich swings in the dark and addresses the stranger. "Subject RW-117, cease and desist! Stand down or we will open fire!"

If this is, in fact, the asset they have been hired to protect, then Argerich has no clue how he exited the pod and ended up behind them without anyone seeing the man. Then again, he's still trying to figure out how poor Dr. Ravi had lost her head, the decapitated corpse still warm on the floor beside them. The man Argerich believes to be RW-117 doesn't move a muscle and shows no sign of understanding.

Alright, we'll try again... "RW-117, I need you to get down on your knees and—"

Then, suddenly, he's *gone.* Argerich has never been so dazed and confused in his life. He didn't so much as blink, and yet somehow, the man who stood before him moments ago has vanished. It's as if he has literally glitched out of existence. Just then, he hears a grotesque noise, like vomit hitting a hard surface and splattering all over the nearby surroundings. He turns to locate its source, and his eyes settle on Owens.

"Sergeant Major, I don't feel so good..." Owens stutters and coughs up blood, collapsing to his knees.

Sweat starts to bead on Argerich's forehead as he takes in the scene. RW-117 now stands behind Owens, a wide bloody gash spread across the young soldier's abdomen, his entrails spilled about the floor. He falls forward with a gut-wrenching splat.

Fuck this and fuck the money, Argerich thinks. "Previous orders are out the window. Put that thing down, *NOW!*" he screams and depresses the trigger on his assault rifle.

Gunfire fills the once-still air around them in an instant. Brilliant white muzzle flashes contrast with the crimson pulses that coat the lab in spurts. Before the rounds can find their target, RW-117 disappears again. Argerich curses under his breath. It's like the damn thing is teleporting around the room; either that or it's moving *so* fast that the human eye can't even register it.

Something is thrown past Argerich and strikes the wall behind him, and then he hears a primal scream. It's Freeland, clutching the blood-soaked pulp at the shoulder joint where her left arm should have been. Instead, the appendage slumps against the wall behind Argerich. He immediately moves to help her but stops short when their attacker materializes in front of her. Argerich watches helplessly as the man lifts her by her throat and clenches tightly, an audible snap ringing through the area as Freeland's body goes limp and her wailing instantaneously falls silent. Their adversary tosses her corpse aside like a ragdoll and vaporizes out of existence again. Argerich's heart pounds in his chest. He's trained for many different situations; this isn't one of them.

"Everyone on me! We're abandoning the mission! Time to get the fuck out of dodge! Kat take up the rear, Isaiah takes point! Vargas watch my six. Go, go, go!" he yells, as they all kick it into high gear, making their way toward the door that leads out of the lab.

He can see the gathering of techs ahead, trying to push their way through the exit in a not-so-orderly fashion. Someone beyond the door is shouting something Argerich can't quite make out. He ignores it, continuing his sprint toward salvation. Argerich immediately feels a million little splatters of warmth strike his face and chest just before something in his path trips him up, causing him to hit the ground hard. When he sits up to figure out what caused him to lose his footing, he sees a semi-auto shotgun on the ground a few feet away from Isaiah's legs. They're severed at the torso, his left foot twitching ever so slightly. Where his upper body has gone is anyone's guess.

There's no time to mourn, no time to react; Vargas is on Argerich's position in an instant, lifting him to his feet. "Let's go! Move it!" she shouts, nearly ripping Argerich's arm out of its socket.

Moments after he's up and running again, he can make out what the voice at the lab's exit is shouting; *seal the doors.* Those sons of bitches plan to trap them in here with this... *thing.* He quickens his pace, with Vargas and Kat close behind him. Somewhere in the depths of his consciousness Argerich is aware of subject RW-117 ripping apart ENDURE employees left and right. The beast blips in and out of reality like a bolt of lightning as they speed through the ongoing carnage, desperately attempting to escape with their own lives. Corpses are piling up around them by the minute. It's too unreal to comprehend the way this monster seems to bend space and time, evanescing out of existence and then materializing before its next victim.

They're close now, only fifty feet or so to go. "Hold that fucking door!" Argerich growls, his throat sore and shredded from barking orders. He isn't ready to die in here, refuses to. Kat suddenly passes him up, the fleetest of foot among them, true to her nature.

She reaches the crowd of employees in an instant, pushes her way through them, and clears a path for Argerich and Vargas. "Hurry the fuck up! Let's go!" she roars at the top of her lungs.

Vargas flinches as one of the techs running alongside her is picked off, just there one moment and gone the next. *Holy shit that could've been me, that could've been me!* Then, just as quickly as the thought crossed her mind, she's through the doors. Kat places a welcoming hand on Vargas's back. They turn their attention in unison to Argerich, but just before he passes through the doorway, he's slung backwards into the lab as if by some invisible force. He hits the ground and skids on his armored backplate before crashing into a nearby desk.

"We need to quarantine this area immediately!" the technician named Elizabeth cries out.

Kat catches her by the wrist as she reaches for the keypad that controls the doors. "Don't you fucking dare!" She screams in Elizabeth's face, shoving the woman back and away from the door controls.

The entrance will stay open until Argerich is either out or dead; she'll make certain of that. Kat watches from afar as Argerich rolls onto his hands and knees, and then the asset appears in front of him, blocking her line of sight. As RW-117 approaches him, Argerich regains enough strength to get a leg under himself.

He's halfway to standing when he looks up through pained eyes and labored breaths, then addresses his aggressor. "What... what *are* you?"

The asset's eyes meet his, but they appear hollow. A wickedly twisted smile forms on the creature's face before it responds, "Reckoning."

Well shit. It was a good run while it lasted. Argerich closes his eyes, accepting his inescapable fate. Then, as if by some blind miracle, RW-117 stumbles backward, clutching its head with both hands. A beastly screech escapes its mouth before the asset collapses to the floor, unconscious. Argerich stares in stunned disbelief, his eyes wide and his trousers more than a little damp with piss.

"Move your ass, NOW!" Kat's voice pulls him out of his shellshocked state, and he's up in a flash, racing as hard and as fast as he can to the exit. The moment he crosses the threshold, Kat finally allows Elizabeth to access the keypad. She turns to

Argerich as the doors seal shut and places a grounding hand on his shoulder. Vargas catches one final glimpse of the bloodbath that remains inside as the doors close at a pace much too slow for her liking; dismembered body parts strewn about, blood and guts spattered on nearly every surface, at least twenty people torn to pieces by whatever had been inhabiting that young man's body. Certainly, regardless of how it appears, subject RW-117 is *not* human.

"You good?" Kat asks Argerich.

He shakes his head in confirmation, inhaling and exhaling sharply. "Yeah... yeah, I'm good... I'm good." He leans back against the wall, slides down it until his ass thumps against the floor.

Vargas and Kat join, taking seats on either side of him while the technicians remain erratic, unsure of what to do next. They sit in shocked silence for a long time, unable to process what they have just experienced.

After what seems like an eternity, Argerich collects his thoughts and picks himself up off the floor. "We're going to see Atticus Cais, *right fucking now.* Let's move."

CHAPTER 39

Waste

Time and location (372 days post-cryostasis): Unknown

"...Welcome home, Royce." Disembodied yet somehow near, Mallen speaks to me, deceitfully soothing in his tone.

"What... Where am I?" I ask, too preoccupied with the flood of memories I am trying to categorize and resolve. Having your entire past life thrust into your mind all at once was a lot to navigate.

His voice envelops me. *"Surely you recognize it, Royce; it's your home. We're in your bedroom."*

I could've sworn that there was nothing around me, that I was floating in a deep, ebony void. Yet now, as I gather my bearings, it feels as if I'm seeing for the first time. I'm indeed in mine and Lena's bedroom; the walls are painted a soft grey, and light filters softly through the sheer curtains hanging in front of the window. I glance down as our cat weaves lovingly between my legs. Somewhere deep down, I'm certain that none of this is real, and yet the uncanny attention to detail draws me in, nonetheless. Everything is just as I remember it: the television caddy-cornered on a wall mount across the room from our bed, matching floating nightstands with stacks of books on them flanking either side of the mattress, a small tank on top of our dresser full of colorful fish, and even the stain from where I had spilled coffee on the carpet in front of the closet doors is present. I grip my head, trying to ground myself in reality; this isn't my room in the home I shared with Lena; it's Royce Wilko's, and I'm not Royce. In truth, I have never shared a room with Lena outside of my quarters at ENDURE; I have never really been here at all.

"You seem perplexed, Royce. What's eating you?" Mallen presses on, feigning concern once more.

"This isn't my room, it's his..."

A harsh laugh reverberates through Mallen's mental simulation. "True... you aren't the original, but who's to say you aren't Royce Wilko? The real Royce is dead and gone, his life is yours for the taking. It could all be yours. It's what you want, isn't it? Who's going to stop you? Who's to say you aren't him in the eyes of those who matter the most?"

The door handle suddenly rattles, and then a brunette-haired woman with startling green eyes enters the bedroom. She's elegant and radiates warmth. Her eyes meet mine, and I feel my heart drop into my stomach. "Royce... you're home... I thought you were dead..." The woman's eyes quickly fill with tears as she cups her hands over her mouth in disbelief.

"Lena?" I ask as tears of my own begin to stream down my cheeks. She hurriedly makes her way across the room and embraces me fiercely. I hug her back, and all my worries melt away. For the first time in recent memory, things feel okay, feel right, feel like home.

"I'm so happy you're here! Come downstairs, your parents and your sister are here. They'll be so excited to see you!" she says excitedly. I know she isn't truly here, yet I can feel Lena's arms around my body.

Mallen's treacherous voice enraptures me once again, caressing my ears like a soothing melody. "Your family is waiting to see you, Royce. Go on... follow Lena downstairs and reunite with them. It's been so long since you've seen your parents... don't you want to see Rory? Tell your sister how much you've missed her? It can be like this forever, this can be your life— all you need to do is choose to stay."

I pull away from Lena's embrace and look into her eyes. Somewhere beyond the viridian greens of her irises lies something darker, something soulless. I hear a cracking sound behind her and turn to the wall. As if struck by some invisible force, the paint begins to chip and peel away. Following suit, the bedframe starts to erode. One by one, every item in the room begins to deteriorate into ash.

I look back at the woman Royce loved... the woman I love, her expression frozen in place, gleeful and yet daunting at the same time. "I'm not Royce Wilko... and you, you're not Lena."

"Royce... I don't know what you're talking about... Please, let's just go downstairs; the others are waiting for you."

"What is this place really, Mallen? Am I dreaming?" I ask, unwilling to be lulled deeper into this comatose state by the Boundless.

Lena's smile slowly fades into a grimacing frown as Mallen's voice exits my mind and enters Lena's body. "So be it, Royce. We refer to this void as 'The Waste'. It exists in a place between space and time. You aren't dreaming; your consciousness is merely split in two. I promise; you are very much awake in your dimension, just not in control."

"What are you talking about?" I feel my heart rate increase instantaneously.

"You'll see when we're done here. It is clear to the Nine that your persistence knows no bounds; You will serve our purposes no longer, we will find another."

The creature that looks like Lena turns to leave, but I quickly jut out an arm and grab her by the wrist. "Wait! I want answers Mallen!"

She swivels around quickly and grabs me by the throat, pressing me against the wall. "You dare to make demands of the keeper of the Nine? You are powerless in this dimension, human. You are still alive by my will, and my will alone; do not forget your place."

Struggling for even the slightest breath of air, I respond. "The Nine... you mean the monoliths, right? What are they?"

Mallen looks at me through Lena's eyes. Then, with what appears to be curiosity, her grip around my neck loosens and I fall to the floor. "You truly are tenacious... So be it. I will divulge our story to you. It will make no difference in the end; you and your kind will be eradicated all the same."

I'm coughing and hacking when I notice Lena's hand reaching out toward me through my peripherals. Hesitantly, I take hold of it, and then Mallen speaks. "Humans were not the first to call this planet home, that much you may already know, courtesy of that pest, Atticus; but there were others prior to the archaic creatures your kind thought to be the earliest lifeforms to inhabit the Earth. This world was originally ours, uncontested by any other beings, and it was paradise."

"I... I'm not following." My head is pulsating as I sit down upon the half-deteriorated bed.

"Tell me Royce... growing up, did your parents read you stories?"

"Of course."

In the form of Lena, Mallen came to sit beside me. "Some stories are happy and full of lessons, some are sad and riddled with tragedy, what most have in common though, is a protagonist. Sometimes, that protagonist perseveres and saves the day. On other occasions, they lose, maybe even die, because the things that go bump in the night are too powerful to overcome. Who this savior might be though, usually depends on the perspective of the reader. From your point of view, we are the things that go bump in the night, Royce."

I hesitate, then look at the shadow of Lena sitting beside me. "So that's your grand explanation? Monsters are real and I'm looking at one?"

The Boundless known to me as Mallen, cackles, a garbled, disgusting sound. "Monsters, no. It's much more complex than that. As I mentioned earlier, it all depends on perspective. We've always inhabited your world, claimed our stake here long ago. However, it wasn't until your species came into existence, until humanity gave us purpose, that we truly began to thrive."

I'm becoming agitated. I know no more than I did at the start of this conversation.

"Think in terms of energy Royce, positive and negative forces, and a balance in between. You need that balance to keep everything flowing the way it should be, too much weight in one direction and things can go catastrophically wrong. That's what's happening here; humankind tipped the scale beyond the point of no return long ago. Now that a doorway between our reality and your own has been opened via Atticus' experimentation on his brother, we can reverse the harm your species has wrought upon this planet. The visions Mason suffered were never going to come to fruition, not until Atticus Cais came into the picture and inadvertently assisted in our cause..."

"Wait, you don't mean..."

"Atticus Cais gave us the means to carry out our will, to cull this world of your species and thus return it to the utopia it once was. All we had to do was plant the seeds in Mason Cais' head. We'll admit, his condition was a fluke, truly a mutation of DNA coding without which we would never have been able to speak with one another. Once communication was established, however, we were able to telepathically tether our consciousness with Mason's. The melding of our minds created a resonance, one that signaled the awakening of the Nine, thus the mutation in his genes had served our purpose. Mason's mind was too weak to occupy two realities at once though, and eventually, he succumbed to his affliction instead of embracing it. We used Mason as a stratagem to lure Atticus along, to fool him into recreating the circumstances that first gave us entry into your dimension."

I nod in understanding. "And Atticus being Atticus, he walked right into your trap, because doing so furthered his own agenda."

"Correct. He took the bait like a starving animal, like a hungry animal to a piece of meat. We knew we had to find a way to replicate those conditions before it was too late; before Mason perished. So, we manipulated Atticus into cloning his brother's genetic code, and therefore the defect that allowed us into your reality. What was once intangible to us became palpable through the Echoes created by Atticus. They became a shell for us to inhabit, a means of transportation and physical perceptibility, albeit flawed vessels at best. That is until your DNA donor came along. You see Royce, you are Mason's replacement, as Jonathan had been before you; so long as you are alive, so long as you carry the Deus Molecule within your genetic code, so too, do you carry us."

"Jesus Christ..." I hold my head in my hands. If what Mallen is saying is true, then Atticus has unwittingly created the very scenario he has dedicated his life to preventing. "So, once you finish calling forth the rest of the Nine, you'll use them to eradicate humanity? As what? A means of punishment for our shortcomings and mistakes?"

"Though our dimension is positioned parallel to yours, the world we share is one in the same. A world that your kind is killing, slowly but surely. If we continue to allow you to grow, it will lead to Earth's ruin."

I don't respond, but instead sit in silence, trying to process what's being said. "Why are you so intent on destroying us? Why not help us see the error of our way? Help us change?"

"This is our grand purpose in the universe. All sentient beings seek purpose; it's what drives every individual organism forward on its journey through life. We have spent the whole of humanity's feeble existence watching you stumble and fall. Without failure, every time you dusted yourselves off, soon thereafter your kind would make the same mistakes that sent you tumbling to the ground prior. Repeatedly performing the same miscalculations again and again, always choosing the wrong path forward. There is no hope of change. Humans hunt and kill creatures they consider beneath them for sport; we do so to restore balance."

I scoffed at the nature of the statement. "You're nothing more than a parasite. Far more advanced than the likes of any we've seen before, but a parasite, nonetheless."

"Quaint; from where we stand, the parasitic party is mankind. You rape and pillage, have spent centuries murdering your own kind in mindless wars, and to what end? You have squandered the Earth, overused its resources, and polluted its atmosphere, shown complete and utter disregard for the species whom you share this home with. Humankind will eventually destroy itself if left to its own devices, that is inevitable. All we're doing is expediating the process and minimizing casualties to other species of Earth."

"I..." the words escape me at every twist and turn as I struggle to think of a valid response. Everything Atticus Cais has poured his heart and soul into, all the horrid things he has done, have been for nothing. Just as Mallen says; Atticus murdered time and time again for a fruitless cause. He and I will die all the same because it's the will of the Nine and the Boundless who follow their doctrine. Desmond Luther, Matias Castellón, Lena Cais, everyone will cease to exist. Yet here, in this moment, I'm not so sure that Mallen is wrong... The part of my brain that instills fear in my heart tells me I have to stop the Nine, and yet the part that breeds logic tells me they're right; humans had been on a destructive course long before ENDURE unknowingly opened a gateway to proverbial hell. Maybe the execution of the will of the Nine was for the best...

"No." The words fall from my mouth almost involuntarily.

"No? Elaborate," Mallen demands.

I stand up from the bed, and it continues to deteriorate at an accelerated rate. "I won't let you. Maybe you're right about us; Maybe we are destined to be our own downfall, but that isn't your decision to make. Besides, there's something you're not telling me, something you don't want me to know, but I do."

Mallen smiles; a sinister gesture. "And just what might that be?"

"You said so long as the Deus Molecule lives within someone, so to, will you. That's not entirely true though. You need it to be couriered by someone who can withstand its adverse effects, someone who can utilize its abilities. You need someone like me, but there is no one else like me."

"True; you hold the potential to hone the latent ability within you, and there is no one else who can. It's why you're able to bridge the gap between our realities the way you are in this very moment."

I step closer to Mallen as he stands up, still wearing Lena's skin.

"Then that makes me superior to you and your kind."

The Boundless leans in, a grave expression upon Lena's face, and yet there's something else there... fear? "You are foolish, human. We are omniscient and omnipotent where your kind is concerned; we are eternal, and you cannot hope to kill that which is intangible to you. Even now, we are using your body as a vessel to carry out our bidding. And my, my, Royce, you do slaughter humans with so much enthusiasm. Superior? You are nothing more than our sword."

There's a moment of panic as I weigh how much of what Mallen is saying is true and how much of it is manipulation. If I truly am being used as a weapon in my reality, I can't spare any more time on this existential debate. "Yeah, well... we'll just have to wait and see about that." I thrust my hand up and toward Lena's throat, a swift and decisive movement. When I pull it away, blood begins to pour from a puncture wound in her neck. She stumbles backward, collapsing onto the floor, eyes wide and panicked. Glancing down, I notice a large steel blade gripped confidently in my hand, not dissimilar to the knife that had killed Jonathan McAllister. Where it came from, I don't have the slightest clue. It seemingly appeared solely by the volition of my thoughts.

Lena cups a hand over the wound, gasping, as Mallen struggles to take air into her lungs. "How did you? This isn't possible..."

Releasing the blade, it falls from my hand and disintegrates just before hitting the floor. Mallen, inhabiting Lena's body, draws one final breath, and then she does the same, dissipating into ash before my eyes. It was never Lena, that much I know, yet I feel a pang in the pit of my stomach all the same.

"Wake up... Royce, wake up..."

Once more, a voice speaks from a distance, but this time it is different; sweet and loving in tone. Its cadence captures my attention. The false environment that had surrounded me slowly finishes fading, and just as suddenly, my eyes grow heavy with fatigue.

"Please Royce, you have to wake up..." One final plea, and my eyelids shut, thrusting me not into darkness, but instead, into light.

C H A P T E R   4 0

Slaughter

Time and location (372 days post-cryostasis): 12:06 pm,
ENDURE Secure Sublevel

"Wake up Royce, please God, wake up! He has a pulse, why won't his eyes open?! Come on, come on... WAKE UP!"

With a deep, labored gasp, I jolt upright. I struggle to breathe, choking as if sand has been poured down my throat. The taste of chemicals leaves a chalky residue in my mouth. It takes some time for my body to stabilize and regain my bearings. When I finally do, I realize I'm naked and cold, with nothing but a lab coat draped over my shoulders. I pull it around me tightly, doing my best to maintain any shred of dignity and modesty I can.

I look up and see a familiar face—one I never thought I would see again. Lena is crouched beside me, firmly gripping my hand. Her touch grounds me and helps me process my memories better. Two men stand at a distance, flanking either side of the door that leads into the area, dressed from head to toe in tactical military gear. They hold assault rifles at the ready. When I look back at Lena, I notice a sling resting across her chest, attached to the stock of one of those rifles peeking out just behind her right shoulder. She, too, wears armor and tactical gear. The sound of alarms reverberates throughout the facility, and everything is bathed in the red glow of emergency lights once again.

"Oh, thank God, I thought I'd lost you. How do you feel? Can you walk?" asks Lena.

It isn't until that very moment that I notice her face has tiny splatters of blood on it, barely visible in the crimson lighting. Bracing my hand against the ground, I begin to lift myself up, but withdraw it when I feel something odd; it comes away wet. As I steady my hand in front of me, I see that it too is covered in blood. Something isn't right, and Lena seems to have noticed the confusion on my face. "Royce, take it slow, we don't know what happened here."

I lift myself up to stand, clenching the lab coat shut, and Lena rises alongside me. I struggle to comprehend the gruesome scene as I take it all in; we're clearly in a lab of sorts, and there are bodies *everywhere*. They're chaotically scattered across the room. A few of them are clothed in lab coats like the one that blankets me—staff members of ENDURE, no doubt. There are others, however, who are dressed in body armor. Some are wholly intact, but others are torn to pieces, appendages and organs strewn about the area like confetti. There's blood *all over,* so much so that I can *smell* it. The heavy scent of iron fills the air, threatening to trigger my gag reflex. It appears as if a wild animal had gotten loose within the lab and wreaked havoc on everyone and everything in its path.

I turn around and notice a tube of sorts behind me, large enough to fit a human body. Crystalline shards of ice still cling to what remains of its glass cover; something had broken out from within. Inspecting myself for injury, I glance downward. As I stroke my forearms, I feel a grainy substance on them. I rub my thumb and index finger together. When I separate them and inspect the surface of my fingers, they come away with a small bubble of blood, as if I had been pricked for a sample; the grains are splinters of glass. Lena stands in silence, studying my every move. I can tell she has come to the same conclusion I have. "Royce, listen to me," she says softly.

"Did I... did I do this?" I ask shakily.

"We don't know who or what did this, but right now that's not important. What's important now is getting you out of here," she says, attempting to calm me.

I'm still staring at the spot of blood on my thumb. "Lena, what have I done? *How...*"

She centers herself in front of me, grips my shoulders, and shakes my body. "Royce, we are on borrowed time here. I can't explain everything right now, but I promise you we'll cover it all later. We are currently in lockdown on a sublevel of ENDURE, beneath the main facility you're accustomed to. You've been in cryostasis for a little more than a year. During that time, two more monoliths have appeared across the globe, bringing the total count to four. When I found out the extent of Atticus' wrongdoings, I knew I couldn't be a part of his research any longer; I knew that I had to stop him. So, I helped Matias escape, and in return, he led a strike force back here to rescue you and Desmond. I didn't find out until later that Aiden was... well... I guess you already know, Desmond told me as much... I'm so sorry."

I recall Aiden's death; how I hadn't been quick enough to prevent it. Then, something else Lena said pulls my thoughts away from our late friend's early demise. "Wait... *Matias*? He's *alive?*"

One of the two men by the door interjects. "Sure am, but there's no time for pleasantries. Lena, wrap it up. We've got maybe ten minutes before this lab is crawling with PMCs."

I realize then that these two men aren't strangers; they're Desmond and Matias. All at once, the gift Oakley had given me that day in my quarters made sense. It had been one of Matias's fingernails. Oakley must have done unspeakable things to him during the time he was held hostage, and I curse myself for not doing more to find him. Though, what could we have done? Aiden was a prime example of what happened when we repeatedly defied Atticus.

Lena nods to Matias, then continues bringing me up to speed as we make our way to the two of them. "Over the course of the last year, we've built a network of people dedicated to stopping my uncle and burning ENDURE to the ground. I recruited several ex-employees of the company, people within the corporation who shared my ideals and the idea that this project was dissolving into something we could no longer support. That's how we gained access to the gear and weapons. When Matias escaped, he killed Oakley and liberated his credentials, which I then used to hack into ENDURE's systems and siphon a considerable amount of funds from multiple offshore accounts. Once I got what we needed, I planted more than a few trojan horses within their programming; we have full access to the facility's controls from our own headquarters."

Lena pauses as we approach Matias and Desmond. They line up, one in front of the other, and begin assessing each other's gear. Matias checks Desmond, who checks Lena, who then circles around to check Matias while she continues talking. "Roughly six months ago, ENDURE went public. They revealed a 'new division' of their company dedicated to using science to find a way to stop the monoliths. It was a farce to obtain more funding from multiple parties, with the darker aspects of the company we're familiar with still being kept under wraps, but of course the masses ate it up. Atticus has become far more powerful and influential than ever before; I'm not sure we'll get another chance to stop him anytime soon. An hour or so ago, we initiated an attempt to coerce him to surrender, threatening to use force if he did not comply. From that point on... all hell broke loose. He has a large team of private military contractors onsite whose sole purpose is to wipe out any and everyone associated with our organization, known as the Coalition."

She stops again, gets down on one knee, and checks the clip in her weapon. Satisfied with its contents, she snaps it back into the gun. Then, she reaches over to a large hard case a few inches away and slides it toward me. "Royce, take this. There's an M4A1 assault rifle in there and gear fitted to your measurements."

I unlatch the case, reach inside, and take hold of the weapon. There's a hesitancy within me as I place it at my side. My eyes study the firearm; I'm fearful of it and of what I might do while it's in my possession. I haven't been the same since taking Jonathan's life, yet that death occurred under different circumstances. It had been a life I didn't intend to take. I certainly wasn't a stone-cold killer, but maybe... maybe I could kill for the right cause.

"The United States government is backing Atticus; we are the only thing standing between him and the destruction he will cause," Lena continues. "Royce, my uncle has lost his grip on reality, lost any ability to rationalize. Once we leave this lab, you're stepping into a warzone. Coalition forces are doing their best to push back, but the men and women working for Atticus are highly trained and have far more experience in warfare than most of our people. Our team won't be able to hold them off for long..."

I'm dumbfounded—a mixture of my delirium and the sheer weight of information that has just been dumped in my lap. *Another year gone just like that.* Have I really been on ice for that long? It seems that spending time in a comatose state is becoming par for the course. At the very least, Matias has gotten his revenge; Jordan Oakley is dead, and the world is better off for it. I take another look around the room and silently hope that I wasn't responsible for the carnage surrounding us. I recall my conversation with Mallen, his words ringing aggressively through my head as if I'm hearing them all over again...

"You aren't dreaming; your consciousness is merely split in two. I promise; you are very much awake in your dimension, just not in control."

Had Mallen done this with me as his vessel? In my gut, I already know the answer, but something in my heart refuses to accept it.

"Get dressed, quickly," Lena says, gesturing back to the hard case. I nod and remove the matching set of armor and clothing from inside it. As I slip into the suit and secure the Kevlar plates, Lena surveys the area once more, unaware that I'm watching her. The scene we find ourselves in is truly horrid and vomit-inducing. If I'm the one who caused this, then perhaps I'm capable of more violence than I previously anticipated. It pains me to see the look on Lena's face, a look that tells me she feels the same. I shake the thought away. If this slaughter had been committed by my hands, there are unknown circumstances at play that need to be considered before guilting myself into oblivion. After all, I clearly have no recollection of the events that led to the massacre. I pull one final strap taut and then approach the others at the door.

"Hey man, it's good to see you, *really* good," says Desmond, patting me on the back.

"Glad you're okay," is all Matias can muster while focused on the task at hand.

I nod to each of them, still struggling to grasp the situation, still feeling woozy. I fight through the daze and speak. "Alright, so what's the plan here?"

Matias smirks without much enthusiasm. "Survive, for starters."

Desmond elaborates. "We're not quite sure what we're up against. Like Lena said, there's a ton of soldiers on the premise who weren't here initially, hired-out firepower working for Atticus. They're highly trained, and we obviously aren't, so the odds are... well, they aren't great. We're working with what we've got, even if it isn't much."

Matias agrees. "Best not to take these guys head-on, target soldiers who are distracted or engaged in separate altercations, and move from cover to cover. No one wants to be caught in the open; it doesn't take guys like this long to find their targets and drop 'em."

As far as plans go, this one is rather poor. "So that's it? We just run and gun our way out of the facility? Surely, you've thought of something more... tactical?" I direct my question at Lena.

Her gaze drops to the floor. "No... this really is our only option. With the limited resources we have at our disposal on site... this is the only way."

I nod solemnly. "Okay, and then what? What happens when we get out? *If* we get out? These monoliths need to be destroyed; how are the four of us going to accomplish that?"

"That all depends on how the Coalition comes out of this. If we suffer limited casualties, then the potential we gain to grow as an entity all our own is substantial. I've recruited supporters from all areas of ENDURE, including biologists, chemists, and engineers; the list goes on. As a joint force, I'm positive we can figure out a way to prevent whatever damage the monoliths have yet to cause."

I freeze, the mention of the monoliths reminding me of the information I had obtained in the Waste. Unfortunately for me, Lena notices. "Royce, what is it?"

With a sigh, I delve in, doing my best to explain things quickly and concisely. "I know why the monoliths are being used to wipe out humanity. Mallen explained it to me while I was stuck in that canister. There's this… plane of existence he calls the Waste. It felt like a kind of limbo between life and death… I spoke with him there, and he told me what the monoliths are capable of, what their purpose is, all of it. I know all of it."

Matias and Desmond are guarding the door, but now their attention is divided, their eyes firmly locked on me as I continue. "From what Mallen told me, the Boundless were the planet's first inhabitants, and they never died off. They've been here for literal eons, existing on a parallel plane of reality to ours, unable to communicate or interact with humankind. They had no way of crossing over into our realm until Atticus began experimenting on your father. He said he developed some sort of mental tether with Mason. It transmitted a signal that caused the monoliths to rise. They intend to utilize the bodies of Deus Molecule carriers as surrogate vessels to usher in the arrival of the Nine, the monoliths. So far, though, I'm the only one the active Deus Molecule hasn't killed. Their options for vessels are exactly one. Mallen said their aim is to use the monoliths to wipe out our species so that the Earth can return to its natural state. He referred to it as a 'utopia' before humankind came into existence and blames us for the planet's decline. Once they finish summoning the Nine, it'll mean the extinction of humanity."

Matias responds promptly. "Before I put him down, Jordan Oakley told me something just as insane; that the three of us and Aiden were all clones. Called us Echoes. Then, when I linked up with Lena, she substantiated those claims with video footage. I saw... *me,* many of me, floating inside tubes like the one behind you. So, all in all? I'm not ruling anything out as unbelievable anymore."

It's true; nothing seems too outlandish or far-fetched to be accepted as fact now. The lingering silence that followed signified our acceptance of this truth.

Lena's father was the first to be born with the Deus Molecule active in his DNA and the first to fall prey to Atticus' cloning experiment. Mallen jumped at the chance to spread the gene and, in doing so, spread himself. When Mason came to Atticus talking about apocalyptic premonitions, he proved to the doctor that his clairvoyant abilities were real, though not entirely accurate. Mallen only needed Atticus to believe that his brother's vision would come to pass. Once Atticus was convinced of that, Mallen used Lena's father to manipulate her uncle into replicating the Deus Molecule through cloning. Atticus thought that finding a carrier of the gene who could harness its abilities was the only way to stop the monoliths. That may still be true, but it's also true that someone capable of harnessing the Deus Molecule's abilities also runs the risk of being Mallen's gateway into our dimension. That's where our DNA donors come into play. Atticus tried again and again, but the Echoes could never withstand the adverse effects of the activated gene—not until, well... me."

Lena says nothing, simply shakes her head in disgust. Desmond looks at me. "So, you're saying that..."

I reply as he trails off, staring down at my hands, the idea of what I might've done in this room knocking on the back door of my mind. "It's me, I'm the new clairvoyant. Before they killed Aiden, I had a vision; I knew someone was about to die. By the time I pieced together who, though, I had been too late. I haven't figured out exactly how it works or how to control it entirely; I only see bits and pieces, but it's me. All the other donors were missing a set of balancing traits that would allow the Deus Molecule to evolve without the deterioration of the host's body and mind, except for my donor, except for the real Royce Wilko."

"Jesus Christ..." Matias sighs under his breath. "Where does that leave Desmond and I then? If you're what Atticus was seeking, wouldn't that imply the two of us are failed experiments? Doesn't that mean we're doomed to lose our minds? That we'll be dead sooner rather than later due to rapid deterioration?"

After what seems like an eternity, Lena finally re-enters the conversation, trusting that Matias and Desmond now understand the parameters of the situation they find themselves in. "It's far from an exact science. The original Desmond, Matias, and Aiden all had almost as much potential as Royce did. For whatever reason, while the three of you could never communicate with the Boundless no matter how many Echoes my uncle ran through, you also never suffered from the deterioration issues the other

Echoes did. At least for now, that isn't something I would worry about. If we make it out of this alive, we can return to headquarters and run tests of our own, try to get some more solid answers."

It's a lot to absorb, but then again, that's how our entire existence has been.

"Back to the monoliths, how do we stop them?" Desmond asks me.

"As far as I can tell, we don't. Even if it's possible, I think I'm the only one capable of doing so and like I said, I don't know the first thing about whatever abilities I've gained from Atticus' experimentation," I say, reading the growing defeat on Desmond's face with every passing word.

Lena scratches her head in frustration. "Why? Why only you?"

I shrug. "I don't know. I might be our only shot at stopping this, but I have no idea where to start. The Boundless are interdimensional beings. There are moments when it seems like I'm able to... I don't even know how to say it... project myself into that void Mallen refers to as the Waste. I think all those nightmares I was having weren't nightmares at all, but interactions with Mallen in that place. It's like I'm able to bridge the gap between our reality and theirs. Whether that's something I have control over or not, I don't know. It could be that I can only enter the Waste when Mallen allows me to. I woke moments ago because I think... I think I killed Mallen in the Waste. At the very least, I wounded him. I don't believe I can do that from our plane of existence, but if I can figure out how to get back there on command, maybe that's the key to stopping all of this. If the Boundless can get ahold of more host bodies strong enough to survive though, if they find a way to use humans as vessels... who knows what they'll be capable of."

Lena takes the reins once more. "Alright, well right now our main problem is Atticus and escaping this facility. We can figure out how to stop the Boundless and destroy the monoliths with The Coalition's help after we regroup."

I nod, and begin to say "Okay, but—"

A loud bang echoes off the lab door from outside. Matias aims his rifle at the entrance, snapping into his DNA donor's role as a marine. "Shit, we've got company. Dez, start flipping desks and anything else large enough to shield us; we're gonna need cover." Desmond immediately complies, sprinting away while Matias shifts his focus to Lena and me. "Royce, Lena; Get behind cover and check your weapons. Lena, give him a rundown on how to operate that thing." I've fired a gun before, or at least Royce has, but those were handguns, not assault rifles. Lena shows me where the safety is, and how to release an empty clip and reload, among other things.

Desmond flips a desk over beside us, its contents loudly clattering onto the bloodied floor. He crouches behind it, resting his rifle on the edge of the furniture. The pounding at the entrance to the lab grows louder and more consistent; what we believe are hired guns will be entering the room in mere moments. This is it, the culmination of our search for the truth and our subsequent escape; live or die, everything is about to change.

CHAPTER 41

Trenches

Time and location (372 days post-cryostasis): 12:21 pm,
ENDURE Secure Sublevel

The doors separating us from our aggressors are solidly constructed; I expect them to hold for much longer than they do. I silently hope for a moment to prepare myself for what comes next when the barriers explosively burst open, flying off their tracks and into the lab only minutes after the siege has begun. A plethora of footsteps can be heard shuffling through the destroyed threshold, and from the sounds of it, we're heavily outnumbered.

I look to my right. Immediately beside me, sharing the same overturned desk for cover, is Lena, and beyond her, behind a separate makeshift shield, is Desmond. Where, though, has Matias gone? The last I saw him, he was standing directly in front of the doors. No one has fired a shot, at least not yet. Did he surrender? No; I highly doubt these men came here with any qualms about taking lives; Matias would have been shot on sight.

Then again, if I were in the position of contracted help and entered a lab filled with blood, guts, and body parts, I'd be inclined to shoot first and ask questions later as well. It isn't exactly the scene you'd walk into without feeling threatened. They certainly aren't here to take prisoners; they're here to eliminate the threat, shoot to kill. If I know that, Matias has certainly deduced the same.

A semi-automatic burst of gunfire rattles through the air. I look back at Desmond and realize, much to my surprise, that he fired first. Immediately after, a cacophony of gunfire fills the room, mixed with the sound of rounds ricocheting off the steel desks and equipment like hail striking a parked car. Had our improvised protection not been made of steel, Desmond would have already been filled with holes.

A soldier falls to the floor beside me, his balaclava drenched in blood that oozes out onto the floor. I nearly jump out of my skin, initially unsure if the man was dead or alive when he came into view. Glancing back to where Desmond is posted, I notice he's ducked down with his weapon held tightly to his chest; neither he, nor Lena, had fired a single shot. It must have been Matias who took out the soldier, but where he is firing from remains a mystery. The clamor caused by the bullets is becoming less overbearing; is Matias winning this fight? All on his own?

One of the intruders suddenly rounds the corner of the desk behind which Desmond is positioned, but luckily, he has seen the enemy approaching. He fires the rifle, and I watch as the bullet finds its mark in the man's chest. The injured soldier collapses to the floor, and Desmond swiftly places another round in his skull with precise accuracy.

Lena and her Coalition had certainly spent what little time they could training for this, and it showed in their preparedness for the situation. The gunfire has now all but stopped, apart from a singular weapon still expelling bullets from its current clip; no doubt Matias is picking his targets and methodically disposing of them. Another moment passes, and silence fills the room. The firefight felt like it lasted forever but couldn't have lasted more than five minutes.

I peek out from behind my protection, slowly but surely. There's even more blood pooling up around the lab than before, a feat that had previously seemed impossible. I'm grateful that the sublevel's version of a lockdown seems to differ from Atticus' prior definition of the event, also swathing everything in a crimson wash. If everything is bathed in red, I can almost trick myself into thinking the carnage isn't quite as bad; almost.

The intruders lie motionless, at least seven of them. I stand, extending a hand to Lena, who hesitantly takes it and slowly rises to stand beside me. Desmond follows suit once he's certain that the threat to our lives has been neutralized. Just then, the shattered door of the pod that had been my home for the past year flips open, splinters of fractured glass clattering upon the floor. Out of the container pokes a familiar face, Matias.

"You were... *in* the pod?" asks Desmond.

Matias steps up over the ledge, dropping from the casing and hitting the floor feet first. "Amongst other unsuspecting locations around the room, but yeah. When Lena told me we were clones, she also told me that I had never truly been in the military. That was an experience the original Matias had, but I *do* have his memories, and he was quite the tactician."

"Interesting," adds Lena.

"Care to elaborate?" Matias asks, intrigued.

"The memories of your DNA donor; they're supposed to be just that, memories. You are only supposed to remember the skills they had during their lifetime, not be capable of utilizing them. What you just did though... one man against seven trained soldiers? I'd say it's safe to assume your *body* remembers how the original Matias utilized it just as well as your brain does, almost like there was a transference of muscle memory..."

"Six," Desmond interjects. "One man against six; I got one of them."

Lena rolls her eyes at him. Desmond walks over to one of the unconscious soldiers and inspects him. "Hey, Mr. military tactician, wouldn't be such a bad idea to reup on gear before we leave, right?" he asks Matias, crouching to tap the dead soldier's vest.

"Not at all. From the looks of it, these guys are packing Kevlar and M4A1s, the same as us. You're just lucky those rifles weren't loaded with armor-piercing rounds, or that desk would've been shredded like paper, and you'd be dead. Royce, gear up too. We went through hell to get to you; the last thing we need is you getting shot and killed."

Desmond freezes for a moment at the remark. "Comforting, but I agree. Let's stock up on ammunition and armor and get out of here before we have more company."

Matias nods and finds a body while Lena and I do the same. The soldier who had fallen immediately beside me during the firefight seems as good a place to start as any. When I look him over, my suspicions are confirmed; these men aren't playing around. Along with the Kevlar vest and M4A1 carbines are some frightening pieces of equipment. I had played more than enough video games, or at least the real Royce had, to recognize most of it: frag grenades, spring-loaded ballistic knives, C4 charges. When I remove the man's helmet, I take note of an attachment bolted atop it. "Hey, are these—

"Night vision googles, USNV PVS-7 Gen 3's, standard issue for U.S. military," Matias confirms.

"Should we take them?" I ask as Matias finishes strapping on a Kevlar vest.

"Could be useful, but it won't give us any kind of advantage if the enemy has them too."

I nod, placing the helmet on my head and tightening the strap under my chin. "These goggles, do they work pretty much the same as they do in video games?"

Matias responds to me with a blank stare as he removes a radio from the soldier's hip.

"Sorry, I'll elaborate. In games, they enable the player to see in the dark, but once you enter a brightly lit room, all you see is white. Is that how they function in real life?"

"Sort of. They magnify light to make things visible in the dark, so when presented with a light source, it's almost like shining a flashlight in your eyes. Why?"

I turn my attention to Lena. "Can we get the regular lights back on in the facility with this lockdown active? What's with the emergency lights anyway? Atticus had told me those were only used in Code Red scenarios."

"Things operate differently on the sublevel. Emergencies down here are treated as such since there isn't a façade to maintain. Regardless, we'll have to lift the lockdown to leave the facility once we're topside. To do that, we need to access the server room."

I nod and study Lena's face between flashes of ruby light. "So, if we can get to this server room, rather than only shutting down the system's emergency responses, could we also kill the power entirely, then access it remotely at will?"

Matias seems to catch on to the idea I'm proposing. He grins as he picks up one of the M4A1s, releasing its clip to check if it's filled to maximum capacity. "That's not a bad idea, pretty brilliant actually."

Desmond raises a brow as he puts on a utility belt fitted with grenades. "I'm not exactly following here, care to explain?"

Royce aims to use the NVGs to level the playing field since these guys outnumber us ten to one. If we can find a way to access the building's electrical grid remotely, we can instantly power down the entire facility, leaving us in the dark. This will encourage the opposition to activate their NVGs. Then, we'll remote back in and turn the power on, temporarily leaving them blind and stunned by their own equipment. It gives us a split-second window before they power down their goggles or before the goggles' automatic shut-off triggers. If it works, though, we can do some real damage to these guys before they even know what hits them."

Desmond looks to me, and I confirm that Matias hit the nail on the head. "That pretty much covers my idea, only I was thinking we strobe the lights, have them constantly flashing on and off if possible. They'll eventually remove the NVGs and rely on sight, but either way it will give them quite a bit of vertigo in the interim. A dazed opponent is better than a stable one. Lena, is it doable?"

"Better than that, the maintenance crew is all equipped with tablets programmed for remote access. If we find one of them, we can confiscate the device. Come to think of it, we can shut down power via the tablet as well and skip the server room altogether. There's most likely one in this lab; we just need to..."

Her voice trails off as she looks around us; one last photograph of the gruesome scene to sear into her brain. I realize then that, apart from our attackers, there's a good chance Lena knows some of the dead here. Taking gear from soldiers bent on killing you is one thing, but I can tell she's struggling with the idea of looking into the cold, lifeless eyes of her former colleagues to find that tablet.

"Alright, let's finish gearing up and get a move on. Lena, I'll look for a tablet," I say, placing a hand on her shoulder. She smiles weakly, but it's genuine. Even if I had somehow unconsciously brutalized half the people in this room, she still appears to love me. As she turns away to gather equipment, I crouch and pick up an M4A1 lying on the floor in front of me, slinging the extra rifle over my shoulder. I replace the spent magazine with a fresh one pulled from a pouch in my vest, just as Lena had shown me earlier. Whether my natural ability to adapt comes from a place of intelligence or an experimentally altered one, I'm not sure.

Either way, it pays to be one of Atticus's experiments in this particular moment.

I carefully navigate through the bodies, one by one. Some are completely intact; those are the ones I can look at and search without feeling queasy. The others, however... It takes seven bodies before I find the tablet, and every fiber of my being to hold it together for Lena's sake.

Matias gestures towards the door, grabbing our attention. "Alright, time to clear out. I'll take point, Desmond will bring up the rear. I want you and Lena between the two of us just in case things get hairy."

Neither Lena nor I have any objection to the notion.

"Alright," says Matias, pausing to take a deep breath, steadying himself for the hell to come. "From here on out, we operate as a unit if we want to survive. Do what I say, when I say. We're headed for the trenches now, so keep your weapons loaded and at the ready. Let's move."

Abaddon

Time and location (372 days post-cryostasis): 12:33 pm,
ENDURE Secure Sublevel

"Lena, which way?" Matias whispers, quiet as a church mouse. "Down the hall, then take a right," comes her answer, the tone of her voice even lower than his. She's studying the tablet I had pulled from one of the bodies in the lab, mapping our quickest exit path. We can hear the chaos in the distance. The halls reverberate with gunfire, harrowing screams, and explosions. There's no mistaking it; inside this building, there is a war raging, and by the sounds of it, fiercely so. The area of the facility we're passing through is nearly empty, aside from the occasional body scattered here and there. Wherever they had been keeping me stored away, it's evident that only a select few ENDURE staff had access to this space, most of whom are lying obliterated back in the lab we had come from. If that weren't the case, there would have been many more dead along our way.

We reach the end of the hall, wait for Matias to signal that it's clear, and then hang a right. A few more paces down, Lena taps Matias on the shoulder. He stops and turns around to face her. "What is it?" he asks.

"Take a left up ahead, and then at the end of the corridor, there will be an elevator that we can take up to the main level," says Lena. It dawns on me then that the mayhem sounds so distant because most of it, if not all, is happening far above us.

Matias nods, and we continue forward in unison. As we near the corridor that leads to the lift, I reflect on Matias's display of tactical prowess in the lab. He had nearly single-handedly taken down multiple soldiers utilizing skills that he shouldn't have been capable of. Once again, I wonder if my own ability to adapt is engineered by Atticus and his scientists. Were all the Echoes designed to operate under any circumstance with incredible precision and efficiency based on the expertise of their DNA donor?

It makes sense after all. To a certain degree, Atticus's goal was to create us as weapons, a counterattack to stave off what Mason's visions had predicted to be the end of humankind. Perfecting my clairvoyance is what Atticus strives to achieve. If he can also make soldiers of us Echoes in the process, giving us the brawn to match our brains, then all the better. If he manipulated our DNA in more ways than one, I can't even blame him. The more I reflect on what the doctor has done to me overall, the more conflicted I feel. Maybe if Atticus had approached his work more delicately, I could have agreed with it, considering what was at stake...

At the mere consideration of pardoning the doctor for his sins, I'm reminded of all the suffering left in Atticus's wake, all the death he consciously permits in pursuit of his goals. Justifying his actions is impossible. Every time I try to find reason in his decisions, I come to the same conclusion: Atticus must die for the betterment of mankind. He has become just as much a threat to our survival as the Nine. The idea of killing as a necessity seems morbid but grows less and less abhorrent with each passing day. If I have to end the doctor's life myself to ensure he never takes another, then so be it.

I refocus as we approach the end of the corridor. Finally, after all these years, freedom from ENDURE and Atticus's twisted clutches is within reach. Though I harbor no illusions about the threat that remains, it's a gratifying feeling all the same. We certainly still have much larger fish to fry, but I'll worry about that later. Just before we round the corner to our left, Matias suddenly raises his arm, a single clenched fist held in the air. All of us halt at once. My stomach drops, and the thought occurs that maybe we won't make it out of this place; perhaps the bowels of ENDURE will be my tomb.

"What's wrong?" Desmond whispers from the back of our line.

"I heard something," Matias answers. The hallway splits into a T-shape up ahead. To the left is the elevator that leads to our liberation. To the right, however...

"I can hear that you've stopped, which means you know we're here," the voice bounces off the walls down the hallway to our right, causing us to sink in and hug the corner tightly. I break out in a cold sweat; we're trapped.

"Here's the deal," the voice continues, "you walk out into the open slowly, with your hands on the back of your heads. In return, I give you my word that my men aren't going to open fire. We'll take you into custody and sort this all out. You know as well as I do that we need Royce alive; we aren't going to hurt any of you. Seems like a fair shake given the wake of destruction you all left back in that lab."

I bristle at the mention of my name, then steel myself before responding. "You're outnumbered! Give it up and let us leave!" I shout back.

"Well, speak of the devil, I'd know that chatterbox anywhere... Trust me, we're not outnumbered. There's what, four of you? I've got a six-man squad with me, all highly trained and deadly. Come quietly, please, for your own sake. If not for your own, then for your friends and for the whole of humanity. You hold the key to our survival, Royce; it's time you decide what to do with it." I'm pretty sure it's Elliot Shaw speaking now. I disregard his attempts to lure us into the open.

Matias speaks over his shoulder to the rest of us, keeping his eyes focused ahead. "Remember what I said earlier about listening to me and getting out of here alive?"

Lena interjects, "Matias, don't do anything brash," she warns.

He puts on a barely perceptible nervous smile. "Sorry sweetheart, brash is what I do best. Desmond, give me a few of those frag grenades."

Desmond protests. "For *what?* We're underground with a building on top of us. Why don't we just think this through for a minute?"

Matias shakes his head from side to side. "No. On my command, I'm going to lob a few grenades to our right. Once they go boom, the three of you need to cut left and make a break for that elevator."

Desmond scowls at him. "Are you out of your damn mind?" he asks, but the question is clearly rhetorical. "Matias, setting those off down here could compromise the entire infrastructure of the compound. There's no way you'd make it out before the place collapses."

Matias lets out a resigned sigh. "Royce is the only one who *needs* to make it out; the rest of us are disposable as long as he survives."

My skin crawls, and there's a buzzing in my ears. Reality sets in once more, and I go numb. His words feel like a punch to the gut. We've already lost Aiden, and now Matias is trying to sacrifice himself. This colossal, hardheaded, stubborn as hell brute of a man is ready to die to save us, to save *me*.

The man we believe is Shaw interrupts again. "We don't have all day. Last chance, come quietly or we'll have no choice but to advance. If we do, this ends in more unnecessary bloodshed," he warns from down the hall, a hint of agitation in his tone.

Time is running out, but I plead with Matias nonetheless. "Let's just think for a second, I'm sure there's another way."

Finally, Matias turns to face us all, looking us in the eyes. "You heard him, they're six men deep. Seven including who sounds like Shaw, and he's a force to be reckoned with all on his own. Every second we waste chatting is another second towards them deciding to take us down by force. I told you all from the get-go; do what I say, when I say."

I watch Lena's gaze drop to the floor as she shakes her head in disbelief. Deep down, we all know this is our best option. Matias extends his left hand. "Desmond, the grenades."

Desmond reaches for his belt, hesitantly removing two frags and placing them in Matias's hand. The two of them lock eyes for a moment before Desmond says his farewell. "You get out of here alive, got it?"

Matias nods. "I'm right behind you."

I feel tense as I watch the exchange between them. This is really happening. "Matias, *please* don't do this," I whisper in desperation.

He looks at me, and in an instant, seems to embody the essence of my father, Charles. "You just worry about the others. Protect them. You can't stop me, but you can make sure that what I'm about to do serves its intended purpose. I've spent my entire life wallowing in regret, wanting to right my wrongs. I can't change the past, but I can do some good *right here, right now.* Let me have this, Royce."

There's a fierce stubbornness in his eyes, like a bull determined to eviscerate a matador. I search them for any trace of compromise but find nothing. Matias is going to do this, and no one will stand in his way.

"Okay," I finally say, "but if there's even a sliver of a chance that you can make it out, you find us. I want you to look me in the eye and *promise* me that you'll find us."

The callousness fades from his face. "I promise. Now back up and cover your ears. On my go, you run like hell, all of you."

I swallow hard against the knot in my throat. I hadn't prepared to leave anyone behind, especially a friend. I've lost so many people already, and the thought of losing anyone else is excruciating.

"One," Matias starts counting down.

"Two," he continues as I glance at the others. Desmond's gaze is fixed on the floor, unwavering, with anger etched on his face. He grips his M4A1 so tightly that his hands tremble. When I look at Lena, I see tears streaming silently down her face. All three of us are thoroughly broken. I squeeze my eyes shut and hope this is just another vision, that this isn't my reality.

"Three!" Matias pulls the pins from both grenades and tosses them around the corner as far as he can. I accept the facts; this is no vision, and there is no turning back now. The grenades explode, shaking the ground beneath our feet and kicking up a plume of dust that tumbles down through the intersection of the halls.

"GO!" Matias shouts as he briefly turns the corner, laying down heavy covering fire with his assault rifle.

None of us hesitate; we'd honor what could very well be his final wish and dash through the smoke to the left before the soldiers have time to recover. Sprinting at full speed toward the elevator, the cacophony of warfare grows increasingly louder. The enemy has recuperated and begun to exchange fire with Matias. I stop and turn around just in time to see a bullet hit him in the shoulder.

"NO!" I shout in desperation. Suddenly, a hand grips my forearm, pulling me away from the terror.

"We need to go, Royce! He made his choice; don't let him die in vain!" It's Lena's voice. I mobilize, forcing my legs to work as I turn on my heel and run. Before I can even process it, we're in the elevator, rising toward the surface of the facility. Everything around me mutes, becoming utterly void of sound aside from a ringing in my ears. I'm aware of Lena consoling me, though I can't hear the words she speaks. We're almost there, almost free; yet all I can think about is how this hell, this Abaddon, would be Matias' final resting place.

CHAPTER 43

Cloth

Time and location (372 days post-cryostasis): 12:33 pm,
ENDURE Secure Sublevel

"You hold the key to our survival, Royce; it's time you decide what to do with it." Elliot Shaw stands in the middle of the hall, rifle aimed steady and true toward the open crossing ahead. On either side of him are three PMCs, making six in total. They're paid-for-firepower, hired by Atticus due to the paranoia he developed shortly after Lena had quit and disappeared.

Although Shaw isn't sure that the doctor is sound of mind lately, his precautionary decision paid off; Royce's colleagues launched a full-scale attack, recruiting like-minded former ENDURE employees as their own soldiers. Most of the PMCs beside Shaw now are ex-military from every imaginable branch; SEALS, Army Rangers, PJs, you name it. Not only are these soldiers much more skilled with a weapon than any former

ENDURE employee, but they also have no scruples about the tasks they undertake as long as they lead to a paycheck.

Shaw tunes into the opposing group's whispered conversation down the hall to his right but can't make out anything specific. Enough is enough; he isn't going to continue standing idly by, waiting for them to come peacefully. Holding up two fingers, he flicks his wrist in a forward motion and signals his team to advance. They do as ordered, slow and silent like serpents underwater. Shaw follows closely behind, but not too close; these guys are the fodder, and while they provide an extra tactical advantage, Shaw brings intellect. Atticus needs him alive more than ever if they're to finally unlock the secrets of the Deus Molecule once Royce is back in their possession.

They're about ten feet from rounding the corner when two small spherical objects fly into the hall, bouncing off the wall and clattering to the floor at their feet. One of the PMCs yells, "Shit, fall back!" but it's too late. As soon as the soldier finishes his sentence, both frag grenades detonate, sending up a storm of blood-infused dust and debris. The force of the combined blast sends Shaw flying, and he lands hard on his back. Gunfire fills the air before the dust can settle, and, much to his dismay, it's incoming fire.

"Crazy son of a... you trying to bring the whole place down?!" Shaw screams in agitation. He struggles to his feet as what remains of his company attempts to return fire. Staying as low as possible, he begins to retreat down the hall. About seven steps in, debris trips him up. Shaw stumbles and falls, his ears still ringing and the vertigo from the explosion all-encompassing. Whoever had started the assault did so with barely a shred of a plan, if any at all.

Surprisingly enough, it had worked. These mercenaries had been trained in tactical warfare, but this was pandemonium: someone on a suicide mission. They don't even have time to react. Shaw rolls onto his stomach and glances back toward the T-split in the hall as the sound of bullets finding their targets fades. Smoke finally begins to clear, if only a little. The grenades wiped out at least half of his squad, and what remains of them is shredded apart by enemy fire almost immediately thereafter, regardless of their efforts to prevent this outcome. In an instant, they're all dead; only Shaw remains.

A silhouette begins to form through the remaining dust. Whoever has attacked them is making his way down the hall toward Shaw, though he has a good idea of who it is. He doesn't have any line of defense; his rifle was lost in the initial commotion. Laying his head flat, he slows his breathing and plays dead. More rounds sound off, but this time in smaller, more controlled bursts; the assailant is cleaning house, ensuring every one of the hired guns is down for the count.

Instantly, Shaw knows his guess is correct: it's Matias Castellón's clone. He served alongside the original DNA donor and even came close to considering him a friend. From what he knew of the real Matias' skillset, pulling off some half-assed, one-man army bullshit was right up his alley. Though the Echo shouldn't have been able to mimic his donor's acquired skills, it's a miscalculation—one he fears he'll pay dearly for.

A final burst of fire echoes through the halls, filling an otherwise silent void. This is it; the enemy's footsteps grow closer; Shaw will have only a millisecond's chance to save himself. He steadies his breathing, remaining calm and collected. The Echo's footsteps halt just short of his head, and then he hears heavy steel clattering against the concrete floor. The crazy bastard has tossed aside his weapon.

"Get up," Matias' clone demands.

So much for playing possum. The clone takes after Matias more than Shaw gives him credit for; he's intuitive. With hesitation, Shaw tucks his arms under himself, pushing up into a kneeling position. When he lays his eyes on the clone, he notices that the Echo didn't come through the firefight unscathed; there's a bullet wound in his left shoulder.

Shaw takes a deep, ragged breath. "So, what's your plan here? Kill me too? You already put yourself in quite a bind when you offed Oakley."

"He wasn't the first, and if you look around, he *clearly* wasn't the last. I told you to *get up,*" the would-be Matias repeats.

Shaw stares him down, searching for any leeway, but all he finds is grim resolve. He stands up and leans back against the wall, the Echo's eyes locked firmly on his. They stay like that in silence for a while, and Shaw begins to wonder if maybe the clone didn't plan this far ahead.

Just when he's about to break the awkward silence, the Echo finally speaks. "Oakley... from what I remember of the two of you during our service days, you weren't exactly two peas in a pod. Why the hell would you work with that lunatic, Elliot?"

"You *aren't* Matias," Shaw snaps back.

The Echo glances briefly at the floor. "No... no, I suppose I'm not. Though you could have had this conversation with him, if you had not abducted and murdered him in the name of a better tomorrow."

"I wouldn't expect you to understand, clone. What we're doing here is *important*."

The Echo scoffs. "Spare me. You can fool yourself, but you can't fool me. You may not think of me as your old buddy Matias, but I have his memories. I *know you*, and I know when you're bullshitting. You don't *really* believe that, not anymore."

Shaw is momentarily stunned into silence before replying. "I... I have a job to do."

The clone rolls his neck and shakes his arms loose. "I know you do, Elliot. That was always your problem; you ran to wherever the money was and followed orders with no room for a moral compass… but when you do that for so long? The regret starts to eat you alive from the inside out. You're going to do what you need to do, and I'll respond in kind. I just wanted you to know in advance that I'm sorry for it, even if you aren't. There's one thing I need to know, though," he pauses, waiting for Shaw's response.

Shaw shakes his head, feeling disgraced and exhausted. "What do you want to know?"

The Matias clone sighs, and to Shaw's surprise, appears emotionally drained before asking, "Were you there when he did it? Someone else was, but the feed was blurry, and I couldn't tell who. Was it you?"

Shaw raises an eyebrow, confused. "The fuck are you talking about?"

Like lightning, the Echo throws a right hook, connecting like a bag of bricks with Shaw's cheekbone. He slides down the wall and onto the floor with a thud. After taking a moment to regain his composure, he lifts himself onto all fours, spitting blood.

Matias' Echo points an accusatory finger at him. "Don't play stupid with me, Shaw. Were you there when Oakley killed Aiden? Did you let it happen?"

Shaw stays down on all fours, wipes the spattered mix of saliva and blood from his bottom lip. He hesitates to answer, but when Matias' doppelganger delivers a swift kick to his ribs, he feels a couple crack, and that's enough to change his stance. "Yes. Yes, I was there. Is that what you want to hear? I entered his quarters with Oakley during lockdown. We had a conversation and when it was all said and done, Oakley put a bullet in his head. Then we disposed of the body and cleaned house. Alright? Now you know, so what do you intend to do about it?"

The Echo bends down, grabs hold of Shaw's vest with both hands, then lifts and presses him against the wall. "Nothing personal Shaw, you didn't pull the trigger. Either way, though, Aiden didn't deserve that, and you could have stopped his death from happening. Consider yourself lucky; you saw what I did to Oakley."

With Shaw's vest held tightly in his grip, the clone's left fist presses firmly against his chest, crushing his sternum against the wall, leaving his right fist free to inflict massive damage. When the first punch connects with his jaw, it's enough to make Shaw see stars. By the second and third blows, he's out like a light, but the fourth brings him back to consciousness, and the cycle repeats over and over again. It's a nightmare; Shaw knows how to take a beating, but the Echo's blows carry all the force of Matias Castellón's fists and feel like two cinderblocks connected to pistons every time they hit their target. The flurry continues, and Shaw starts to lose any faith that the Echo will stop. Somewhere in the back of his mind, he hears the clone screaming violently, wails of a man tormented by the pain and agony of loss.

When he finally stops, it takes Shaw a while to react, having lost sensation in most of his body many moments earlier. He opens his eyes as best he can, his swollen and battered lids and the blood from his split brows threatening to blind him.

Through ragged, broken breaths, he speaks. "Go on then... finish it. You wanted to prove you were human... prove you were better than Atticus... better than me. Look where your self-righteous journey has brought you... You and me? We aren't so different... we're both monsters... molded by the horrors of our past...cut from the same cloth..."

The Echo stares hard at the mangled man before him, his fist still cocked and ready to fire, quivering in wait. His breathing is heavy and quick, like that of a rabid animal. Shaw can tell the clone wants to punch straight through his face, feel his fist collide with the concrete as it passes through his skull. Every fiber of his being seems to twitch with the urge. The Echo grits his teeth, his fists shaking with tremors of pure rage, and then he lets one last punch fly free. Connecting with the concrete directly beside Shaw's head, his anger is suddenly replaced by pain, and just as quickly as it had built up, it subsides into calmness. He looks Shaw in the eye one last time.

"No... I'm not you, and I never will be. You sold your soul, Elliot." The Echo pushes him sideways to the ground with the hand that had kept Shaw pinned to the wall.

Lying there, like an animal struck by a car, Shaw takes shallow breaths. He struggles to move, willing his muscles to pick himself up, urging his brain to signal the proper synapses to get his body functioning again. His struggle yields no favorable results. Shaw has been beaten, and that seems to be enough to put the clone's weary mind to rest. Matias' Echo steps back, crouches down to retrieve his rifle among the shredded bodies of the PMCs. He then stands and slings it over his shoulder.

The giant turns to leave but stops short, glancing back at Shaw. "I don't know if you're listening, or if you can even hear me. Just know this; I chose to show you mercy today; you owe me your life."

Seemingly having found closure, the Echo walks down the corpse-riddled corridor toward the elevator. Shaw remains behind in the midst of the massacre, now contemplating his choices and affiliations more than he ever expected. That clone *isn't* his former squad mate; he *isn't* Matias. So why does he seem so familiar? Why does the Echo remember him as if they had served together side by side all those years ago on deployment? Shaw ponders this for a long while as he lies there, a crippled mess, and then wonders yet again if Atticus is wrong. Maybe they had turned into the villains ENDURE sought to destroy all along.

CHAPTER 44

Ashes

*Time and location (372 days post-cryostasis): 12:57 pm,
ENDURE Center for Rehabilitation*

The scene on the ground level of the facility is a wasteland of its own. When the elevator doors open, we exit quickly, ducking into the nearest room to regroup and formulate our exit strategy. Much like the setting of the sublevel, this floor is also ripe with the deceased. The number of bodies on the main floor is nearly triple what we saw below.

Now, above and with the lockdown still active, the lighting is normal. It seems ironic considering the jig is up, but the facility itself can't differentiate between when ENDURE's act is or isn't in play. With steady fluorescent lighting, I observe just how much destruction and havoc have been wreaked here. Millions of fragments of glass from shattered panes that had once been office walls flanked either side of us almost immediately when we first stepped out of the lift.

The room we currently occupy is cluttered with broken chairs and tables, perforated with bullet holes, and littered throughout the area. Still, even from within this momentary haven, I can hear the sound of gunfire blaring continuously in the distance. When I peek through the glass window in the door that leads to the lobby, I see people engaged in violent close-quarters combat. PMCs in their matte black full-body armor clash with Coalition fighters dressed in whatever gear they could scavenge. The only thing that levels the playing field is that Lena and her cohorts have raided their guns and gear from ENDURE itself. Even if their skill level is inferior to that of Atticus's forces, at least they're waging war with similar weapons and firepower.

The gimmick is up, and it seems that anyone who previously wore a lab coat in an official capacity has either left the facility or is among its dead. Even amidst this chaos, I can't shake Matias from my mind; I can't accept that we left him behind... Did we make the right choice? Regardless of the man's wishes, should we have found another way?

As I check my surroundings, the realization that I'm unsure of our location pulls me away from my horrid thoughts. I nudge Lena from behind while she tries to map a way past the altercations in the lobby with the tablet. "Where exactly are we?"

She glances back and then responds. "Staff break room, you wouldn't have ever been here in the past. The area is off limits to everyone else."

That explains why I hadn't recognized it.

"So where do we go from here?" Desmond asks Lena as he stands watch by the door.

"We use the tablet to cause Royce's strobe effect via remote access. I won't be able to offer any supporting fire in the meantime, so the two of you are our only riflemen. This is it, though; once we exit that door, we're diving headfirst into the fire. We move, and we don't look back until we're outside the facility, through the courtyard, and miles away from here. The Coalition has a safe house set up for us at an undisclosed location. They'll send coordinates once we're clear of the area."

Desmond nods. "Alright then, Lena will handle the power. Royce, I want you to watch our backs and make sure no one attacks from the rear. I'll take point, and if I need your assistance, I'll call for it. You two ready?"

Lena exhales heavily. "Not at all," she says as she looks at me, and I try to give her as reassuring a nod as I can.

"Good enough," says Desmond. "Let's go."

About twenty feet separate us from the exit of the break room, but the walk there feels like a ten-mile hike on hot coals. The closer we get to the door, the louder the persistent gunshots ring in our ears, and the more pronounced the violence beyond becomes. We reach it, and Desmond takes hold of the handle, glancing back at Lena. She has the tablet in hand, ready to puppeteer the electrical grid.

"Do it," Desmond orders.

In an instant, everything goes dark. I look down, barely able to see my own hands or the M4A1 I'm holding. Lena's tablet glows like a beacon, and the muzzle flashes on the other side of the door and down the hall light up in sporadic flares. I swear we've been washed in the glow of the sublevel's lockdown for so long that even in the darkness, everything still has a tinge of red to it, as if stained by the vermilion luminescence.

"Give me a second, hold on," Lena says, fingers tapping away fervently.

Waiting in the dark, I feel the tension setting in, as if the vastness of it all is trying to swallow me whole. Then suddenly, the lights flash rapidly, only to return to blackness briefly afterward.

"Alright, I've got it," says Lena. "Let's equip the NVGs for now. When you remove them, drop your targets as quickly as possible. The lights will strobe in forty-five-second intervals, then go dark for ten seconds before the cycle repeats. I figure giving us an extended period of darkness now and then will lead to greater confusion for the enemy. Try to maintain a mental count to avoid blinding yourselves and to know when to re-equip your goggles. That's pretty much all there is to this plan."

"Got it," I say uncertainly.

Desmond and I shift the goggles down from atop our helmets to cover our eyes. We then switch them on and are instantly granted the gift of sight. I look at Desmond, who gives me a thumbs-up. Lena sets the tablet down on the floor, seemingly struggling to power on the NVGs. I walk over and place my hand gently on her shoulder. She jumps, a momentary pang of embarrassment washing over me for having forgotten that she can hardly see me coming.

"It's just me, sorry," I say, a trace of laughter in my voice.

"Christ, you nearly gave me a heart attack!" she says in an angry whisper.

"I'm sorry," I repeat. "Let me help you." My hand finds her goggles, and I toggle them on. "Better?"

She nods sullenly, so I ask her, "Are you okay?"

"Yeah, just… scared, I guess," she says in response.

It's a reasonable response, one I wish I'd seen sooner. "You have every right to be, I am too."

Crouching down, I pick up the tablet and offer it to her. Lena grabs it from me gingerly. Her confidence is wavering, so I'll exude that confidence for her. "Dez, are you ready?"

"Just waiting on you two," he replies.

"Alright, open the door," I say, bringing my weapon to the ready.

Desmond pushes the handle down and gently guides the door forward to avoid making noise. He holds it open while Lena and I exit the breakroom, then takes the lead. As we move forward, a familiar sensation washes over me. Somewhere deep in my subconscious, I can feel him again; *Mallen*, clawing at the gates, threatening to break loose and take control. Apparently, he isn't as dead as I had hoped. I fight against his urges, as violent as they are.

Desmond suddenly raises a hand, commanding us to stop and shifting my focus away from the potential internal threat of the Boundless. Shortly thereafter, he gives us a signal that the lobby is clear. As we pass through, I notice the fresh corpses that litter the area. They're the still-warm bodies of the combatants I had seen fighting just moments ago from the window in the breakroom door. I notice Lena peering at each one we pass and tap her arm. When she glances back, I simply shake my head no, as if to say, *"don't look."* She steadies her gaze straight ahead, silently accepting my suggestion.

When we reach the other side of the lobby, Desmond once again signals to wait. He walks ahead, skimming the wall until he reaches the spot where it opens into a final exit leading to the front doors. Columns line either side of the wide gangway roughly every six feet, providing plenty of cover. This can be good or bad for us depending on how much opposition we're about to face. Desmond glances around the corner, scanning the area with his goggles. "This is our final push before we make it to the front courtyard. What are we dealing with beyond that, Lena?"

"About a two-hundred-yard dash through a heavily wooded driveway," she says, not too excited at the prospect. "Atticus had the trees planted at the inception of every facility in operation to ensure privacy until the domes were erected. After that, we reached the front gate, which I should be able to bypass with the tablet. There will be a getaway vehicle with a driver waiting for us on the other side."

"Domes?" Desmond asks, uncertain of her meaning.

"We're essentially in a snow globe," Lena begins explaining. "The dome is the glass above, or in our case, highly sophisticated projection panels that show people looking in from the outside whatever ENDURE wants them to see. They're a contingency meant to provide an artificial environment should the monolith's spores affect the area."

Desmond shakes his head, checking our pathway once more. "Jesus Christ, this place is a literal house of horrors," he says under his breath.

"Let's hurry up and get out of here then." I agree.

Before we can get moving, however, the front doors swing wide open. Desmond quickly returns to cover. "Shit, I count another six hostiles between us and the exit, their NVGs are equipped."

There's suddenly more commotion at the front door, culminating in gunshots and shouting. With full confidence that they're concealed well enough in the dark and that the soldiers are otherwise engaged, Desmond steals another glance. "A couple of our allies ambushed them; they're preoccupied for now. Let's trigger the strobes and try to sneak past. The second one of those PMCs looks our way though, we put them down. Everyone understand?"

Lena and I recognize his orders.

"Good, goggles off," says Desmond.

We all power down our NVGs, returning them to their upright positions atop our helmets. Desmond glances at Lena. "Hit it."

She turns her attention to the tablet. Immediately after, the lights begin to flash excessively.

"Move!" Desmond yells as he advances under the erratic pulse of the lights.

Lena and I follow suit, not wanting any distance to come between us. We pass through the security checkpoint and into the spacious area just beyond the receptionist's desk. The two Coalition fighters who ambushed Atticus's hired soldiers are using the strobing lights to their advantage. On the left side of the pathway, they're trying to wrestle away rifles from the military contractors. Another pair of PMCs has their M4A1s trained on the altercation, likely trying to find a clear line of sight to take a shot that won't hit either of their squad mates.

Clinging to the right wall and staying far away from the spat, we quietly pass behind them, using the columns for cover and avoiding the conflict. When we reach halfway to the entrance,

I get tackled from the left, just before the strobing lights stop, leaving us to fight in the dark. There's no time for me to equip my NVGs as my attacker and I both go down hard, causing me to lose my M4A1 in the process.

Somewhere nearby, I hear Desmond shout, "Let them go!"

This indicates that Lena has also encountered confrontation, and my heart begins to race with panic. The lights start to strobe again just in time for me to see another PMC a few feet to my left. He holds Lena from behind, one arm wrapped around her chest while the other presses the muzzle of a sidearm against her temple. I can see Desmond a few feet behind them, his goggles raised and his weapon at the ready while I grapple with my opponent. Lena's goggles are also up, implying she hadn't found the time to put them on either before she was attacked; our plan was already unraveling.

"Easy there, pal," says the man holding Lena hostage, "just drop the weapon and come quietly. You don't have to die today." He tightens his grip around Lena's chest.

"Sure, just drop yours first," Desmond responds, earning a laugh from Lena's oppressor.

"That's not how this works," says the PMC. "You can put the weapon down, or we can shoot these two in the head and then put a bullet in yours. What's it going to be?"

Without Mallen's assistance, the contractor I've been struggling against has the upper hand. She successfully disarms me of my secondary weapon and then walks me to stand beside Lena and her captor. The woman forces me to my knees as I place my hands on the back of my head. The man holding Lena hostage shoves her down to join me. Now, with our backs facing the entrance leading to the courtyard, one of the weapons is aimed at Desmond, and the other is pointed at both Lena and me. The male soldier takes a step toward Desmond.

"Don't... stay where you are, or I'll fucking end you." He warns the PMC.

The man just grins in return. "You could try, but I promise you, I'm quicker on the trigger."

I can see the sweat beginning to bead on Desmond's forehead. He has to make a move, and quickly at that, or Lena and I are as good as dead. I glance to our left, back to the point of our origin. Through the glinting light, the other four PMCs have seemingly gained control of the coalition fighters they were squabbling with and vanished from the area. Not good; it means they'll be returning shortly, and we'll be heavily outnumbered.

"What's it going to be, old man? My patience for your antics is wearing thin. Decide," the PMC demands with conviction, and I can't help but think he's moments away from pulling the trigger and ending Desmond's life.

Darkness descends again, earning a fresh exclamation of, "shit!" from the woman covering me. All I can do is hope Desmond had kept a mental count, equipped his goggles, and found his window. As if to answer my silent inquiry, gunfire flashes from his location, and I hear a body hit the floor beside me.

I can still feel the woman's hand on my shoulder, so I take the opportunity to throw myself backward into her, knocking her down. Quickly equipping my goggles, I notice she hasn't lost her M4A1 during the fall, but it's now sandwiched between her body and mine, unable to find a target. Lena jumps in out of nowhere, scrambling for the PMC's sidearm holstered on her right thigh. After a moment, she manages to unclasp the strap that secures the gun. Ripping it free from its housing, Lena presses the muzzle against our adversary's temple and pulls the trigger, spattering skull fragments and brain matter across the floor.

Just as quickly as it began, it's over, and all is quiet, except for our combined strained breathing and the ringing in our ears. Desmond turns and aims his weapon back toward the lobby we came from as fresh gunfire rings out in the distance. It takes just moments for the gunfire to stop, leaving us in a deafening silence once again.

The lights begin to strobe once more as we hear heavy footfalls approaching from the lobby. There's no time for a reprieve from the traumatic fight we've just barely survived. The tapping of boots on the ground stops abruptly around the corner to our right; whoever it is knows we're here. Lena stuffs the tablet into her Kevlar vest, and we both grab the closest weapons available on the floor, taking aim alongside Desmond.

"Come out with your hands raised or we'll shoot!" Desmond demands as Lena and I both struggle to steady ourselves.

The perpetrator steps out from behind the corner, his hands raised in front of him. "That's no way to treat someone who just saved your lives. Four more PMCs were heading right for the three of you." Desmond can't help but smile as he lowers his weapon. "Son of a bitch… I never thought I'd be so happy to see you."

Like a phoenix rising from the ashes, Matias closes the gap between them, pulling Desmond into a brotherly embrace. "Good to see you too," Matias says, patting him on the back before releasing him.

He then looks at Lena, who gives him a nod of approval, a small but noticeable grin on her lips. I lower my rifle and walk over to him, reaching up slightly to place a hand on his right shoulder. The wound on the other is now crusted over with blood. "Thank you, but no more hero shit. We stick together from here on out."

Matias smirks and agrees. "Alright, we stick together."

Lena comes in closer to the rest of us. "This is it boys, we're almost out."

We turn our attention to the entrance where giant double doors lead to the front courtyard. It feels like a looming threat, like some mystical beast guarding a trove of treasure that we have given everything to unearth. Lena is right; this is it. Once we pass through that threshold, we're just a short sprint away from freeing ourselves from Atticus, freeing ourselves to hopefully make a difference in the coming conflict. Only then can we face the larger storm brewing in the background, one that holds unprecedented and unfathomable trials and tribulations.

It has taken everything we had to escape ENDURE, and even now we aren't entirely sure how we'll stop Atticus from continuing his horrific experiments once we are gone. The doctor is a *human* adversary, one who has proven incredibly difficult to overcome. How then, can we hope to defeat the Nine and the Boundless who protect them? How can we possibly prevent a future that seems inevitable? Just then, as if attuned to these thoughts, Mallen's voice returns full-force, overwhelming my mind.

"You can't, and deep down you know it. You're in over your head, Royce, a man playing at being a warrior. The only place you will lead these people is to a quicker, more excruciating death."

I push his voice aside, keeping the beast at bay. "You're not in control anymore, I am."

"Think what you will, but you are only prolonging the inevitable. Soon your species will cease to exist, and there is nothing you can do to prevent that. A tsunami pays no mind to the obstacles in its path, and you are barely an obstacle to begin with."

"We'll see about that," I say aloud. "I'm coming for you next."

Lena places a hand on my shoulder. "Royce? You were talking to yourself... are you alright?"

I blink rapidly, as if awakening from a deep slumber. All three sets of concerned eyes are focused on me. "Yeah, I'm sorry... everything is fine."

"Are you sure? Because—"

"It's fine," I interrupt her, not wanting to pull focus from the task at hand. "Let's scavenge for ammo and get moving." I turn and walk away, making my way to the PMC that Lena shot earlier.

Matias and Desmond both shrug it off and follow suit, seemingly uninterested in anything other than completing our mission. Lena can't help but worry, and I understand completely. After what they discovered in the lab when they came to rescue me, I know there will be an underlying suspicion between us. I think she senses something ominous within me and is acting as if I'm a ticking time bomb, and she's right to.

She knows all there is to know about Mallen and his ilk. Even though I told them he might have been slain by my hand, Lena knows there's a chance he's survived... but right now isn't the time for that revelation. I need her focused and sharp. Sooner or later, we'll need to have that conversation, and I know I'll dread every moment of it.

CHAPTER 45

Apogee

Time and location (372 days post-cryostasis): 1:17 pm,
ENDURE Courtyard

More bodies and carnage await us outside. Blood, severed limbs, and corpses as far as the eye can see; I'm not quite sure what I had expected when we exited the facility and entered the courtyard, but I now know one thing for certain; I hadn't been prepared. The annihilation I may have caused back in the lab seems minor compared to the horrors here. We've entered a genuine war zone outside, nothing short of trekking the beaches of Normandy during World War II.

What makes matters worse is that at just a glance, the Coalition's efforts seem to be failing. The fighting has ended just outside the facility, but the Coalition forces scattered along the driveway in the distance are severely outnumbered. Most of their soldiers have either been subdued or slaughtered. I glance downward, catching a flash of what used to be someone's lower half, blown apart at the torso with intestines spread about the surrounding area.

Choking back the urge to hurl, I address the others. "The fighting is too heavy down the middle of the courtyard; I say we pick an outer wall and trail our way down alongside it until we hit the gate."

"Either route has its disadvantages," Desmond adds. "If we take a path on the outskirts, we're more exposed and likely to be spotted. If we shoot down the middle, we'll be in the thick of it all and risk injury or worse, but it would be easier to blend in, keeping attention off ourselves."

"He has a point," Matias says.

I glance at the bloodshed just a few feet ahead of us again. "No, we shouldn't risk losing anyone in that chaos. Let's stick to the outer wall and deal with any opposition we may face along the way together. Agreed?"

Desmond and Matias both nod, and I direct my attention to Lena. The tablet is still tucked away in her armored vest, and she has unslung the M4A1 from over her shoulder. We need more firepower than anything else in the moments to come.

"You okay with that plan?" I ask her.

"If you can call it a plan, sure," she responds. Lena's right after all; much like our previous endeavors, it isn't much of a strategy, but it's all we have.

"It's the best I've got, unfortunately," I say.

"Then I guess we don't have much of a choice," she shrugs, showing little to no confidence in her tone.

Looking back at Desmond and Matias, they both seem eager to get the hell out of here. The two of them had been captives of ENDURE far longer than I had, and their determination to escape is evident.

"Alright then, let's get this over with... for Aiden," Matias says, his voice hitching audibly. Even with Oakley dead by his hand, I can tell he's still stricken by the loss of Aiden. Matias had been closer to him than any of us. With the considerable guilt and pain I feel over the loss, I can only imagine the strain it's putting on him.

"Weapons up, let's stay vigilant," Desmond says, taking charge and refocusing our group. "I'll take point, Matias take the rear. Royce and Lena in between."

He seems more stoic than usual, a characteristic undoubtedly born from the idea that he'll soon escape this place and be reunited with his family... a family that was never truly his to begin with, and one that may no longer exist. I refuse to pay it any mind any longer; the thought of it all physically pains me. Taking position behind Desmond, I check to ensure that Lena is behind me, and Matias after her. When I'm certain we're in formation, I tap Desmond on the shoulder, giving him the okay to move.

Like a well-oiled machine, we make our way to the leftmost outer wall of the facility, a solid concrete mass at least fifteen feet high. In that moment, I'm entranced by our objective, and my vision starts to tunnel. My breathing grows louder in my head as all external sounds become muted, blocking out the battle a few yards to my right. We have to move swiftly and stay on objective because at this rate, ENDRUE will have our remaining forces managed in little to no time. If we aren't fast enough, we'll be facing Atticus' entire army on our own. If that happens, there isn't a chance in hell we'll win this battle.

We make it about thirty yards down the courtyard driveway when we first encounter trouble, albeit indirectly. A group of Coalition soldiers is going head-to-head with a few PMCs who aren't outmatched, but are definitely outnumbered. The mass of bodies pushes and shoves their way out of the main crowd of chaos and crashes into the wall a few feet ahead of us like a wave hitting a jetty.

Desmond stops before colliding with them. "We're going to have to go around," he suggests, as I scan our alternate route.

When I do, I immediately detest the idea; it will place us between the large fight blocking our current path and the more significant, menacing gathering that has taken over most of the courtyard and driveway. Straying from our course means risking being overwhelmed by the very violence we originally aimed to avoid. "I don't like it, it's too dangerous," I respond.

"We don't have time to find any other option, Royce," Matias says from the back.

Lena squeezes my shoulder from behind. "It'll be okay."

With a moment of hesitation and a heavy sigh of dissatisfaction, I concede. "Alright, lead the way," I tell Desmond, tapping him on the shoulder.

He immediately mobilizes, heading for the small opening between the chaos ahead and the maelstrom to our right. I feel uneasy, almost claustrophobic as we approach the bottleneck that should lead us through the tumult, or so I hope. The moment Desmond starts to pass between the two groups of people locked in savage warfare, everything goes completely sideways. The smaller group fighting against the wall shifts, working their way back toward the larger mass they had broken away from. Desmond is separated from us in an instant.

I try to push my way through, only to be engulfed in flailing limbs. A frightened voice cries out, and I instinctively turn in its direction; I know it, I'd recognize it anywhere. I catch the slightest glimpse of Lena and Matias before she goes down, presumably having lost her balance and fallen. Matias willingly dives into the swarm after her, a desperate attempt to pull her back up from beneath the sea of human bodies.

"Lena! *Lena!*" I scream, but there is no reply.

Despite the potential death all around me, my complete focus is on finding the others, especially Lena. An elbow drives down hard onto my shoulder, causing me to almost stumble and fall, but I manage to catch myself against someone's back. The last place I want to be right now is on the ground, terrified that the overwhelming stampede will trample me. Something slices my arm, and a burning pain starts to spread through it. I turn to my left and see one of Atticus's men, combat knife in hand. The blade has cut my forearm, but not intentionally.

The soldier is currently facing off against a Coalition-aligned woman. I steady my M4A1, with my sights aimed at his head, then reconsider my actions. I don't *want* to kill anyone, not unless I have to. After flipping the rifle around in my hands, I bring the butt of the stock down hard into the back of the PMC's neck. The man collapses onto the grass beneath our feet, unconscious. The Coalition woman glances at the unconscious soldier and then at me, nodding her thanks before vanishing into the crowd.

Peeking above the mosh pit, I search once more for the others, but I can't make visual contact with any of them. Part of me feels panicked, while the *other* part remains calm, trying to pull my darkest thoughts from the recesses of my mind. Mallen wants nothing more than to make me feel like pulling the trigger is my only option. I can hear him speaking from within.

"Raise the rifle, Royce, mow them down. They stand between you and your salvation. Friend or foe, it does not matter; kill them all."

"Shut up," I say aloud, unheard by anyone else over the chaos of the skirmish.

I wrestle with my thoughts, trying to replace those coming from Mallen's mind with my own. I doubt I'll achieve victory, but at the very least, I can put up a decent fight. As I strive to maintain control, I realize that my chances of finding the others are slim to none; I have no choice but to head for the courtyard exit and blindly hope they have done the same. So, I turn around and start to push and shove my way to what I hope will be our rendezvous.

Elbows and fists strike me repeatedly in the frenzy, some from PMCs, some from Coalition fighters. They have all turned rabid, desperate to survive at this point. Paying attention to your targets is apparently out of the question. It's like being caught in a fight between two packs of stray dogs. I brush aside the pain as best I can, pushing through the pile. The wall of bodies in front of me seems to be thinning as I struggle past, and soon, I can see the first hint of a clearing through the flailing limbs and clashing weapons.

Finally, I find myself on the outskirts of the combat, relatively unscathed except for the knife wound on my arm. My best guess is that the front gate is merely forty yards away, and I have a clear line of sight to it. There are a few people up ahead, too far away to recognize, and I fervently hope that it is Lena and the others. Without another moment's hesitation, I take off, running as fast as I can. The first ten yards fly by in a flash. Another five down, and before I know it, I'm almost there. I'm within the final fifteen yards when I suddenly stop. My muscles tense and seize all at once, my teeth gritting and threatening to shatter. I tip over and crash into the ground like a felled tree, writhing and twitching.

"You have been quite the thorn in my side, almost more trouble than you're worth, Royce." Through the agony, I recognize the voice and the inflections in his tone; Atticus. The son of a bitch had somehow found his way back to me once more, had somehow thwarted my efforts yet again. "A standard stun gun packs a punch of 50,000 volts, but we've made some adjustments to ours. Not enough added power to kill, but just enough to make you wish you were dead." Atticus releases the trigger, allowing me to breathe and giving my muscles a chance to relax.

"Rip his throat open Royce, this is your chance! Take your vengeance, thrust your hand through his chest cavity and crush his beating heart in your palm!"

"No! I won't give you control!" I scream into the air.

Atticus moves closer to me. "Ahhh… Mallen… it's speaking to you, isn't it? Becoming more prominent… I can help you, Royce, but only if you cooperate."

Somehow, I find the strength to tuck my arms underneath myself and begin to push up onto all fours as I speak. "I'll never cooperate with you... you're sick... in the head."

Atticus scoffs. "You converse with a voice only you can hear, and I'm the one who's sick?"

I'm not backing down, not now. I won't let Mallen control me, but it feels like I'm sapping some of his strength. The longer the conversation goes on, the steadier my responses become, and the quicker I recover from the volts that surged through my body moments ago. "Don't pretend that this is some psychotic break. You and I both know what that voice is... there's a bigger threat coming, Atticus. We need to stop it, but not this way... not your way. *This* isn't the answer." I manage to get one knee under myself as I slowly rise from the foliage.

"You've surprised me with your persistence time and time again; you shouldn't even be able to move. I need you to understand something," Atticus pauses, then squeezes the trigger of the stun rifle once more, electricity coursing up its tendrils to the prongs embedded in my abdomen.

Burbling in torment, I crumble and find myself face down in the grass once more, muscles tightly wound like metal fibers as Atticus continues. "*My way* is the only way. I've dedicated years of my life to finding a solution to the current predicament the world faces, as well as an alternative to the impending extinction that looms over us all. There is no other way, and I will see this project through. I prefer to do so with the two of us seeing eye to eye. As you know; you are our most successful candidate to date and our most promising asset in our fight against the Boundless. However, if I must terminate you and start fresh, I will, pressed for time or not. You and I can no longer stay stagnant and at an impasse; this moment is the apogee of our rivalry, Royce."

Atticus releases the trigger, anticipating my answer. It's an opportunity I desperately want to seize, but I can't. My muscles won't respond; my brain can't send the proper signals or communicate with my body to control basic motor functions.

Helplessly, I watch as Atticus tosses aside the stun rifle and draws his sidearm. "These are lethal rounds Royce, time's up. You need to choose; with me? Or against me? Live? Or die? What will it be, RW-117?"

CHAPTER 46

Traitor

Time and location (372 days post-cryostasis): 1:21 pm,
ENDURE Courtyard

Matias quickly finds Lena's hand after the mortal torrent pulls
her under. Pulling her back to the surface takes hardly any effort
for a man of his build.

"Where's Desmond and Royce?!" she shouts with her first
gasping breath of fresh air.

A mixture of fear and concern is etched across her face. Matias
firmly grips her forearm as he struggles to navigate through the
pileup of bodies. "I don't know, we got separated. Don't worry,
we'll find them. Sling your rifle over your shoulder and keep
hold of the back of my vest!" he shouts back over the crowd and
releases her arm.

Lena does as she is instructed, slipping her hand into his vest
and clinging to it as if it were her only lifeline in a hurricane.
Matias can navigate through the congregation much more easily

than she can, hulking above nearly everyone around them and parting the crowd like the Red Sea with a simple sweep of his arm. Every now and then, Lena hears his rifle fire, the distinct sound of live rounds ringing in her ears. Each time she does, she steps over a dead PMC just moments later. Enduring the bloodbath surrounding them isn't easy for her, but she is grateful to have Matias at her side. The man is supremely effective at utilizing the skills perfected by his DNA donor during a lifetime long since passed.

"Shit, I'm out of ammo! We're almost through, hang in there!" he shouts back to her, tossing aside the M4A1, as it has outlived its usefulness.

Lena swings her assault rifle around from behind her with her free hand and tries to pass it forward to Matias, but it's immediately knocked from her grip. It vanishes beneath their feet. She curses under her breath; they're completely unarmed now. Eventually, they find their way out of the chaos. Once they've put enough distance between themselves and the main group of combatants, they take cover behind a large oak tree and reassess the situation.

"I didn't see Desmond or Royce back there," says Matias, nodding his head toward the commotion behind them.

"Neither did I," Lena agrees, deciding that they're just as lost now as they had been before.

Silence stands between them for a moment, like a brick wall isolating them from any solution to the problem at hand.

"Wait... where's your rifle?" Matias asks.

"I lost it back there," she shakes her head, visibly disappointed in herself.

"Well shit... no sense worrying about what we can't change," Matias says to console her. "Maybe Dez and Royce broke for the gate and assumed we'd do the same? It would be the logical thing to do."

Lena ponders the idea. "Maybe... but what if they didn't? We can't leave them behind." She knows that Matias is most likely right; it's what she would have done if she had been separated from the group and alone. Yet she can't shake the worry that they're still somewhere in the chaos behind them.

Matias touches her shoulder to get her attention. "We need to make a hard call; we can't just wait here; we're sitting ducks. We either head back into the thick of it and attempt to find them, or we break for the courtyard gate and hope that they're waiting for us when we get there."

"Shit," she utters in frustration. Matias is right; the clock is ticking, and time is running out. They need to come to a decision, and fast.

A shout from behind them breaks her concentration. "Matias! Don't you take another fucking step!"

He glances back to where Lena's gaze is already fixed. On the outskirts of the fighting stands a single man. Matias sighs in disbelief. "He just doesn't quit..."

It's Elliot Shaw again, and he looks worse for wear. His gear is tattered, and dried blood cakes the side of his face. In Shaw's hand is a sidearm, a military-issued Sig Sauer from what Matias can tell.

He positions himself between Shaw and Lena, subtly and slowly, then raises his hands as he speaks discreetly to her. "You need to leave, find the others. Run as fast as you can in a straight line behind me, use me to block Shaw's line of sight so he can't get a bead on you."

"What? No!" Lena says angrily. "We all agreed, no more hero shit, Matias!"

He shakes his head slowly. "It's not about that. Atticus and his men almost have this situation under control; either we get out now, or this was all for nothing. I'd rather have some of us make it than none of us. Please, just go. This is my fight; Shaw has always been my problem. I promise I'll be right behind you if circumstances allow it."

Lena feels herself tearing up, whether from anguish or frustration, she can't tell. She doesn't want to leave him again, but what choice does she have? "Okay, just hurry up and deal with him. There's only so long we'll be able to wait for you once we reach the evacuation point."

Matias nods his head in agreement. "I'll see you on the other side of that gate."

Lena smiles at his blind optimism and then takes off, ensuring she stays aligned with his body.

Matias sees Shaw's eyes dart to Lena for a moment. "Uh-uh; your fight is with me. She's none of your concern. I didn't think I'd see you again. You could've walked away with your life, Elliot."

Shaw laughs, releasing an exhausted breath. "The way I see it, I'm holding all the cards here, and you haven't a single hand to play."

They approach each other, gradually closing the gap between them. "There isn't time for this, Elliot. You and I both know what comes after this. Royce is the *only* thing standing between humanity and otherworldly eradication. You've seen it; Atticus is off his rocker; he's lost himself to this endeavor. If you don't let Royce leave, we *all* die."

Shaw raises his other arm, gripping the Sig with both hands to steady his aim. "I'm no traitor, and Atticus isn't the only one who has devoted years of his life to this campaign. We're on the brink of a breakthrough with subject RW-117; we just need a little more time."

"Not a traitor? Elliot, look at yourself! You've betrayed your own humanity! Do you truly believe more time will change the outcome of what ENDURE has done here? Royce's mental state is already questionable, possibly deteriorating as we speak. How long before he can't hold back that… whatever it is inside his head? Your methods aren't working, but ours just *might*." Matias pleads, reflecting on all the times he's witnessed the aftermath of Royce going berserk.

He feels like there's a demon caged within Royce. If that thing takes full control, then it's game over for everyone and everything in its path. Something explodes behind them, grabbing both of their attention. A plume of smoke begins to rise from the facility, clearly the work of the remaining Coalition fighters.

"God damn it!" Shaw yells.

Matias tries to regain his attention. "Shaw; let me go. Hell, come with us if you want. I'm trying to help us all, but you need to let me go."

For only the second time during their many encounters, in this life and the one he only holds memories of, Matias can see the man faltering. The gun he holds shakes visibly in his hands, and his eyes dart around frantically.

"I promise you, we will stop what's coming," Matias continues, "but you need to let me walk away."

Shaw's eyes lock onto Matias' gaze and remain steady. He seems to be holding his breath, immersed in quiet contemplation with himself. Then, to Matias' relief, Shaw lowers his weapon slowly, still at the ready but no longer aimed at center mass. He looks as though he has more to say but can't find the words.

Reaching for a radio clipped to his chest, Shaw issues orders. "Alpha squad; gain control of the courtyard. All other squads fall back towards the facility. Regroup and await further instruction regarding fire hazards and containment. This sector is lost, I repeat, sector seven is lost."

Matias nods in solidarity with his enemy. "Thank you, Elliot."

Shaw simply shakes his head. "Don't make me regret this decision… Matias." He hangs on the name of his former fellow marine as he says it, as if it feels unnatural to use it in reference to the Echo before him. For so long, he has refused to call the clone by that name. It is a subtle change in his demeanor, but one that Matias feels could have huge ramifications in their conjoined future, should there be one.

Shaw turns and runs back toward the burning building, disappearing into the dwindling group of warfighters. Matias had been sure that he was just buying time for Royce and the others to escape, that Elliot Shaw would kill him. Somehow, he had evaded death once more, and he wouldn't waste this chance. He knows he must catch up with Lena quickly, or he won't make it out before their exfil leaves the area.

Taking off in a full sprint toward the courtyard gate, his mind races with a flurry of thoughts. How he managed to break Shaw down and change his mind remains a mystery that triggers a whole new wave of guilt. If only Aiden had been able to reason with the man first, then maybe, just maybe… Matias pushes the thought aside and focuses on his footing. It's a tragedy, but Aiden is gone; he needs to concentrate on the people he can still save.

CHAPTER 47

Sacrifice

*Time and location (372 days post-cryostasis): 1:33 pm,
ENDURE Courtyard*

As Atticus stuns me a second time, I catch the briefest glimpse of Desmond watching us from behind a nearby tree. How he managed to find Atticus and me in the heavily forested and crowded terrain is nothing short of dumb luck. Now that he has, it seems he is waiting for a moment to intervene, which may be my only way out of this mess. Unless I plan on being his hostage again, it doesn't seem like Atticus intends to let me leave this situation alive. By all accounts, the stress induced by the nature of his work has clearly taken a toll on the doctor's last shred of sanity; Atticus is unhinged.

Desmond watches me from a distance until Atticus drops his stun rifle in favor of a sidearm. Only then does he take off in a full sprint from behind the tree. He approaches from Atticus's right side and has the advantage of being in the doctor's blind spot. By the time Desmond reaches him, Atticus has only a moment to turn before he's shoulder-tackled to the ground, the handgun slipping from his grip and bouncing across the grass. Desmond struggles to subdue him while yelling to me, "Get the hell out of here, now! Get to the gate, I'll meet you there!"

I'm still curled in the fetal position, the voltage from the second lengthy jolt rendering me immobile. I hear Desmond but can't respond or react. Atticus throws an elbow into Desmond's ribs. I watch helplessly as he grumbles in pain but doesn't relent, doesn't loosen his grip on the man's throat.

The doctor seems abnormally strong for his age; fit as he is, I briefly wonder if the deranged man has somehow altered his own DNA. "I will not let him leave here. He will come with me willingly or he will die," Atticus utters a garbled slur against Desmond's hold, expending what little air he has left in his lungs.

Ignoring his bleak promise, I watch as Desmond clamps down even harder on Atticus' trachea. Finally finding the strength to move, I manage to gradually rise to my feet. Instead of running away as Desmond suggested, I begin to approach them.

"No! Find Lena and Matias and go!" He screams.

I try to shout back, but my voice is hoarse and my response is terse. "I won't leave you... let me... help!" I say, dazed and confused, still not fully recovered from the shock.

Atticus throws another blow to Desmond's gut, and he looks like he's fighting back the urge to vomit. "You need to leave, you're the only hope we have of stopping the Nine! Go Royce, please!"

Dizzied and disoriented, I try to make sense of the situation. My whole body aches as if I've fallen from a rooftop; my vision is blurred, and I'm struggling to find my footing. As if that isn't enough, I can see a squad of at least ten PMCs making their way toward us, scattered among the trees. A bullet whizzes past my head, hitting the bark just behind me and causing adrenaline to surge through my veins. I make my decision; leaving Desmond isn't an option; not now, not when we're so close. I take a few unsteady steps toward Desmond and Atticus as they grapple on the ground.

Before I can reach them, I'm struck, tackled by someone who sweeps me off my feet and now carries me in the opposite direction. It's Matias, who has reappeared out of nowhere and hefted me over his shoulder. Lena runs up beside us, sliding to the ground to retrieve the sidearm that Atticus had dropped during his altercation with Desmond. As soon as she hits the ground, she's back up and firing mid-sprint. The bevy of bullets is growing heavier as the ensemble of PMCs trails us. I struggle to free myself from Matias's powerful grip.

"Put me down, we can't leave him!" I bellow.

"We don't have a choice; we need to go now or we're all dead!" Matias yells without slowing down.

"No!" I scream again and start hitting him in the back of the head as Desmond drifts further away from us.

Matias curves sharply to his right, throwing me down behind a sturdy oak tree while Lena takes cover next to us, providing what little cover fire she can with her handgun. Matias grabs my shoulders and screams at me in agitation. "Listen to me, Royce! We need to go, and you need to make it out. The rest of us are expendable. You need to live, or everything we've done here is pointless!"

I can hear bullets striking the backside of the tree as Matias urges me to make a decision, emphasizing his point. "I heard what Desmond said, he told you to leave him! It's what he wants, and it's what needs to happen!"

He extends a hand to help me up from where I sit slumped at the base of the tree. My breaths are so rapid that I'm nearly hyperventilating. Tears fill my eyes; we've already lost Jonathan and Aiden, and I can't bear to say goodbye to Desmond as well, but there's no alternative. I take Matias's hand and let him pull me to my feet.

"Can you run fast enough?" he asks, observing my less-than-ideal condition.

I nod, the adrenaline overpowering my affliction. Matias looks at Lena, who understands his silent gesture immediately. The three of us take off in unison, bobbing and weaving through the maze of trees to avoid the hail of gunfire aimed at us. When

I glance over my shoulder, I see two PMCs split from the group pursuing us. They rip Desmond from Atticus, holding him at gunpoint; then he disappears from our line of sight forever, his sacrifice doubling as our salvation.

It takes Lena just three minutes to bypass the gate's locking mechanism, thanks to the malware she installed in EDNURE's security software long ago. Just as she promised, there's a getaway vehicle waiting for us on the other side in the form of an armored Humvee, undoubtedly the repurposed property of ENDURE. A coalition member named Dane is ready and waiting at the wheel to escort us to safety.

As we pile into the vehicle and it jerks forward, my heart's still pounding, half-expecting to hear gunfire or see Atticus in the rearview mirror. But the further we drive, the quieter it gets, no more explosions, no more shouting, just the hum of the engine and the heavy silence between us. After a couple of hours, we realize no one's coming. For the first time in what feels like forever, we can actually breathe. We're finally free, but not all of us. That truth sits heavy in the silence.

I gaze out the window of the Humvee as it speeds along the endless asphalt. Buildings rush by, and actual civilians stroll through the streets, completely unaware of the horrors that have occurred miles away from their quaint little town... If only they knew the terror to come. How the air they take for granted will soon be unbreathable, how the monoliths will rain down spores of death on their doorsteps...

I can't stop thinking about Desmond and can't help but wonder if he's alive... or if Atticus chose to play God yet again, just as he had with so many lives before. Mason Cais, Jonathan McAllister, Aiden Buckley... hell, even Jordan Oakley had all been pawns in a game only Atticus knew how to win... until now. Not knowing Desmond's fate pained me, but at least now the tables have begun to turn.

A hand gently settles atop my own, and I turn to look at Lena sitting beside me. "I'm sorry," she softly says. It isn't enough to stop the aching inside, but the small comfort it provides is welcome.

Matias interjects from the front passenger seat of the vehicle. "It's what Desmond wanted; you know that as well as I do. His sacrifice will mean something, we'll make sure of that."

I have nothing to say in response, so I don't. Matias decides to change the subject, turning the conversation over to our driver.

"Where are we heading, Dane?" Matias asks.

"We're leaving the capital of the Czech Republic, Prague, and heading to an FOB we set up in Berlin," the driver responds.

That finally solves the mystery of the location of the ENDURE facility, information I'm sure Desmond and Matias had been made aware of during my last stint in cryostasis.

"We're only going to Germany?" Matias questions. "Seems a little close for comfort, don't you think?" He clearly wants as much distance as possible between us and our former home.

Lena intervenes in the discussion. "Berlin is about four and a half hours away from the main facility we just escaped. They'll find us no matter where we go if it's the play Atticus chooses to make. We're still on borrowed time, albeit much more than we were previously allotted."

"Fair point. What's the plan once we reach the FOB?" Matias asks.

"With what I managed to siphon from Atticus' offshore accounts before ENDURE caught on and cut me off, we'll be up and running for quite a while without interruption," Lena responds, a proud smile on her face. "We have more than enough resources to sustain ourselves and our supporters. So, we are planning for the coming storm. We'll figure out what we can regarding the Nine and the Boundless, and make sure we're well defended against any disturbances we may encounter from Atticus and ENDURE."

"He's still alive you know... your friend, Desmond."

I perk up, glancing briefly at Lena to see if she's paying attention, but she's deep in her conversation with Dane and Matias. I turn back toward the window, shuffling up against it, and speak to Mallen telepathically. *"Are you going to elaborate on that?"*

I receive no response, only silence. Frustration begins to brew within me. *"Answer me, Mallen."*

Still, there's no reply. "God damn it, I said answer me," I growl, a whispered yet verbal demand.

"Royce, did you say something?" Lena suddenly asks. I stop hugging the window and jerk around to face her.

"Uh… no, it's nothing. Never mind." I reply quickly, a hint of nervousness creeping into my voice.

She nods after giving me a confused look, then returns to the conversation with the others.

"Desmond Luther is being held captive by Atticus. Will you save him, Royce? Or leave him to die like you did Aiden Buckley?"

"Why should I believe you?" I ask, ensuring my mouth is shut and my mind is open.

"Think of it as an act of good faith. We help you save your friend, and you don't interfere with our plans."

I scoff mentally. *"What happened to nothing being able to stand in your way? Besides, even if we save Desmond, not interfering with your plans would lead straight to our collective deaths. Your deal is a shit one."*

Once more, silence from Mallen. Then, all of a sudden, it becomes clear: I had harmed the Boundless before, inflicting a wound that Mallen was quite possibly still reeling from.

"*This is rich... you're scared. I've hurt you when you claimed to be intangible, and you're afraid of what I might be able to do if I harness these abilities, come to understand them fully... I'll save Desmond and stop Atticus. After that, it's just like I told you before; I'm coming for you next, Mallen.*"

The Boundless' voice thunders furiously in my head. "*You... insolent little insect, you are nothing but a speck of dust, we will—*"

"*Silence,*" I command him, and just like that, Mallen falls silent. At least for now, Mallen goes catatonic. I grin to myself; for the first time in a while, it feels as though I'm in full control, as if I'm finally beginning to understand how to subdue this demon.

Just then, static crackles over a CB radio mounted on the ceiling of the Humvee, followed shortly by a voice that could only belong to one man. "This message is encrypted and being transmitted to Royce Wilko and company. We have Desmond Luther in our custody. Bring me Royce, and we will spare Desmond's life and release him to you. You have forty-eight hours to consider my offer."

The airwaves go dead before we can respond, the static lingering. Matias turns around and locks eyes with Lena, who then looks to me.

"What do we do?" she asks.

"If we go back now, there's no question in my mind that we'll be ambushed and captured. We can't take Atticus' word for shit," argues Matias, a valid point as far as I'm concerned.

"We can't leave him there either, Matias, especially now that we know he's alive," Lena pleads.

He sighs deeply in response. "I know, I'm not suggesting we do. I just... I don't know what the right move is here. Neither option is great."

"Atticus gave us forty-eight hours to decide," I interject. We will meet with Atticus, and he will hand Desmond over to us."

Matias raises an eyebrow. "It isn't that simple, Royce. Or have you already forgotten what he and ENDURE are capable of?"

I meet Matias' gaze, and I can tell he recognizes the fire in my eyes; it's the same fire that had ignited behind his own when he vowed to hold off Shaw while we escaped the facility's sublevel. Staring sternly into his eyes, I tell him, "don't worry; I have a plan."

Epilogue

Time and location (372 days post-cryostasis): Redacted

"You know this isn't right, you don't have to keep following his orders, Shaw..." Desmond pleads with the man as he fastens the shackles that bind his arms securely behind his back.

Shaw leans in and whispers to him. "Just keep your mouth shut, and you might live through all of this. Do what you're told."

Atticus finishes delivering his thinly veiled threat to the Coalition. Desmond knows that if Atticus gains custody of Royce, humanity will be doomed. The Boundless will undoubtedly win this battle. The three of them stand in a dimly lit room, one of its four walls interrupted by a large one-way mirror.

Atticus approaches Desmond, studying him from head to toe. "Our message has been sent. So, for now, we wait. I've given them forty-eight hours to respond."

"And if he doesn't?" asks Desmond, reluctant to hear the doctor's answer.

"Then we terminate you and hunt him down," Atticus answers. "If he does, however, the outcome will remain the same, save for Royce; his life will be spared, if only out of necessity. When they arrive to rescue you—and we both know those fools will—we'll take him into our custody, and you and your allies will all be killed, including Lena. She's chosen her side."

Atticus turns his back on Desmond, ignoring the clear disgust on his face, and wanders over to the fake mirror. When he reaches it, he walks along its length, his hand trailing lightly across its frame. "In the meantime, we will break you. You see, I know my dear niece Lena is responsible for the birth of this 'Coalition', and I also know that you have information that could be valuable to me regarding her organization. Considering this, there's someone I'd like to reunite you with..."

At the end of Atticus's diatribe, Desmond glares at Shaw, who stands directly to his left. The man avoids his gaze.

"What the hell is he talking about, Shaw?" Desmond asks, his voice growing louder.

Unwilling to make eye contact, Shaw speaks under his breath. His voice is a barely audible murmur. "I... I'm sorry."

He spoke so softly that Atticus didn't even hear him. Shaw's discretion sent chills down Desmond's spine. Witnessing Atticus's most trusted colleague's hesitancy can only be a sign of terrible things to come.

Desmond shifts his focus back to the doctor, who resumes the conversation. "The young man on the other side of this wall has a few questions for you, Desmond…"

At the mention of Desmond's name, the mirror phase-shifts, replacing his reflection with a view into the adjoining room. He doesn't recognize the man standing before him on the other side of the glass. He's a young adult, at most in his mid-twenties. Then, all at once, it strikes him. Desmond feels his heart sink as he recedes into himself. His lip quivers, and warm tears roll gently down his cheeks. It can't possibly be… and yet something innate in Desmond knows it is. Through shaky lips and broken speech, he utters the name he and Nora had given to their child. "Dom… Dominic?"

END OF BOOK 1

About the Author

The Deus Molecule is a sci-fi horror novel I've been working on for roughly a decade. It's grown and evolved with me as a writer—originally written in third-person, now fully reimagined in first-person. This is Book 1 in a planned five-part series, and I've worked hard to make it stand apart from anything else out there. From the beginning, my goal was to create something entirely original. If I ever came across a story that felt too close to The Deus Molecule, I went back to the drawing board and pushed it further. Now, after years of meticulous shaping, I'm proud to share a story unlike any other—one that draws you in with its mysteries and leaves you craving answers with every twist and revelation.

Publish with Us

619-565-8281
https://www.seerendippublishing.com/